31016000013650

D0350379

WITHDRAWN

Hastings Memorial Library
505 Central Avenue
Grant, NE 69140

1/31/14 #26.95

ORFEO

ORFEO

a novel

RICHARD POWERS

W. W. NORTON & COMPANY

NEW YORK | LONDON

Copyright © 2014 by Richard Powers

All rights reserved
Printed in the United States of America
First Edition

For information about permission to reproduce selections from this book,
write to Permissions, W. W. Norton & Company, Inc.,
500 Fifth Avenue, New York, NY 10110

For information about special discounts for bulk purchases, please contact
W. W. Norton Special Sales at specialsales@wwnorton.com or 800-233-4830

Manufacturing by Courier Westford
Book design by Chris Welch
Production manager: Anna Oler

Library of Congress Cataloging-in-Publication Data

Powers, Richard, 1957–
Orfeo : a novel / Richard Powers. — First Edition.
pages cm
ISBN 978-0-393-24082-5 (hardcover)
1. Composers—Fiction. 2. Time travel—Fiction. 3. Music—Quotations,
maxims, etc.—Fiction. 4. Musical fiction. I. Title.
PS3566.O92O74 2014
813'54—dc23
2013031952

W. W. Norton & Company, Inc.
500 Fifth Avenue, New York, N.Y. 10110
www.wwnorton.com

W. W. Norton & Company Ltd.
Castle House, 75/76 Wells Street, London W1T 3QT

1 2 3 4 5 6 7 8 9 0

ACKNOWLEDGMENTS

For my account of the creation and premiere of Olivier Messiaen's *Quatuor pour la fin du temps*, I am indebted to Rebecca Rischin's excellent book *For the End of Time*.

ORFEO

An overture, then:

Lights blaze from an American Craftsman home in a demure neighborhood, late on a spring evening, in the tenth year of the altered world. Shadows dance against the curtains: a man working late, as he has every night that winter, in front of shelves filled with glassware. He's clad in mufti, protective goggles, and latex hospital gloves, and his Giacometti body hunches forward as if in prayer. A gray but still-thick Beatles mop hangs in his eyes.

He studies a book on the gear cluttered workbench. In one hand a single-channel pipette, raked like a dagger. From a tiny refrigerated vial, he sucks up no more colorless liquid than a hoverfly might take from a sprig of bee balm. This pellet goes into a tube no bigger than a mouse's muzzle, a dollop so small he can't be sure it's really there. His gloved hands shake as he shoots the used pipette tip into the trash.

More liquids go from the beakers into the dollhouse cocktail: oligo primers to start the magic; heat-stabilized catalyzing polymerase; nucleotides that fall in line like enlisted men for a five a.m. reveille, a thousand bonds per minute. The man follows the printed recipe like an amateur cook.

The brew goes into the thermal cycler for twenty-five rounds of roller-coaster flux, swinging between near-boiling and tepid. For two hours, DNA melts and anneals, snatches up free-floating nucleotides, and doubles each time through the loop. Twenty-five doublings turn a few hundred strands into more copies than there are people on Earth.

Outside, budding trees submit to the whims of a light wind. A wave of holdout nightjars skim the air for bugs. The do-it-yourself genetic engineer removes a colony of bacteria from his incubator and sets it under the laminar flow hood. He stirs the flattened culture flask and dispenses the loosened cells into a twenty-four-well sample plate. This plate goes under a microscope, at 400x. The man puts his eye up to the lens and sees the real world.

Next door, a family of four watches the denouement of Dancing with the Stars. *One house to the south, an executive secretary for a semi-criminal real estate development firm arranges next fall's cruise to Morocco. Across the double expanse of backyards, a market analyst and his pregnant lawyer wife lie in bed with their glowing tablets, playing offshore Texas hold 'em and tagging pictures from a virtual wedding. The house across the street is dark, its owners at an all-night faith-healing vigil in West Virginia.*

No one thinks twice about the quiet, older bohemian in the American Craftsman at 806 South Linden. The man is retired, and people take up all kinds of hobbies in retirement. They visit the birthplaces of Civil War generals. They practice the euphonium. They learn tai chi or collect Petoskey stones or photograph rock formations in the shape of human faces.

But Peter Els wants only one thing before he dies: to break free of time and hear the future. He's never wanted anything else. And late in the evening, in this perversely fine spring, wanting that seems at least as reasonable as wanting anything.

> I did what they say I tried to do. Guilty as charged.

On the tape, the hum of deep space. Then a clear alto says: *Pimpleia County Emergency Services, Dispatcher Twelve. What is the location of your emergency?*

There comes a sound like a ratchet wrapped in a towel. A hard clap breaks into clatter: the phone hitting the floor. After a pause, a tenor, in the upper registers of stress, says: *Operator?*

Yes. What is the loc—

We need some medical help here.

The alto crescendos. *What's the nature of your problem?*

The answer is a low, inhuman cry. The tenor murmurs, *It's okay, sweetie. It's all right.*

Is someone sick? the alto asks. *Do you need an ambulance?*

Another muffled bump turns into static. The silence ends in a stifled O. Rapid words shear off, unidentifiable even with digital filtering and enhancement. The sounds of failed comforting.

The dispatcher says, *sir? Can you confirm your address?*

Someone hums a muted tune, a lullaby from another planet. Then the line goes dead.

> I was sure that no one would ever hear a note. This was my piece for an empty hall.

The two officers who pulled up in front of 806 South Linden in an indigo squad car had already dealt that evening with an antidepressant overdose, a molar-breaking scrum in a convenience store, and a eugenics debate involving small arms fire. Life in a Pennsylvania college town flexing itself, and the night was still young.

The house belonged to Peter Clement Els, an adjunct professor who'd been released from Verrata College three years before. The police database had nothing; it seemed Mr. Els had never even jaywalked. The two officers—a young man with a shot-putter's gait and an older woman who gazed around bewildered as she walked—headed up the path to the front steps. Maple branches clicked in the spring wind. Dampened hilarity spilled out of a nearby house and across two dark lawns. High overhead, the twin jets of a short-haul flight shrieked toward the regional airport. Cars scythed up and down the state highway four blocks away.

The front porch was littered with things on the verge of being put away: a wood chipper, a pair of chewed-over rawhide bones, nested flowerpots, a bicycle pump. The male officer held open the screen, and the woman knocked, braced for anything.

Something flickered behind a half-moon window, and the door swung open. A gaunt, monkish man stood in the wedge of light. He wore rimless glasses and a plaid work shirt pilled around the collar. His gray hair looked as if a pioneer woman had cut it using an inverted bowl. An archipelago of food stains speckled his corduroys. His eyes were way elsewhere.

Mild disarray ruled the room behind him. Mission chairs sat ringed by bookshelves. Books, CD jewel cases, and stalagmite-coated candles covered every surface. A corner of the worn Persian rug was flipped up. The evening's dinner dishes sat stacked on a magazine-covered coffee table.

The woman officer surveyed the scene. *Peter Els? You placed a call to Emergency Services?*

Els closed his eyes, then opened them. *My dog just died.*

Your dog?

Fidelio.

You dialed 911 for your dog?

Beautiful golden retriever. Fourteen years old. She started hemorrhaging out of the blue.

Your dog was sick, the policeman said, her voice sagging under the weight of humanity, *and you didn't dial a vet?*

The guilty party dropped his eyes. *I'm sorry. A stroke, I guess. She was sliding around on the floor and howling. She bit me when I tried to move her. I thought that if someone could help restrain . . .*

Behind a gate, down a hallway leading from the living room, a green quilt covered a lump as big as a curled-up child. The male officer pointed. Peter Els turned to look. When he turned back, his face was an anagram for confusion.

She must have thought I was punishing her. He held the half-open door and studied the ceiling. *I'm sorry to have bothered anyone. It felt like an emergency.*

The officer nodded toward the lump. *Can we have a look?*

Els flinched. *At what? She's dead.* After a clumsy pause, he stepped aside.

In Els's living room, the uniforms looked harsher and more hardware-laden. The three walls of floor-to-ceiling shelves stuffed with books and CDs unnerved the male officer. He stepped over the gate and down the hall to the covered lump lying on the floor, where he turned back the sheet.

That dog trusted me, Els said.

Goldens are good dogs, the woman said.

That dog loved everybody. I'm surprised she lasted fourteen years.

The male officer pulled the quilt back over the corpse. He retreated down the hall and stepped back over the gate. He fingered his belt: baton, handcuffs, communicator, keys, pepper spray, flashlight, gun. His brass name bar read Mark Powell. *You'll have to contact Animal Care and Control.*

I thought I'd . . . Els thumbed toward the back of the house. *Give her a decent burial. She loved it back there.*

You have to call Animal Care and Control, sir. Reasons of public health. We can give you the number.

Ah! Peter Els raised his brows and nodded, as if all kinds of mysteries at last made sense. The woman gave him a number. She assured him that the law required the call and that nothing could be easier.

Officer Powell scanned the shelves of CDs: thousands of discs, the latest obsolete technology. A large wooden frame, like a freestanding coat rack, stood against one wall. Several sawn-off water-cooler bottles hung from the frame by bungee cords.

Powell touched his belt. *Judas Priest!*

Cloud chamber bowls, Els said.

Cloud chamber? Isn't that some kind of . . . ?

It's just a name, Els said. *You play them.*

You're a musician?

I used to teach it. Composition.

A songwriter?

Peter Els cupped his elbows and bowed his head. *It's complicated.*

What do you mean, 'complicated'? Techno-folk? Psychobilly ska?

I don't write much anymore.

Officer Powell looked up. *Why not?*

A lot of music in the world.

The communicator on the policeman's belt hissed and a woman's voice issued phantom instructions.

True, that. A lot of everything.

The officers swung back toward the front door. Off the dining room, a study stood open. The room's shelves swelled with beakers, tubing, and jars with printed labels. A half-sized refrigerator stood next to a long counter, where a compound microscope sat hooked up to a computer. The white metal body, black eyepieces, and silver objective looked like an infant Imperial Stormtrooper. More equipment covered a workbench on the far wall, glowing with colored LCDs.

Whoa, Officer Powell said.

My lab, Els explained.

I thought you wrote songs.

It's a hobby. It relaxes me.

The woman, Officer Estes, frowned. *What are all the petri dishes for?*

Peter Els wiggled his fingers. *To house bacteria. Same as us.*

Would you mind if we . . . ?

Els drew back and studied his interrogator's badge. *It's getting a little late.*

The police officers traded glances. Officer Powell opened his mouth to clarify, then stopped.

All right, Officer Estes said. *We're sorry about your dog.*

Peter Els shook his head. *That dog would sit and listen for hours. She loved every kind of music there is. She even sang along.*

When the police left the house, the wind had died and the insects paused their eerie explorations. For half a measure, as the officers headed down the sidewalk, there came a softness bordering on peace. The dark calm lasted all the way to the car, where the pair at once began placing calls.

What was I thinking? I wasn't, really. I've always been guilty
of thinking too much. This was doing, pure and simple.

The dog answered only to Fidelio, from the moment Els first
used the name. Music launched her into ecstasies. She loved
long, held intervals, preferably seconds, major or minor. When
any human sustained a pitch for more than a heartbeat, she
couldn't help joining in.

There was method to Fidelio's crooning. If Els held a D, the
dog went to E-flat or E. If Els moved to Fidelio's pitch, the dog
slid a semi-tone up or down. If a human chorus held a chord,
the dog sang a note that wasn't in it. Whatever pitches the pack
served up, Fidelio found one that hadn't yet been taken.

In the creature's howling, Els heard the roots of music—the
holy society of small discord.

The few solid studies Els could find on the musicality of
dogs suggested they resolved only about a third of an octave.
But Fidelio always came within a whole tone of any pitch
Els sang. Research into the effects of musical genres on dogs
claimed that heavy metal agitated while Vivaldi sedated them.
No great shock: Els had once declared, in one of the few
interviews he'd ever been asked to give, that *The Four Seasons*
should come with the same warning label as any powerful
tranquilizer. This was years before the birth of the calm-a-pet
industry: *Music Dogs Love, Vol. 1, Soothe Your Animal, Tunes to
Play While You're Away.*

At twenty-one, Els had worshipped at the shrine of Wagner.
So he knew about Peps, Wagner's spaniel muse and the cowriter
of *Tannhäuser.* Peps would lie at Wagner's feet under the piano

while he worked. If a passage didn't please Peps, the dog leapt up on the desk and howled until Wagner abandoned the idea. There were years when Els could have used such a candid critic, and Fidelio might have obliged. But Els had stopped writing music by the time Fidelio came along.

Like Peps, Fidelio was good health to her owner. She reminded Els when to eat or walk. And she asked for nothing in return but to be part of the two-dog pack, loyal to her alpha and free to howl whenever the music played.

Els read about other musical dogs. There was the bulldog Dan, immortalized in the eleventh of Elgar's *Enigma Variations,* who growled at out-of-tune singers. The bull terrier Bud had performed a Stephen Foster medley in the White House for Eleanor and Franklin D., five years before Peter was born. Thirty years later, as Els wandered through a John Cage Happening in Urbana, Illinois, Lyndon Johnson and his mutt Yuki performed a duet on camera for a stupefied nation. In the three short decades from Bud to Yuki, biplanes had given way to moon rockets and Aldis lamps had become the ARPANET. Music had gone from Copland to Crumb, from "A Fine Romance" to "Heroin." But nothing at all had changed in the music of dogs.

Fidelio's appetite for singing never wavered. Not for her, the insatiable need for novelty. She never tired of warhorses, but neither did she recognize anything Els played her, however often she heard it. A permanent, moving dance, in an eternal Standing Now: that's how she took in every piece they listened to together, night after night, for years. Fidelio loved all the great landmarks of the twentieth century, but she perked up just as happily to the digital chimes of an ice-cream truck from blocks away on a summer's evening. Hers was a connoisseurship Els would have traded his for, in a heartbeat.

I had no idea what might happen. That's the trouble with making things. You never do.

Was tonality *out there*—God-given? Or were those magic ratios, like everything human, makeshift rules to be broken on the way to a more merciless freedom? Fidelio became Els's lab animal, his experiment in musical universals. The dog got excited simply watching Els fetch the scuffed clarinet case of his childhood. Duet time again: she'd start baying before Els played a note. The first thing to check was octave equivalence. Els held a tone, and the dog answered in a mournful interval. But if the clarinet jumped an octave, the dog held steady, as if the pitch hadn't changed at all.

The experiment convinced Els that his dog heard octaves much as humans did. Octaves were built into the body, a truth that held not only across cultures but over genomes. Run from *Do* to *Do*, no matter how you divvied up the steps in between, and even other species heard the pitches double back on themselves, like a color wheel.

Only a crazy person would care. But Fidelio's response thrilled Els. It returned him to all those years in the wilderness, pushing the human ear toward places it wouldn't gladly go, searching through musical math for a shortcut to the sublime. Fidelio, that happy creature baying at the whims of Els's clarinet, hinted at something in music beyond taste, built into the evolved brain.

Els had staked his life on finding that larger thing. Something magnificent and enduring hid under music's exhausted surface. Somewhere behind the familiar staff lay

constellations of notes, sequences of pitches that could bring
the mind home.

He still believed the thing was there. But with his dog dead
and he himself on the waiting list, he no longer believed he'd
find it in this lifetime.

Maybe I made a mistake. But Cage says: A "mistake" is
beside the point. Once anything happens, it authentically is.

He went out to the backyard with a flashlight, a shovel, and
a lump wrapped in a quilt. He picked a spot by a line of box-
woods that Fidelio had loved to mark. Already, the little plot
was covered over with a dense mat of weed species. Life traded
in a profligate overkill that never failed to stun him. Els set the
flashlight into the crook of a honeysuckle, took up the shovel,
and dug.

The thump of his sole on the rung and the snick of the shovel
whiffing into stony earth set a calming two step. When the hole
was deep enough to hold the companion of his late years, he
put down the shovel and picked up the body. Fidelio now felt
light, like something had left her in the hour and a half since
she'd died.

He stood on the edge of the hole, considering the quilt. His
ex-wife had made it from their spent clothes more than forty
years ago, in the happiest stretch of their shared years. The
quilt was large and luminous, in deep shades of cerulean, jade,
emerald, and chartreuse. The pattern was called Night in the
Forest, and Maddy had taken almost two years to complete
it. Alongside the set of cloud chamber bowls, it was the finest

thing Els owned. Sanity demanded that he salvage, clean, and leave it on a shelf for his daughter to find when he died. But Fidelio had died in this quilt, the most uncomprehending of deaths, comforted only by the familiar coverlet. If humans had a soul, surely this creature did. And if humans did not, then no gesture here was too fine or ridiculous. Els apologized to Maddy, whom he hadn't seen in decades, and placed the bundle into the earth.

The quilt-wrapped corpse nestled in the pit of loam. By the flashlight's glow, Night in the Forest glistened in rich, cool tones. For a moment, those dark greens redeemed all the pain that he and Maddy had ever inflicted on each other.

Humming to himself a slowly unfolding upward phrase, Els picked up the shovel again. Six times in the course of his seven decades, he'd been forced to remember how grief made you love the smallest, most mistaken thing. This was the seventh.

A voice said, *What are you doing?* Els gasped and dropped the shovel.

Startled by that startle, the voice called out, *It's me.*

Standing on a lawn chair, the neighbors' eight-year-old peeked out over the slats of the wooden fence. Eight-year-old children, wandering around unsupervised in the middle of the night. Els couldn't remember the boy's name. Like all boys' names in the age of social networking, it began with a J.

What's that? J asked in a silky whisper.

I'm burying my dog.

In that?

It's like a grave offering.

J knew all about grave offerings from multiplayer online games.

You can bury them in your yard?

She liked it back here. Nobody has to know, right?

Can I see it?

No, Els said. *She's peaceful now.*

Els picked up the shovel and scooped dirt into the hole. J watched, rabid with interest. He'd seen several thousand deaths already in his young life. But a careful burial was the wildest novelty.

The hole became a modest mound. Els stood over it, looking for the next step in this ad hoc service.

She was a good dog, Fidelio. Very smart.

Fidelio?

Her name.

That's long for Fido or something?

This dog could sing. This dog could tell pretty chords from harsh ones.

Els didn't mention that she preferred the harsh ones.

J looked suspicious. *What did she sing?*

Everything. She was very broad-minded. Els took the flashlight and waved it toward the fence. *You think we should try to sing something for her?*

J shook his head. *I don't know any sad songs. Except for the funny ones.*

I wanted to remember how life really worked and see if chemistry still wanted something from me.

Eight-year-old Peter hides in the pantry of his mock-Tudor home, cowering in his Gene Autry pajamas, spying on his parents, flouting every law of God and man. He doesn't care about being caught. He's doomed already, anyway. The Reds had

exploded an A-bomb weeks before, and Karl Els has told the
assembled fathers of the neighborhood, over ribs barbequed in
an enormous pit, that the planet has another five years, tops. The
cookout is the neighborhood's last hurrah. With the ribs gone,
all those condemned fathers and their wives gather around the
Els Hammond chord organ, a gin glass in every other hand, a
chorus of sloshed innocents singing goodbye. They sing:

> There's a bower of roses by Bendemeer's Stream,
> and the nightingale sings 'round it all the day long.

Big brother Paul is asleep in the attic bedroom, one story
above. Susan frets in her crib at the foot of the stairs. And Peter
stands in the surge of these chords, listening to America's fare-
well song. The notes float and rise. They turn speech as pointless
as a radio ventriloquist. Light and darkness splash over Peter at
each chord change, thrill with no middleman. The pitches top-
ple forward; they fall beat by beat into their followers, obeying
an inner logic, dark and beautiful.

Another milky, troubled chord twists the boy's belly. Several
promising paths lead forward into unknown notes. But of all
possible branches, the melody goes strange. One surprise leap
prickles Peter's skin. Welts bloom on his forearms. His tiny
manhood stiffens with inchoate desire.

The drunken angel band sets out on a harder song. These
new chords are like the woods on the hill near Peter's grand-
mother's, where his father once took them sledding. Step by step
the singers stumble forward into a thicket of tangled harmonies.

Something reaches out and trips the tune. His mother's fingers
lose their way. She stabs at several keys, all of them wrong. The
gin-waving singers tumble laughing into a ditch. Then, from

his hiding place, the pajama-boy sings out the pitches of the lost chord. The ensemble turns to face the intruder. They'll punish him now, for breaking more rules than anyone can count.

His mother tries the suggested chord. It's startling but obvious —better than the one she was searching for. The gin-soaked singers cheer the child. Peter's father crosses the room and nips him on the rump, sends him back up to bed with a suspended sentence. *And don't come back down unless we need you again!*

TWO MONTHS LATER, young Peter stands clutching his clarinet in the wings at his first citywide competition. Every pleasure, he has already learned, must turn into a contest. His mother wants to spare him the gladiator ritual. But his father, who—so claims brother Paul—killed a German rifleman in the war, declares that the best way to protect a boy from public judgment is to subject him to heavy doses.

Someone calls Peter's name. He stumbles onstage, his head full of helium. Bowing to the room of utter blackness, he loses his balance and staggers forward. The full house laughs. He sits down to play his piece, Schumann's "Of Strange Lands and People." His accompanist waits for a nod, but Peter can't remember how the tune starts. His arms ooze jelly. Somehow his hands remember the way. He blows through the piece too fast, too loud, and by the time he finishes he's in tears. The applause is his cue to run offstage, humiliated.

He ends up in the bathroom, puking his guts into the toilet. Vomit flecks his clip-on bow tie when he comes out to face his mother. She wraps his head into her breastbone and says, *Petey. You don't have to do this anymore.*

He pulls free of her, horrified. *You don't understand. I have to play.*

He wins second prize in his age group—a pewter G clef that his parents put on the mantelpiece next to his brother's 1948 little league Division B fielding trophy. Three decades later, the thing will turn up wrapped in newspaper in his mother's attic, a year after her death.

I'd been hearing that tune for sixty years. Musical taste changes so little. The sound of late childhood plays at our funerals.

Carnegie Elementary, Fisk Junior, Rockefeller High: Peter Els survives them all, propelled from Dick and Jane to gerunds and participles, the *Monitor* and *Merrimac*, Stanley and Livingstone, tibias and fibulas, acids and bases. He memorizes "Hiawatha's Childhood," "Ozymandias," and "The New Colossus"; their rich dotted rhythms fill the dead spots of his late afternoons.

By twelve, he masters the mystic slide rule's crosshair. He toys with square roots and looks for secret messages in the digits of pi. He calculates the area of countless right triangles and maps the ebb and flow of French and German armies across five hundred years of Europe. Teachers rotate like the circle of fifths, each of them insisting that childhood give way to accumulating fact.

He loves his music lessons best. Week by month by year, the clarinet yields to him. The études his teachers assign unlock ever more elaborate and enchanted places. He seems to be something of a native speaker.

It's a gift, his mother says.

A talent, his father corrects.

His father, too, is obsessed with music, or at least with

ever-higher fidelity. Every few months, Karl Els invests in clearer, finer, more powerful components until the speakers cabled to his vacuum tube stereo amp are bigger than a migrant worker's bungalow. On these he bombards his family with light classics. Strauss waltzes. *The Merry Widow.* The man blasts, "I am the very model of a modern Major General," until their pacifist neighbor threatens to call the police. Every Sunday afternoon and four nights a week, young Peter listens to the records spin. He combs through the changing harmonies, now and then hearing secret messages float above the fray.

And it's on his father's stereophonic rig that Peter, age eleven, first hears Mozart's *Jupiter.* A rainy Sunday afternoon in October, boggy hours of excruciating boredom, and who knows where the other kids are? Upstairs listening to *The Blandings* or *The Big Show,* playing jacks or pickup sticks, or spinning the bottle down in Judy Breyer's basement. Deep in Sunday malaise, Peter works his way through his father's micro-groove records, looking for the cure to his perpetual ache that must be hiding somewhere inside those colored cardboard sleeves.

Three movements of Symphony 41 pass by: destiny and noble sacrifice, nostalgia for a vanished innocence, and a minuet so elegant it bores the bejeezus out of him. And then the finale, its four modest notes. Do, re, fa, mi: half a jumbled scale. Too simple to be called invented. But the thing spills out into the world like one of those African antelopes that fall from the womb, still wet with afterbirth but already running.

Young Peter props up on his elbows, ambushed by a memory from the future. The shuffled half scale gathers mass; it sucks up other melodies into its gravity. Tunes and countertunes split off and replicate, chasing each other in a cosmic game of tag. At two minutes, a trapdoor opens underneath the boy. The first floor of the house dissolves above a gaping hole. Boy, stereo, speaker boxes, the love seat he sits on: all hang in place, floating on the gusher of sonority pouring into the room.

Five viral strands propagate, infecting the air with runaway joy. At three and a half minutes, a hand scoops Peter up and lifts him high above the blocked vantage of his days. He rises in the shifting column of light and looks back down on the room where he listens. Wordless peace fills him at the sight of his own crumpled, listening body. And pity for anyone who mistakes this blinkered life for the real deal.

At six minutes into the amazement, the five galloping melodies align in a quintuple fugue. Lines echo and overlap, revealing where the music has been heading from the opening Do. They plait together too tightly for Peter's ear to make out everything that happens inside the five-way weave. The sound surrounds him, and Peter is immanent, inside it all, a small but crucial part of everywhere.

When silence sets him down once more, he no longer believes in the place. He wanders around dazed for the rest of the afternoon. The family house denies that anything just happened. His lone proof is on the record, and for the next three days, Peter wears out the vinyl with dropping the needle onto it. Even his father yells at him to listen to something else. He falls asleep nightly to the cascade of notes. All he wants to do forever is to take the magnificent timepiece apart and put its meshed gears back together again. To recover that feeling of being clear, present, *here*, various and vibrant, as huge and noble as an outer planet.

Jupiter beckons, but each visit is a little weaker. Within a month, Peter gives up, trapped again on the unrelenting Earth. He rattles through the rooms and slams the doors of the split-level ranch. He bikes in fury, up and down the cluster of streets lined with homes just like his, streets that twist along each other like a thumbprint whorl. Tunes trickle out from kitchen windows, melodies as savory as the scent of brisket and cabbage. But Peter has no patience for them anymore. His ear has left and gone elsewhere.

He falls out of step with the neighborhood. The pleasures of others begin to baffle him, given where he's been. Sports feel like pointless seesaws, movies grow way too cheery, and loud cars depress him. He hates the gray, flat, fake, cardboard worlds of TV, although once, to trance himself, he sits and gazes for half an hour at a screen of boiling static, a message from deep space. And even after he kills the tube, he goes on staring at the shriveling periscope in the center of the screen, a portal to that place he can't get back to.

By thirteen, Peter Els is out of sync with the whole eight-cylinder, aerodynamic zeal of America. He no longer cares whom his tastes embarrass. He needs nothing but his math and his Mozart, the maps back to that distant planet.

One endless June Saturday in Peter's fourteenth year, his brother Paul and friends abduct him from his bedroom and drag him down to the half-finished basement, where they lash him to a barstool and make him listen to 45s on a portable turntable the size of a steamer trunk. "Maybellene." "Earth Angel." "Rock Around the Clock." They force-feed him hits, sure that they can break the kid and remake him into something a little less square. They even toss around the idea of shock therapy.

Come on, cat. Pull your head out of your ass and listen.

Peter tries. *That one's great*, he says. *Nice walking bass.*

He does his best to sound enthused, but the posse sees through him. They drill another tune into him: "The Great Pretender."

It's a catchy sing–along that turns into Chinese water torture after the first chorus.

So what's the problem this time, knucklehead?

There's no problem! It's just that . . . He closes his eyes and calls out, downbeat by downbeat: *Tonic. Subdominant. Dominant. Those guys need to learn some new chords.*

Criminetly. What's wrong with the chords they got?

Nothing at all, if those three make you happy. But what's happiness, compared to an earful of forever?

It's not about the chords, Paul spits.

It doesn't go anywhere, Pauly. It just sits there, circling the drain.

Circling . . . ? Are you bat-shit deaf? His brother gets that faraway look: the sledge, the sex, the drill of infant rock. *You can't hear that? Freedom, you dried-up little turd!*

Peter hears only harmonic jail.

The tribunal puts on "Blue Suede Shoes." Peter shrugs: Why not? Peppy dimestore fun. His refusal to swoon maddens his older brother. Paul cocks back his arm to brain the punk with a Magic 8-Ball. But an ecstasy of backbeat sweeps him up, and he calls out, *Listen to that. Jeez! Does music get any better?*

He flicks the cannon shot across the drum-flooded basement. Peter catches it, bows his head, and reads the plastic fortune-teller's reply:

CONCENTRATE AND ASK AGAIN.

All my life I thought I knew what music was. But I was like a kid who confuses his grandfather with God.

A boy treads in the shallows of a summer lake. Sky and pine in all directions, the buzz of noisy relatives. The air has the heft of vacation, with Peter back in the early rehearsals for his life.

Call it late afternoon, but hours before dark. This far north, near the solstice, the sun hangs for days near its zenith before dropping into dusk. The lake fills with swimming children: an Elsfest—that annual jag that his errant family branch rarely dares attend. Elses from across the States lay claim to the southern shore of this northern water. Thirty yards out, kids swarm a plywood float lashed to empty oil drums, like ants massing a melting sugar cube. Shore-hugging uncles fish beer bottles from an ice-filled zinc trough and open them on the trough's handle. Aunts and worse stretch out on beach blankets in a suntan assembly line. Elses in all directions. Not even Peter's father can identify the whole bevy of relatives. One tiny Russian device—even a conventional one—would finish off the family name.

Midsummer comes with a crystalline theme that Peter has been practicing to death for days. He woke this daybreak and woodshedded for hours, up in his hillside hideout, on the Evette & Schaeffer clarinet his father found for him at an estate sale. By the time he joined the others down at the lake, summer's theme was burned deep into his brain.

His clarinet is the one thing Peter would take with him to the moon or a desert island or prison. His fingers come home to the keys; he practices even here, under the waves of this summer lake. He can swell, launch leaps, race up and down the tube in runs that feel invincible. Playing is like solving a perfect proof—QED.

The tune under his fingers this summer is the new national anthem of his desire. He'll perform it next month in his downtown debut, with twelve older players. The piece is everywhere, in the bobbing water, in the raft-swarming chatter. He loves that dance suite like he loves his mother, who lies up on the shore of this upstate lake in her gappy one-piece suit with the little skirt that makes her look like a Ponchielli hippo ballerina. He knows the music better than he knows his father, there on his lifeguard rotation, Lucky Strike in one hand and Carling Black Label in the other, conducting the Els uncles in a verbal brawl.

Peter can't name the secret of the suite's power. But somehow its first few notes, like the rays of sunrise over eastern mountains, lay down a foundation for all the developments to come. They return at the end, layered against an old Shaker hymn tune, to make a sound bigger than any country. He can't say how that simple return produces a release so spacious and shattering. He knows only that the piece predicts even this blazing afternoon, these bracing lake breezes. Peter has tried to imitate them, jotting down his own chords on systems of clean staff paper—a boy's pencil sketch of the stupor that dizzies his head each time he hears this piece's openness.

He will love this music to death. In a few more years, he'll snort at its sentiment and mock its stirring progressions. Once you've loved like that, the only safe haven is resentment. Peter won't realize until too late that all he ever wanted was to move a listener the way these variations moved him.

But the throats of his dozens of younger cousins scream another soundtrack altogether. One by one they scramble up on the raft, swivel their broomstick hips, shout, *I'm all shook up!* and jackknife into the water. The older kids take up a game called smear the queer, dunking whoever dares hold an orange beach ball. Bodies plunge. Yelps spatter the air. Peter clings to the float's algae-coated ladder, keeping his fingers safely underwater. Horseflies as big as hummingbirds nip at his nape.

He watches Minnesota cousin Kate carve her manic path
through the swarm. Who knew that such surprise could move
about on two bare legs? Peter has scribbled her name with ball-
point deep down in the soles of his All Stars, where no one but
he will ever know the word is hidden. He has dreamed of her
haunches and the backs of her knees. Now she's everywhere
at once in this water war, colluding, colliding, cannonballing
through the air, crawling back onto the float and hitching up
a slipped strap as if her apricot tit didn't just go sunning. Her
Mayday cries quicken Peter's flesh, and the kick of her scissoring
legs matches that ballet suite running through his brain. Her
smile plots the next escapade even before her last one is finished.

Up on shore, around the hissing grill pits, the Els patriarchs
wage a war of their own. Their words reach Peter above the
shrieks of the raft battle. The women, from their sun chaises and
mah-jongg tables, shout at their spouses to give it a rest. Can it.
Or better: bottle. *Hey Mabel—Black Label!* Peter's three favorite
aunts—two real ones and one aunt's companion, a trio who
sing each night around the campfire, reliving the glory years of
their Andrews Sisters knockoff act, when their shiny-tight added
sixth chords once backed for Sinatra himself—start belting out
"Ac-Cent-Tchu-Ate the Positive." Half the Els Tabernacle Choir
joins in on, "Don't mess with Mister In-Between."

But Mister In-Between is everywhere, messing with them.
The men wade into current events. They determine what went
wrong in Korea. Peter's father—self-made insurance sales force
manager with a captured Nazi flag hanging in his subterranean
rec room—declares that America should have bombed its way
up both banks of the Yalu until the Chinese saw reason. Elses
of all stripes parry him with snub beer-bottle lances. *Get a load
of this guy! He's off his nut!*

A squeal from lissom Kate dispels all politics. She launches off the raft, arcing into the air with a C# of delight, a missile aimed to land with deadly precision inside a ring of Pittsburgh male cousins.

When Peter turns his ears back shoreward, the adults have crossed the bloodstained map to Hungary. Uncles decree that going up against the Russians for nothing would have been suicide. *For nothing?* Peter's father shouts. *We egged those people on; we then left them for dead.* But he's outgunned, scoffed at even by the chorus line of sunbathing aunts.

The uncles jump from Hungary back home, drawn along by the family need to fight. They squabble over the buses down South, the black and white chess game for the nation's soul. Karl Els pokes a bottle in his brother Hank's chest and says that blacks have more right to North America than whites. Uncles swat the air, dismissing him and his whole blighted branch. *Aw, go raise your rabble in the Congo.*

Awful names ring out onshore, words from the forbidden list. Peter's mother starts to cry. Her husband tells her to grow up. The Elsfest threatens to go the way of world affairs. Peter searches the lake for help. His hundred cousins are hammering out the rules for a game of tackle water polo. His mother sits wrapped in her French towel, sobbing. His father sucks a cigarette through the cup of his hand. Peter glances at brother Paul, who glares back a warning shot. Paul has never been so popular as he is today, and he will not let this party end. On the far side of the raft, little sister Susan, already addicted to giddiness, spins herself silly in her inner tube.

The music dies. His mother combs the beach, gathering up her things and crushing them into her beach bag. Peter slips from his seat on the slime-slick ladder and starts to breaststroke back to the beach. But a voice from behind hooks him.

Hey, licorice stick. C'mere a sec.

Cousin Kate, sleek and shiny as any marine mammal, splits him with a smile. Her challenge unfolds as it has a hundred times already in Peter's private theater. But she doesn't wait for a response, just paddles around to the hidden cove on the raft's deep side. Peter follows, helpless in her wake. The great adventure of his life is beginning at last, and the tune unfolds just as he has practiced it.

He draws near to where she floats, her hand on the raft.

Licorice stick. You like me?

He nods, and she plunges through the water onto him. Her legs wrap around his chest, pulling him down. Her clasping weight swamps him, and they go under. In the green cloud, her coiled body inches over his. Her tongue probes his mouth, filling him with the taste of lake. A thigh whacks his groin. Pain shoots up his whole length, and with it, a filament of sharpest pleasure. He paws her slippery skin and snags a fallen strap. She pushes away, back toward air. A foot catches his face on their scramble upward, and his nose fills up with water. He tastes the murk of whatever comes after life. Liquid goes down his windpipe, and he starts to drown.

Rising, he rams a slimy mass. He comes up underneath the raft. The green-smeared oil cans bang him. His head pounds with the need to breathe. He jerks sideways, frantic for an opening, but tangles on the seaweed-coated anchor chain.

At last he snaps free. He surfaces, coughing up algae, grappling on the raft's edge and sucking air. Nearby, a pair of California cousins laugh at this, the most hilarious thing they've seen all day.

His vision clears. He looks around for Cousin Kate. She's leagues away, bobbing in the waves and singing at full voice for an admiring crowd. *Come smoke a Coca-Cola, drink ketchup cigarettes. See Lillian Russell wrestle with a box of Oysterettes!*

His mother stands calling at the water's edge. *Petey! Are you okay?*

A California cousin shouts, *Only his hairdresser knows for sure.*

Peter waves; he's fine. More green water issues from his lungs. The air fills with shrieks that pass for laughter. He thinks he might be dead, still thumping against the underside of the raft. His father looms up onshore and blasts his metal lifeguard whistle. *Everybody out for a head count. Chop-chop.*

Sister Susan doesn't hear. She's trying to force every part of her inner tube underwater at the same time. Brother Paul, enjoying a brief reign as king of the raft, yells back, *Five more minutes!*

Not five minutes. Now! You don't bargain with your father.

In fact, every exchange with the man since their infancy has been a haggle. A couple of nervous aunts rise from their beach blankets and count their kids. Another calls her daughters from the lake. There's a general summoning, and the whole surly group, crushed again by adult whim, readies to swim in.

Then, on some invisible cue—a shift in the wind, a cloud across the sun—the group will changes to won't. The ringleaders detect a fatal softness in the adult demand. *Coming!* they call falsetto, half compromise, half jeer. They swim back to the raft, across a moat too wide for any beer-addled old man to ford. Karl Els blows the whistle again—two violent blasts for no one.

One of the Pittsburgh lieutenants snarls, *He's gonna swim out and drag us all back one-handed?*

Kate's mountainous brother Doug sniggers from his roost on

the edge of the float. A line of dark hair runs from the dimple of his sternum all the way to his navel. The fur gives him dominion over the whole raft. *Let him try.* His grin declares the whole great span of human events to be Howdy Doody time.

Karl Els calls his sons by name. Paul studies the landlocked man, and Peter studies Paul. Too many seconds click off for life ever to come right again. Even if they submit now, the weakest imaginable punishment will be terrible.

His father's shame reddens Peter. A bankrupt government of one, mocked by a lake full of children . . . One short swim to shore and Peter might still rescue the man, help him pretend that nothing has changed in the order of things.

A sneer from Paul freezes him. Kate, too, holds Peter with a look, threatening bottomless contempt if he surrenders and promising prizes if he stays true. Everything alive wants his loyalty.

Treading water, Peter eyes his father. He wants to tell the man: It's nothing. A summer game. Patterns on the air—over before you know it. Queasiness engulfs him. How easy it would be, to kick out into the center of the lake until he can't kick anymore. But Peter can only bob, weightless, between this rebel raft and the imperial shore. The music in his head, that Shaker tune of his green practicing, scatters into noise. He will dog-paddle in place, a lone child, waving his stick arms and kicking his feeble legs until strength fails him and he goes down.

The day fragments into frozen shards. His father, beet-red, staggers, sheds the cigarette and beer. He plunges into the lake. But he doesn't swim. There's rushing, shouting, confusion. Uncles in the water, dragging the thrashing bulk back onto land. His crushed father, clutching his chest, propped against a cabin, ashen and sneering at the wisdom of crowds. That crowd, on the beach, like statues, heads bowed. Too late, Peter swims in, as hard as he can. But he hangs back from the pallid man, terrified, and soon they have his father in a car and heading to a doctor.

Music forecasts the past, recalls the future. Now and then the difference falls away, and in one simple gift of circling sound, the ear solves the scrambled cryptogram. One abiding rhythm, present and always, and you're free. But a few measures more, and the cloak of time closes back around you.

The fatal heart attack followed an hour later, in a rural clinic where the lone GP with his shelves full of gauze bandages, tongue depressors, and rubbing alcohol was helpless to do anything but put Karl Els in an ambulance for Potsdam. He died in transit, miles from anywhere, still blowing his lifeguard's whistle, leaving behind a son convinced he'd helped to kill him.

In middle age, Peter Els would spend years writing an opera, the story of an ecstatic rebellion gone wrong. For years, the piece seemed to him like a prophecy of End Time. Not until the age of seventy, an old man burying his dog, did he recognize it, at last, as childhood memory.

Crumb: "Music is a system of proportions in the service of a spiritual impulse." My spirit's impulse just happened to be criminal.

Els brushes off the dirt, goes inside, and looks for something to play for his dog's funeral. He lands on Mahler's *Kindertotenlieder*: five songs lasting twenty-five minutes. Fidelio used to go nuts with the cycle, back in her puppyhood. At the very first measures of the first song she'd start crooning, the way she did when Els took her to the park on a fall night under the full moon.

The choice feels a little maudlin. It's not as though a human has died. Not Sara, the three a.m. call he can't even imagine well enough to dread. Not Paul or Maddy or a former student. Not Richard. Only a pet, who had no clue what was happening. Only an old dog, who gave him unconditional joy and loyalty for no good reason.

He and Fidelio often attended imaginary musical funerals —preemptive memorials of pure sound. Nothing was more invigorating than dark music, the pleasure of a practice run, the chance to make imagination the equal of death. But tonight is no rehearsal. He has lost the one listening partner who could return to the same old pieces and hear them afresh each night, for the first time. *A little lamp has gone out in my tent. Hail to the joyous light of the world.*

The recording sits on his shelf, a prophecy from a hundred years ago. These five songs first taught Els how music might work. In the half century since, he has gone back to them through every sonic revolution. No music would ever again be as mysterious as this music was, the day he discovered it. But tonight he can listen one more time, take in their wild noise the way an animal might.

He fumbles the disc out of its jewel box while doing the math: an eight-year-old who heard Schumann's *Scenes of Childhood* in the year it was published could, at seventy-five, have attended the premiere of Mahler's *Songs on the Death of Children*. From the spring of Romanticism to Modernist winter in one life. That was the curse of literacy: Once you started writing music down, the game was half over. Notation touched off a rush to uncover

every trick hiding out in the rules of harmony. Ten short centuries had burned through all available innovations, each more
fleeting than the last. The accelerating vehicle would one day
have to hit the wall, and it was Els's luck to be alive at the
moment of smash-up.

By the time Peter first heard Mahler's songs, his own childhood had long since died. It ended with his father's heart attack,
the raft uprising. For a long time, nothing softened Peter's guilt
about that day more than listening to the best of his father's
records: the *Jupiter*, the *Eroica*, the *Unfinished*. Once or twice,
the music reopened that purer world, just alongside his own.
Then his mother got rid of all his father's records, all his clothes,
every possession that gave memory any power over the present.
Without even asking her children, she donated the music to
Goodwill.

Way too fast, Carrie Els got remarried, to a casualty actuary who'd worked with Peter's father. Ronnie Halverson, a
big, friendly man whose Bennett Cerf puns and quid pro quo
morality were as inexorable as death, took gentle possession of
the Els home. He filled the house with big bands on Saturday
mornings while he fried up hash browns and omelets for all, and
he never understood why his gifted stepson refused to hear, in
the sweet, swinging liberty of Woody Herman and Artie Shaw,
how the clarinet ought in fact to be handled. Peter made peace
with the intruder, did his homework, delivered his newspapers,
practiced, played in the local youth symphony, smiled at adults
whenever they smiled at him, and scribbled down furious,
revengeful tutti passages for enraged full orchestra, which he
hid in a spiral-bound music notebook between his mattress
and bed slats.

At fifteen, he fell in love with chemistry. The pattern language of atoms and orbitals made sense in a way that little else but music did. Balancing chemical equations felt like solving a Chinese puzzle box. The symmetries hidden in the columns of the periodic table had something of the *Jupiter*'s grandeur. And a person might even make a living with the stuff.

Then, on the first day of senior year, from across a packed homeroom, Els spotted Clara Reston and recognized her as coming from a planet even more remote than his. He'd watched her with pained lust across the bowl of the high school orchestra the year before, primped up behind her cello in muslin skirts and thin-ribbed pullovers that the school should have banned, drawing her bow across her instrument with an all-denying smile. Slim-framed, her posture like a bookend, and with four feet of hair that fell below her knees, she looked like a Tolkien elf. And she could play the silliest arrangement of the state song as if it were the first tune ever to spring from Apollo's lyre.

He gazed on Clara across the classroom in a stupor of admiration. As if he willed it, she lifted her eyes to intercept his and tilted her fine head, knowing everything. Her look said: Took you long enough. And in that glance, the morning of his life changed into blustery noon.

Two days later she came up to Peter in the hall and stepped on his right foot with the tip of hers. *Hey,* she said. *What do you think of the Zemlinsky Clarinet Trio?*

He'd never heard of Zemlinsky. She appraised him with a smile that hinted at a very long list of things he'd never heard of.

The next week, she had parts for them to sight-read. They spent two hours working through the Andante. Just the pair of them: the school had no pianist who could handle the piece. The movement started with an extended solo piano passage that Peter figured they'd skip. But Clara insisted they sit and count their measures of shared tacet. She could hear the ghostly keyboard as clearly as if it were there, playing alongside them. And soon enough, so could he.

They read through a dozen pieces that way—trios, quartets, quintets—their two lines sailing out over the hush of the missing instruments. Once they read a piece, they followed up by listening to a recording.

Listening alongside her, he began to make out the muted message that he'd always suspected lay underneath the surface of sounds. And watching Clara listen, he saw that she possessed a key that he did not.

Sometimes, she told him, *when I listen? I'm everywhere.*

Soon they were listening together two or three evenings a week. And before long, listening turned to another kind of playing.

In November, when Clara decided he was ready, she gave him the *Kindertotenlieder.* Els knew Mahler's name, but had shunned the music. He'd accepted the prevailing opinion about the man: too long-winded, too banal, too neurotic, too twisted up in marches and ländlers and pub songs. How teenaged Clara came to love the still-little-heard composer, Peter never knew. Truth was, once she dropped the needle down on the first track of those five blighted songs, he had more urgent questions.

They listened in Clara's room, with the door cracked open wide enough for propriety, while her parents prepared dinner a floor below. A night in November 1959: Earth's first artificial moons threaded the black sky above them. The phonograph spun, the song began its chromatic wanderings, and Peter Els never heard music the same way again.

As the songs played, Clara hovered over him. Her four feet of hair, which hadn't been touched by a scissors since she was six because of the pain she claimed to feel, draped him like a tent in the wilderness. Flushed and confused, her face a little cloudy, she undid the buttons of her pink seersucker blouse and placed his hand inside. And they sat stock-still, blood pounding, tangled in each other, listening to the muted reds and russets of dying children.

The story would stay with Peter better than the details of his own childhood: How in the first year of the new century, Mahler the wanderer, three times homeless—a Bohemian in Austria, an Austrian among Germans, and a Jew throughout the world—collapsed from a massive hemorrhage brought on by overwork. Only hasty surgery saved his life. During his forced convalescence, he fixed on a collection by Friedrich Rückert of more than four hundred poems to his two young children, who died of scarlet fever within two weeks of each other.

The poems had poured out of Rückert, two or three a day— thousands of raw and compulsive stanzas. Some of them were stillborn. Some were filled with a sick calm. Some sank into the hackneyed, while others talked to themselves in an airless crypt. Rückert hid them away for private use. None were published in his lifetime.

Fresh from his own near-death, Mahler read the poems like a lost diary. Seven of his thirteen siblings were dead by the age of two. His beloved younger brother died on the threshold of puberty. And here was the field guide to those deaths. The forty-one-year-old bachelor consumed the hundreds of lyrics like a parent come loose with grief.

The songs took shape, an exercise in convalescence. Then came Mahler's whirlwind marriage to the child bride, Alma Schindler. In quick succession, they had two healthy children. When, in the summer of 1904, Mahler returned to work on the songs, his wife was horrified. Incomprehensible, setting the death of children to music, when the man had kissed his own daughters good night moments before. *For God's sake, don't tempt fate!* But tempting fate was music's job description.

Els goes to the kitchen, pours single-malt scotch into a jelly glass, and takes it into the front room. He sits in the Eames chair and pushes away the footstool, making space at his feet for the dog. He goes limp, closes his eyes, and hears Clara whisper to him. *These songs are the death knell of tonality.* Where did a self-taught, eighteen-year-old virgin get such grandiosity? Els, an ignorant hick with a gift, had believed her. He'd loved her for her eager, bright pretension. And hers were the first girl's breasts he'd ever touched.

A click on the remote, and the music starts up. And one last time, in the bare opening notes, Els makes out the sounds of a death foretold. The death of a child he spent his life trying to revive.

AT FIRST, THERE'S only a thread of frost spreading across a pane. Oboe and horn trace out their parallel privacies. The thin sinews wander, an edgy duet built up from bare fourths and fifths.

The singer enters, hesitant, hinted by bassoon. She channels a man wrung out after a sleepless night, a father with nothing left to keep safe. *Now the sun will rise so brightly . . .*

The sun rises, but the line sinks. The orchestration, the nostalgic harmonies: everything wrapped in the familiar late nineteenth century, but laced with the coming fever dream. Bassoon and horn rock an empty cradle. Scant, muted violas and cellos in their upper registers enter over a quavering harp. The line wavers between major and minor, bright and dim, peace and grief, like the old hag and lovely young thing who fight for control of the fickle ink sketch. The voice sings, *It's almost as if nothing terrible happened in the night!*

Nerves gather in the broadening orchestra, joined now by clarinet and bass clarinet. Then the killer touch, the daub that Els would have traded his soul to make. The ensemble falls away to two pianissimo strikes on the glockenspiel. Then two more. A child's toy, a funeral chime, a light in the night all rolled into four soft, ringing high D's.

The lines of entwined oboe and horn return, but colored now with small, stray variants. The singer comes back, to claim that death is no more than a blot on a day that is everywhere bright and gathering. But she protests too much: When the chopped-up echoes of the opening duet reprise, shadowed now by the remorseless glockenspiel, the notes begin to go astray. The lines haunt each other in parallel intervals, perseverating, like a lone figure rocking in the corner, biting his sleeve.

The verse starts again, but the tune veers off into a vacant elsewhere. Now the voice rises where it once fell, clashing against the oboe's mirror inversion. *You must not fold up the night inside you. You must drown it in eternal light!* The singer struggles to do just that. The words try to push toward grace; the music drowns in grace's opposite. Yet the whole ensemble holds out the hope that death itself may be a brilliant light, and kinder than anyone can suppose.

In the fourth return of the instrumental interlude, the song turns deranged and the twentieth century begins. The orchestra sets off in a frantic ecstasy, gusting through chromatic swells and counterswells, shaking loose of all center, anchored only by a deep, droning pedal point in the horn.

The frenzy breaks. Flute and oboe attempt the opening lines

again, but they're dogged now by the tolling glockenspiel. A small voice says, *A little light has gone out in my tent*. The notes set a path where their offspring must go: upward into the light, over the surrender of the strings and hollow harp. But the song stutters and catches. The voice drops out, while the surging orchestra carries the melody forward. Two measures too late, the singer rallies—*Heil!*—to welcome in the joyous light of day. The orchestra obliges, pushing toward redemption. But at the last moment it falls back into minor. The last word belongs to the glockenspiel, repeating the singer's final note three octaves higher, throwing off glints from a place unreachable by grief or consolation.

At eighteen, hearing these songs while holding Clara's breasts was like graduating from the Crayola eight-pack to the rainbow box of sixty-four. At seventy, alone in the house with an untouched glass of scotch, Els can still make out, in the songs' recesses, the germ of a freedom that isn't done with him.

Why should bottomless grief feel so bracing? *The day is lovely; don't be afraid.* Over the decades, he'd read many theories about why sad music lifted the listener: The antibody theory. The sanctuary theory. Shadowboxing. Mastery by habituation. Mahler himself expressed pity for a world that would one day have to listen to these songs. Yet the cycle has sweetened Els's life beyond saying.

Don't be afraid; the day is lovely. They have only gone out, and do not feel like coming home again.

Els swirls his scotch and listens through the other four songs. His favorite passages shine and die. The second song, shifting through keys and meters, between clarity and cloud. The third song, with its Bach-like trio sonata that mimics the mother's unsteady steps: *When your mother walks through the door by the candle's light, you always come in too, slipping in behind her . . .* And that song's end, its wayward cadence on the dominant: he knows it cold, but still the run-up chills him. Someone came up with these chords. Someone remembered the sound of false recovery.

The fourth song, in radiant E-flat, always felt like the first flash of real light in the whole cycle. But tonight it's a klezmer-tinted, lurching folk dance. *They've just gone out for a long walk. They've only gone on ahead of us. The day is beautiful.* The final phrases ascend into bright uplands, the music almost escaping to the distant sunny hill the words describe, alongside two small children who can't be bothered to turn around and wave.

Then the storm. Does it make him a depressive, that he loves the storm best of all? The thrill of lightning, of an ambulance, of safety crumbling away. The full orchestra, at last—the wrenched strings, the plummeting winds—pumps out a tempest. In the interludes between each stanza, the storm blows out of control: at first nothing, then four bars, then eight. The voice ratchets up—*in this weather, in this weather, in this weather*—rising in each successive entry, from a monotone D to an E to a G. *In this raging, in this horror, I would never have let the children out!*

Guilty survivor, beating up on himself. The music locates the storm inside the singer's mind, like the one in *Peter Grimes*, another work that Clara gave Els in that year of miraculous discoveries. The song's storm isn't the one that takes the children; this is a later gale, long after the fact. *I would never have let the children out in such weather. I'd worry that they might die. Now there's no reason to worry about anything.*

Fifty-two years of listening, and Els still can't say how the thing is done. How the notes find that precise signature of doubt and hope. The bliss of giving up. Grief too great to be bought off by the promise of an afterlife. A song that predicts the end of its own tradition. But this time through, near his own cadence, Els no longer hears the prediction buried in the songs, but only the memory of discovering them once, at the end of youth. Of Clara stroking him, the storm of eighteen.

Clara laid it all out for him, after the songs ended: How two years after the premiere, Mahler's own five-year-old Maria died of scarlet fever. How the composer's shattered wife took up with another man. How Mahler himself died soon after, of a diseased heart, at fifty. And three years on: the war, the death of a generation, the collapse of the absurd empire whose end his music had long foretold . . .

Peter learned the sequel soon enough: How the dead Maria's half-sister, Manon, the daughter of Alma and the man with whom she betrayed Mahler, died three decades later, of polio. How Alban Berg brought the dead sister back to life in his Violin Concerto, an atonal miasma that climaxed in a chilling Bach chorale. How music blurred the line between prophecy and recall.

Els wraps himself in the rising storm, feeling the madness one more time. *The children were taken away from me. I had no say.* The crazed gale draws up short. It hangs on a diminuendo; the clarinet, contrabassoon, and harp shrink to nothing. And here is where Clara broke off in mid-caress and grabbed him. The skin on the old man's forearm puckers, where the ghost of the girl takes hold.

Then the damning glockenspiel, mute for three songs, silent for so long that the ear forgets the forecast from song one. Child's toy, funeral chime, a light in the night. A bell from out of the pitch-black; a shock but no surprise. A sound that makes hope sound primitive.

Hear that? Clara said, her voice as serene as the singer's now is. *A music box. From the nursery.*

The music turns sickly sweet. The storm lifts in a heartbeat, and the sky in all directions clears. The singer says, *They rest, they rest in their mother's house.* But everything about the eerie music box insists, *You dream.*

For years after that first listen, Els read everything on the *Kindertotenlieder* he could find. He even struggled through articles in German. Every analysis insisted that the last song ended in otherworldly consolation. He knew beyond a doubt that it did not. Something more was happening in those final measures, and to hear it, all a person had to do was listen. He searched for a long time for someone to confirm the eviscerating lilt of that final, music-box lullaby. Years passed, the articles piled up, and at last Els reached the one possible conclusion: music said only what the ear could bear to hear.

Listen, Clara said. *These are the deaths that start everything.*

Mahler to Bruno Walter: "How dark is the foundation on which our lives rest!"

He killed the player and called his daughter. Stupid superstition. But a simple enough safeguard, with no downside. It was three hours earlier on the Pacific Coast. She would already be hard at work, preparing for tomorrow morning. They had talked three days before. But that was then.

Sara was VP for research of the second-largest data-mining firm in the Northwest. Her company figured out how to make advertisements chase their target users around the Web and read their minds. In her spare time, she competed in standard-course triathlons. Her fortieth birthday present to herself had been surviving a double Olympic distance out in Hawaii. She sat on the board of two museums. She spent her vacations volunteering for an NGO that transferred obsolete supercomputers to sub-Saharan countries. She wasn't married; she wasn't even single. Men who weren't scared of her were usually sociopaths.

Els got her voice mail. Lifetimes ago, in the seventies, when Sara was still a child and Els was still her father of record, he'd hung up in alarm the first time he called a friend and got a machine. It took him years to stop bellowing at answering tapes—repeating, spelling out his name, falling into fatuous improvisation or flustered silence. These days, it shocked him to get a live person.

It's your father, he told the machine. *Give me a ring.*

He hadn't even crossed the length of the room to the kitchen when she called back.

What's wrong?

It's Fidelio, he answered. *She's dead.*

A pause came across the line. For decades in the classroom, Els had told his composition students that rests were the most powerful elements in a composer's palette. The negative space, that little, ambiguous leap before the *Heil.* The silences were the thing that the notes were powerless to reach.

How?

A stroke, I think. I didn't get an autopsy.

I'm sorry, she said. *She was good to you.*

Another prolonged fermata, the only sound he could bring himself to make. At last she said, *Are you okay?*

Sar? he managed. *I've been thinking. There's an opening at Shade Arbors.*

You've taken up golf?

A gated thing, south of the college.

Gated thing.

A condominium association. You know. There's a bar and a restaurant right there. They even have a gym.

You want to move into a nursing home?

Not a nursing home. Retirement community. The nurses are only there if you need them.

Are you crazy?

You told me you don't like me living alone.

I meant rent out the back bedroom or hire a girlfriend. Not move into some assisted living death trap.

This house has a million stairs. You don't want me falling and breaking a hip.

Please. No one falls and breaks their hips. That was, like, a nineties television scare campaign. You're seventy years old. Seventy's nothing. Seventy is the new forty-five.

Do you remember how you could never go to bed without hearing Saint Anthony preach to the fishes?

Don't change the subject. You don't need this. You're young. Healthy. I can get you a new dog.

How's your mother? he asked.

She has a Facebook page, Dad. You can stalk her there.

What are you listening to these days? He'd always relied on Sara to tell him what was happening in the world of real music.

Listening? She laughed. *I listen to Bloomberg. When I have time. Swear to me you aren't moving anywhere.*

He swore.

I'm so sorry about Fidelio, she said. *She was a good one.*

She's only gone out, he wanted to say, and doesn't feel like coming home.

I'll find you another. I'll get on it tonight. How do you feel about border collies?

He could hear her clicking keys, already searching, even before he said good night.

I wanted to believe that music was the way out of all politics. But it's only another way in.

The thermal cycler, acquired for a few hundred dollars online, was getting some good PCR product yields. He couldn't wrap his brain around what happened inside the quarter-thimble reaction tube: the fragments cleaving, the jumbled bases assembling themselves onto the exposed templates, the strands of DNA doubling and redoubling, exploding into incomprehensible numbers. The thought of it made him feel religious.

For raw materials, Els relied on a pair of online shops that would have struck him as insane two years ago. One was named Mr. Gene, like some bargain reseller or used-car salesman. Between the two sites, he could buy all kinds of made-to-order materials without breaking the bank. Do-it-yourself bio: the latest mushrooming cottage industry. A computer, a credit card, and a little patience, and a person might customize a living thing.

Life at the smallest levels, its pointless overabundance, the sheer profligacy of its chemical signaling: he had no wilder an art to witness, before he died. As he worked, a line from a letter that Mahler once sent to his faithless Alma hummed in his head: *We are brought back to ourselves by solitude, and from ourselves to God is only a step . . .*

He went to bed late and woke soon after falling asleep. Fortunately, he needed little sleep anymore. When the sun came up the next morning, it was almost as if nothing at all had happened in the night.

Once, I'd hoped to make thousands of runaway pieces. They failed to run away. This one did. It's all around you now, in the billions.

Two men in navy two-button suits, one of them holding a leatherette portfolio, appeared at the front door a little past eleven o'clock, the morning after the improvised funeral. They looked like counterfeit Jehovah's Witnesses. Electioneering was still months away, and the pair were too well dressed for fund-raising. *Someone must have been telling lies about Peter Els.* The line occurred to Els and broke across his lips. He was still grinning when he opened the door on the overdressed duo.

They handed him business cards: Coldberg and Mendoza, with the Joint Security Task Force. Coldberg rubbed the fingernails of his right hand with his thumb. Mendoza had a tiny smear of egg yolk in the crook of his lips.

Mendoza said, *We've received a police report about bacterial cultures in the house.*

I see. Els waited for the question.

Coldberg fiddled with his ear, searching for some miniature audio hardware that had been swiped while he wasn't looking.

Is that accurate? Mendoza asked.

Yes, Els said. *That's accurate.* Lots of bacterial cultures in the house.

Can we come in? Coldberg asked.

Els tipped his head sideways. *It's a hobbyist lab. I'm not stealing anyone's patents.*

The agent asked again. Els stepped aside and watched two pairs of Blüchers cross the transom.

At the sight of the back room, Mendoza stopped. *What's all this gear for?*

Els's turn to be nonplussed. *You don't know?*

We're not scientists, Mr. Els. You're the expert, it seems.

Els showed them the PCR machine. He tried to explain how it worked—the cycles of denaturing and annealing—but the agents lost interest.

Coldberg pointed. *That's your centrifuge?*

I made it from a salad spinner. And I modified the rice cooker to distill water.

And that over there, with the wires?

That's for gel electrophoresis. It's . . . it tells you how big your molecules are.

Your molecules?

Your snippets of DNA. What have you.

You work with DNA?

The question was so artless it made Els laugh. *It's everywhere, these days.*

What's behind the door?

Before Els could object, the two agents stepped into his clean room and contaminated his homemade laminar flow hood.

Coldberg waved a thick black pen around the room. *Where'd you get all this?* His voice had a note of admiration.

Els told him. There was nothing—nothing at all—that a person couldn't get from some obliging five-star vendor.

How much did this set you back?

Less than you think. It's amazing what you can get for nothing, in auctions. All those bankrupt biotech start-ups . . . Penn State was dumping a bunch of perfectly good scopes just because they were a few years old. I picked up a three-thousand-dollar cell incubator for two hundred and ninety bucks on eBay. The low-temperature freezer was my biggest-ticket item, believe it or not. Everything together cost less than five thousand dollars.

Five thousand?

Els shrugged. *That's one Mediterranean cruise. Or one big-screen television, five years ago. Of course, the reagents can add up, depending on where you get them.*

The word had a bad effect on Mendoza. Els regretted using it. But he'd broken no laws. No serious ones, anyway.

What reagents do you work with? Mendoza asked.

Els listed a few. Coldberg drew a pad from his portfolio and addressed the tip of his pen. *What kind of bacteria are you stocking?*

These days? Serratia marcescens. It's a motile, short-rod anaerobe.

Coldberg asked for spelling. Mendoza ran his finger across the top of a twenty-four-well microplate sitting on the table.

Is it a pathogen? Coldberg asked.

Els stood still and composed himself. *No offense, but this stuff is all over your bathroom. The grout in your shower. The water line in your toilet tank . . .*

You don't know my wife, Mendoza said.

Coldberg glared at his partner, then at Els. *Is it harmful to humans?*

Everything was harmful to humans.

It can give you infections, yes. Urinary tract. Conjunctivitis. But

*you'd have to work hard to hurt yourself with it. They used it in
school labs, back when I was a kid. The Army sprayed it on San
Francisco.*

When was this?

I don't know. Fifty years ago?

You're not the Army, Coldberg said. And Els realized that he
might be in trouble.

Coldberg waved the pen again, as if it were a laser pointer.
What exactly are you doing with all this?

The question that should have been asked some time earlier
hung in the air. Els waved toward the pipettes on a wall rack
he'd made from kitchen clamps. *Learning about cell biology. It's a
hobby. It's a whole lot like cooking, to tell you the truth.*

You're not a biologist?

Els shook his head.

But you're manipulating the DNA of a toxic organism?

I . . . If you want to describe it that way.

Why?

There were scores of good reasons, and not a single one
would be credible to this pair. In the year of Els's birth, no one
had even known what a gene was made of. Now people were
designing them. For most of his life, Els had ignored the greatest
achievement of his age, the art form of the free-for-all future
that he wouldn't live to see. Now he wanted a little glimpse.
Billions of complex chemical factories in a thimble: the thought
gave him the cold chill that music once did. The lab made him
feel that he wasn't yet dead, that it wasn't too late to learn what
life was really about.

He said nothing. Coldberg picked up a petri dish. *Where'd
you learn how to manipulate microorganisms?*

You know, genetics is not all that hard. It's a whole lot easier than learning Arabic.

A grace note passed between the agents. Coldberg's scribbling stopped.

Where'd you learn Arabic?

I don't know Arabic, Els said. *It was a figure of . . .*

Then what's that?

Coldberg pointed to a framed manuscript page hanging on the wall in the dining room: half domes with smaller half domes tucked in line underneath them, like the scalloped arches of a Sinan mosque. Each niche was emblazoned in flowing Arabic.

Els pressed his right temple with two fingers. *That's a sixteenth-century Ottoman manuscript showing an old system of musical notation.*

Coldberg took out his phone and began snapping pictures.

Mendoza asked, *You called Emergency Services last night?*

Els nodded.

Your dog died? The police told you to call Animal Control?

Els shut his eyes.

Animal Control has no record of any call from you.

God, Els said. *You think I nerve-gassed my dog?*

Where's the body? Mendozza asked.

The body. The evidence. *I buried her out back.*

You were instructed not to do that.

I was, Els agreed.

They're in there? Coldberg pointed at the incubator with his chin.

Els considered the question. He crossed over to the unit. *They're harmless, if handled right.* He moved to open the cabinet door. He wasn't sure what he meant to do. Open up a cell culture flask and sniff it, maybe. Prove that it was no worse a threat than most pets.

The agents rushed him. Mendoza placed his ample body between the incubator and the seventy-year-old anemic composer. Coldberg came up behind. Els froze.

Coldberg shut the incubator with one thick hand. *We'd like to take this with us.*

Els stood waiting for the request to make sense.

Are you saying I . . . ? Do you have some kind of a warrant?

No, Coldberg said. *We do not.*

Is this legal? Am I being charged with anything?

No. You are not.

Everyone waited. The agents didn't move. Their deference surprised Els. He seemed to have some kind of power of refusal, a power that might be fatal to use.

It shouldn't be unplugged, Els said.

The agents waited. Els clasped the back of his neck and nodded.

Coldberg and Mendoza unplugged the incubator, wrapped it in duct tape, and carried it off. Els stepped aside, hearing the stacks of culture flasks rattle as the incubator went by. The colonies would be smashed and scattered before the two opera buffa extras got the box down to Anti-Terror HQ.

They passed the cloud chamber bowls, that seven-foot rack of sinister-looking, sawn-off carboys invented by Harry Partch, the hobo outsider. The agents set down the incubator long enough for Coldberg to snap more pictures. Els tapped the chimes, which rang out with excruciating microtones. It reassured no one. The agents carried the incubator out to the trunk of their black sedan. Els followed them out.

We're going to ask you not to go anywhere for a couple of days, Mendoza told him.

Els stood in the parkway, shaking his head. *Where in the world would I go?*

Partch on the piano: "Twelve black and white bars in front of musical freedom." I found an instrument free of all such bars.

He sat at the dining room table, stunned. He had to do something, but there was nothing useful to do. It crossed his mind to call an acquaintance, Kathryn Dresser, who worked on constitutional law at the college. But home invasion wasn't Dresser's field, and Els didn't know her all that well. He'd never engaged a lawyer for anything, not even his divorce. Calling one now felt criminal.

He felt like suing. But righteousness would only incriminate him. Coldberg and Mendoza's cards bore the address of a government building in Philadelphia, a generic email contact, and a phone. He'd failed to get any other information. He'd let two strangers come into his house and walk off with his lab equipment, no questions asked.

It wasn't clear how much trouble he might be in. Perhaps the impounding was a routine precaution. The best thing was to keep still and see how things played out. Let the Joint Security people run their checks on him and on *Serratia*, his bacterium of choice. Let them comb through every datum collected on him in the course of seventy years and discover that he'd never even gotten a speeding ticket. Nine or ten days from now, long enough to punish him for making them waste valuable public resources on a false alarm, they'd ship the incubator back, dinged up and emptied out.

The day was shot for any real effort. His last week of work was ruined. Els drained off his nervous energy in the yard, deadheading daffodils and splitting the early hostas. He moved half the huge Blue Angel that filled the bed under the front bay window to the center of Fidelio's grave. It would be beautiful there, by this time next spring.

When he could move no more plants around without doing damage, Els went inside and got on the computer. There, he made the rounds of his bookmarked DIY bio sites, to see whether the community of amateur researchers had any advice for a situation like this. One site mentioned a recent rise in legal confrontations. It linked to a grassroots group for citizens' rights to do science.

A few clicks, and Els found himself scanning a recipe for getting ricin from castor beans. Botulism from stockpiles of cosmetics. Ebola from any of half a dozen obliging cults. Fifty minutes on the Net and he wanted to arrest himself.

But all the garage genetics sites agreed: a person could assemble a respectable plague for far less than five thousand dollars, without needing any fancy gene splicing. Spreading the plague, however, would be a problem. One link led to another, and before long, Els was lost in the whole Amerithrax saga, its byzantine plots—all the mysteries surrounding those seven spore-filled letters. He'd forgotten about that nightmare—one of the largest investigations in history. The topic might have made a first-rate CNN opera.

Amerithrax led him to the 1995 sarin gas attack on the Tokyo subway. From Tokyo, two clicks landed him on a rooftop in Miyako City, watching cars and trucks and warehouses and apartment buildings turning into driftwood on a hump of gray water that would not stop surging inland. A whole neighborhood tore loose and shot down the rapids. As the cell phone film panned, a stack of frothing water overtook the camera and the shot went black.

Els scanned down the long columns of related videos: *Latest eyewitness. Tape captures eerie sounds. Most dramatic compilation. Survivors recount terror.* Some clips had been clicked on a million times, some once or twice. Overnight, this carousel of catastrophe.

Among the hundreds of two-minute clips, right between *Moment tsunami hits* and *Japan bids to save power plant,* a prodigious automated sorting algorithm had inserted the bleakest of errors. Or maybe a human curator planted the link, a sadistic joke on the theme of disaster: a video that had gone viral on the day of the quake, racking up 62,700,312 views in the few days since. Els clicked and became number 62,700,313.

At his click, the room filled with a vivacious, pitch-corrected, and jaw-droppingly sunny little song. On Els's screen, a thirteen-year-old singer woke up, went to the bus stop, joined her friends in a convertible, and visited a suburban house where an upper-middle-class teen party was in full swing. As the clip rolled, the hit count rose by ten thousand viewers. Shaking off the song, Els searched for an explanation. The Web teemed with ten thousand parodies, reactions, tributes, covers, homages, analyses, and news segments about the global phenomenon.

He looked up. It was past dinnertime, and he was starving.

· · ·

THE LEBANESE MEZE restaurant not far from campus was hopping. But the oblivious crowd was just what he needed after his morning's run-in with the law. Noises everywhere— ice sliding from pitchers, a rumble of silver on stoneware, the diffuse, rolling chorus of clientele swapping their strands of gossip—like one of those mad Stockhausen pieces composed in a fireworks-testing facility. Drink your wine with a glad heart, for God accepts your works.

Els asked for a table near the center of the room. Maddy had always accused him of being a closet extrovert. *You are the Thomas Merton of music. You want to live in a hermitage in Times Square, with a big sign pointing to you reading, hermit.*

Els smiled at the accusation, decades downstream. He imagined his wife across the table, shaking her head at the fix he'd gotten into. They had lived together for a handful of years, each year leaving them a little less explicable to each other. And still he sometimes joked with her ghost or sounded her out on the latest strangeness. Once Maddy had admired his compulsive need to make music; by the end, it merely baffled her. Garage genomics would have struck her as total madness.

You don't hate the public, Peter. You need it. You want people to come drag you out of your cave and make you play them something.

Once, in his late twenties, in the full flush of skill-driven freedom, he wrote a hermetic, harmonically adventuresome song cycle for piano, clarinet, theremin, and solo soprano on texts from Kafka's "The Great Wall of China." The third song ran:

You do not need to leave your room.
Only sit at your table and listen.

Don't even listen;
simply wait, be quiet,
still and solitary.

The world will offer itself to be unmasked.
It has no choice;
it will roll in ecstasy at your feet.

The songs were performed twice, seven years apart, for a dozen puzzled listeners each time. That was the kind of music Els wrote: more people onstage than in the audience. Sometime in the late nineties, after the disaster of his three-hour historical drama *The Fowler's Snare*, Els destroyed the only copies of many of his scores, including "The Great Wall" songs. The cryptic music now existed nowhere but in his ears. But he could hear it again, even above the restaurant din. He'd forgotten how jagged and eerie the whole cycle had been, how bent it was on its prophecy. He regretted destroying the piece. He could brighten the songs now. Give them room to breathe. A little light; some air.

He lifted his water glass and toasted the ghost sitting across the table from him: *Guilty as charged.* No one in the noisy room heard him.

AT HOME, HE had no lab to occupy his evening. He switched on the giant flat-screen. Sara had gotten it for him for his seventieth birthday, to keep him on progress's forced march. On the vibrant high-def screen, a cloud of radiation drifted toward the largest urban conglomeration on Earth, just as in the worst disaster movies of his youth.

Els switched to a documentary on western wildlife. The soundtrack—a mythic, pentatonic meandering—bugged him, and he switched again. One click, and he landed on a corral full

of string-bikini models whacking each other with giant foam
hands. He killed the set and vowed to remove it from the room
tomorrow, as he'd promised the doctor at the insomnia clinic
he would do, months earlier.

The book on his nightstand opened to where he'd left off the
night before. He stopped each evening at the top of the left-
hand page, the end of the first paragraph—one of a thousand
foolish, useful habits Madolyn had taught him. His wife was
still so present in his habits that he couldn't believe they'd been
apart now for four times longer than they'd been together.

Els lay on his back in the enormous bed, trying to conjure up
Maddy's face. Her features had become one of those cheerful
études from another century whose melodies he could remember only by spelling out the intervals.

He took up the open book, and once again, for another
night, he trained his mind to settle in and read. It took some
time to build up a rhythm. The sense of concentrated elsewhere
filled him with that primal pleasure: seeing through another's
eyes. But after some paragraphs, a clause swerved and slid him
sideways into a drift, a soft passage several pages on, in the middle of the right-hand page, a sense-rich description of a man
and woman walking down a street in Boston on a July night,
reprised, in misty da capo, again and yet once more, his eyes
making their closed circuit, hitting the right margin's guardrail,
looping back around and trying the line again, tracking along
the circuit of text, slowing then slipping down the stripped cog-
way of slick subordinate clauses, retrying the sequence until his
dimming sight again found traction—the man, the woman, a
moment of regretful truth along the esplanade—before snagging
and starting the fuzzy looping climb all over again.

At last, after who knows how many round trips, he jerked

awake. And the words on the page, before Els's now-focused but disbelieving eyes, marshaled like troops on a parade ground and solidified, only to reveal no man, no woman, no night, no Boston, no exchange of intimate insight, but merely a Bulgarian writer describing the secret will of crowds.

He put down the book, shut off the light, and settled his head deeper into the pillow. As soon as the room went dark, he came wide awake. The floorboards snapped and blasted like an exchange of gunfire, and the furnace shuddered like a great engine of war.

I chose my host organism for the most naïve reason: it had a colorful history. That color was red.

Of love's Pangaea, no more than a few scattered islands remained above water. And of Clara Reston, who listened to eight-hundred-year-old conductus as if it were a news flash, he remembered little that couldn't fit into a five-minute student song. But she had turned Els into a pilgrim listener. Before Clara, no piece had any real power to hurt him. After, he heard danger everywhere.

The composers Els returned to at seventy—Pérotin, Bach, Mahler, Berg, Bartók, Messiaen, Shostakovich, Britten—were the ones that Clara taught him to love at nineteen. But along the way from exposition to coda, he'd betrayed them all. There were years in youth when all Els wanted was to write a piece so perfect it would cripple Clara with remorse. In middle age, he'd wanted only to give her back something, for all she'd given him.

He never thought it strange that she had no friends. She'd

jumped out early and alone into adulthood, long before he himself glimpsed their coming eviction from adolescence. He wondered sometimes if her life hid some spooky domestic secret that left her so precocious. She had life's concert and all its program notes memorized, long before the performance started. *Peter! You'll love this one.*

She applied to college in Indiana, to study cello with Starker in America's best string program. Without a second thought, young Peter followed her. He didn't even have a fallback school. His stepfather wouldn't pay for him to major in music; Soviet science threatened the country's very existence, and as Ronnie Halverson saw it, any able-minded eighteen-year-old had a duty to join the counteroffensive. And so, deep in the late fifties Midwest, Els set off after a bachelor of science. Better things for better living through chemistry.

Freshman year exhilarated him. He sat in the auditorium alongside four hundred other chemistry students while the lecturer scribbled down blackboards full of spirit writing from the world inside this one. The labs—titrating, precipitating, isolating—were like learning to play a wayward but splendid new instrument. Matter was thick with infolded mysteries waiting to be discovered. Coming from the lab, stinking of camphor, fish, malt, mint, musk, sperm, sweat, and urine, Els smelled the heady scent of his own future.

He still studied clarinet. In his second semester, he bested a dozen performance majors for a chair in the top undergraduate orchestra. The other woodwinds refused to believe he was wasting himself on test tubes and Erlenmeyer flasks. Clara just shrugged at his perversity. She glanced at him sometimes from across the orchestra, at her stand in the cellos, her patient smile waiting for him to discover what she already knew.

To Els, music and chemistry were each other's long-lost twins: mixtures and modulations, spectral harmonies and harmonic spectroscopy. The structures of long polymers reminded him of intricate Webern variations. The outlandish probability fields of atomic orbitals—barbells, donuts, spheres—felt like the units of an avant-garde notation. The formulas of physical chemistry struck him as intricate and divine compositions.

Alongside courses in structure and analysis, he sneaked in an elective in music composition. Harmonizing chorales and realizing figured bass felt a bit like algebra. He wrote minuets in the style of Haydn and imitation Bach da capo arias. For Clara's twentieth, he scored "Happy Birthday" à la late Beethoven. For New Year's Eve 1961, he gave her his most elaborate trinket yet: a Brahms intermezzo treatment of "How About You?" Clara read through the gift, shaking her head and laughing at a thing so obvious to everyone but its maker.

Oh, Peter. For a bright boy, you're so clueless. Come on. Let's play through it.

He tried to explain the plan to Clara. He could graduate with a guaranteed bench job in industry while still making all the music body and soul needed. But she looked away with her maddening sextant look, out to the horizon and over the curve of the Earth, at a future that she could see and he could not.

They spent their every spare minute together. Clara got them reviewing music for the *Daily Student*. Under the anagram byline Entresols, they championed dozens of new recordings as if they were Adam and Eve naming the animals. Their friends—those who didn't throw up their hands in disgust at that breakaway state of two—called them the Zygote. While the best and brightest headed for civil rights sit-ins, Peter and Clara camped out in the music library listening room, following along in the score of Strauss's *Four Last Songs* while Schwarzkopf sang "Im Abendrot": *We've gone through need and sorrow, hand in hand . . .*

Clara ran point in their discoveries, reconnoitering. She brought Els prizes for dinner: crazy Gesualdo madrigals or brilliant horn passages from late nineteenth century tone poems. And even as Peter scrambled to master her expanding repertoire, Clara blew on ahead of him and found more.

They sang up close, right into each other's mouths, bending pitches into near-miss dissonance. The grate of those beats sawed straight into their brains. They had not yet seen each other naked. But that shared resonance in the plates of their skulls was as intimate as any sex.

Clara knew her destiny and never wavered. She studied with the demanding Starker, and although the man made her weep almost every week, he led her to tricks of the mind and the wrist that left her playing like an angel.

Music alone, for Clara, had the power to peel away the lie of daily life. She wasn't sure who Adenauer was, and she didn't understand why Glenn deserved a ticker tape parade. But a few measures of the *Grosse Fuge* held more raw truth than a month's worth of headlines. The force of her pitch-driven Platonism gave her a power over Peter. He had hunches; she had convictions. It was never much of a contest. She had only to smile at his churchgoing, and from one Sunday to the next, he quit his family's faith. With little more than a cocked eyebrow, she got him to grow out his flattop and trade in his button-downs for pullovers. And on a late March night near the end of his sophomore year, she took the war for his soul into the heart of the enemy camp.

She asked him to meet her after dark on the bank of the Jordan River. He arrived after a miserable three-hour failed struggle to identify an unknown in his Advanced Organics lab. She lay back on the damp, grassy rise, forever staining the back of her blue pencil skirt. He stretched out with his head in her lap, wrecked. *They want me dead.*

Her face curdled at the chemical reek of him. She combed back his hair with two fingers. *Who does?*

All of them. The alkenes, the alkynes, the paraffins . . .

Peter? She leaned down over him, and her silver lyre necklace charm grazed his cheek. She tugged on the hint of sideburn she'd gotten him to grow out. *Who told you that you were a chemist?*

Well, I'm not half bad at it, you know. Tonight's disaster excepted.

And you're ready to spend your whole life doing it?

He pressed his fingertips into the cold soil. The idea of spending a whole life doing anything filled him with something between wonder and panic.

Are you trying to please your father?

He rolled away, up onto one elbow. *You mean my stepfather? My father's dead.*

I am aware. And you're aware that no one can satisfy a ghost?

I'm not trying to please anyone. I'm learning chemistry. It's not a bad way to make a living.

He wanted to add: For two, if that interests you.

Peter, it's 1961. You're a white man in college. And you're worried about making a living? That's what dance and wedding bands are for. No musician with your talent ever ended up in the gutter.

He tried to tell her: Chemistry made sense. Its problems had clean and repeatable answers. Its puzzles read like cosmic rebuses. Manipulating fundamental stuff, shaping whole new materials with properties that could raise the quality of life . . .

But Clara wouldn't see the splendor in the system. She bent

her arm along the crease of his chest. *You think the chemistry won't get done if you don't do it?*

You think no one's going to play the clarinet if I don't?

Clarinet? Who said anything about clarinet?

Her whole insane plan for him took shape and buzzed around his head. He swatted it away. She snared his wrists and held them to the chill ground.

Put away the Lincoln logs, Peter. Playtime's over. Music pours out of you when you snap your fingers. That's called a vocation. You don't get a choice.

He sat and tilted his head at the girl Platonist, like he was the RCA dog and she the inscrutable gramophone. Then he started to hear them, those souls lined up in the celestial anteroom, awaiting reincarnation: all the preexisting sounds that only he might bring into being. The deep symmetries, the forms and formulas of chemistry that had so absorbed him for two years, turned into a mere prelude. It was true: he'd been trying to please someone. But that someone called for another pleasure.

He lay back in her lap and looked up at her inverted face. She opened her shawl to settle it again around her shoulders. Her draped arms were wings as wide as the night sky.

These pieces you want me to write, he said, awash on pure possibility. *How many do you suppose there are?*

She leaned down to answer him. How easy it would be, he thought, to kick out into the center of the lake until he couldn't kick anymore.

FOR THE NEXT five weeks, when he should have been studying for final exams, he worked in secret. He stole hours from labs, from classes, even from Clara, who turned giddy with concealed suspicion. He took to working in lightning shorthand, sketching out music in quick, clean strokes, the way a child might scribble a crayon moon, a loopy forest, and a gash of campfire, and call it night. There was no time for orchestration. The thing unfolded on the simplest scale, for solo piano and voices. But he heard every line in massed banks of instrumental color. The wayfaring winds, the swelling support of brass, a raft of low strings bearing forward.

He had the perfect text, the end of Whitman's "Song of Myself." Clara had recited the stanza from memory on a freezing picnic in Cascades Park, during winter's last hurrah. They'd lain wrapped up together in a cotton sleeping bag, cradling a thermos full of hot tomato soup between them, their lashes dusted with fresh snowfall while she spoke:

What do you think has become of the young and old men?
And what do you think has become of the women and children?
They are alive and well somewhere,
The smallest sprout shows there is really no death,
And if ever there was it led forward life, and does not wait at
the end to arrest it,
And ceas'd the moment life appear'd.

All goes onward and outward, nothing collapses,
And to die is different from what any one supposed, and
luckier.

He studied the words for days, listening to the sounds contained in them. Then the phonemes and accents led him forward. Note by note, phrase by phrase, he relived that picnic in the snow: the sun low in the sky through the bones of an oak, promising some hidden continuance, and that shivering girl holding a thermos in her mittened cellist's fingers, challenging him with a few chanted and expanding words, her face hungry, pale, and amused, already knowing what would become of all the young men and daring the old ones to look back. Each measure he wrote changed the ones he'd already written, and he felt them all, already being altered by the unformed noises of the years to come.

As his pencil spilled lines onto the blank page, all Els had to do was listen and guide each new note to its foreordained place: *They are alive and well somewhere.* He could write for forever; he could write for no one. He wasn't choosing: simply detecting, as if he were running a dozen different assays to determine an unknown that, by reactive magic, precipitated out in the bottom of his test tube, solid and weighable.

The song took shape; he focused the nub of his will to a sharp point. Fear lost all traction, and that current of well-being he'd experienced a few times before in life, listening to the *Jupiter* or stumbling into Mahler, flooded into him. A cherry-picker taller than a redwood plucked him out of the rubble-filled culvert where he lay and lifted him to the watch room of a lighthouse. The worst that could happen in throwing his life away revealed itself to be a blessing. Only keep still, wait, and hear, and the world will open.

The piece was simplicity itself: a triplet-driven, Phrygian figure in the high voices, while beneath, arpeggios moved in contrary motion, in wide slow waves. Each new entry took the evolving figure into higher registers. The blend strained toward something archaic, a folk tune an ethnographer might find in a remote mountain village of a failing monarchy, to bring back to his studio in the decadent capital and flesh out with volunteer harmonies.

He stole from Mahler, to be sure: the blurred boundary between major and minor. The shaky key regions that wheeled off, before the end, into wildness. A spinning waltz, a distant brass band. Slow ascent tumbling down in a heartbeat, only to climb again in the reprieve of the next measure. All the individual components had a familiar air. But the thing as a whole had never quite existed before Peter wrote it down.

Building toward the climax, Peter discovered that he'd laid its foundation well in advance, in the germ material of the opening phrases. A four-note figure, drawn from the original triplets, rose and expanded into a five-note one, which overflowed into the full, rising, seven-note assertion of certainty:

All goes onward
Onward and outward
Outward: nothing collapses . . .

Then came the transforming final phrase, the one that was waiting for him when he reached it, almost as if he'd envisioned it all along.

Teasing out the piece on a baby grand in a music building practice room gave him a pleasure so complete it might as well have been illegal. Clara was right: he was shaped to do this work, even if the work had no use for anyone alive or dead. Paying off his stepfather's wasted investment, putting in years of scut work at minimum wage, playing to empty auditoriums peppered with a handful of listeners hostile and indifferent: his entire misspent life spread out in front of Peter. Drunk on birthing up this first-time thing, he saw the future, and he recognized it from way back when.

For weeks, turning and shaping, Els saw everything: the

young men and the old, the women and children, alive and well, needing no one but him to spring them. He stepped off into the void and felt no fear. It didn't even feel like a choice. Chemistry died an easeful death. But that death was different from what anyone might imagine, and luckier than even an old man of seventy could yet suppose.

He surprised Clara at semester's end, with a fresh copy. She sat on the foot of her dorm room bed, under the poster of the young Casals, reading and nodding in silence. When she looked up, her wet eyes looked almost timid. Still, she smiled that all-foretelling smile. *Well,* she said. *Bravo. Encore.*

Pythagoras, discoverer of harmony's math, also discovered my bug: *Serratia marcescens*. It looked like blood seeping out of old food.

Clara's reward waited for him at the year-end concert. The program was some attempted Cold War rapprochement: Borodin, Rimsky-Korsakov, Stravinsky's *Firebird*. Els loved it all, even those baggy exotics. Something had happened to his ear, and in that month, everything from Machaut to the "Mickey Mouse Club March" struck him as a masterpiece.

Playing in orchestra felt like sitting in the general assembly. Each section set off on the agenda of its own private timbre, but all combined under one baton into a surprise leviathan. From his perch in the center of the winds, Els glanced to his left, over the lip of his music stand, past the conductor, to see Clara in profile, second chair, her cello nestled in the vee of her long black concert skirt, her white silk blouse tightening against her breasts as the instrument rocked and breathed. She played like a distracted Firebird, her graceful neck pressed against the fingerboard of her instrument, her bow arm tracing out sideways-eight infinities in the air. As the slashing accents set off Kashchei's infernal dance, Clara glanced over her shoulder and caught him looking. And as if it were scored into the note heads on the staves in front of him, Els saw what dance waited, later that night, when the music ended.

What had they done together, until then? Incandescent things. Crimes against their upbringing that left Els stunned by the cunning of his lust and wracked with holdover Lutheran guilt. But these were the early days of the New Frontier. His own daughter would giggle her way through worse by age sixteen. No self-respecting thirteen-year-old in 2011, keeping public stats on her social network page, would even consider it sex.

After the concert, Els found Clara in the orchestra rehearsal room, putting her cello into its coffin. The Russian music and her bohemian soul left her so flushed she couldn't talk. The night's plan was so obvious in their furtive faces that Peter was sure her resident director would detain them both for questioning when they snuck into her dorm to borrow her rich roommate's Beetle. They had no route. Clara sat abandoned in the car, still in concert clothes, feet up on the dash, open to fate and free of the Earth's pull. Peter's hands shook on the wheel. They drove to the quarries outside of town, left the car on a pull-off in front of a dense stand of pines, and walked into the thick dark.

Leaf stuff tripped her up, and Clara had to carry her high heels. Deep in the copse, she staggered into him and whispered, *Time to get serious.* The tip of her tongue followed the words into his ear canal.

She pulled Els to the ground onto a bed of Scotch pine needles six inches deep. She swept her pleated black concert skirt to her waist and straddled him. Her silk blouse billowed open, and her four feet of hair tented him in a Botticelli skein. She lowered herself with a strange, sharp cry of elated betrayal that he'd try to re-create in various combinations of instruments for the next forty years. She gripped his shoulders and pushed them against the needles, a bare threat: Do we understand each other? He cuffed her neck and made her look at him. He nodded.

As she took him, a bright light pulsed in his temples. It struck him that he was having a stroke, and he didn't care. Two more flashes, and Els focused. The white turned into a high-beam searchlight, sweeping the woods. On the far edge of the pines, two policemen were peering into the windows of the parked Beetle.

His legs jerked; he tried to push her off. But before he could scramble to his feet and surrender, she pinned him back against the earth. Her eyes were manic, swimming. Her lips moved. Something criminal and pianissimo came out of them. *Don't move.*

An officer called, twice, *Hello?* Els twisted, and Clara fought him down again.

Don't. Move.

A beam sliced across the nearby grass. Pinned under Clara, Els went slack. His skin heard her body-long pulse. She was shuddering now, her mute mouth open, and it took Els several heartbeats to understand that shudder. Searchlights swept through the black grove. A voice called out again, now farther off. At last the police gave up, retreated to their vehicle, and drove away. Peter and Clara lay as narrow as death, on the floor of a night forest distilled by cold. The whole dark woods were speaking, and nothing said a thing.

Blood trickling out of bread at the siege of Tyre rallied Alexander's beaten troops to victory.

Eighteen months pass: three short chamber works and two small song cycles. A young man huddles in a phone booth outside the student newspaper office. In his pocket is a wrinkled blue onionskin aerogram that has taken two weeks to reach him. The world has just escaped annihilation by a few beats. Nuclear silos in an aerial reconnaissance photo of an impoverished tropical island: Peter Els has other worries.

The aerogram is covered in a wispy, Elvish script. "Peter, Dear. Please don't think I've turned promiscuous, here in Merrie England, but life seems to have gotten complicated."

He waits to place the call until well past midnight, when the rates are low. It's morning on the other side of the planet. No phone at the dorm, and he must come to this public booth with a fistful of coins. Judging by the abandoned campus streets, that nuclear exchange has already come and gone. The air is so bone-crushingly cold that his bare hand sticks to the metal phone faceplate when he takes off his gloves to dial.

She answers mezzo, muffled, and time-lagged, the gap it takes her voice to travel the length of the transatlantic cable. *Peter?*

He shouts into the receiver, and his own voice echoes back at him in a canon at unison.

From the first phoneme, it's a terrible mistake. They speak like people playing bughouse chess. He asks for clarification, then elucidations to her clarifications, then glosses on her elucidations. His quarters pour into the slot at a staggering rate and he hears himself say things like, *First of all, I'm not shouting.*

A week's rent, then two, then three disappear, and still he can't tell what this blithe woman is saying to him or what he's supposed to do with a worthless degree in music composition and a minor in chemistry, without the sole audience that matters. He asks her what's changed and she answers: nothing.

So everything's finished, then? Dead?

Her silence says that even early death might be luckier than he thinks.

There's something playing in the background, on her stereo, in her little stone room in a medieval college cloister on the other side of the globe. Mahler. Mahler at breakfast, and although she denies it, he knows she has company. Another set of eager, learner's ears.

But even now, in this frosted phone booth, under a streetlight that steams in the sublunary cold, melodies occur to him— devices and forms he never could have come up with on his own. His swollen, graying fingers fumble with the aerogram. He wants to scribble out a mnemonic to help him retrieve these sounds, once the concert is over, but he's too numb to grip a pen.

So it was all a lie, he says. *It all means nothing.*

The echo turns her voice into a stretto. *Peter. This has to happen. It's something good, for both of us.*

So this is it.

Stop being so dramatic. You'll see me again. Life isn't all that—

He needs two tries to settle the receiver back on the hook. His fingers are too weak to yank open the phone cabin door and free him. He fumbles out of the booth and starts to walk, down a street slick with black ice and empty of a single soul. His spine stiffens against the shock of the gelid night. He exhales, and air freezes to his upper lip. He breathes in, and it crystallizes on the walls of his lungs. He needs to go only six blocks. After two, he thinks: I'm in real trouble. He considers knocking on the door of the nearest house. But he'd be dead by the time anyone let him in.

He reaches his apartment, where his claws try to gain entry. His limbs are frostbitten, and by the time he gets inside, his face is numb. Even the icy tap water scalds like flame. His back has sprained itself from shivering. He crawls in bed and stays there for sixteen hours.

When he gets up, it's to throw himself into work. Nothing can save him but a new piece—something bright and brutal and unforgiving.

Music, he'll tell anyone who asks over the next fifty years, doesn't mean things. It *is* things. And for all those years, in fifty-four pieces from fragments for solo flute and tape to full orchestra and five-part chorus, his music will circle around the same vivid gesture: a forward, stumbling surge that wavers, sometimes in a single measure, between the key of hope and the atonal slash of nothingness.

We will not sleep, but will all be changed, in a moment, in the twinkling of an eye. *You'll see me again.* But you'll never know when. Hear that shifting, ambiguous rhythm, that promise of all things possible, and the ear is on its way to being free.

The miraculous mass at Bolsena, 1264: A fallen priest watched the host bleed on his robe during Communion. Faith restored.

The night was short and fitful, and his brief stint of unconsciousness did little for Els. In the worst of his suite of dreams,

he had to defend Shostakovich's third string quartet from a
public tribunal. The tribunal accused the piece of being elit-
ist, irresponsible, formalist, and full of coded misanthropy. Els
tried to show the judges how rich the thing was, how full of
splendid horror. But the tribunal only added those qualities to
the charges.

Then the prosecutor turned the case against Els himself. He
produced letters to Clara and Maddy in which Els confessed
to loving certain kinds of music because most people found
them worthless and ugly. The case went against him as he
watched, and jurors from all over the Web weighed in with
contempt and proposed humiliations. The dream took Els by
the throat, and he woke up sucking air. Even surfacing in his
raided house felt like a relief.

Joint Security Task Force: a federal outfit. No real threat had
happened anywhere in the country for half a dozen years. A
retiree with a kitchen lab in a rural college town was the worst
they had to deal with.

He rocked himself out of bed and attended to his body. In
the bathroom, he decided to make some inquiries after all. He'd
send an email to that colleague of his in the Law Department.
Safer: he'd visit her office and lay out everything. Then he'd
call the numbers on the business cards Mendoza and Coldberg
had given him and begin the whole process of straightening
things out. Dealing with bureaucracies required no more than
the patience of an animal and the simplicity of a saint. He could
fake both, for a while.

But first, his Monday ritual: the Crystal Brook walking loop,
followed by blueberry pancakes. Then he could place some calls
before the midmorning class on twentieth century landmarks

that he ran each week at Shade Arbors, for people so old they were landmarks themselves.

Way too late in life, Els learned that the time to concentrate yourself was right before sunrise. His greatest art now was to walk two hours before the neighborhood woke. Moving his legs left him blissful. Had he discovered the routine in young adulthood, he might have long ago amassed a portfolio of playful, exuberant creations that pleased him and gave delight to others.

He threw on his workout clothes—baggy gray painter paints and maroon waffle shirt—and drank his tea in his traditional happy silence. Then he grabbed the Fiat keys from the hook by the back door and called the dog. The dog didn't answer.

It made no sense in a grand, American way: driving a mile to walk three. When he pulled up to Crystal Brook Park, the predawn sky was beginning to peach. Someone in the throes of early womanhood was already out jogging on the macadam loop. Wildflowers covered the ground, their colors soft in the sentinel light. White snowdrops, yellow aconite, and a carpet of crocuses almost indigo ran alongside scattered blooms whose names Els didn't know, although he'd seen them every spring for decades. The morning air smelled silly with possibility.

As soon as he began to walk, yesterday's debacle softened and grew manageable. Coldberg and Mendoza now seemed like the bumbling twin bowler-hatted inspectors in Tintin. He fell in a hundred yards behind the jogging woman and started on his own small steps to Parnassus. Every few yards he caught himself looking for Fidelio, as if the dog had run off somewhere.

The park could have been a seventeenth century landscape painting. Nothing tied Els to the present except for the jogging woman. She had on a sports bra and shorts of some shiny, environment-sensing tech material. She ran like an anatomy lecture. In Els's youth, a woman dressed like that in a town like this would have been arrested for subverting public morals. She seemed to Els preternaturally desirable. Happily, he no longer felt desire.

She lapped him as he reached the central transect. He picked up his pace, jogging for a while behind her. An old man of seventy chasing an almost nude girl through a dawn glade: a scene straight out of Baroque mythological opera. The shining form in front of him pulled away again, laying waste to sloth, anomie, idle thought, and metaphor.

White wires ran from the cuff on her arm into her ears. Jogging and the portable jukebox: the greatest musical match since tape hit the V8. A thousand and one nights of continuous hits, all inside a metal matchbox. When this woman reached Els's age, mind-controlled players would be sewn into the auditory cortex. And not a moment too soon, because the entire nation would be deaf.

It seemed to Els that Mahler would have loved the MP3 player, its rolling cabaret. His symphonies, laced with tavern music and dance tunes, were like a vulgar playlist. The fifth Kindertotenlieder had its eviscerating mechanical music box, and *Das Lied von der Erde* was inspired by one of the earliest cylinders recorded in China. Real composers didn't fear the latest mass-market recording. They used it. But how to use one and a half million new songs a year?

Once, Els had spent months cutting quarter-inch reel-to-reel tape with razor blades and splicing the snips back together. He'd programmed a computer to generate a string quintet using probability functions and Markov chains. At this jogging woman's age, he'd believed that digital technology might save art music from the live burial of the concert hall. Now the concert hall itself needed saving.

He drifted underneath the giant trunks, their branches drift-netting the dawn sun. The hundred trees had all gone into the park at the same time, and, in a long largo, they'd begun to leave the place together. Every high wind now brought down another hulk. The park would be a very different proposition—a sunny, trivial one—by the time Els, too, vacated the neighborhood.

The goddess had no use for trees. Her knees, like twin pistons, rose high and clean. Tiny daubs of sweat coated her olive limbs. Through the trees, Els glimpsed her in profile. Her face, resolute but neutral, focused a good hour or two into the future. She looped back up the path behind him, a bright, cyborg *Thanks* issuing from her as she flowed past.

A tinny munchkin backbeat trailed from her earbuds in her wake. Els couldn't make out the flavor of her bliss. This park, these advance spring flowers, the sixty-degree air stolen from paradise, were colored for her by invisible instruments that no one but she could hear.

She ran down the path ahead of him, now and then reaching across with her right arm and grabbing at the arm cuff, as in a tricky cross-hands Chopin étude. It dawned on Els: she was canceling songs.

At the wooded edges of the pond to the south, the spring migration was gathering. Els counted the different calls, but lost track around eleven. Fresh, surprising music that escaped all human conventions: the very thing he'd spent his life searching for was here all along, free for the listening.

Off to his left, a crow cawed in the branches of a gaunt pine. Nearby, something small began to trill: an invisible soloist reinventing melody, as it had done for millions of years before human ears. Els trotted, light in the scattered racket of the morning chorus. The jogger appeared again through a clearing, still executing her merciless verdicts. She averaged half a minute between swipes—judge and jury in a kangaroo court. Every few dozen steps she condemned the Now Playing to the dustbin of history.

Her player must have contained thousands of tracks tagged by artist, year, genre, and user rating. A few menu clicks and she could be the Minister of Culture for her own sovereign state of desire. Yet she turned away twenty times as many auditioners as she let through. The explanation came to Els after another quarter mile: shuffle—the Monte Carlo game that had changed music forever. She was running through her several thousand tunes like random speed-date suitors. Songs were breaking over her in waves of wild accident—the mix-and-match mashup that was her birthright.

She rounded the southeast corner of the park, toward the high school, flicking away tunes like evolution's demiurge. She was looking for something, the perfect sonic drug. And the medicine chest was endless: the laughing gas of a forties big band, a highball of brassy show tunes, punk heroin, techno-ecstasy, folk songs like a pack of tobacco, the hashish trance of Pali chanting, a caffeinated Carnatic raga, cocaine-tinged tango . . .

A player filled with her private reserve, and still the random shuffle produced dozens of songs in a row that had to be killed. Or maybe she was streaming on mobile broadband—3 or 4 or 5G, or whatever generation the race had reached by that morning. A server farm on the far side of the planet was piping down one hundred million tracks of recorded music into her blood pressure cuff, and none suited. The job of taste was to thin the insane torrent of human creativity down to manageable levels. But the job of appetite was never to be happy with taste. How many tunes did anyone need? One more. The next new one.

All the bogus bacterial blood is a pigment called prodigiosin. From *prodigiosus*—strange, remarkable, wondrous—a prodigy.

The sun had risen and the neighborhood was waking. Car wheels a block away thrummed on the asphalt. Els rounded the park's southwest corner and passed the driveway of a mock-Tudor house, where a man in navy sweats and a T-shirt—Gravity: Not Just a Good Idea—was putting two plastic trash cans the size of a Mercury space capsule out on the curb. The man waved to Els as if they knew each other. Els waved back, in case they did.

He'd see what he could discover, online. Maybe the ACLU had a hotline. Coldberg and Mendoza had no warrant. His rights had surely been violated.

The goddess came up behind him again, her step matching the latest beat coming through the thin white wires. A Persian tar improvisation to cure melancholy. A Ukrainian funeral lament. Every tune in creation lined up in her shuffled stream, waiting to take its ten-second turn.

Els stepped off into the grass as she shot by. Above him, in the branches, the air still rang with birdsong. Check the day. Drop it, drop it, pick it up, pick it up. What cheer, what cheer, cheer, cheer, cheer? Why don't you come to me? Messy sprung rhythms spilled out over every bar line Els could draw for them.

If any grand, guiding rule held these rhythms together, Els was too crude and long-lived a creature to hear it. The racket was like the local combined middle schools set loose with a copy of GarageBand. Surplus bothered no one here. The noise washed over him, brisk and urgent and shining.

Through that clatter came a news flash. Three strong notes descended in a major triad, then riffed on the tonic in a dotted rhythm:

Sol, mi, do-do-do-do-do-do-do . . .

A thing no bigger than a child's fist was asserting a chord as brazen as any that a kid Mozart might plunk out prior to taking it through a maze of rococo variations. Els scanned the trees, but the perp hid. Maybe the bird had ripped off a playing child or heard the notes spill out of a summer convertible. Birds were big on mimicking. Mozart's pet starling liked to mock the theme from his G Major Piano Concerto, K. 543. Australian lyre birds could mimic camera shutters, car alarms, and chain saws so perfectly they passed for real.

With two brisk tweaks of pitch the bird launched another descending arpeggio, like a pranking Beethoven having one over on the audience:

Fa me do-do-do-do-do-do-do . . .

The bird might as well have chirped *Eureka* or sketched out a circle in the dirt with a twig in its beak. Much of twentieth century music had been lost to the idea that the diatonic scale was arbitrary and exhausted, part of the bankrupt narrative that had led to two world wars. Nothing mattered but finding a new language. Now this feathered thing sat up in the branches, singing its triads and making a fool of him. Evolution had its innermost needs, tens of millions of years old.

The goddess startled Els; he couldn't imagine how she'd lapped him again so soon. She saw him standing paralyzed under the trees and stopped. She pulled the white wires from her ears.

Are you okay? Her accent—thick, nasal, and Mid-Atlantic—came straight out of Philly.

Els pointed. The bird answered for him, its perfect phrase. The goddess's eyebrows pulled down; her lips twisted.

White-throated sparrow! She opened her mouth wide, and a clear, bright alto poured out. *Poor Sam Peabody-peabody-peabody . . .*

The bird answered, and the imitator laughed.

Thank you, Els said. *I've never heard that one.*

Oh-migod. I love that bird. I wait for him, every spring.

She backed away, turning on one heel as if she'd never broken stride.

Wait, Els said. The lone benefit of age: you could ask anything and frighten no one. He raised both hands and pointed at each ear. *What are you listening to?*

She should have jogged off without saying another word. But the young knew that life would henceforth be forever lived in a fishbowl, and they liked it that way. The names of her tracks were doubtless being beamed to her social networking page, even as she nixed them.

The buds lay draped across her shoulder, like a stricken stick insect. She took them in her fingers.

I'm sorting through some new stuff. Tagging things for later.

I hope you have a tag for "sooner," too?

The words wrinkled her forehead. Song came from the trees.

Sam tried out a fresh new triad. Delight distracted the girl, and she forgot the question.

When she looked back down, Els grinned. *Why listen to anything else, if you can hear that?*

The goddess laughed, not getting the joke.

You have a lovely voice, Els said. He wanted to say: Worth waiting for every spring.

Pleasure reddened the jogger's face. *Thanks.*

She edged away. Els ached to call her back. Faust's parting shot to life: Stay awhile; you're so beautiful. But then, he felt like saying that to everything, these days. She smiled, put the buds back in her ears, waved, and looked again up into the tree, at the invisible maker. Then she turned back to the jogging track, and, like so much else that Els took for granted on that disastrous morning, vanished forever.

Prodigiosins kill fungus, protozoa, and bacteria. They might even cure cancer. Their red is the color of pure possibility.

It's 1963, Els's final month at that massive musical factory pumping out performers from the fields of rural Indiana. All winter long, he's studied with Karol Kopacz, and now it's spring, his last undergraduate May. Old *Klangfarben* Kopacz: Polish by way of Argentina, one of those aging terrors from the era of cultural giants who died in the war and were resurrected in the Americas, the marble guardians of a lost art. From what Els can tell, Kopacz hasn't put a note in front of the public for twenty years. The man seems to care nothing for music anymore, though he knows it better than most people know how to breathe.

Els sits in his mentor's office in a corner of the Old Music Building. Every surface of Karol Kopacz's lair, including the baby grand, is heaped high with moldering books and papers, loose scores, records long divorced from their cardboard sleeves, brass Shiva Natarajas, a broken bandoneón, a stringless oud, plates of forgotten sandwich, and a framed photo of an almost handsome younger man underneath the bear paw of Stravinsky that Kopacz has never bothered to hang. Channels through the clutter lead from the door to the desk, the desk to the piano, the piano to the veined leather love seat where cowed composition students sit and take their weekly beatings.

Every seven days, Peter Els brings the man the best that his green soul can generate. Kopacz sits and scans Els's systems in silence. Then he tosses the scores back, saying, *Lots of traffic and no cops*, or *Too many peaks, not enough valleys*. For days afterward, Els rages against the man's glib dismissals. But a month later, he's always in complete agreement.

Today Els brings a thing of antic splendor for solo piano. It feels fresh, quirky, and young, everything art ought to be. It's an openhearted gamble, keen with both reason and love.

His professor looks at the first measure and grimaces. *What is all this?*

It's a compact chromatic phrase, packed with every one of Western music's twelve available notes, twice over. Els stole the idea from Henry Cowell, who may have stolen it from Scriabin, who surely stole it from someone even older.

Go to the piano, Kopacz commands. Peter does as told. He may be a budding revolutionary, but he's an obedient one.

Hit a key.

Els reaches out one finger. *Which . . . ?*

The émigré presses one hoary hand over his eyes, as if the genocidal century has finally caught up with him and he can flee no farther.

Peter hits a key.

Thank you, his mentor says, oozing grace. *What do you hear?*

C? Peter tries. His brain scrambles for the real answer. *C-two. Great C.*

Yes, yes, Kopacz snaps. *What else? Again!*

Bewildered, Peter restrikes the note.

Well? Mother of God. Just listen.

Els strokes the key. He doesn't understand. It might be a foghorn at night. It might be the singing radiator from his childhood bedroom. It might be the first note of the first prelude of the first book of *The Well-Tempered Clavier.* He strikes again, harder, but says nothing.

His teacher hangs his head and groans for civilization's sad waste. *Just listen*, he begs. *Stay inside the sound.*

Els does. The building's torrent of heating switches off, audible now that it stops. He hears the plosives of two people bickering. Down the hall, someone runs through the Adagio from the *Pathétique.* Someone else grinds out four measures from the Elgar Cello Concerto until it sounds like Fluxus. A soprano vocalizes in rapid chromatic swells and dips, the cartoon cue for seasickness. Something that sounds like a large cardboard box knocks against the brick wall at six-second intervals. Outside, a young couple flirts in muffled Spanish. Blocks away, a siren makes its way toward someone's life-erasing disaster. Through it all, Karol Kopacz sits slumped at his desk, face in his hands, drowning in bitter music.

Els blocks him out and listens. He focuses until the note he keeps striking breaks in two. Obvious, what else is there, now that he stops assuming that there's nothing else to hear.

I also hear C-three.

He braces for abuse. But his teacher barks in triumph.

Thank you. Maybe your ear does function, after all. What else?

Relief turns back into panic. Surely there's more to the game. But since Peter can now hear the G above that octave C, a perfect fifth shining out like a ray through cloud, he's forced to say so.

Go on, the displaced Pole commands. Now the game is flushed out into the open. Above that perfect fifth, a perfect fourth. Els has never before taken the fact seriously: hovering above any tone is twice that tone, and triple it, and on up the integers.

He has the map; he knows what islands must be out there, farther off at sea. He stops breathing and concentrates himself. Soon he thinks he can hear the C above the G above the C above the original C ghosting in his ear. He claims as much, and glances at his teacher for a reward. Kopacz's curled fingers wave lazy ellipses in the air: Don't stop now.

Higher still, there hides a major third, then a minor one, and out above that, the entire harmonic series. Els knows the sequence; he could cheat with impunity. But he's still a beginner in his own life, saddled with virulent idealism. He won't claim any pitch he can't in fact hear.

It dawns on Els that even a newborn must feel suspense and resolution, tensions drawn from this series of concealed pitches that the ear detects without knowing. For a beat or two, he flirts with apostasy; maybe the laws of harmony aren't a straitjacket imposed by random convention, after all. He strikes the key harder. It blots out the performance students down the hall, struggling to master their craft. He strains to extract that E above the third C, high up the rainbow of this single note. But the longer he listens, the more that pitch is lost in the angry hum of the fluorescent lights.

E, Kopacz taunts, in a half reverie. *Another G. B-flat above that.*

Peter can't tell if the man claims to hear those pitches, or if, like a high-energy physicist, he's simply asserting their theoretical existence. Audible or not, they're all present: every pitch in the chromatic scale. Sweet stability and crashing discord, the palette for everything from sultry seduction to funeral mass, and Peter has gone his whole life hearing nothing but the fundamental.

Kopacz holds Els's composition up in the air with his left hand. He smacks it with the wiggling fingers of his right. *How many busy little notes do you need to play at once? Use a single C, and be done with it.*

Peter glares, but his teacher doesn't notice. The man busies himself with pushing back the frenzied referendum of his white hair. He slumps in his broken Bauhaus chair and commands, *Now: C-sharp.*

When the bell rings, ending the lesson, it sounds to Peter Els like the *Tristan* chord. He drops the score of his frenetic piano prelude in the green dumpster behind the Music Building, on top of scraps of drywall, a broken desk, and bales of waste office paper. He retreats to his dorm cell and digs in. From behind the union, the bullhorn-led call-and-response of a demonstration floats across Dunn Meadow. The chants for justice sound, in his ear, like ardent folk choruses begging to be orchestrated.

He works late, purging his style of all its superfluous flash and dazzle. He lets the phone nag on, a burr that becomes a whole parfait of pitches. Unanswered knocks on the door ring like tympani. The muffled joy of two new LPs released that very week seep through his cinder-block walls, two wildly different records that will go on to remake the world and leave a wake of nostalgia for decades to come. He hears these sounds the way Debussy heard his first gamelan band.

His desk drawer squeak turns into a tone poem and the hinge of his dorm room door soars like a Heldentenor. Briefly, Els's music retreats into a staggering simplicity. But two months later, he's back to his arcane self, the lesson lost, or not so much lost as tucked away, in a whole spectrum of overtones beyond his ear's ability to hear.

M. H. Gordon gargled *Serratia* and recited Shakespeare in the House of Commons, 1906, to see if speech spread germs through the air.

In the Fiat on the way back, Els resisted the urge to turn on the radio. Not that the news frightened him anymore: by the time the Apocalypse came, we'd all long since have habituated. But the ride home took only five minutes, and anything he might learn about the Libyan no-fly zone or the Fukushima radiation cloud was not worth the further atomization of his brain. Two years earlier, he'd come across the first reports about chronic focal difficulty, from a source he could no longer remember. Since then, he'd tried to take his media in nothing smaller than fifteen-minute doses.

The account of the thirty-eight-year longitudinal study had shaken him: Two researchers, one now dead, had spent thirteen thousand days in blinding tedium, testing people. The study was more rigorous than elegant. But the brute data were undeniable. Over almost four decades, people in every North American demographic had lost, on average, somewhere around one-third of their "sustained focusing interval." The two researchers —whose names Els failed to retain—documented significant declines in how well people could filter out distractions and attend to simple tasks. The country's collective concentration was simply shot. People couldn't hold a thought or pursue a short-term goal for anywhere near as long as they could a few years before, back in the waning days of analog existence.

The blogs bounced the story around for half a dozen days. Then chronic focal difficulty disappeared into its own symptoms. Collapses in phytoplankton and fish populations and honeybee hives, bedbugs and cyberworms, obesity and killer flu: life was awash in too many disorders to pay any one of them more than a few minutes' mind. But the study gave Els the same shudder he'd felt the day he first saw a list of the top one hundred terms that passed through the world's largest search engine. Soon afterward, he began choosing silence over any kind of background listening.

In silence, he drove back home. He saw the commotion just before turning onto Linden. His first thought was that his next door neighbor had had another heart attack. Two cream-colored, windowless vans sat in Els's drive. A sedan stretched alongside them, in the parkway. Streamers of yellow tape cordoned off his house in a geometric proof gone wrong. The repeating, black, all-caps words—DO NOT CROSS— hummed in the wind.

Men in white hoods and hazmat suits carried equipment out of his front door. A trio in business suits directed traffic. Coldberg stood at the top of the concrete steps, swiping at a mobile device. Through the gap between the houses, in the far corner of Els's backyard, two more hazmat suits were digging up Fidelio's grave.

Els edged the car to the curb, his hands fighting the wheel. The scene might have been a European shock-opera staging of the final scene of *Boris Godunov.* Men in puffy white space suits stacked his belongings in storage bins, which they labeled and photographed and placed in the backs of the vans. They moved with practiced efficiency in their hoods and gloves, like biohazard beekeepers. One of the hooded foot soldiers toyed with Els's digital lab scale. Another cradled Els's computer tower as if rescuing an infant from a fire. A box of lab glassware sat in the front lawn. On top of it, in a sealed two-gallon Ziploc, lay Els's sixteenth-century print of Arabic music.

The squad went about stripping his house, as if in an installment of bad reality TV. Els wanted to run out of the car and shout down the intruders. Instead, he sat watching the impossible scene in a haze of presque vu. The middle-aged flight attendant across the street stood in her yard shooting pictures with a cell phone until one of the dress-suited men crossed over and made her stop. A triumphant shout came from the backyard excavation. Els slouched down on the car seat, shading his face. When the man in the suit turned back to the house, Els eased the Fiat away from the curb and out into the open street.

He had to think. In a sweep of left turns, he rounded the adjacent block. A wartime image of the inside of his house popped into his head: CD jewel cases strewn on the floor, books riffled and cast around, the cloud chamber bowls shattered, lab equipment and chemicals confiscated in a hundred labeled baggies. Pictures and papers, sketches for aborted compositions, all picked over by white-suited troops.

Four turns on, he nosed back down Taylor, up to Linden. From half a block away, he watched a hazmat suit on his roof stick a pole down his chimney. Another was testing Ziploc samples with a handheld meter out of the rear of one of the vans. In the backyard, two men scraped mud from his ex-wife's quilt and collected it in sample bottles. At their feet was a ten-gallon plastic storage box filled with a lump of muddy ochre. Fidelio.

Els hung at the corner stop sign. He needed time. He'd broken no laws. Coldberg and Mendoza had charged him with nothing. They'd only told him to stay close. He needed an hour to calm down and prepare a story. The Fiat pulled straight through the intersection and kept on going.

He drove at random. To clear the static in his head, he flipped on the radio. An Emmy-award-winning actor was holding his ex-wife hostage in her Aspen condo. Els found himself on the western edge of campus. He could park and go find Kathryn Dresser, for legal advice. But she'd only tell him to put his faith in the hands of the same authorities who were gutting his house for no reason.

Campustown's commercial strip loomed up on his right, and he turned in. Students drifted in front of his car like targets in the easy levels of a video game. The street stank of fried food. He'd had nothing to eat since the night before. He parked at a meter that still had forty minutes on it, and for an instant he felt like this was his lucky day.

In the corner of a chain coffee shop he sat and nursed breakfast: frothy almond milk and a blueberry muffin as big as a small ottoman. Tension turned his waffle shirt rancid with sweat. Through speakers mounted around the room came a thumpy, hypnotic, overproduced, swollen, irresistible river of lust. The groove looped around three pitches—tonic, minor third, and tritone—while a singer chanted dense, allusive words in shift-ing, irregular rhythms.

The best thing to do was to turn himself in. His picked-through belongings would prove his innocence. But Joint Security agents had his notebooks, full of their fantasias on bacterial modification. They had his computer, with its cache and brows-ing history. Hours from now, they would identify the sites he'd visited the previous afternoon—the ricin recipes; the anthrax.

Back out on the sunlit street, campus felt foreign and dif-fident. Students in shorts and tees, their bared limbs sporting wholesome tattoos, swerved around him without looking up from texting. Els took the diagonal path toward the Music Building. A small, voluble, promiscuously friendly professor of violin walked toward him, waving. Coming here was madness; he spun around and fled.

He hurried back to the car and headed to an ATM on the other side of campus. The screen of the drive-up cash machine threatened him with several choices. Els withdrew two hundred dollars. How soon would the transaction be traceable? A video camera behind the smoky glass gaped at him, and he brushed the bangs from his eyes.

He drove to the public library, three blocks away. It was empty at this hour, except for mothers with small children, other retirees, and street people. In a carrel near the first-floor periodicals, he settled in to clear his head. Two months before, in this same spot, he'd read a magazine article about new Patriot Act provisions. Something about the government being able to keep citizens confined indefinitely on no evidence. All he could remember from the story now was the phrase "hold until cleared."

In another few hours, the news would break. Els headed

to the stacks on the second floor. He stood in front of the life
sciences, running his finger down the spines, inventorying the
titles he'd checked out over the two years since his obsession
began. A memoir by the top scientist in the Soviet Union's biological weapons program. A social history of plagues. A book
called *Escape from Evolution*. With a few keystrokes into the right
databases, an investigator could find every incriminating title
that Peter Els had read over the last ten years.

A groan escaped him. The sound startled an ashen librarian
with dancer's hands who sat at the reference desk near the top
of the stairs.

Is everything all right?

Yes, Els said. *Forgive me.*

He got back into the car and drove. Coming down Linden,
he saw the local news channel vans from two and a half blocks
away. He panicked and turned left on Taylor. The crime scene
shrank to nothing in his wake.

Researchers sprayed *Serratia* in hospitals, to study bacterial drift. Biology students rinsed in it, to watch it travel by
touch.

Clara had told him how Mahler sent the young Alma Schindler the manuscript of the Adagietto from the Fifth Symphony
without any explanation. Alma sent it back, inscribed with the
word "Yes." Weeks later, they married. That's how it was to
have been for Peter and Clara. Then Clara went to Oxford to
study music on a full scholarship, where, in quick succession,

she chalked up a trio of men whose accomplishments made Peter's look like amateur hour.

Clara never bothered to tell Els the rest of the Mahler courtship fable. Only when Alma entered Gustav's life did his music descend into real despair. Battles, lies, betrayal, death. All the stoic affirmation of the young songs and symphonies—*What the Universe Tells Me,* etc.—ran smack into incurable bitterness. Adorno called Mahler *ein schlechter Jasager*: a poor yes-sayer. Once Alma entered his life and the two of them began flaying each other raw, Mahler could do nothing but continue saying the word, with less and less conviction or cause. And deep in his own free fall, young Peter kept listening to the music, well beyond the point where its poor and desperate *yes* could help him.

The Army used *Serratia* for decades to test bioweapons: San Francisco, New York subways, Key West. But I'm the wanted criminal.

Until Els stood in that phone booth after midnight, pleading with a stranger on another continent, the coins freezing to his hands, he had nothing like a *yes* of his own worth saying. Then Clara left, and the real music came. It was one of those arcane exchanges people in operas make with mysterious visitors. The moment the woman with the four feet of hair abandoned Peter to life alone in the barren Midwest, strange, vital, viral creations began pouring out of him.

Every one of those pieces was a message aimed at that now-alien woman. *All goes onward and outward, nothing collapses.* If the least of his manuscripts had ever come back to him penciled with so little as an exclamation mark, Els would have been at Heathrow two days later, in debt to the tune of a transatlantic flight, ready for whatever hope Clara wanted to dangle in front of him.

Instead, he headed off alone to make a new base camp in that little Darmstadt in the prairies. Champaign-Urbana in the early 1960s: an island in the archipelago of I-80 avant-garde, a breeding ground for mutant musical strains surrounded by hundreds of miles of corn, soybean, and rural, religious America in every direction. The perfect place for six more years of school.

A golden age was breaking out in that progressive boondocks. The adventurers who taught composition—Hiller and Isaacson, Johnston, Gaburo, Brün, Hamm, Martirano, Tenney, Beauchamp—made up new rules as fast as they could break them. The infamous Festival of Contemporary Arts and the first electro-acoustic facility in America turned the whole scene into a brilliant party. The spell of math and the pull of charged particles: Els recognized the place even before he hit town.

That self-inventing outpost on the edge of the endless cornfields felt like a new Vienna. In his first five days as a graduate student, Els met more composers than he'd met in his previous twenty-two years. Overnight, his ear grew wanton, and he gorged on things that had only recently terrified him. He joined a listening group studying Persian dastgāhs. He attended talks on music and information theory. Music and the social contract. Music and physiology.

Then, education. In the sixth week of his twentieth century formal analysis class, he arrived breathless over the previous night's performance of Barber's *Hermit Songs*. The class hooted. A stunned Els appealed to the professor.

It's a great piece, don't you think?

The man stifled his amusement and looked around for the hidden camera. *Sure, if you still dig beauty.*

Els sat through the session humiliated. He raged against the man at the grad student Murphy's happy hour, but no one backed him up. When he checked out a recording of *Hermit Songs* from the music library the following week, he found them banal and predictable.

He'd learn the truth from Thomas Mann later that semester: Art was combat, an exhausting struggle. And it was impossible to stay fit for long. Music wasn't about learning how to love. It was about learning what to disown and when to disown it. Even the most magnificent piece would end up as collateral damage in the endless war over taste.

The idea sickened Els. He flirted with dropping out. He lay in bed until noon, planning to head back East to a job sweeping floors or delivering the mail. He could start over in chemistry. But bewilderment forced him back onto campus. Bewilderment and the need to hear whatever that hooting consensus was hearing.

He was sitting in that same formal analysis in late November, staring at the professor's winklepickers as the man danced around the Carter *Variations for Orchestra*, when the door to the classroom flew open. A senior doctoral candidate in musicology burst into the room saying, *They've killed him. They've killed him.* The oldest principle of composition: repeat everything. The messenger's face was as washed out as an unfixed Polaroid, and his right hand traced odd, gnostic signs in the air. *The president,* he said. *They shot him through the head.*

Someone said, *Jesus God.* Els looked to the professor for an explanation, but the man's face fisted up in fear. The co-ed at the desk behind Els began to sniffle like an engine that wouldn't turn over. Someone said, *Get a radio*. Someone put his arm on Els's shoulder, a last awkward innocence. And the thought—three parts dread and one part thrill—passed through the mind of the beginning composer as if one of them had spoken it out loud: Make what you want, now. The place is up for grabs.

You carry around ten times more bacterial cells than you do human ones. Without their genes, you're dead.

Els returned to school after that Christmas break with a single-movement octet—cello, violin, viola, clarinet, flute, horn, trumpet, and trombone. Music for uncharted times. The piece had started out studious, even reverent, but something happened as he fleshed it out. The lines insisted on more room, more play, more heat and light. The thing turned demonic, as reckless and motor-driven as those rock and roll anthems that his brother once forced him to admire.

He assembled a group of grad performers and cajoled them through several rehearsals until he produced a satisfying tape. The piece felt strong enough to win him lessons with any of the faculty's alphas—those men who locked themselves into the Experimental Music Studio for days at a time, outdoing even the north campus scientists in rigor and formal perfection.

For his pedagogical parricide, Els settled on Matthew Mattison. A working-class boy from Lakehurst, Mattison went about in bomber jackets, three-day stubble, and loosened ties that looked like sliced-up Pollock canvases. The man was a dervish of dark energy, not yet forty-four, but his music had been performed in a dozen countries; he seemed to Els like a study for a bust in tomorrow's Museum of Iconoclasm. His most recent twenty-five-minute tour de force was a contrapuntal pitched-speech chorus for virtuoso verbal ensemble built from the phrase, "So what if it's so?"

Mattison invited Els to his house to listen to the octet. The home of a real composer: it wasn't possible. Els stumbled on the loose, weed-covered flagstones twice while coming up the front walk.

The meeting began at eight p.m. and didn't break up until one in the morning. And in those five hours of vicious back-and-forth, Els found himself defending a musical philosophy he never imagined anyone having to defend.

Els liked arguing as well as the next rebel acolyte. He and Clara had once stayed up all night fighting over which three piano concertos to take down in the fallout shelter for the final stay. But Mattison meant war. He began with a ferocious volley, not merely against the octet itself, but against all the foundations that Els took for granted. He called it cheap of Els to hide behind a melody that the audience would leave the hall humming. That meter so regular you could skip rope to it, those thrilling chord progressions: Why not just send a cozy Christmas card?

The front room where the two men clashed was almost bare aside from three wood-plank chairs, built by Swedes for mannequins. A stand near the window held a fishbowl filled with cobalt marbles. In the middle of the room a wrought-iron cube supported a thin surfboard of glass, a coffee table that had never seen coffee, let alone magazines. On a ledge jutting from one wall sat a sculpture made of bolts and washers and nuts that looked like an engineer's upgrade of an elephant. Taped to the wall were unframed newsprint printouts—skeins of radiating black lines, generated by Illinois's massive mainframe computer. Three years later, every child in America would be making similar webbed designs with their toy Spirographs.

For hours, Els and Mattison battled over first principles, and all that time, the master never offered his prospective disciple food or drink. For a while, the student held his own. But at last, herded into a corner, Els broke.

Isn't the point of music to move listeners?

Mattison smiled. *No. The point of music is to wake listeners up. To break all our ready-made habits.*

And tradition?

Real composers make their own.

So Gustav Mahler wasn't a real composer?

Mattison regarded the ceiling of the bare room and stroked his stubble with the back of his knuckles. He considered the question for forty-five seconds—half the length of Els's octet scherzo.

Yes. I would have to say that Gustav Mahler was not a real composer. A songwriter, perhaps. But caught in the grip of the past.

It was beyond late. Els rubbed his mouth and said nothing. He was hearing things, faraway things approaching, faint and impenitent and electric.

If you come study with me, Mattison said, *your very first piece will be about the stop sign at the end of my street.*

Els looked around the bare room. The white plaster walls caught the light of the paper lantern and bent it into a cubist bouquet. He listened to the future for a long time. Then he turned back toward his next teacher and squinted. *Fine. But I'm going to write it in C.*

Life is nothing but mutual infection. And every infecting
message changes the message it infects.

The war between Peter and Matthew Mattison lasted years,
without any hope of peace with honor. They fought not simply over Els's tenderfoot soul but over the whole project of
music. Week after week, Els tried to revive the once-audacious
inventions of the past and make them dangerous again. And
week after week, his mentor dismissed his études as pretty
sentiment.

The wildest things Els dared to make were too tame for
Mattison. And in time, Mattison's constant harping on fresh-
ness began to stale. Still, the rolling clashes taught Els a great
deal about theory and harmony, despite Mattison's contempt
for those spent games. Els learned a lot, too, about the human
ear, about what it would and wouldn't hear. But above all, he
learned how to weaponize art.

Els grew; he broadened, under the attack. At last, the jagged
terrain that Mattison pushed him toward opened up its cold
magnificence. And like the businessman who finds one Friday
that he might enjoy dressing up as a woman and heading to a
dark cellar club on the other side of town, Peter Els embraced
his panic and thrilled to realize that he might be free to make
anything at all.

For years, the crisis lay in choosing Schoenberg or Stravinsky. By 1966, both those men sounded old and quaint. European postwar weirdness, American pop ballads, magnetic tape,
advertising ditties, and gnarly microtones all collided in one big

free-for-all. Yet the wider the choice, the more every conscript in the program wanted Els to declare allegiance. He grasped this one night in a campus bar, while Dylan wailed "Desolation Row" on the jukebox, that reworking of the old United Mine Workers anthem: *Everybody's shouting, "Which Side Are You On?"*

He knew no earthly reason why he should have to choose. Yet he now saw—crazy late—just how the pecking order worked. The high-concept men got all the performances. The twelve-tone formalists got all the cachet. And with new Ph.D. programs in composition sprouting up all across the country, to compete for grants, you needed a system as pure as physics. And so the choice came clear to Els: radiant versus rigorous, methodical versus moving.

For as long as he could, Els crept between camps like a Swiss diplomatic courier. But the fray said declare, or be despised by all. And soon enough, the fray began to excite Els.

It was his pure dumb luck to be alive in the morning of that revolution. For one more time, music had causes to champion, utopias to foster, and idols worth demolishing. Not since *ars nova* in the fourteenth century or the development of sonata-allegro form at the end of the eighteenth had there been a better time to be a beginner.

And beginnings were everywhere for the taking. One Saturday, out scavenging his week's stock of TV dinners in the freezer aisle of the Jewel, Peter heard a girl, no more than ten, in pink shorts, flowered peasant blouse, and flip-flops, humming to herself while bathing in the cold clouds that poured from the open door of a Popsicle case. The tune hit Els like a distilled Magnificat. Over the span of two manic months, he took the girl's ditty and turned it into the twenty-minute *Rapture,* for chamber orchestra, soprano, and four reel-to-reel tape machines. The six pitches of that singsong fragment, combined and recombined, slowed, sped up, inverted, reversed, stacked into evolving rhythms and incanted in banks of antiphony, blossomed into a fantasia.

Mattison condemned the finished piece as decorative. Johnston liked the virtuoso reach, but wanted something more purged of familiar harmonic gestures. Hiller found it intriguing but inchoate. And Brün wanted to know how such music helped bring about a more just society.

Els squirreled away his teachers' cavils and crafted his revenge. He spent nights in the electronic studio, coaxing the theremin, splicing tape loops, and learning how to program. The computer made it possible to shape any pitch, amplitude, timbre, and duration, and combine these into the voiceprint of the early space age. But omnipotence made Els sad. He yearned for the clumsy, freighted flights of earthly instruments.

In secret, he returned to the exhausted vocabularies of the old masters, looking for lost clues, trying to work out how they'd managed, once, to twist the viscera and swell whatever it was in humans that imagined it was a soul. Some part of him could not help believing that the key to re-enchantment still lay in walking backward into the future.

Picasso: "Art is dangerous. Art is not chaste." Ellington: "When art ceases to be dangerous, you don't want it."

There were women in those years, one brittle and misgiven, the other glad and loud. Each had a music, though neither was Clara, whom Peter now hated with such force it left little room in him for other need. There were entertaining men, too, friends whose crackpot ideologies seemed just the thing for a month or two. Above all there was his growing technique, the greatest chemistry set a boy could want.

By demented but rigorous Cold War logic, composing kept him out of the jungles of Southeast Asia. People in marble buildings out East vowed to beat the Communists at every available proxy war: athletics, chess, showpiece architecture, even high culture. And that meant deferments for student composers. The State Department and the CIA even sent the best of Els's colleagues on concert tours to Thailand, Argentina, Turkey, and other contested world hot spots.

Back in his first year in graduate school, Els had sat in a TV room at the Illini Union, surrounded by giddy students, watching a bulky, grainy, rabbit-eared black-and-white set bolted to the wall as the Beatles played *Ed Sullivan*, their infectious seventh chords electrifying the room. By the time he started his doctoral portfolio, a great feedback loop of influence had swept him up. Everyone was picking everyone else's pockets: the Fab Four stealing from Stockhausen for *Sgt. Pepper*; Andriessen and Berio rearranging Lennon and McCartney. For a few bright months, high and low, timid and adventuresome, coarse and intricate, all braided around each other in complex counterpoint. But by the year Els left school for good, the gods were fumbling around up on a London rooftop, trying and failing to get back home.

For three years, Peter lived in a graduate flophouse in West Urbana—a majestic old turn-of-the-century American Gothic carved up into separate units, each serviced by its own fire escape, with a dozen mailboxes in a police lineup on the front porch. There, in the fall of '66, his roommates clamped him in a wing chair, fed him hash brownies, and launched him on a marathon listening session that seemed to spread out across days. They started him on *The Well-Tempered Clavier.* Kaleidoscopic lines burst in Peter's head like tangled stairways in a Piranesi labyrinth. Indescribable arcs separated themselves from the flood of music and struck off on lives of their own. Those independent lines in turn formed—in the surprise intervals they struck when gliding over each other—further unheard melodies, airs folded perpendicularly inside other airs, or buried like cryptic cross-word hints that hid the keys to their decoding inside another would-be clue. The weave staggered him—a two-minute proof of time's divine design.

Who's playing? he shouted, with an urgency that sent the group into hysterics.

He was disappointed to learn that it was Gould. *I always hear all the counterpoint, with Gould. Try me with Richter.*

The secret weaving was still there, even in Richter's pedaled blur.

Six more hash excursions with much careful note-taking ended in disillusionment. Pot was a private aha. All the glories were sealed in the locked room of the smoker's brain, and turned to a joke when he sobered. Els was after something more solid, a priori, shared—durable wonder raining down on whole roomfuls of listeners at once.

Then a summer night, a gram and a half of *P. cubensis*, and Els found himself swimming upright, propelled by thought through a field filled with what announced itself as filaments of pure life stretching out much farther and deeper than the mere world. The stars spoke in patterns of brilliance so obvious he'd forever overlooked them. The field was pure music, *Jupiter* unbound, one of an endless, renovating series of *theres* that the brain might live in, were it not shaped so mercilessly for here.

Music has killed more people than *Serratia* ever did.

Babbitt asked the question to the country's face: *Who Cares if You Listen?* His manifesto made the rounds, drawing more readers than his music had listeners. Music knew things. It had its expanding toolkit, no less than chemistry. If you wanted to go deep, to make the full journey, you had to study the language.

The great mystery of those days was how many people still thought the journey worth the effort. Audiences sat for hours in somber black-box theaters to listen to a rash of abstruse blips and bleeps. Even downstate Illinois crawled with people—bright, energetic, hip, inventive explorers in loud stripes and madras and sideburns the shape of Idaho—people on the verge of a newfound America of sound.

In the middle of this efflorescence, the Imp Saint came to town. He walked into that wasteland of corn like the Apostle Paul wandering into the boonies of Lystra. A chance toss of the I Ching led Els to John Cage. Yet chance was just an order that you hadn't yet perceived. The Imp Saint himself had written as much: every item in existence was linked to every other.

But then, the man had also written, many times in many ways, *I have nothing to say, and I am saying it.*

Music is awareness flowing in through the ear. And nothing is more terrifying than being aware.

He wanted to go home, shed his walking clothes, take a shower, and eat lunch. But camera crews encircled his house and lab techs were autopsying his dog for biotoxins. His face would be all over the local news by afternoon. Renown had evaded Peter Els his whole life. Now he had only to drive home and wave his arms, and he'd become America's most famous living composer.

His brain was pure noise. Els drove at random, turning often, his eyes on the rearview mirror. The strip mall where he bought his groceries swung into view. He turned in. The familiar gauntlet of shops felt like the set for a comic operetta: tanning salon, weight loss clinic, dentist-in-a-box, Pretty Nails, Eyemart.

Els sat in the parked car, hands under his armpits. At last, he fished his phone out of the glove compartment. Sara had made him swear to keep one there, for road emergencies. She failed, however, to make him promise to keep it charged. The green phone button did nothing; the screen reflected his face in a postage stamp of black. He rummaged around for the car adapter among the piles of books and CDs in the backseat, without luck.

Something like the space shuttle pulled into the slot next to him. Its running board came up to the middle of the Fiat's window. Waves of pounding bass passed through the hulls of both vehicles and shook Els's torso like a Vitamaster belt massager. Whole windshield-shattering subcultures had grown up around that sonic violence: dB shoot-outs, video sites featuring women whose hair whipped about in the winds of sound. Deafness as the price of ecstasy: any composer had to admire the bargain.

The van's engine cut out, the body-bruising waves ceased, and the parking lot reeled under the sudden evacuation. A close-cropped, thirtyish man in work shirt, chinos, and huaraches got out, peering at a shopping list as he headed into the supermarket. He looked like one of the stalwart patrons of those extravaganzas in abandoned SoHo sweat shops that Els had helped mastermind decades ago.

The dashboard clock jerked Els back. At that moment, eight people with four feet in the grave were convening in the Shade Arbors main common room, notepads in hand, waiting for their teacher to come run their ninth music appreciation class of the season. Twentieth Century Landmarks. God knew he had an excuse to miss. Were his students to die in their sleep tonight without this week's lecture on classical music and the Second World War, they would still pass the final exam.

A gutted phone booth, dead these last few years, sat in the strip mall parkway. All the nation's public phones had vanished. He considered bumming a cell phone off of someone in the supermarket. It didn't seem advisable, given his morning.

He had to get to a lawyer. He needed to prepare an explanation, something to justify those few casual experiments that now seemed criminal, even to him.

He started the car and pointed it toward the gated retirement community. If someone there heard the news already and called the police, then that's how the piece would play out. He, at least, would have hit all his marks, met all his obligations, and followed the printed score.

Be grateful for anything that still cuts. Dissonance is a beauty that familiarity hasn't yet destroyed.

Els stood in the coral foyer of Shade Arbors in front of the curving reception desk. His pulse was presto and he felt as furtive as a walking mug shot, as if he were wearing a bandolier of yellow police tape draped across his chest. But the receptionist greeted him like an old friend.

He cut through the reception area, flinching each time a logo-emblazoned staffer passed. A woman shaped like the letter *f* walking into a stiff headwind cut across his bow. Another skipped alongside him, toting a mini-oxygen cylinder in a crocheted sling. The place had the air of an Ensor carnival, and Els was just another mummer in the monstrous parade. Flesh kneaded loose by gravity, vessel-popped limbs pushing tartan-wrapped aluminum walkers, liver-spot continents that floated on oceans of pallid face, spoon-wide gaps in smiles, necks thinned out to tendons above colorful golf-shirt collars, heads crowned in bony domes: each of them as awed by age as children by their first snowfall.

Els's students waited for him in the main common room. Two sat in wing chairs by the fake fireplace, testing their memory with a deck of famous-painting flash cards and cursing like Sicilian dockworkers. Six others sat on the couches flanking the kidney-shaped central table, deep in an argument about whether trees pollute. They dressed in bright tracksuits and knockoff cross trainers—games day on a landlocked cruise ship. The Q-tips, they called themselves. *White at both ends, with a stick in the middle.*

The group brightened at Els's entrance. *You're late,* someone said. *Culture's waiting.* Someone else said, *So what train wreck are we listening to this week?*

Els leaned against the river-stone wall, breathing hard. The too-warm room stank of floral-scented hand sanitizer. Triclosan: antibacterial in a hundred consumer products, probable carcinogen, breeder of bacterial super-races. But no one was closing down that lab.

What happened to you? Lisa Keane asked.

Els shrugged, still in his painter pants and waffle shirt. They'd never seen him more casual than oxford button-down. *Forgive me. My morning has been a little . . . avant-garde.*

They waved off his apologies. No one seemed to have heard a thing. On a flat-screen TV behind the couches, a famous ideologue adulterer embezzler with his own nationally distributed brand was sticking pins into the groin of a presidential voodoo doll for the entertainment of thirty million people. The next local news came on at noon. Els had until then.

Could we . . . ? He waved at the screen and twisted an imaginary knob, though no TV in the Northern Hemisphere had used knobs for years. William Bock, erstwhile ceramic engineer, jumped up from the love seat and doused the set.

Els looked out the big bay window onto a stand of pines. He had the distinct impression of having disappeared into one of those Central European allegorical novels that Clara always urged on him, years ago. Those books had always filled him with a dread hope, a feeling between falling in love and dying. He looked around the room at his companions in decrepitude, on their last-minute search for cultural burial swag. Some finish-line respite from the present's endless entertainment.

It's been a hell of a morning. I locked myself out of the house. And I'm afraid I locked my notes in. Can we reschedule?

Disappointment rippled through the room. Piccolo and pizzicato violins.

You don't love us anymore?

Locked yourself out? Time to book a room with us.

We're all here, Lisa Keane said. *Let's listen anyway. We don't really need the lecture.*

They didn't really need the music. Yet the pattern was as

old as dying. A sudden turn in the aging body after the back straightaway, a need for more serious sound. Els had seen it in every uptown concert he'd ever attended: everyone in the audience, old. Auditoriums a whitecapped sea. For years he'd thought that these incurables were the survivors of another time, the children of early radio's doomed project of cultural uplift. But the years passed, the old died away, and more old people came to replace them. Did something happen to the fading brain, some change in meter that made it turn away from the three-minute song? Did old people think that *classical* held the key to deathbed solace, an eleventh-hour pardon?

I'm sorry, he said. *I didn't bring a single disc. They're sitting in a stack in the living room, on top of my lecture notes.*

Klaudia Kohlmann, the retired clinical therapist who'd talked Els into this teaching gig, tipped herself out of her overstuffed chair, crossed to where he stood, and drew a small black slab out of her Incan shoulder bag. She held out the weapon as if she meant to phaser him. He took it and flipped it on, watched by the eight people who'd come for their next installment in the further adventures of an endlessly dying art.

Els gazed at the tiny black rectangle. Like a detonator in an action film, it possessed one button. He pressed it, and the screen filled with a white-shrouded figure in a small rowboat near a rocky outcrop covered with cypresses.

He fingered the miracle again. All of recorded music—a millennium of it—nestled in his hand. Els looked out across the sleeper cell of ancient pupils who waited for their payoff. It crossed his mind to tell them that the Joint Security Task Force wanted him and he really must be going. He glanced back down and flicked at the screen. Two more menus flashed by, leaving him with a patient prompt and a tiny thumb keyboard.

Although he no longer believed it told a coherent story, Els had given the group the last century's major milestones in rough chronological order. He'd led them from Debussy to Mahler, from Mahler to Schoenberg, revealing the parent's genes still hiding out in the child. He described the riots at the premiere of *The Rite of Spring*. He played them *Pierrot Lunaire,* those whispers on the edge of a moonlit abyss. He took them down into the Great War. He raced them through the frantic twenties and thirties, Futurism and free dissonance, Ives and Varèse, polytonality and tone clusters, and the scattered attempts to return to a home key that had been forever blown away. And still, each week, his clutch of core listeners kept coming back for more.

The group followed his account like it was an old Saturday serial—*The Perils of Pauline*—a footrace between triumph and disaster forever coming down to the wire. And as the sessions unfolded, Els found himself cheating, stacking the deck. He cherry-picked the evidence, the way NASA had done when they sent their golden record billions of light-years through space and wanted to make a good first impression on the neighbors.

In this way, he'd taken his eight pupils up to the year of his birth. And today, he'd wanted to give them a piece that proved how catastrophe might be luckier than anyone supposed.

Kohlmann handed him a cable to the room's speaker dock. *Come on. Don't leave us hanging.*

Els pecked into the search box: F-O-R.

A drop-down list leapt ahead of each keystroke, predicting his desire. The top of the list had the most likely suspects: *Howlin' for You. Three Cheers for Sweet Revenge. For All We Know.* The bottom of the list: there was no bottom.

He fed in more letters: T-H-E. The thinned list was still

infinite. *Ain't No Rest for the Wicked. Sing for the Moment. For the First Time.*

Els typed on: E-N-D. The planet-sized catalog zeroed in on several dozen suspects. *For the End. Waiting for the End. Ready for the End of the World.* Two more letters—O-F—and there it was, in the middle of the drop-down list, in a dozen different performances: *Quartet for the End of Time.*

All my music ever wanted was to tunnel into forever through the wall of Now.

The last day of spring 1940. The Nazis pour into France. Just past the crumbling Maginot Line, the Wehrmacht captures three musicians fleeing through the woods. Henri Akoka, an Algerian-born Trotskyite Jew, is caught clutching his clarinet. Étienne Pasquier, acclaimed cellist and former child prodigy, surrenders without a struggle. The third, organist-composer Olivier Messiaen, a weak-eyed birder and religious mystic who hears in color, has saved nothing in his satchel but a few essentials: pocket scores of Ravel, Stravinsky, Berg, and Bach.

Days before, all three Frenchmen were playing in a military orchestra at the citadel at Verdun. Now their captors march them at gunpoint, with hundreds of others, to a holding pen near Nancy. They walk for days without food or drink. Several times, Pasquier faints from hunger. Akoka, a big-hearted, hardheaded man, pulls the cellist up and keeps him going.

At last, the prisoners arrive at a courtyard where the Germans distribute water. Fights break out among the captives. Packs of desperate men battle each other for a few swigs. The clarinetist finds Messiaen seated far from the fray, reading a score from his pack.

Look, the composer says. *They're fighting over a drop of water.*

Akoka is a pragmatist. *We just need to get some containers so they can distribute it.*

The Germans round up their prisoners and force them on. At last the column arrives at a barbed-wire enclosure in an open field. The three musicians mill about with hundreds of others in the summer rain. Their country is lost. The entire French Army is routed, captured, or dead.

The rain stops. A day passes, then another. There's nothing to do but wait under an indifferent sky. The composer produces a solo for clarinetist, saved from the captured citadel. Akoka sight-reads it, standing in a field full of prisoners. Pasquier, the cellist, serves as human music stand. The piece, "Abyss of the Birds," grew from Messiaen's dawn military watches, when the day's first chirps would turn into a morning orchestra. It passes the captive time.

Henri Akoka is a good-natured joker, who likes to say, *I'm going to go practice now*, when he's off to take a nap. But this music disconcerts him. Impossibly long crescendos, tumults of free rhythm: it resembles no music he has ever heard. Six years before, Akoka took the *premier prix* at the Paris Conservatory. He has played for years in the Orchestre National de la Radio. But this piece is the hardest solo he has ever seen.

"I'll never be able to play it," Akoka grumbles.

"Yes, yes, you will," Messiaen tells him. "You'll see."

FRANCE FALLS WHILE they rehearse. Giant swastikas drape from the Arc de Triomphe. Hitler hops out of a Mercedes and trots up the great stairway of the Palais Garnier, the first stop on his private Paris tour.

THE MUSICIANS LIVE for three weeks under the stars in the enclosed field. After the disgrace of the armistice, they're shipped to Stalag VIII-A—a camp on a five-hectare lot outside the town of Görlitz-Moys, in Silesia. There, the trio is stripped and processed, along with thirty thousand other prisoners. A soldier with a submachine gun tries to confiscate the composer's satchel. The naked Messiaen fights him off.

The speed of France's defeat surprises the Germans. Stalag VIII-A can hold only a fraction of the tens of thousands who pour in. Most live in tents; the lucky trio find space in the barracks, which at least have toilets and earthen stoves. Food is scarce: ersatz coffee for breakfast, a bowl of watery soup for lunch, and for dinner a slice of black bread with a lump of grease. The cellist Pasquier gets a job in the kitchen, where he takes to stealing scraps to share with his comrades. The man who works next to him is killed for stealing three potatoes.

Messiaen goes to bed at night faint and famished. Starvation brings rainbow visions filled with pulsing colors: great bursts of blue-orange lava, flares from another planet. He wakes to the gray of meaningless work, hunger, and monotony.

Another prisoner lands in Akoka's bunk: a grim pacifist named Jean Le Boulaire. He was on the front in May when the French Army panicked and dissolved. He made his way to Dunkirk, where a fishing boat evacuated him to England. From there, Le Boulaire returned to Paris, just in time to suffer another, final rout. Akoka instructs his new bunkmate in camp life and introduces the violinist to his friends. Le Boulaire remembers

Messiaen from his days in the Paris Conservatory. And so the trio becomes a quartet.

The tens of thousands of prisoners in Stalag VIII-A pool their books into a small library. They form a jazz band and a tiny orchestra. They start a newspaper called *Le Lumignon—The Candle*. Every story is censored to shreds, but writing holds at bay the crushing boredom of days.

The musicians lose weight and hair and teeth. Messiaen's fingers swell with chilblains. Fed up, Akoka decides to escape. He devises a way to slip past the guards. He stockpiles provisions and acquires a compass. He tells the composer that everything is set for a break-out the next day.

No, Messiaen says. *I'm staying. God wants me here.* Demoralized, Akoka abandons the plan.

The Germans send Pasquier to work in the Strzegom quarries. But a camp administrator recognizes the cellist from the famous Trio Pasquier and commutes his assignment. The other musicians, too, get a little more food, a little lighter work. War is war, but for Germans, music is music.

One of the camp captains, Karl-Albert Brüll, now and then smuggles Messiaen extra bread. Hauptmann Brüll hunts down fresh music paper: pages lined with pristine staves, rescued from the war's bedlam. He gives Messiaen the sheets, along with pencils and erasers. Who knows his reasons? Guilt, compassion, curiosity. He wants to hear the unborn music of his enemy. He wants to know what kind of sounds a man like Messiaen might bring into so damned a place.

Brüll takes Messiaen off of all duties and places him in solitary. He posts a guard at the barrack entrance to prevent disturbance. And Messiaen, who thought he'd never compose again in this life, slips back into the spell of patterned sounds. He needs nothing else—only notes, added pitch by pitch toward some obscure whole. As summer dies and fall follows it into extinction, something begins to fill the empty pages: a quartet from beyond all seasons.

Sounds swirl from out of Messiaen's malnourished dreams. He works through the fall of France, the Nazi triumph, the horror of camp existence. An eight-part vision takes shape—a glimpse of the Apocalypse for violin, clarinet, cello, and piano, freed of imprisoning meter and full of rainbows.

Messiaen reworks from memory two pieces that he wrote in another life, before the war. To these he adds sounds from a remembered future. Here in this camp, in the middle of a wasted Europe, the notes come out of him like the creature of light revealed to John:

> And I saw another mighty angel come down from heaven, clothed with a cloud: and a rainbow was upon his head, and his face was as it were the sun . . . And the angel which I saw stand upon the sea and upon the earth lifted up his hand to heaven, and sware by him that liveth for ever and ever, who created heaven, and the things that therein are, and the earth, and the things that therein are, and the sea, and the things which are therein, that there should be time no longer . . .

Akoka's clarinet is the one decent instrument in the camp. The commandants scrounge up a cheap violin and a collapsing upright piano whose keys go down but don't always rise again. Hundreds of prisoners pass the hat and collect sixty-five marks for Pasquier to buy a cello. Two armed guards take him to a shop in the center of Görlitz, where he finds a battered cello and bow. When Pasquier brings it back to camp that evening, the prisoners assail him. He plays them solo Bach, the "Swan" from *Carnival of the Animals, Les mignons d'Arlequin*—everything he can remember. Prisoners who care nothing about music make him play all night.

The quartet rehearses in the camp lavatories. Every evening at six, they leave their jobs and huddle together for four hours. Winter sets in, animal and effective; temperatures plummet to minus twenty-five Celsius. Prisoners die of exhaustion, malnutrition, and cold. But the Germans give the quartet wood to make a fire and warm their fingers.

Messiaen coaches the others through the world he has made. The piece is too hard for them; even the virtuoso Pasquier struggles. Messiaen demonstrates from the piano, but the players fall into a thicket of rhythms. The music is Messiaen's escape from the grip of meter, from the plodding thump of heartbeats and the ticking of clocks. His jagged lines struggle to defeat the present and put an end to time.

The tools for this escape come from everywhere: Greek metrical feet—*amphimacer* and *antibacchius*. North Indian *deśītālas*. Rhythmic palindromes that read the same forward and backward. The jerky syncopations of Stravinsky. Medieval isorhythms—huge metrical cycles within cycles. At times, meter drops away altogether and demands the freedom of birds.

But flight eludes the players. Raised on their tame regular beats, they stumble in the chaos of liberty. The rapid unisons, those wild swells, trip them up. *Hold the note until you can't blow anymore*, Messiaen says. *Enlarge the sound*. He demands absurdly high pitches and brutal, scattering runs. He marks the score with commands like *infiniment lent, extatique*—infinitely slow, ecstatic. He wants a sound softer than a bow can make. He wants every color that can be teased out of the wood, from chill shouts to fierce silence, and he insists that every manic rhythm be perfect. The shabby violin, the sixty-five-mark cello, the out-of-tune piano with the sticky keys, the clarinet melted by resting against a hot stove: together, they must produce the angel and all the shimmer of the Celestial City.

The players rehearse with frost-crippled fingers. For two months, they work the same impossible passages again and again. Thrown together for so long at this fevered music, while winter comes down on Silesia and their camp blankets them in death, the four of them alter. Their technique pushes into a new place. Even-tempered agnostic, gloomy atheist, messianic Catholic, and Trotskyite Jew crouch over the parts of the recalcitrant piece by dim light, in a prison bathroom, and locate, in their shared focus, birdsong's answer to the war.

THE CAMP PRINTS programs for the premiere:

Stalag VIII A–Görlitz
PREMIÈRE AUDITION DU
QUATOUR POUR LA FIN DU TEMPS
D'OLIVIER MESSIAEN
15 Janvier 41

Against regulations, the commandant authorizes even the quarantined prisoners to attend. Something is happening in this corner of confinement, far away from the annihilating front, the wolf pack strikes, the desert pendulum offenses, the fire raids on London, the steady gearing up of machinic carnage on scales no human can comprehend. The next world's debut.

The day opens like hundreds before it. Ersatz at dawn. A

morning of mind-fogging work at the assigned duties. A lunch of cabbage soup, and more forced labor all afternoon. For dinner, another cup of ersatz, a slice of bread, a little *fromage blanc*. No messenger comes to break open the eternal tomb.

The concert starts at six, in Barrack 27, the camp's crude theater. Half a meter of snow carpets the ground and buries the roof. Snow gusts through the barrack doorway. The dim house is packed, a few hundred prisoners of several nationalities, from every class and profession—doctors, priests, businessmen, laborers, farmers . . . Some have never heard chamber music before.

The audience crowds together on the benches, wrapped in gray-black coats. Clouds of frozen breath fill the room, whiffs of rotting gut exuded by malnourished men in oil-stained rags. What heat the barrack manages on this bone-numbing night comes only from these wasted bodies. Infirm men from the hospital block are borne in on stretchers. The music-loving German officers take their reserved seats in the front rows.

The quartet shuffles out onto the improvised stage in tattered jackets and bottle-green Czech uniforms. Wooden clogs are the only shoes in camp that can keep their feet thawed for fifty minutes. Messiaen steps forward, his suit bagging. He tells the audience what they're about to hear. He explains the eight movements, one for each of the six days of creation, the day of rest, and the Last Day. He talks of color and form, of birds, of the Apocalypse, and of the secrets of his rhythmic language. He speaks of that moment when all past and future will end and endlessness will begin.

The prisoners cough and squirm on their benches. Hardened faces turn suspicious. No one knows what this scarecrow is raving about. Pasquier caresses his cello. Le Boulaire nurses his violin. Akoka, clarinet on his lap, looks out at his comrades and smiles a joker's last smile.

The lecture ends, the musicians raise their instruments, and the crystal liturgy begins. Two birds start a predawn song they've sung since long before human time. The clarinet channels a blackbird; the violin, a nightingale. The cello skates about in a fifteen-note loop of ghostly harmonics, while the piano cycles through a rhythm of seventeen values, divided into a pattern of twenty-nine chords. This whirling solar system would take four hours to unfold its complete circuit of nested revolutions. But the movement lasts a mere two and a half minutes—a sliver between two infinities.

A shimmer of sound, according to Messiaen's program notes. *A halo of trills lost very high in the trees . . .the harmonious silence of Heaven*. But before the dazed prisoners can tell what they hear, morning is over.

Then the angel appears, one foot on land, one on the sea, to announce the end of time. Bright, crashing chords, a race of doubled strings. Violin and cello, in a unison chant, wander as far from this camp as imagination can reach. The piano descends in waterfalls of chords. Fanfare returns, jarring the audience. No one can say what on earth these four performers think they're doing.

Music drifts past the bundled listeners, through the snow-buried barrack, beyond the last twist of barbed wire that seals this camp in. The movement ends, releasing a fit of coughs. Numb listeners shift on their benches, and the third movement starts. This one reworks that fantasia for solo clarinet that Akoka sight-read out in the empty field near Nancy, so long ago. The abyss of birds. *The abyss is Time*, Messiaen explains, *with its weariness and gloom. The birds are the opposite of Time. They are our desire for light, for stars, for rainbows, and for jubilant songs.*

The clarinetist who once played in a wallpaper factory band now plays himself into the future. He chirps and trills. His crescendos swell from silent to shattering, like an air-raid siren issuing its final warning. The song demands staggering control. It asks even more of the audience, who begin to divide, in the gaslight, between those who hear escape and those who make out only tedium.

The fourth movement, a little music-box trio, lasts ninety seconds. It could be a trifle from before the war, a lark from back when the largest crisis facing civilization was still skirt length. Eternity, too, needs its interludes.

Bombs fall tonight in the south of England. A cordon tightens around Tobruk. The savage tank battles across North Africa pause for a few hours, delayed by darkness. In Berlin, a two-hour drive northwest, Hitler's staff work late, firming up the invasions of Yugoslavia and Greece. But here in Barrack 27, Stalag VIII-A, halfway through Messiaen's fever dream, the cello spins a melody out of itself. It rides on the waves of the piano, which wanders through endless, patient modulations. Each sprung chord pushes the duet into a new color.

Anywhere else, this movement would last eight minutes. But here in this barrack, with its drafty rafters and frosted windows, packed with men who'll live here for years, who'll die in this hole unable to recall the look of home, the beat between any two wandering chords gets lost for hours. For some, the pulsing phrase is a shade less deadly than the boredom of their captivity. For others, it's a bliss they'll never find again.

On the shoe-box stage, the quartet digs in, releasing the "Dance of Fury, for the Seven Trumpets." All four instruments chase each other around in jolting cadences of jagged unison, a mounting game of crack-the-whip. *Music of stone*, says Messiaen, *formidable granite sound; irresistible movement of steel, huge blocks of purple rage, icy drunkenness.*

The angel returns, tangled in cloud and rainbow. There have been elations in the piece before now, but none to match these raptures. For Messiaen: *I pass through the unreal and suffer, with ecstasy, a tournament; a roundabout compenetration of superhuman sounds and colors. These swords of fire, this blue-orange lava, these sudden stars . . . !*

The end of the End, when it arrives at last, comes as a solo violin above piano throb. Pared back to its essence, the melody abides, burnt pure in the crucible of the war. Out of a cloud of shimmering E major chords—the key of paradise—the violin hints at all a person might still have, after death takes everything. The violin rises; the piano climbs along toward some final immobility beyond human patience and hearing. The praise wanders higher, into C minor, through a frozen minefield of ambiguous diminished and augmented chords, rising again to another E major, then one more in the octave above. From out at the edge of the key- and fingerboards, the line glances back at a lost Earth on a cold night, when there is time no longer.

When the last notes die out in the frozen air, nothing happens. The captive audience sits in silence. And in silence, awe and anger, perplexity and joy, all sound the same. At last there's applause. The prisoners in their clogs and bottle-green Czech uniforms fall back into the world and make an awkward bow. *And then*, Le Boulaire will recall decades later, *lots of unresolved discussions, about this thing that no one had understood.*

. . .

TWENTY DAYS AFTER the premiere, fifteen hundred Polish Jews in Stalag VIII-A are rounded up and sent to Lublin
for destruction. Akoka is saved by his French uniform. Two
weeks later, Messiaen, Pasquier, and Akoka try to board a con-
voy, with papers forged by the same Captain Brüll who made
the quartet possible. A German officer stops Akoka: *Jude*. The
clarinetist pulls down his pants, hoping his botched circumci-
sion will look like gentile integrity. The officer arrests him and
brings him back to camp.

In March, the Algerian-born Akoka passes for an Arab in a
group being shipped out of the camps. He ends up in Dinan,
Brittany. He's put on another freight heading back east. He
jumps from the moving train in the night, still cradling his
clarinet. Somehow, he makes his way across the Demarcation
Line to Marseilles, in Vichy. There, a note reaches him in his
father's hand, tossed from the window of another moving train:
I'm leaving for an unknown destination.

Le Boulaire flees the camp late in 1941, with papers covered
in official-looking stamps made with a carved potato. Soon
after his escape, the violinist breaks down. He abandons his
musical career and changes his name to Jean Lanier. He starts
a whole new life, free from a past he doesn't care to remember.
He commences a distinguished acting career, including a role
in the wartime classic *Les Enfants du Paradis*. The men with
whom he played on that night of January 15, 1941, will become
total strangers. A stroke in his eighties leaves him hallucinating,
believing that the war is still going on, that he's being chased by
the Germans, that he's hiding in a deep cellar, afraid to move.
Jean Lanier, born Le Boulaire, dies a prisoner of war.

Pasquier returns to occupied Paris, where he premieres the

Quartet for the End of Time. He plays it countless times afterward, throughout a long and distinguished career. Until his death, he carries in his wallet a faded card:

Stalag VIII A Görlitz
PREMIÈRE AUDITION DU
QUATOUR POUR LA FIN DU TEMPS
D'OLIVIER MESSIAEN
15 Janvier 41

The back of the program is inscribed by Messiaen, urging the cellist to remember the rhythms, the modes, the rainbows, the bridges to the beyond.

Messiaen passes through the conflict hearing sounds beyond all earthly politics. He lives out his life writing music of spectral harmonies and birdlike rhythms. But no piece will reach more listeners than the *Quartet*. He sees Pasquier and Akoka now and then. Captain Brüll tries to visit him in Paris, decades later, but the concierge turns him back, saying Messiaen does not want to see him. Brüll goes away devastated. Later still, Messiaen tries to contact the German who gave him paper and pencils, the man who, at great risk to himself, faked the composer's exit papers. But by then Brüll is beyond the reach of time.

If I composed this quartet for anything, Messiaen will write, *it was to escape from the snow, the war, captivity, to escape from myself. What I gained most of all from it was that, among three hundred thousand prisoners, I was perhaps the only one who wasn't a prisoner.*

And of that night in January 1941: *Never was I listened to with such attention.*

The best music says: you're immortal. But immortal means
today, maybe tomorrow. A year from now, with crazy luck.

Eight days after that winter Stalag concert, Peter Els is born.
Over the course of seventy years, he hears the piece a hundred times. He ages with it, and the notes change each time
he listens. The piece, forever a week and a day older than he
is, grows from an elusive puzzle to a venerated classic. In an
undergraduate lecture, his professor calls it one of the three
seminal works of the war. In graduate school, his circle of
friends take it for granted, a thing that has always existed and
needs to be escaped from, like the pitches of the major scale—
music lost forever in lore and reverence, too classic to trouble
anyone.

Cage: "Nothing is accomplished by writing, playing, or
listening to music." Hear that or miss everything—even
what's within earshot.

That was the story Els told his eleventh-hour pupils, from
memory, with his notes sealed up in a Ziploc bag on their
way to a government crime lab in Philly. He heard himself
talk, weirdly calm despite the morning, like one of those cool
criminals who duck into matinees five minutes after the mur-
der, drawn in by the promise of air-conditioning and popcorn.
The lede of his arrest would write itself: terrorist caught while
giving lifelong learning class on dead music to dying people.

He warned the group that the work would last fifty minutes.

Klaudia Kohlmann blew a raspberry. *At this age? It takes me fifty minutes to tie my shoes.*

I have one word for you, Will Bock told her. *Velcro.*

Els didn't mention that federal agents might come and arrest him midway through the piece. He pressed the play button on the phone's screen and settled in to his last chance to listen at liberty.

The crystal liturgy spread through the group like flu moving through a day-care center. Chris Shields, a pizza parlor owner who liked to play "Fascinatin' Rhythm" and "Somebody Loves Me" on the Shade's upright piano, shooting the last notes with the gun barrel of his index finger, grappled the conference table and Fletcherized the tangle of notes in his clenched jaw.

Prisms of sun slid across the almond ceiling. The swish of nylon and muffled complaints passed down the hall. A gray head poked through the common room's double doors, listened for a moment, then withdrew in giggles.

Fred Baroni, financial planner forced into unwilling retirement, using the course to try to hold dementia at bay for another week, shot Els a scared look at the sound of the pulsing lines: Go on without me. Leave me here, by the side of the road, in the falling snow.

By the Intermède, Paulette Hewerdine was cradling her face in her hands. The year before, her eldest son had been killed when an oncoming truck shot across the highway median. A month later her husband sat up in bed, complained of a headache, and died. She listened now, face covered, as if the sinuous music announced the long-expected trifecta.

Sounds filled the room, none of them real: Rain spattering a tenement roof. A girl on a wobbly swing set. The rustle of cotton dresses in a dance hall in wartime. The wind over a Nebraska wheat field. A stone dropped down a well with a long-forgotten wish tied to it. Crickets in a November cupboard.

Lisa Keane, who took notes throughout Els's impromptu lecture, kept taking them during the music. The week they did Ravel, the apostate nun turned junior high science teacher confessed to the group that music was her North Korea—an unfathomable country that refused her a visa. She heard no more in the average masterpiece than a person might see in a pile of soggy cardboard. She didn't want to face oblivion deaf to something that made life bearable for so many people.

Hearing the ex-nun's confession, Els had wanted to tell her: Don't start here, at the story's end. Start back where the harmonies are fresh and clear all the way to the horizon. But Keane was stuck with Els and the music of her own failed century. And so she sat pushing her pen across the page like a pilgrim slogging to Compostela.

A burst of color stopped her hand. She lifted her head. Yes, Els willed her. This is it: nothing else to hear but these blocks of purple rage, this icy drunkenness. But a moment more, and Keane's pen began again.

William Bock gazed out the plate-glass window, where a gray squirrel corkscrewed up the trunk of a white pine. The battle for the soul of twentieth century music struck the former ceramic engineer as an amusing shaggy dog story. He cocked his head at the Messiaen as if it came from an outpost colony on a remote but hospitable planet in a backwater star system on the edge of a galaxy straight out of the pages of *Astounding Stories,* the pulp bible of his childhood.

Klaudia Kohlmann huddled against the music, a hand like an ice tong on her temple. She kept a violin in a battered case under the dresser in her Shade apartment, although rheumatoid arthritis made playing it impossible. She'd held that instrument on her lap in the backseat of her father's Opel Kapitän P1 as her family sped west through the junction of the Heinrich-Heine-Strasse and the Sebastianstrasse in Berlin, three days before the Wall went up.

Retirement had shrunk her, and she looked now like an apprentice pixie. Once she'd been Els's therapist—until a mad mistake made that impossible. Their fling was brief and their joint repentance long. Neither could remember whose fault the autumnal wrong turn had been. Later, they sometimes ran into each other at concerts on campus, two cultural recidivists. He stood with her once in the concert hall lobby as she smoked three cigarettes during a ten-minute intermission, trying to fill her veins with enough nicotine to tide her through the all-Rachmaninoff second half. *Doesn't it bother you?* she'd asked. *Eight-tenths of every piece performed in a major venue, written by one of twenty-five composers?*

I'd be fine with it, if it were the right twenty-five.

She sucked in burning air and shook her head at his stupidity. But she, too, was a late-life backslider. The music she loved should have died at that Berlin Philharmonic concert in 1945: Beethoven, Bruckner, and Brünnhilde's immolation, while bombs rained down and Hitler Youth passed out cyanide. On that afternoon, five-year-old Klaudia was two neighborhoods away, under the family piano, her customary bomb shelter, listening to her father play Hummel's opus 18 Fantasy. Now she listened to the *Quartet*, fingers pressed to the side of her skull, with the look of someone who'd just discovered that she still had work to do but not enough remaining time to do it.

In fifty minutes, the sun shed enough energy to power

civilization for a year. Six thousand people died; thirteen thousand were born. One hundred days of video were uploaded to the Web, along with ten million photos. Twelve billion emails went out, eight-tenths of them spam. A dozen of them involved terror plans, real or fantastic. The angel came and passed over again—eternity in an hour.

During the last *louange*—that slow violin climb beyond the top stair—the group of old people sat lost in their own listening, braced against the rising pitch. They were an outlawed sect, a church-basement AA meeting, a study group prepping for the pop quiz of death.

The music climbed up into nothingness, and ended. Els shut off the phone and looked up. His house was surrounded by yellow bunting reading do not cross. He'd sleepwalked across town to teach a class, when he should have driven straight to the main police station half a mile from his home and turned himself in.

Well, he began. But someone shushed him.

Lisa Keane held up one palm. *Could we please just . . . ?* Paulette Hewerdine pressed three fingers over her mouth, ambushed by the thought of an old and careless cruelty. Shields swung his head like a searchlight. Each held on, a little longer, to the silence of their choosing.

The engineer Bock was first to speak. *Holy crap. That was fifty minutes? I now know how to double my remaining life.*

No one seemed to need anything more from Els. For the better part of an hour, they'd done nothing but listen. There was nothing to do now but come up slowly enough to avoid the bends.

The eight of them stood, shaking off one of those spells of syncope that old people grow skilled at covering up. They grinned at each other: What the hell was all that? Then the flood of talk, the partisan atmosphere of a première.

Shields and Keane stood near the coffeepot arguing like undergraduates. Bock and Baroni were already halfway down the hall to the cafeteria, their arms windmilling, when Klaudia Kohlmann grazed Els's shoulder. *You going to give us homework?*

Her words woke Els. He called out to the stragglers, *Listen—I may have to cancel next week.* He pointed at his left wrist, which had not seen a watch for fifteen years. *If you don't hear from me by Wednesday, assume I'm tied up.*

Or (more Cage) "the mind may give up its desire to improve on creation and function as a faithful receiver of experience."

A Friday night in winter, late in '67, and Peter rides shotgun in the borrowed secondhand microbus, a little frantic because the Happening started at eight—fifteen minutes ago—and neither he nor the luminous Madolyn Corr has the faintest idea where the Stock Pavilion is. They're looking for a beaux arts, barrel-vaulted, red-brick, pre-slaughterhouse animal show rink on the south campus, down toward the round barns. No such place seems to exist.

Maybe Cage made it all up, Maddy says. *He'd do that, wouldn't he? Some kind of Zen koan?*

Els peeks out from behind his fingers. *I'm pretty sure that was a stop sign,* he whimpers.

We're good! Maddy turns to him sidesaddle as the microbus swerves, and she gives his biceps a reassuring squeeze. *We're good!*

Only weeks ago, this assured, game, knowing girl from the
North Country landed in the middle of Els's life, and the film
went from black-and-white to Day-Glo in a single jump cut.
Last night, in her bed, that fresh new continent, she perched
over him, mock-worried, taking his face in her hands like
a surgeon takes a wound under the loupes. She squinted at
him, cooing, *Mr. Composer. What is it? What's wrong?* Behind
the muscles of his own face, he could feel the evidence she
laughed at—the perilous open prospects, the wonder bordering
on pain, and how could he explain it? This bright confusion,
the discovery that he might have a real companion in this
life, after all.

I'm happy, he told her.

You sound surprised.

You have a good ear.

She took his hand in the dark. *What is it that you do with your
fingers all the time?*

What?

She showed him, tapping out rhythms with her second finger
on the pad of her thumb.

Oh, that! Nervous habit.

You look like the Buddha making a mudra.

He hadn't done it for years, not since Clara. He didn't even
realize he'd started up again until that moment. The taps—
miniature pieces, rushing out to populate the future.

I'm singing.

Mr. Composer, she said, crawling on top of him. *You got something to sing about?*

He does. And the somethings are all her. She can blow away a
year's worth of his fear with a single amused pout. She pulls him
out of himself, into the broader neighborhood, the worldwide

scavenger hunt. Her groove is wide and sure enough to hold them both.

A BITTER NOVEMBER night, the pitch-black edge of campus, and Maddy guides the microbus filled with amplifiers and cables belonging to the band she sings for—a psychedelic quintet called Vertical Smile—across the frozen sheets of street as if she's piloting a one-seat Skeeter ice boat across the frozen lakes of her Minnesota childhood. All the while she hums, under her breath, the B-side of the Byrds' "Eight Miles High": "Why."

Oblivious, she chants the tune, as if her id were mumbling a sexed-up rosary. Her humming is what has set this hook so deep in him. Six weeks earlier, Els tacked up a three-by-five card on the notice board at Smith Hall. *Looking for clear-voiced high soprano to read through four hard new songs. Must not be afraid of strange.* Madolyn Corr was his lone responder. She showed up at the practice room at the arranged time, overly confident of her attractions: five-foot-four, with a pageboy, in a green velour miniskirt. They read through his piece together from the pencil-scrawled score. Peter struggled through the accompaniment and Maddy Corr stopped every few measures to say, *I'm not sure the human voice can do that.* Soon the score bore so many corrections that reading it was like doing paleontology.

Her sound was witty, almost comical. She had a nice, warm soubrette, but a hint too light and Papagena for his Borges songs. What he wanted was spinto, or even a coloratura. But Els was grateful for any voice at all that could hit the notes. They woodshedded together for two hours, he for his piece and she on the promise of nothing but pizza and beer. When they got to the end of the fourth song, she stood next to the piano bench, happy-frowning, the look that, years later, he'd call her frog face.

Well?

Well, what?

Well, what do you think?

She considered the question for too long.

Pretty eerie.

And that was all she gave him—a kiss-off reply that should have furled his sails for good. He would have sent her away with professional thanks and never seen her again, if not for that promise of pizza and beer. Half an hour later, waiting for their deep-dish mushroom and running out of gossip about the local musical pecking order, she started humming to herself, happy but unaware, her eyes periscoping the crowded room, checking out the men. She looped through a little four-bar phrase, again and again, and the phrase she looped through, without thinking, was from Peter's third Borges song, the sudden lyrical announcement:

He did not work for posterity,
nor did he work for God,
whose literary preferences were
largely unknown to him.

And Peter, who'd written the songs for forever and for no one, but also to strike remorse in the heart of the woman who'd cut him loose from across the Atlantic four years earlier, now wanted only to put his ear up to the clavicle of this other, warmer woman and hear what there was inside her so worth humming about.

Doing anything later? he asked.

Depends, she answered, her mouth full of melted provolone. *How much later?*

For two weeks they walked everywhere, under the color-shot trees and out into the harvested fields. The last few deciduous flares of October played against clear eggshell skies, and Els's adopted town had never looked so beautiful. Maddy Corr told him about her favorite harebrained scheme.

Know what would be a total trip? Take a dozen friends up to my family's fifty acres in Crow Wing County and farm it. It's sandy as hell, but you could grow cranberries. There's a cottage, a barn. The chicken coop could be winterized. Farm by day, make music under the oaks at night!

Els shook his head at the miracle of her. *You have a dozen friends?*

She laughed, thinking he was joking. *How about you? Forbidden fantasies, Mr. Composer?*

But Els had none, unless it was to have already written Ligeti's twenty-part, micropolyphonic *Requiem* before Ligeti did.

Maddy's eyes crossed a little when he went on too long about harmonic structure. She had no need to talk about music, only to make it. But in her presence, Els couldn't help himself. He told her about every sketch lying dormant in his workbooks. She laughed and dared him toward her, fingers fluttering underhand. *Bring it on, champ. Let's see what you got.*

She showed him her latest art: a quilt bigger than both of them, pinwheels of azure and ochre. She wrinkled up her nose. *Learned how to do this from my maiden aunt when I was twelve. Kind of an old lady hobby, isn't it?*

Something magical to it: rags into riches, scraps into art. Els ran his fingers over the intricate design, its moons and suns and stars. *Does it mean something?*

Maddy snorted and wrapped the thing around him. *It means you don't have to be cold at night, if you don't want to.* That night they slept under it together, and it turned out she was right. Soon after, she began to steal his shirts and work them into her next, more dazzling design.

Nights with Maddy were a slow build. In a few small steps, she taught Peter the cadence of her desire. They moved on her kapok mattress like a single, eight-limbed thing. All the fragments of Els's desire came together like that effortless fugato Mozart's *Jupiter* had predicted, back in childhood. And for the first time in years, Clara's decision to leave Els for dead felt luckier than anyone could have guessed.

Without meaning to, he told Maddy Corr about a pan pipe dream all his own. They were lying in bed, site of all their best discussions. *I want to write music that will change its listeners.*

Change how?

Move them beyond their private tastes. Bring them to something outside themselves. He lifted one arm into the air, the wistful reach of a thwarted lover. *Does that sound crazy?*

She reached up, too, and drew his skyhook hand back down to her chest. *Crazy's up to you.*

I'm not sure what that means.

Those hundred thousand peace protesters, trying to levitate the Pentagon?

Okay, Els said. *I get it. Crazy.*

No! She crushed his fingers in hers until he winced. *They could have done it, if they'd really wanted to. Science is built on stranger things.*

He rolled over and draped his arms over the fall of her hip. *Keep talking, he told her. I'm listening.*

Cage again: "What is the purpose of writing music? . . . A purposeful purposelessness or a purposeless play."

Four weeks on, Els and this humming woman slalom in the dark, late for the evening's spectacle, searching for a building they can't find. They have directions, but the hopeless kind of directions midwesterners give: north, south, east, west. *Left* and *right* would be too easy. It's as if the brain of every farmer out here in the endless Cartesian plan of prairie is magnetized. Maddy is a bubble of tantric bliss behind the wheel, forever a sightseer in her own life. She pilots the microbus like a dog-sled, and Els won't live to see twenty-seven.

Her ear always hears him, in every key. She turns to look, takes his elbow, and smiles. The microbus skids sideways down the street, sending an oncoming car to the curb.

You're worried about being late? For somebody who consults the I Ching to answer journalists' questions?

I don't want to miss anything.

A week ago, at a gathering in the student union, Els heard Cage tell a distraught composer, *If you want to order creation around, that's your problem, not mine.* Well: guilty as charged. Creation is much in need of ordering. That's what Els thought composing meant. But Cage's creation has other plans, and Els just wants to understand them.

Three months ago, at the performance of Cage's *Concerto for Prepared Piano*, Els watched the pianist crawl under the instrument and wallop it with a mallet. Someone in the audience began to scream. The widow of a venerable School of Music professor stormed up onstage and started hurling chairs at the soloist. The police arrived and hauled the widow away as she shouted, *Ladies and gentlemen, this is no laughing matter!* But everyone around Els in the hall just chuckled and applauded, sure that the antics were all part of the piece in question.

There! Els yelps, and points off into the dark, where clumps of people converge on a dappled brick cow palace wrapped in pools of light. The Stock Pavilion. That afternoon, the building was full of sheep being led through a ring in front of a judges' reviewing stand. Tonight, it's the venue for *Musicircus*, a multi-media extravaganza staged by the master of chance, who has, for the last half a year, been leading this land-grant university to hell twelve ways to Sunday.

Maddy coaxes the microbus into a parking spot. The pavilion throbs when they step out, even from half a block away. They make their way to the crowded doorway, where bursts of thunder and light escape the building every time the doors open. A dazed clump of people already bail out of the building, shaking their heads, palming their ears, and discharging some top-shelf profanity.

Inside, it's something out of Dante. The cavernous oval swarms with people gone feral under the waterfalls of light. Bands, dancers, and actors perform on platforms throughout the space. Down on the show floor, milling past the livestock judging stands, spectators jostle, jockey, flinch, and wince, grinning, wigging, gaping, shrieking, and freaking at the happy havoc. They drift in a giant clockwise whirlpool, like Mecca hajjis circling the Kaaba, around a tower of rubber tubes and lead pipes in the center of the show floor, on which they take turns banging.

Maddy clutches Peter's arm. He pulls her close, and together they plunge into the bacchanal. Above them, in the steel trusses, floats a corona of balloons ranging from tiny exclamation points to weather gondolas. An old man presses past them, closer than he needs to, smiling at Maddy and Els as if possessing a great secret. A roar goes up nearby. By the time Els steers them to the cause, the roar has floated farther downstream. A thrilled kelpie races around, trying to herd the wayward humans into something like a flock.

Up on a pipe-fit scaffold, a woman singer in a red velvet gown tries to negotiate a forlorn duet with a dancer on a platform several feet away. Any signals they send each other are swallowed up in the caldera of noise. Nearby, a string quartet saws away at atomized messages for no one. Muffled shouts erupt from a further platform. Els turns to see a scarecrow slashing a silver flute through the air like he's threatening to kill someone.

Maddy points: high on the wall at the far end of the pavilion, like a tender Big Brother or clowning Chairman Mao, a man's giant face sweeps from a scowl to a manic laugh and back again. The film loops, and Els stares at the seamless transformation, three, four, five times in a row. Nothing changes, except for the Imp Saint's litany, playing through Els's head: *If something is boring after two minutes, try it for four. If still boring, then eight. Then sixteen. Then thirty-two. Eventually one discovers that it is not boring at all.* But Els never makes it to eight, let alone sixteen. Maddy, frisky now, draws him deeper into the maelstrom.

They explore, like a vicar and his wife who've stumbled upon the parish's routine underground orgy. They run across three colleagues from the School of Music, an acquaintance from Cine Club, and two neighbors from Maddy's rooming house, blitzed out of their minds and giggling. An alto who sings with Maddy in concert choir snags them from behind. They lean in close to hear her. She points to the dancers on platforms above the turning crowd. *That's Claude Kipnis! That's Carolyn Brown!*

Who're they? Els yells back.

The alto shrugs. *Famous people!*

Children scream in meteoric arcs across the crowded floor, batting at fallen balloons. In the stands behind the oval livestock gauntlet, a few shell-shocked loners take cover, plugging their ears. Part of Els wants to flee, too. But most of him needs to be here, in the belly of this beast.

Each inhalation of craziness fills Els's veins with something dark and viscous. If this is music, then he's lost. If this is composition, then everything he has tried to write is wrong. *Musicircus*: Cage's latest way of saying how noise is music by its maiden name. But in this insane din, Els can't for the life of him remember why that idea held such promise once. This night wants to strip him of every belief, to pull him down into mere sensation, the place of no desire, of pure listening.

But listen to what? To the eve of destruction. To the air raid siren of things to come. To the explosion of Els's own quaint and laughable ambitions. To a deafening freedom.

Then, drifting on the human current, bumming a match to light his cigarette and gossiping with a spectator, there's Cage, twenty feet away. Els has been close to him before, but never like this. He tugs Maddy toward the perpetrator, ready for art. But coming in starboard, hard and low, a gray eminence cuts across their bow. A formidable woman who has attended every Germanic chamber concert Els has ever slunk into confronts tonight's ringleader. She shouts at the startled composer with such stentorian force that she might be yet another circus act, called for by the coin-tossing score.

Mr. Cage. Are you a fraud?

Cage presses his brow, examines his cigarette, and looks off to the strobing lights that bounce off the drifting balloons. His face clears, relieved. *No.*

He casts his cigarette to the pavilion floor and stubs it out with one toe. Something religious to the gesture. Smiling, he slips through the crowd and back up on a performance platform, where he joins a quintet pouring water into different-sized bowls and tapping them, taking their time cues from an elaborate piano roll. Els stands in front of the platform, watching the Kabuki mimes tap at their liquid-filled bowls. For a moment, in some America deep in his neocortex, he can hear every ringing pitch the mute bowls make.

A face brushes his earlobe. Raw charge ripples down his neck and into his shoulders. Maddy, purring, *Had enough?*

He swings around to her. *Serious? It's just getting going.*

She waves at the surrounding chaos, her lips a boggy smile. She shouts something, but the words die halfway across the defile. He leans in, and she shouts again. *I pretty much get the picture, Peter. Don't you?*

The shout, too, is a kind of music. She stands with her head tilted, grinning at the gimmick all around them. The drumlins of her breasts beneath her Elizabethan blouse and the gap at the top of her hip-clinging jeans ought to be all the happening he needs. But there's something here he can't leave yet. His hands improvise in fake sign language: he needs to listen a little longer. She shrugs, asks him with a trill of her fingers if he'll be okay walking home, pulls him to her by the lapels of his ratty bomber jacket, and kisses him. The old man of seventy standing next to them nods in recall.

You do not need to leave your room. Don't even listen.
Simply wait. The world will offer itself to be unmasked. It
has no choice.

Time turns to nothing. His ears dilate. The longer Els stands
still, the more the music pulls apart. His hearing sharpens, able
now to pick out strands buried in the babble. Dixieland trombones. A descending lamento bass played on a fretless Fender.
A psychedelic reworking of "Hand Me Down My Walkin'
Cane," against the ceaseless banging on the lead pipe sculpture. Puccini mocks the furious electronic permutations of
a piece by Matthew Mattison, whose old *épater la bourgeoisie*
sounds housebroken in this surge of crazed elation. It's Ives and
his overlapping marching bands all over again.

Hours pass. Midnight, but the crowd shows no signs of
thinning. Something catches his eye, high up in the flanking
stands: a man seated by himself, conducting. He cues the crowd
with precise waves of his arms, the way young Peter once con-
ducted his father's vinyl Toscaninis. Els knows the man, though
they've never met. Richard Bonner, doctoral candidate in theater
arts, three years Els's senior. Famous for directing last season's
deranged *Midsummer Night's Dream,* set in an old folks' home,
and for coming to a peace rally on the Quad dressed as a sepoy
from the Bengal Native Infantry, circa 1850.

The invisible baton dips. The conductor's fingers curl,
demanding a crescendo. And on cue, the crowd delivers. Els
watches this show above the show, until the lone impresario
holding this spectacle together feels himself being spied on and
turns to face his observer. Bonner's hands point like two cap

pistols at Els and click, like some Rat Pack singer playing the Vegas Sands. Then he waves at Els to come join him up in the stands for the aerial play-by-play.

As Els draws near, Richard Bonner leaps to his feet and grabs his hand. *Peter Els. As I live and breathe! What do you think? Should we all rush out and kill ourselves?*

Els confines himself to what he hopes is a fuzzy grin. The impresario pats the riser beside him and sits back down. Els takes the designated place. They sit and watch, up in the grandstands above the end of the world. Bonner's hands can't help scooping and directing. Now and then he issues a burst of color commentary.

Above the noise of the Happening, Els can make out only a quarter of what the man says. *Under the paving stones, the beach! Meet the fucking Jetsons, man! You know who supplied those weather balloons? Chanute Air Force Base. You know what else Chanute is supplying to the jungles on the other side of the world? No, of course you don't. You're a masterpiece guy, aren't you? Gimme that old-time religion. People getting fragged in your living room, and you're still trying to sweet-talk beauty into a quickie.*

All the while, Richard Bonner grazes on sweets he has squirreled away in half a dozen pockets. Smashed-up oatmeal cookies wrapped in wax paper. Good & Plenty out of the purple-pink box. These he shakes like Choo Choo Charlie and offers to Els, who's surprised to find himself ravenous. They sit chomping candy and watching the revels, like they've known each other since the Pleistocene.

Bonner sighs big, the contentment of someone who has come home at last. *Say hello to the permanent future. You gotta love this shit.*

Do I? Els asks.

Come on, bubala. It's art.

Art is not a mobocracy. It's a republic.

Do let art know that, huh? For its own good.

The party's dying and Els hears himself turning earnest. Still, he wades in. It's like he and this guy have been having this fight all their lives.

People can't stand too much anarchy. They need pattern. Repetition. Meaningful design.

People? People will do whatever the times tell them to. I mean, look at you, man!

Els does: long-sleeve paisley shirt, green bomber jacket, and brown corduroy bell-bottoms. Nothing unusual. Bonner is all black denim and leather, what Els would call a greaser.

You can't make people like psychosis, Els insists.

Oh, please! Bonner points. *I saw you down there digging it. It's after midnight and you're still here.*

You can't even call it a piece. It's a dead end. A one-off novelty.

Bonner's great right eyebrow shoots up, a cartoon arch. *Man. Novelty's our only hope. Surplus leisure time is the single greatest challenge to the industrial state. Right behind property-sharing Asians in black silk pajamas, of course.*

This thing will be finished after tonight. Over and done.

Chunks of Good & Plenty fly from Bonner's mouth. *You jest! They're gonna revive this every year, like* Oklahoma *or* Carousel. *They'll be mounting nostalgic revivals of it in posh London museums in half a century.*

Calm falls over Els. He and this strange man, deep in a new country, the future beyond figuring. What is music, that he needs to bring it to heel? The Stock Pavilion, this backwater town, the whole experimental nation, have all gone stark, raving mod. But this lavish anarchy won't hurt him. He can survive, even steal from it, and fashion a new song he can't yet make out.

Battered by cacophony, he grows huge. The thousand noisy tourists turn into a single organism, and then a single cell, passing millions of chemical signals a minute between its organelles. Plans blind us to the possible. Life will never end. The smallest sound, even silence, has more in it than the brain can ever grasp. Work for forever; work for no one.

Bonner's words yank Els from his trance. *The best part of a piece like this? It doesn't matter what anybody thinks. The whole planet could call this thing a con job. And the man would still be free.*

They get thrown out of the Stock Pavilion with the rest of the stragglers around two a.m., when the organizers of *Musicircus* start striking the set so that the place will be empty again by eight. That's when the cows will be led back onto the showroom floor and the next generation of agricultural scientists—the future's real masters—can go on learning how to keep a ravenous nation in beef patties.

Bonner and Els, cast out into the midwestern midwinter, their ears ringing like mallet-struck glass bowls, make their way back across campus in the swirls of bitter wind. Deep in words, they weave and reel like drunks. They pause on a lamp-lit street corner, Bonner making elaborate points, jabbing Els in the chest for emphasis. Els tells Bonner about his new compositional hopes, with a detail he hasn't yet tried on Maddy. He wants to use regions of cycling pitch groups to create forward motion without resorting to the clichés of standard harmonic expectation, but without falling into serialism's dead formality.

Listen to you, Maestro. You're a damn centrist, is what you are.

Admit it. And fasten your seat belt, baby. Both sides are going to beat your ass black and blue.

Els tells Richard Bonner about Maddy, his bold Sinbad soprano in the tiny idealist's body. He mentions the Borges songs, which he and Maddy are preparing for a recital in the new year. Bonner perks up.

I'll choreograph. The words issue from Bonner's mouth in arctic cumulus puffs.

It's a song cycle, Els says. *She just . . . sings.*

You need a choreographer. Send me the score on Monday.

Els feels hung over, having drunk nothing but mayhem all night. He takes leave of Bonner outside Maddy's rooming house. They shake hands, a grip that Bonner turns into one of those thumb-clasping peace handshakes. *Say yes to how things are.*

You're a damn alien, aren't you? Els tells the director. *Outer space. Admit it.*

Bonner does. With gusto. And hugs his newfound associate good night.

Els climbs the staircase of Maddy's college commune, skirting a cairn of cat turd left in the center of the first-floor landing. She's asleep under her most beautiful quilt, an array of suns and planets. He wakes her up, high on the now-audible future.

You, the sleepy soubrette says. She presses her hair into the dip of his sternum. *What time is it?*

Time for every freedom the miracle year offers. Maddy is logy at first, but game, won over by his need, so fresh and fierce, here, a few hours before dawn. She falls asleep again the minute they're over the finish line. He lies, arms around her, frantic with hope and eager for a future that fills with astonishing new things.

Saturday morning is on him, from one measure to the next.

When light pours in through Maddy's hand-made curtains, he rises and dresses and heads across the Quad to campus town, where he forages for breakfast. Coffee, donuts, two oranges, and a *Daily Illini*. The proof of what already feels like a brief mass hallucination splashes across page one: "Musicircus Rocks Stock Pavilion." Below it, a smaller headline proclaims, "Johnson Demands Honorable Peace."

He brings his breakfast treasures home to a woman just now stirring. She opens her eyes on him as he hovers over her student bed, breaks into a grin, and throws her arms around his neck. An old folk song crosses his mind, one that will take him thirty more years to turn into variations: What wondrous love is this, oh my soul?

Partch: "I went south toward any god who softly whistled . . . the one spot where I would 'choose to abide' was already far behind."

He sat beside Klaudia on the bench in Shade Arbors' front oval. Soon-to-be-dead people gardened in nearby plots, and clouds of pollinators grazed the air like it would be everywhere forever spring. Els's erstwhile therapist and late-life fling faced him and grimaced. *Have you been handling farm animals?*

I'm sorry. My workout clothes.

Sweating like a pig. Something's the matter.

He rubbed his face. *Seems I'm in a little trouble.*

She looked at him slant. What trouble could such a man get in? Reckless archaism. Arpeggiating under the influence. Presto in an andante zone.

He told her of his morning. The facts came out of his mouth, as implausible as any sounds he'd ever made.

She shook her head. *They raided your house?*

A squad in hazmat suits, yellow police tape circling his lawn: all a bizarre invention. The agents had been after someone else. Someone dangerous.

The police raided your house, and you came to teach your class.

You were all waiting. Nowhere else to go.

I don't understand. Laboratory equipment? Some kind of fancy chemistry set?

He wanted to tell her: there were, in a single cell, astonishing synchronized sequences, plays of notes that made the Mass in B Minor sound like a jump-rope jingle.

What on earth were you doing?

He'd been trying to take a strand of DNA, five thousand base pairs long, ordered to spec from an online site, and splice it into a bacterial plasmid.

Learning about life, he said.

Klaudia stared, as if the sweet nonagenarian needle-pointer across the hall from her had pulled out from under the bed a box of merit badges from the Schwesternschaften der Hitler-Jugend.

Why do this, Peter? She'd asked the question often, back when she was still pretending to be his therapist.

Why write music that no one wants to hear? *It kept me out of trouble.*

Don't be coy. What were you doing?

As far as Els knew, the nonsense string would live alongside the bacterium's historical repertoire, silently doing nothing. Like the best conceptual art, it would sit ignored by the millions of trades going on in the marketplace all around it. With luck, during cell division, the imposter message would replicate for a few generations, before life got wise and shed the free rider. Or maybe it would be picked up, inspired randomness, and ride forever.

Nothing, Els said. Call it composing. *Proof of concept.*

What concept?

It didn't seem to matter now.

Are you a terrorist?

His head jerked back. Klaudia appraised him. *Well? Are you?*

He looked away. *Oh, probably.*

Who taught you how to modify cells?

I just follow the recipes.

How did you learn enough to—

I audited a class. I read four textbooks. Watched fifty hours of instructional clips. It's all pretty straightforward. No one seems to realize how easy.

From a lifetime away, he heard himself tell a government agent: *Easier than learning Arabic.*

How long have you been . . . ?

He dipped his head. *I started two years ago. I wasn't . . . doing anything else. I came across an article about the DIY biology movement. I couldn't believe that amateurs were altering genomes in their garages.*

I can't believe people breed poisonous snakes in their basements. But I feel no compulsion to join them.

He couldn't tell her: He'd missed his calling. Science should have been the career, music just a hobby. He'd lived through the birth of biotech, that whole new art. He might have lived a useful life, contributed to the age's real creative venture. Genomics was right now learning how to read scores of indescribable beauty. Els just wanted to hear, before the light in his tent went out.

Kohlmann gazed at him as she had years ago, when he was paying her to dismiss his nameless anxieties. *Are you crazy?*

The thought has crossed my mind.

You didn't think the authorities would be a little jumpy, so near to Jihad Jane's base camp?

I wasn't thinking jihad, at the time.

Kohlmann groaned and palmed her eye sockets. *Peter— couldn't you have taken up bridge, like the rest of us? Continuing ed courses?*

A tremor in her dowel forearm, and Els realized: she had Parkinson's. He'd seen her weekly for eighteen months and had never noticed. They'd spoken about nothing all that while aside from *The Rite* and *Pierrot.*

I'm going to have a cigarette now, Kohlmann said. *I'm fifteen minutes overdue.*

You're smoking? Since when did you start smoking?

Don't nag. I quit for twenty years, by promising myself I could start again at seventy-five.

Kohlmann lit a cigarette and took an enormous drag. They sat silent, combed by a breeze. In the sky above, a contrail spread into frayed yarn. She let out the smoke, sighing.

They raided your house and missed you. Are they total fuckups?

Any other day of the week, they'd have had me. But on Mondays I'm always out before dawn.

Didn't they think . . . ? She read some faint inscription off her fingernails. *You're going to make things a lot worse by running.*

The word shocked him. He wasn't running. He was sitting in a gated retirement community, waiting until it was safe to go home and take a shower.

The task force people said they weren't charging me with anything.

You think there's no warrant for you now?

No one has served one yet.

He had two choices: turn himself in wherever suspected bioterrorists were supposed to turn themselves in and disappear into the wasteland of legal detention, or make himself scarce for a few days while the FBI discovered that he was doing nothing that thousands of other garage genetic engineers around the country weren't doing. By Friday, the fire drill would be over.

He told Klaudia as much.

You might as well sign a confession. They'll ruin what's left of your life, just to make a lesson of you.

I haven't broken any laws. They're not going to waste their time on sunset hobbyists. They have real terrorist networks to go after.

Klaudia turned her cigarette around and peered into the burning end. Her face wrinkled and she shook her head.

What? he demanded.

Her hand traced the air, pointing at threats on the horizon. *Excuse me, but a lot has happened in this country while you've been away.*

He looked off toward the garden plots, where a doddering field gang prepared the beds for tomatoes and squash. It seemed a substantial leap of faith, to believe you'd still be there for the harvest.

Kohlmann waved the glowing cigarette at him like a laser pointer. He remembered why they weren't a couple.

Everyone's an enemy now. The Swiss detained Boulez for something he said in the sixties about blowing up opera houses. John Adams told the BBC that his name is on a list. The authorities harass him every time he flies.

You're joking. Why?

Because of Klinghoffer.

Els had to laugh: the name John Adams, on a sedition list.

Ironies turned on ironies, like the moons in a hand-cranked toy
solar system. Once, he'd sat on a panel at Columbia, a fatuous
firebrand of thirty-seven, claiming that composers had a moral
obligation to be subversive. The best music, he pronounced,
was always a threat. He winced now at the manifesto. But still,
his skin prickled at the news that a composer had made the
government watch list.

Adams, Els said. *Fabulous music. A handful of transcendent works.
He'll live.*

Klaudia stopped making love to her cigarette's last millime-
ter. *Live?*

Her voice was thick with sardonic notes. Music with intricate harmonies, complex rhythms? You might as well write a
medical thriller in Mayan glyphs.

She waved her hand over him, the Pope rescinding a blessing,
and launched into an account of a terrorism arrest in Albany—a
missile sale where all the missiles belonged to the FBI and all the
terrorists were bribed into purchasing them. Els didn't hear. He
was savoring the idea that art—an Adams masterpiece—could
still be dangerous. It gave him unearned cachet, being dogged by
the same Homeland Security hounding Adams. At that moment,
someone was combing through the archives for data about Peter
Els, scanning his scores to see if he'd ever written any music that
might alarm the Joint Security Forces.

Then he remembered. He *had* written such a thing: his disastrous historical drama, *The Fowler's Snare.*

I think I should make myself scarce, he said. *A couple of days. Give
them some time to sort my laundry.*

Her look iced him. Els rubbed his nose and tried again.

It's just . . . I've got this thing about handcuffs.

Kohlmann stubbed out her cigarette on her shoe sole and

slipped the butt into her back pocket. She fished in her striped Incan jerky bag and removed the smartphone.

I suppose this makes me an accomplice after the fact. She handed him the device, waving it away. *There's a map thingie in there. Knows where you are. Let me give you an address.*

He took the device and played. He stroked and pinched the screen, typing with his thumbs the way Fidelio used to sing. He pulled up the mapping app. The former music box was now a compass needle floating above the site of Shade Arbors, Naxkohoman, Pennsylvania. She dictated an address, which he keyed in. A thin green line materialized, running from the needle off the screen.

Klaudia Kohlmann smacked her forehead with the butt of her hand. *Shit. You'll need the charger.*

She rose and hobbled toward the facility. At the automatic glass door, she wheeled around. *Don't even think about moving.*

More Partch: "I heard music in the voices all about me, and tried to notate it . . ." That's all that I tried to do, as well.

Els cradled the four-inch screen. Driving instructions unfurled alongside the postage-stamp map, too small for seventy-year-old eyes to read. He looked up, toward the garden plots. The air droned like the tinnitus that had plagued him in his sixties and made him want to mercy-kill himself. One low trill split into two, a minor second. The interval turned metallic. A moment more, and the pitches collapsed back into unison.

The ringing resumed, a Lilliputian air raid. The new chord bent into more grating intervals—a flat third, widening to almost a tritone—a glacial creation like Xenakis or Lucier, one of those cracked Jeremiahs howling in the wilderness, looking for a way beyond. The sky-wide trill filled the air with sonic pollen, like the engines of a fleet of interstellar space-ships each the size of a vanilla wafer. It filled the air at every distance, too sweet for locusts or cicadas. Bats didn't shriek in broad daylight, and birds didn't sing in chorus. Something abundant and invisible was playing with harmony, and Els turned student again.

A quartct of Shade residents came through the sliding glass, William Bock among them. Seeing his teacher, the ceramic engineer stopped to listen. *Holy crap! What's that?*

The guessing began, but no theory held up. In the distance, children with pennywhistles, wind clacking the branches, the hiss of pole-mounted power transformers, a murmuration of starlings, rooftop ventilation units, a muffled marching band drilling on a school football field miles away.

That's how Lisa Keane, dressed for gardening, found them, a geriatric flash mob standing on the front walk, looking sky-ward at nothing.

Frogs, she told them. *Tree frogs. Singing to each other.*

Amphibians improvising, toying with fantastic dissonant choruses: it seemed no less outrageous to Els than his own life.

I can't tell you what species, Keane said. *Two dozen dialects, in these parts.*

Els asked, *What are they saying?*

Oh: The usual. It's cool and moist. We're alive. Come here. What else is there to sing about?

This was the woman whom music didn't move. Els closed his eyes, transcribing airborne harmonies from a time when sending a message over distance was life's best feat. Listen to this: listen to *this.*

How long have they been going?

Oh, I don't know. A hundred million years?

No. I mean . . . how long, this year?

The ex-Benedictine calculated. *Off and on every morning for the last month.*

Bock said, *Get out of town!*

In another minute, the miracle wore thin and the group wandered off to the shuttle bus. Soon only Keane, Els, and a bent man who moved like a broken-winged eagle were left clinging to the harsh serenade.

At last Kohlmann returned, dangling a power adapter. *Oh, geez. What now?*

Els pointed treeward at the strobing sound. Kohlmann scowled.

Ach—nature, again? The whole thing is out of control.

Tree frogs, Keane said.

It surprised Els: the ex-nun had a crush on the transactional analyst.

Okay, Kohlmann conceded. *Tree frogs. And we need to know this . . . why?*

Lisa Keane grazed Kohlmann's forearm and shot her a crumpled smile. Amphibia would not trouble anyone much longer. She waved goodbye and headed down the walk toward her square of cultivated earth.

Klaudia handed Els the adapter. *You figure it out. Just do what the Voice tells you, even if you think she's wrong. Her ways are mysterious, but the Voice has a higher plan for you.*

Els said, *Can you tell me where I'm going?*

My son's cabin, in the Alleghenies. He and his swarm go in for that kind of thing. Grazing in the poisonous plants. Picking diseased ticks out of each other's scalps. Got it from his father.

I can't camp in your son's house.

They love having other crazies use the place. The four of them are cutting their way through Indonesia with machetes at the moment. You should see my grandchildren. It's all the bovine growth hormone.

You don't want the federal government . . .

Kohlmann clucked her tongue and wagged her finger like a tiny wiper. *Phhh. The key is stuck in an abandoned wasp's nest in the rafter above the back door. I think there's a telephone hiding in that thing, somewhere. If you get in trouble, punch the little phone button and tap "Me."*

I can't take your phone.

I've got two more.

But your mail. Your music. Your Web.

I've been trying to get off the thing for five months. You're helping me manage my addiction. She sat up on the bench, pretending to rejuvenation. *Hey! Listen. You hear that? Little reptiles, singing!*

Els stared down at the device in his lap. *Why are you doing this for me? I mean, considering . . .*

Shut up and use it. I've got unlimited everything. None of this minutes shit.

I'll get it back to you. This weekend.

She waved him off. *Fine. And when you get to the cabin? Do me the favor and shower.*

He stood and stepped toward the parking lot, now far away. He glanced back at Kohlmann. Her right hand visored her eyes.

Thank you? she asked.

He didn't understand the question. *For what?*

She hooked a thumb back toward the entrance.

For today. I've listened to that thing a dozen times and never heard it until this morning.

My cultures can't be called back now. They're off and doubling, like the brooms of the sorceror's apprentice.

Richard Bonner took Els's four art settings of Borges texts and turned them into madcap theater. He made Maddy and the ensemble—horn, oboe, cello, piano, and percussion—start all over again. At first Els tried to manage the damage. He stood at his new friend's elbow during rehearsals, pointing out what might not be realistic. But realism was Bonner's punching dummy. *Let's try this*, he'd say every few minutes, and if Els or Maddy or any of the players objected, the giant Texan son of an abusive evangelist shot back, *A little experiment is going to kill you?*

Richard paid Maddy strange court, wooing her for a larger plan. Els didn't get it; he expected his wholesome, quilting girlfriend to shrink from the man's mania. But Maddy lapped up Bonner's every attention. He brought her jewels—rococo things that no sane person would let touch their body: a varnished gecko skull on a brass stick pin. A clasp made from a cicada corpse. Guileless Maddy wore them with gusto.

Look at you! Richard said. *You look like a vestal virgin in heat.*

But she held her own against him. Once, when he was trying to get her to walk like a robot, Maddy grabbed Richard by the chamois shirt, twisted the cloth in her fist, and asked, *You need this? I could make something interesting with it.*

Richard doled out props at every rehearsal: gas masks for the players to wear during the third song. Malay shadow puppets to wave in the air. Kalimbas, which he got Els to write into the percussionist's part. Els prayed that the Salvation Army would run out of treasures before the players ran out of patience.

Long after the performers headed off to Murphy's each night, Bonner insisted that he and Els huddle up and keep tinkering. He had other obligations—thesis, theater performances, maybe even a personal life, though Els saw no hint of one. And yet, for this one volunteer project—someone else's graduate recital—he had endless energy. Els wondered if he might be addicted to pep pills. But Richard had no need of amphetamines. He ran on sufficient built-in demons—hellfire father, suicide mother, a younger sister sealed up in cortical seizures—that no amount of labor would ever exorcise.

Bonner's plans for the *Borges Songs* called for costumes, a bank of sixteen-millimeter projectors, and dance. He alone saw how all the moving parts would come together. Richard mapped out the steps he wanted from Maddy—the spastic thrusts, flicks, and slashes. He demonstrated, and his clumsiness came so close to unfettered happiness that Els had to look away.

Maddy froze up at the choreographer's weirder requests. *I can't do that.*

You can. It gets easier.

I'll look like a fool.

You look like a force of nature. You'll see.

Els sat in the empty theater, watching his songs turn as strange as death. Maddy thrust out her arms and canted her shoulders, a holy clown. Els wanted to protect the gawky, ambushed soprano from this fate she didn't sign on for. But she needed no protection. The game was already lost, and she meant to face doom bravely.

To Bonner, Madolyn Corr's every inept plié was found art. The man couldn't stop choreographing. He stood in front of the flinching quintet, left hand clasping his right elbow, two fingers pressed to his hairline, smirking as if all history were one long shaggy dog joke whose punch line he was now permitted to deliver. He'd scan the score, regard the palette of possible victims, and swoop.

The percussionist dug Bonner's hijinks; the pianist just laughed. The other three threatened a walkout. Bonner faced them down.

You gonna sit there with a broom up your sphincter, afraid to tap your feet? You've all forgotten where music comes from. Why do you think they're called movements?

And, howling all the way, the musicians turned back into dancers.

The piece was one of those commercial flights to Paris that found itself heading down to Havana. But by December, Els's embarrassment at the hijacking turned into excitement. He expanded the score where Bonner's shambolic theater called for more. The academic piece began to breathe and bleed. The pair of them—pushing and prodding and trumping one another—lifted the notes into a new place.

Fights: Yes. Fits of temper and pique. Too many stressful hours together for anything less. But Richard turned even war into creative charades.

The collaborators were crossing the dark Quad one icy night, wasted by hours of rehearsing, but carried along by the strangeness coming alive under their care. Richard stopped on the long diagonal, his hands conducting the air. *How do you like seeing your cold little fish swimming in the great big ocean?*

Els drew up next to him. *How do you like seeing your random thrashing get some form?*

The choreographer craned toward the gibbous moon. *Maestro. We work pretty well together, don't you think? It seems to me that half of life's problems would be solved if one of us had a vagina.*

Els recoiled. His boots slid on the packed snow, and he would have fallen if Bonner hadn't grabbed his elbow. Bonner smacked Els in the back of the skull and cackled.

Oh, fuck off! Don't look at me like that, man. You got a problem with something?

Richard snapped his finger and waved the parade onward. After a hundred-yard silence that he seemed to feast on, he grabbed Els again. *Maestro, listen. I'm happy, for you, that she has one. And a marvelous one, I have no doubt.*

Then he was all business again—Borges and Brecht and new plans for getting infinity up onto that cramped little stage.

There's joy in a minor key, a deep pleasure to be had from hearing the darkest tune and discovering you're equal to it.

The performance was set for late January, the day before Peter Els's twenty-seventh birthday. Bonner's notoriety was good for business. Maddy's Vertical Smile groupies turned out to hear the band's lead singer. Peter's composer friends showed up, to gauge the competition. Mattison was there, near the front of the hall, waiting to be unsatisfied. Word had gotten around that the patients were running the asylum. It made for a decent house.

As the room filled, Bonner staked out a seat halfway down the right aisle. When the players came onstage to polite applause, Richard retreated to where Els sat, in the back of the hall. The horn started its stutter-step stall, a figure picked up by the cello, then the oboe. As the three instruments played their patient delaying game, Madolyn crept down the right aisle in a gray tunic—Cleopatra with a gecko-skull brooch and a cicada in her hair. She edged toward the stage, stopped, cringed and recoiled, then retreated to the chair Bonner had vacated. The audience was baffled, but the band played on.

Ratchet and wood block prodded the delaying motif, which cycled through dissonant parallel intervals in the cello, horn, and oboe. Maddy rose from her seat, lurched toward the stage, hesitated, lost her nerve again, and sat back down. The audience tittered, as nervous as they should have been.

The piano blasted through the stuttering material and broke it loose. All five instruments fell into a flowing stream. Maddy bolted from her seat and jerked her unwilling body up the stairs and out to center stage, where, shocked by a sudden rush of will, she sang:

The truth is,
truth is,
truth is . . .
The truth is that we live out our lives
putting off all that can be put off . . .

On a downbeat, the pitch group changed to Hypophrygian, an old church mode. The instruments circled in tight stretti of dense materials. Then the projectors fired up—twin beams from opposite sides of the hall, coating the singer in colors. Near the bottom of her register, Maddy sang a legato line that twisted like a tunnel in an ancient tomb:

Perhaps we all know deep down . . . that we are immortal.

At the word *immortal*, the lines sailed up into a series of ringing forte chords in the piano and a frenzy of handbells.

The three melodic instruments reached a blistering peak of arpeggios, then froze. The projectors blacked out. The sound decayed in the dampening hall. Awkward Maddy beckoned out over the audience's heads. Her grasping hands and desperate glances made half the room turn and look. Then, over the pianissimo horn and oboe, she wove through the four pitches of a diminished seventh:

And that sooner . . .
Sooner or later . . .
Sooner, or sooner or later . . .
Later . . . or later . . . later . . .

The projectors blazed again, along with a choir of antiphonal taped voices. Images pelted the hall's walls in a time-lapse cavalcade that ran from Edison's electrocuted elephant to Edward White tethered to his Gemini capsule by a twenty-five-foot umbilical above the blue Earth. The pianist placed his forearms across the keyboard and undulated. Horn, oboe, and cello built a corona of minor seconds while the percussionist rolled sponge mallets on a suspended china cymbal. On a fixed pitch in the middle of her range, rising three steps at the end of the line, Maddy, motionless, intoned:

Sooner or later, all men will do and know all things.

Who was in the audience that night? Students of cultural
anthropology in tie-dyed kurtas and beards like shoe brushes.
A doctor of philology about to embark on a career selling dis-
count furniture off of flatbed trucks. A long-haired, sloe-eyed
woman with the "Desiderata" on her bathroom wall, who
woke up nightly, convinced she'd burn for what she'd done.
Retired social scientists certain that consumer democracy
had ten more years, tops. An agitator with a mind like lighter
fluid who ended up owning a seat on the Chicago Board of
Trade. A scholar of German idealism who believed that the
universe was coming to know itself. An atmospheric scientist wondering if the planet might be about to slow-cook to
death. An ethnomusicologist who'd spend the next forty years
proving that music evaded every definition. In all, a hundred
people whose offspring would someday know all things and
become immortal.

The first song ended; the audience coughed and shifted.
Giggles rippled through the seats near Els. The woman to his
left leaned toward her companion and pantomimed the wind-
ing of a crank. Els turned to Richard. Bonner's face shone. He
cackled like a melodrama villain and rubbed his hands, keen
for the feast of abuse that only art can bring. Three songs left,
and hot, tourniquet pains were shooting down Els's left arm at
ten-second intervals.

The second song consisted of just two ideas: a dotted trochee
pulse, like a lopsided metronome, overlaying itself at different
intervals, and a cycle of suspensions forever falling into other
suspensions and failing to resolve. Maddy flexed and squared

her shoulders, leaning forward and reaching out while being drawn back, swaying in place, trapped in what struck her as someone else's body.

Time is a river which carries me along,

she sang, on a tone row that flowed by like chant. Then the long phrase's lyric answer:

But I am the river.

Each time the players rested, they passed various colored globes in slow arcs over their heads. Images painted them— stretched and compressed clocks, the throbbing sine wave of an oscilloscope, atomic nuclei, spinning galaxies. The tone row returned, transposed and inverted.

Time is a tiger that devours me.

Then the answering cantilena:

But I am the tiger.

At the third couplet, the images spilled over the musicians and onto the back wall: rebels in Biafra, riots in Detroit, bombers in Da Nang, and the young Che, who'd died only a few months before. Maddy, stilling her trembling limbs, sang like no one would ever hear.

Time is a fire that consumes me. But I am that fire.

The cycle of suspensions faded. The ghostly films, too, froze on a frame of a sinking supertanker, before going dark. The audience coughed and shifted again and checked their watches. Els wanted to slink off and be dead somewhere for a very long time.

Then came the scherzo romp. Maddy sang the words about working for neither posterity nor God, whose tastes in art were largely unknown. The players passed around an eight-note figure, tricked up with every species of counterpoint Els could manage. The antics climaxed with singer and players all threatening to leave the stage in a combined hissy fit, but coming back together for the cadence.

Listening, Els heard the total lie. He wrote for the future's love, and for the love of an ideal listener he could almost see. He saw how he might expand the music, make it stranger, stronger, colder, more huge and indifferent, just as soon as this concert was over.

But a breeze blew through the final song, and the skies cleared onto pure potential. Maddy gathered herself, as if laid out for her own funeral, at peace at last with the previous three outbursts. All dancing stopped, and the back wall hung on a single black-and-white photograph of a few diatoms a handful of microns wide, their silica casings carved like the finials of Gothic cathedrals. Above the piano's pulse, the cello and horn overlaid a tune of outmoded yearning, like the start of Schumann's *Mondnacht,* in disguise. Maddy sang a slow, stepwise rising figure, a blue balloon coming up over the horizon:

We are made for art . . .

The moment Maddy took up the tendril phrase, Els knew she was as dear to him as his own life. Talons gripped his ribs, and he felt a joy bordering on panic. He needed to know how this woman would unfold. He needed to write music that would settle into her range like frost on fields. They'd spend their years together, grow old, get sick, die in shared bewilderment.

She nudged the phrase up another perfect fourth:

We are made for memory . . .

Something seized his arm. Richard. Els turned, but the man's face was fixed on the stage, as if he hadn't already heard the melodic prediction two dozen times in the last two days.

The pianist broke off in the middle of an ostinato, stood up, and left the stage. Maddy reached out, palm up, but couldn't stop him. The reduced ensemble kept turning over notes that now lined up to reveal themselves as a permutation of the delaying fragment that had opened the first song. The horn, too, grew forgetful; he stood and wandered, climbed down the front of the stage and into the audience. Maddy looked on, touching her cheek, unable to call him back. Puzzled, she carried on:

We are made for poetry . . .

The remaining trio turned oddly consonant. The oboist set her oboe on the music stand and left. The cellist carried on for a while, intrepid, with a figure lifted from the Bach D minor suite, while the percussionist haloed him on xylorimba. Then, succumbing to the inexorable, the cellist, too, set down his instrument, and walked up the aisle to the exit. Maddy, lost

in thought, failed to notice. She stood alone onstage with the
percussionist, who stuttered away on the wood block.

Or perhaps . . .

Maddy sang, shaking her head at the baffling melody and
backing away, her arms drawing in as if sieving the wind:

Or perhaps we are made for oblivion.

The percussionist tapped a last dotted rhythm into his block
of wood. The stage went black, and it took the house five enormous seconds to decide that the piece was done. Right before
the applause, Els heard a nearby baritone whisper, *Frauds.*

The clapping came from far away. The musicians reassembled
for bows. Maddy shaded her eyes and stared out into the dark,
looking for the perpetrators and seeing only shadows. Bonner
yanked Els to his feet, where he bobbed several times like a
water-drinking toy duck. Els turned to see his friend regarding
the audience with cool amusement.

People came up to Els after, wanting to take the measure of
this audacity. They wanted to get up close, to see if he'd really
escaped. Someone put his arms around Els's shoulders and said,
That was something. Someone said, *So interesting.* Someone said,
I liked it, I think. Els thanked and grinned and nodded, seeing
no one.

A bald man in a gabardine suit decades out of date slunk up
and whispered an emaciated thank-you. Els offered his hand,
but the man held his up as if they were defective. *I don't often
get to hear,* he murmured, *something so . . .* He backed away,
flinching in gratitude.

A six-foot-tall woman who looked like deposed royalty squeezed his shoulder from behind. Els wheeled, and she asked in a Spanish accent, *What was that supposed to be about?*

Around him in the emptying hall, clots of people were grooming and seducing each other. Els smiled at the majestic woman and said, *About twenty-four minutes.*

Her eyes flashed. *It seemed longer somehow,* she said, and turned into the lingering crowd.

Mattison emerged from a nearby cabal. He saluted Els with two fingers. *You have them all scratching their heads.* The most praise his mentor would ever give him.

Across the thinned room, Els saw Bonner seated in the empty first row, staring at the abandoned stage. Richard didn't turn when Els dropped into the seat beside him.

"*Made for oblivion,*" Richard said, in an odd monotone. *Check. Now what?*

Els sat playing castanets on the pads of his thumbs. *We could take it on the road. Bloomington. Hyde Park. Ann Arbor.*

Could, Bonner said, meaning no. All his mania from the last half dozen weeks had collapsed into mere agitation. His eyes fixed on a series of invisible one-reelers projected in front of him.

Pleased? Els asked.

What's that?

I said, are you pleased?

And I said, what's that?

Somewhere in Bonner's skull, across great, arid expanses all the way to the horizon, the shit-storm of invention was gathering again. The hall had emptied. At last the composer stood and said, *See you?*

Richard nodded, but to some other question.

Els caught up with Maddy, out in the foyer with three of the musicians. She was flushed and floating, astonished to have run the gauntlet and survived.

Well, she said, when Els came up. *That was an experience!*

What she means, the oboist said, *is, "Never again!"*

I liked your chart, the cellist told Els. *But I still think it'd be sweeter without the fire drills.*

The oboist laughed. *You know what Stravinsky said at the premiere of* Pierrot? *"I wish that lady would shut up so I could hear the music."*

The group wrangled for a while over music's soul, as performers will do before heading out for weed and beers. The pianist and horn player were already at Murphy's, half a pitcher ahead of everyone. The percussionist drummed on Els's shoulder.

Time to get wasted. You two coming?

Maddy looked at Els, who begged off. *Mind if I go?* she asked.

Can I talk to you for a minute first?

Meet us over there, the percussionist called over his shoulder as the trio disappeared.

It was good, Peter, Maddy said. *Those songs have something. I heard new things in them, even tonight.*

Els helped her into her long buckskin coat. From behind, he clasped her upper arms. *You were unreal.*

She softened and backed into him. *Was I?*

From another planet. Madolyn. I love you.

She scrunched her neck and smiled. *You love those songs.*

I saw something in you tonight. Something I didn't know was there.

No, she said, and would not meet his eyes. *That was performance.*

We should get married. Join our lives.

She studied the score etched into the linoleum floor, humming, frantic but soundless.

Move somewhere neither of us has ever been. Find a place and make it ours. Read to each other at night. Take care of one another.

He pressed every button she had. Discover America. Turn life's rags into a bright quilt. Levitate the Pentagon.

She shook her head at his list, the way she had at the end of the fourth song. She clamped his wrist in a polygraph grip and scrutinized his eyes.

Let's walk.

Snow was falling, compounding the already knee-high drifts. They walked for a long while, in talk that quieted into something like telepathy. And by midnight, Peter Els was thawing in his love's bed, hurting with a hope he'd never felt. He was twenty-seven, too old now for selective service, and engaged to be married. And the future held music so fine and clear all he needed was to take dictation.

They wed two weeks later at the Urbana courthouse. Richard Bonner was their lone legal witness. They would suffer their families' anger later. No one else had to hear this promise.

Maddy made her own dress, of apricot taffeta, pinned with an orchid that cost a week's worth of Peter's stipend. Peter dressed in cambric and corduroy. Richard wore his usual black leather. He was there with Els, in the courthouse bathroom, for the retching.

If I didn't know better, Bonner said, keeping Els's head from banging the faucet, *I'd say you have stage fright.*

Els could only groan.

What are you afraid of? I'm assuming you've already seen her naked.

Oh, Jesus. Richard. What if I'm wrong for her? What if this isn't meant to be?

Es muß sein, Maestro.

What if I ruin this woman's life?

Oh, that would be awful! Especially after swearing to use your powers only for good.

Richard, what am I doing?

You're leaping, Peter. For the first time in your life. And it's a thing of beauty.

Bonner sponged the flecks off Els's collar with a paper towel, then frog-marched him down the courthouse hall alongside the suspects in blue jumpsuits and handcuffs being led off to their own arraignments. Maddy grabbed him outside the courtroom and shook him. *We're good, Peter. Really good!* She was radiant throughout the service, and every word the judge pronounced threatened to send her into another giggling bout. Afterward, on the street, Richard serenaded them on a silver kazoo wrapped in pink ribbon. Bach's *Wachet auf*: It seemed to Els a very good tune, one that a person might still do all kinds of things with.

And even the least threatening tune will outlast you by generations. There's pleasure in knowing that, too.

That year is a chance-built symphony. A string of scabrous nightclub burlesques. A psychedelic double album made up of the wildest percussive tracks. Els hears about Tet one afternoon after teaching his ear-training class. Johnson's bombshell lands not long after.

Bonner directs a mad, high-speed *Man and Superman,* with incidental music by Els. But his madness is a bagatelle compared to the nightly news: King killed. Rolling riots in every city. The Columbia takeover. The Battle for Paris. Resurrection City on the Washington Mall. Warhol shot. Kennedy killed.

Bonner gets arrested in a campus bar for standing on a table and peeing in a beer mug for Peace. Els and Maddy bail him out.

While yippies trash the stock exchange and the Soviets crush the Prague Spring, Els composes thirty-six variations on "All You Need Is Love," in the style of everyone from Machaut to Piston. He and Bonner stage a play-in of the "Love Variations" in front of Smith Hall, under the frieze carved with Bach, Beethoven, Haydn, and Palestrina. One hundred performers read through a nonstop tag-team performance.

Something's happening here. The world egg threatens to crack open. Els's music cracks open, too, trying to say what's going on. He and Bonner mount a cabaret in the courtyard of the Illini Union for Turn In Your Draft Card Day. They work up an Eisler-Weill drag show called *I'm a Stranger Here Myself.*

On New Year's Eve, Bonner forces the old married couple out on a freezing midnight picnic, deep in the South Farms, under the stars. The trio sit on the iron ground and eat cold lentils, sardines on celery, and frozen Twinkies.

A meal fit for lunatics and saints, Bonner declares. Olympian, he leans back on his elbows. *Who knew a guy like us could have such friends?*

Steam escapes their mouths, and, huddled together, they toast the vanishing year. Maddy pours the champagne into paper cones. Bonner insists they clink. Bubbly spills from the mushy flutes onto the frozen earth.

To putting the past to bed, Richard toasts.

To waking the future, Els says.

To staying in the Beautiful Now, Maddy adds, although they're already leaving.

They come across a cardboard box blowing through the snowy fields. They use it as a three-person toboggan, sledding down the only geological feature for two hundred miles that can be called a hill. Bonner tears the box into three pieces, which he distributes.

Hold on to these. We'll reassemble right here, top of this hill, in fifty years.

Maddy laughs. *Synchronize your watches.*

Walking home in the cold, toting his scrap of cardboard, pressed between his wife and wild friend, Els hears a piece in his head, music like the kind Schumann reported hearing as he slipped into madness—*an instrument of splendid resonance, the like of which has never been heard on Earth.* The harmonies are rich and braided, leading to an unprepared Neapolitan sixth, a rediscovery of naïve sequences, and the melody feels so inexorable that he knows it'll be waiting for him intact when he next sits down to a sheet of virgin staff paper.

But when Peter wakes in the new year, he fails to remember even hearing the piece. By the time he does, a few days later, it's too late to transcribe. All that's left is a blurred contour, disembodied music hinting at something magnificent just out of reach.

I always loved best those tunes written for those who listen on other frequencies.

They're still a trio later that spring, wandering the domed Assembly Hall, that cavernous radioactive mushroom that Cage and Hiller have filled with more happy pandemonium. Seven amplified harpsichords duel with 50 monoaural tape machines and 208 FORTRAN-generated tapes playing Mozart, Beethoven,

Chopin, Schumann, Gottschalk, Busoni, and Schoenberg, all sliced into short genetic chunks then recombined at random. Bonner and the Elses, in their fluorescent overalls—handed out free to the dazed visitors—gawk at a Stonehenge ring of polyethylene screens on which six dozen projectors cast thousands of slides and films. Outside, 48 more enormous screens circle the building's quarter-mile circumference. They turn the whole colossal structure into a pulsating saucer that has come to Earth for refueling and a little galactic-backwater R & R.

The smell of pot seeps from the crowds camped out in the central arena. People lounge or wander about. It's music, Els keeps reminding himself. Music that has reached the end of a thousand-year exploration.

Too much, Maddy says. *My mind's blown.*

Bonner flips his hands in the air, juggling invisible moons. *We could have done this, with a few more bucks.*

But the show is beyond Els. Cage, Hiller, and the army of believers who mount *HPSCHD* have disappeared into liberty. They refuse to impose decisions on any listener. Composition is no longer the goal; all that counts now is awareness, this flickering, specious present, a dive into raw phenomena. And that's a plunge Els will never be able to make. Or so he figures, at twenty-eight.

Maddy strolls around the flying saucer, laughing. She stops to rag-pick the trash for interesting textiles. Peter follows in his wife's happy wake. She has become a season ticket holder for the festival of weirdness Els has inflicted on her these last twenty months. He loves her steady refusal to descend to liking or not liking, those sentimental actions that have nothing to do with listening. Her awe at the range of human desire turns Peter himself back into a spectator in his own life. He falls into orbit beside her; Richard is off buying a poster, for a price determined by the I Ching.

Maddy hums to herself, a snippet of Mozart fished from the randomness. Mozart, the man who invented the musical dice game, two short centuries ago.

Peter, she says, looking away, at a slide of the Crab Nebula. He knows what she'll say before she says it. An oddness has come over her these last few days, a frightened flush, waiting for its moment. What else can it be? Nothing else is big enough for her to keep secret from him for so long.

Peter? Company's coming.

He stops and listens, hearing, above the din, a small, high voice.

Peter?

You're sure?

She spreads her palms, shrugs, and smiles.

When?

I don't know. December? We'll find out. Peter? Don't worry. We're good. We're good! We can do this. Everybody does.

He jerks, objecting. *No, that's not . . . This is incredible. The two of us? Are you kidding?*

She has to laugh at him, standing there, overcome, his eyes like outer planets. And that's how Richard finds them moments later.

Laughing gas? Bonner says. *They're giving away laughing gas somewhere?*

HPSCHD runs for almost five hours. Several thousand people wander through. Two months later, men walk on the moon. Four more weeks, and half a million people gather on a farm in upstate New York for a weekend of rain, mud, and music. By then the trio has abandoned Champaign-Urbana—the Elses for Boston, where Maddy gets a job teaching singing in an

elite junior high, and Bonner for Manhattan, to squalor and a
gauntlet of unpaid positions in experimental theaters.

And on the first day of winter, Els meets his burping, giggling,
raging, laughing, squalling daughter, her tiny foot between his
fingers an astonishment he can't take in. This perfect, working
creature, self-assembling, self-delighting, the brightest whim
that could ever exist, and he'll never make anything to compare
to her for pure wonder.

What do you think has become of the young and old men?
And what has become of the women?

Els followed the Voice. He did as She instructed, down to the
pointless twenty-minute detour through Clarion. The gadget
found its trio of geosynchronous satellite beacons twenty-two
thousand miles high, and triangulated from them the one spot
on Earth where Els could be. From there, it skimmed through
a digitized database of eight million miles of road and took
Els to the one place on Earth he wanted to go. Giving in to
machine navigation was an infantile luxury. And the Voice
came through in the end, dropping him off on the stoop of the
Kohlmann summer cottage just before dark.

The abandoned wasp's nest hung right where Klaudia said. Els
extracted the key and let himself into a room reeking of nature
and vacation. The lodge was lined in cedar-paneled nostalgia
and furnished in cushioned pine from the fifties. The whole
house showed signs of hasty evacuation. Football jerseys and
high-tech sneakers lay scattered about. Stray lights had been

left on, which Els went about turning off before he sat down to collect himself.

He found nuts and cereal in the pantry, and a dozen apples in the refrigerator crisper. He helped himself to a glass of Finger Lakes Chardonnay and some frozen pound cake. The washing machine stood in a utility room off the back of the kitchen. He stripped off his painter pants, waffle shirt, and stale underwear. Then he stood under the shower in the rustic bathroom, naked, sagging, and scalded, waiting for explanation.

Fed and clean, he had no need of anything but sleep. But sleep wouldn't come. He rooted around the possessions of his unknown benefactors, scavenging for diversion. Magazines abounded—old *Smithsonians* and *Outdoors,* as well as scattered issues from more specialized offerings. It seemed possible to append the word *magazine* to any string of words—*Not Your Grandfather's Clock Magazine; Power Balance Holographic Wrist Channeler Magazine*—and still come up with a product that needed only the right focus group to find its way into circulation.

Reading wasn't possible. All Els was good for was music. Shelves in the front room held three dozen jewel boxes—road trip listening, left here in the vacation home alongside battered Parcheesi sets and moldy quiz books. Ripped copies of Ella Fitzgerald's Verve Songbooks, They Might Be Giants, Sonic Youth, Nirvana and Pearl Jam, a smattering of emo, albums by Wilco, Jay-Z, the Dirt Bombs, the Strokes, and Rage Against the Machine. There was a time when the proliferation of so many musical genres left Els cowering in a corner, holding up the *Missa Solemnis* as a shield. Now he wanted alarm and angry dream, style and distraction, as much ruthless novelty as the aging youth industry could still deliver.

He found a disc by a group called Anthrax, as if some real bioterrorist had planted it there to frame him. He looked around the cottage for something to play it on. In the kitchen he found a nineties-style boom box. He slipped the disc into the slot and with a single rim shot was surrounded by an air raid announcing the end of the world. A driving motor rhythm in the drums propelled virtuosic parallel passages in the guitars and bass. The song came on like a felon released from multiple life sentences. The melodic machete went straight through Els's skin. It took no imagination to see a stadium of sixty thousand people waving lighters and basking in a frenzy of shared power. The music said you had one chance to blow through life, and the only crime was wasting it on fear.

Many years ago Els had made a vow to run from no art but let every track play through to its end. He looked out the window, past the gravel drive, through the stand of birches, remnants of the vast, vanished northern hardwood forest, listening to this droll Armageddon. The band had been around for half of Els's life, servicing the need for anarchy written into people's cells. He wondered which of this middle-class, outdoorsy family was responsible for the disc. Probably not Mom, although the thing about music was that you never knew the shape of anyone's desire.

The song was one long, joyous jackhammer assertion of tonic. Surprise was not its goal, and the pattern laid down in the first four measures drove the tune on in a storm surge. But after two minutes, it sprouted a hallucination in the relative minor floating above the thrash, and for several notes Els thought the band, in a fit of real anarchy, had thrown Chopin's E Minor Prelude—the "Vision"—into the cement mixer, like Lady Gaga quoting *The Well-Tempered Clavier*.

Els paused the disc, but the Chopin persisted. Four measures, with a little altered voice-leading at the end, turned back on themselves in an endless, lamenting loop—one of those tuneful fragments that signaled the onset of a temporal lobe seizure. But the sound came from somewhere in the house. He wandered through three different rooms before finding it: Klaudia's smartphone. The one that had guided him here.

Words hovered on the screen: "Incoming Call, Kohlmann, K." He pressed the answer icon, and held the world's portal up to his ear.

You're all over the news, Kohlmann said, trying for sardonic but landing on scared.

Yes, Els said. *I saw the camera trucks this morning.*

This morning. It wasn't possible.

Klaudia said, *Google yourself. The clips are up already.*

Of course they were. Retired professor of music flees scene of terrorism raid. Verrata College officials express dismay.

What else? Els asked. *You sound . . .*

Your bacteria. You said they were harmless.

Something slurred in his brain. *I said the species wasn't dangerous in ordinary situations.*

Storm troopers were assaulting the cabin, from the direction of the kitchen. Els set the phone down and headed toward the invasion. He'd pressed the pause button on the boom box, and the pause had chosen that moment to time out. He looked for eject, and in the onslaught of sound couldn't find it. He yanked the cord from the wall, then walked back to the bedroom and retrieved the phone.

Back. Sorry.

What the hell was that?

Your grandsons' music.

Ach. We're finished, aren't we?

What about my bacteria? Els asked.

Nineteen people in hospitals across Alabama have been infected with your strain. The CDC says nine people dead.

A long caesura, the sound of what terror would be, when it grew up.

My strain? In Alabama?

Kohlmann read from another screen: *Serratia marcescens. That's the one, right?*

There was nothing to say, and Els said it.

The FBI wants to talk to you.

This . . . none of this makes sense. The FBI told the press what bacteria I was culturing?

But he didn't need reminding: Everybody was the press now. Everyone knew everything, as it happened.

The journalists think I . . . ? They can't be that stupid. Were all these patients on IV drips, by any chance?

Google it, Klaudia told him. *That's what the FBI is doing, I'm sure.*

Jesus, Els said.

And call me. They can't trace you to my phone, can they?

About your phone, he said. *Chopin?*

What can I say? It does something to me. Play that at my funeral, please?

He promised. But he wasn't sure an audience with chronic focal disorder would sit through it.

A friend says: "I just heard the strangest song ever." Do you run away or toward?

He sat out back behind the cottage on the edge of a maple grove, his head bowed over the device. In the dark, with that lone beam of white splashed across his face, he read the accounts. Nineteen Alabamans sick and nine dead. Nine people out of a hundred thousand annual American deaths by hospital infection—more than car wrecks and murders combined. The public, drowning in data, might never have registered the story. But he had turned accident into something panicworthy.

All the infected patients had indeed been on a catheter. All six hospitals were in greater Birmingham. All got their IV bags from the same supplier. Either someone had accidentally contaminated a batch, or America was under siege again. In normal times, most people could figure the odds. But the times would never be normal again.

Els's eyes adjusted to the screen, the lone bright spot in the surrounding dark. He searched his name and found student ratings of his teaching, a recent Brussels performance of his forgotten chamber symphony, and old chatter about the 1993 premiere of *The Fowler's Snare*. Searches on the Alabama outbreak led to a gigantic methane dome under the thawing tundra that was belching into the atmosphere massive amounts of greenhouse gas that would speed the process that released them.

Reporters speculated about why a retired adjunct professor of music had been manipulating human pathogens in his den. Neighbors attested to his quiet politeness, although one described him as standoffish and another mentioned the atonal sounds emanating from his house at odd hours. The Joint Security Task Force could not comment on ongoing investigations, but they were interested in any information concerning the whereabouts of Peter Els.

Opera buffa had turned seria. He had no choice. He had to return home and explain, if only to keep a jumpy country from going off the rails again. But he'd already explained everything to Coldberg and Mendoza, and still they'd raided him. Now the Alabama infections vindicated them. Threat once again kept the precarious democracy intact. Els would have to be punished, in proportion to the thrill he'd given the collective imagination.

A hundred yards off, through the dense maples, the windows of the neighbors' cabin threw off an amber glow. The undergrowth on all sides boomed with calls and alarms, an animal *Visions Fugitives*. His frantic flight caught up with him, and Els fell asleep in the deck chair under the trees. The smart screen dimmed, then timed out, then slipped from his hands. Sometime in the night he woke, and, realizing where he was, blundered into the house to a soft bed. Toward dawn, from a sleep filled with epidemics, he heard the E Minor Prelude pulsing again. But not until the next morning—a brilliant, balmy, and innocent thing, like the first day of creation—did he find the phone again, lying on the grass as if it had fallen out of the sky.

There is no safety. There is only forgetfulness.

Even in dried-out memory, those years in Boston are fresh and green. Els and Maddy drive a seventeen-foot U-Haul trailer filled with their combined worldly belongings across Ohio and Pennsylvania to the doorstep of their one-bedroom apartment in the Fens. They port a queen-sized mattress up the stairs on their heads. Els fusses over his gravid wife, making her stop and rest every few steps. She laughs off his anxieties. *I'm pregnant, Peter. Not crippled.* In fact, the thrill of nesting gives her energy for three.

For Maddy, it's an easy commute by T to Brookline and New Morning, the private freedom school modeled on Neill's Summerhill. The starry-eyed school board hired her after she declared in her interview that a rich musical exposure could turn any child into a creator. By the time Labor Day rolls around, she's showing. Her progressive employers pretend to be thrilled.

While swelling Maddy teaches junior high kids how to barrel through dissonant choruses and mallet their way to freedom on Orff instruments, Els picks up odd jobs. He gives private clarinet lessons. He hires himself out as a music copyist. He writes concert reviews for the *Globe*, at fifty dollars a pop.

At night, they watch classic thirties Hollywood films on the oldies station, on a tiny black-and-white set with tinfoil attached to the rabbit ears. Maddy quilts and Peter glances through scores while Barrymore tells Trilby, "Ah, you are beautiful, my manufactured love! But it is only Svengali, talking to himself . . ."

A week after Halloween, he lands a job beyond his boldest fantasies: gallery guard at Mrs. Gardner's fake Venetian palazzo, half a mile down the Fenway. He can walk there in minutes. They pay him to stand motionless all day in the Spanish Cloister or the Gothic Room or the Chinese Loggia, guarding paintings and writing music in his head. Days of silent meditation contribute as much to his musical development as all his years in graduate school. For a decade, he has busied himself with intricate, ingenious forms. Now he begins to hear a stream—simple, broad, and adamant—purling beneath his feet.

He lingers for entire afternoons in front of Vermeer's *The*

Concert, listening to that still trio's silent harmonies. The bowed head, the wave of the singer's curved fingers conduct the strains of frozen music for no audience but him, in this distant future. Soon enough, those players, too, will go missing forever.

Richard Bonner writes letters now and then, from his illegal loft in SoHo. A few times he even calls, despite the ruinous expense of long distance. He's always either euphoric with new projects or ready to press the button that will vaporize humanity. Once, he sends a small commission Els's way—a request for a two-minute piece to accompany a gallery installation. The job pays nothing, but it's Els's first contribution to the downtown scene.

December comes, and with it, a snow that paralyzes Boston. Maddy is huge; she waddles about toting a globe on her outthrust pelvis. When her time comes, their car-owning nextdoor neighbor is nowhere to be found. Peter must run out in the street and flag down a passing Buick, to hitch a ride to the hospital.

Then infant Sara is there, in all her blotchy astonishment. They huddle in their snowbound cocoon: twin parents bowed over a minuscule wailer, who changes by the hour. Els writes no music for two months; he's nothing but diapers and basinet and back-patting, getting that living tube to burp. His daughter mewls and cackles, and that's all the concert he needs. Maddy lies around the apartment languorous, hypnotized, enslaved by this parasite that turns her into a brainless host. They all three do nothing but live. Even yanked awake in the dead of night, Els finds this life finer than any art. These six weeks— the fullest he'll ever live. But the prelude is over in a few brief bars. Maddy's back conducting the chorus at New Morning by Washington's birthday.

Peter takes a leave from the museum to stay home and raise his infant girl. When Maddy returns from work each night to swallow up Sara, Els fusses. *Careful; you're scaring her. Wash your hands first!*

The sea slug learns to locomote, shoving herself across the floor on four floppy limbs. Her lips burble and whir, like her mother's humming in embryo. Peter takes his girl everywhere, in a papoose strapped across his chest. He sings to her all day long. He sings her to sleep each night, as she chants along and reaches for the pitches where they float in the air. "Hot Cross Buns" and "The Itsy-Bitsy Spider": What more music could a person ever need?

From the start, she's her own creature. Everything goes in her mouth. What can't be eaten is there only to test her will. And Sara won't be thwarted. She's born a conductor, and the world is her orchestra. She cues the giant adults with her index finger: *You: get over here! Me: over there!* Life is a puzzle to shift and slide until the solution, so clear already in this infant's mind, comes free.

Her parents find the bossy Von Karajan game hilarious, the first few hundred times. Then exhausting. Then a little scary. One tough night, after a two-hour epic bedtime war of attrition, Peter and Maddy lie slumped against each other, wasted zombies. The air is stained with baby reek—spit-up and talcum. Peter gazes up at the plaster-cracked ceiling, an alternate notation system he can't read.

She has a will.

Maddy flops backward on the bed. *And she always finds a way.*

Plays me like a Strad.

Me, too. How'd she learn that so fast?

Look at us. Remember when the hardest thing in the world was writing a grant?

Maddy breathes out, her soubrette long gone. *Not the life you were hoping for, is it?*

No, Peter agrees, a little surprised. *It's far more.*

"But my lamps were blown out in every little wind. And lighting them, I forget all else again." (Tagore)

He starts to write again. A scribbled gesture one day, then a theme, then a few measures. Over several months, he sketches a short scherzo for small ensemble. In the wilds of stay-at-home fatherhood, music changes. His little tricks and signatures soften and expand. He'll sit working at the electric piano in the corner of the bedroom while his daughter plays on the other side of the wall, rapping at her tiny xylophone, imitating him, chanting the pitchless pitches of infancy.

He crosses over into her room, and she blooms. She slaps the mallet on the shiny metal keys in ecstasy.

What are you saying, Sary-bear?

The name makes her rap faster, gladder. The keys ring out—red, purple, sea-green.

What's that? Say it again!

She shrieks and strikes at all the keys in the rainbow.

Wait. I know! You're saying . . .

He helps her hold the mallet. They touch the keys together in the magic order. He sings.

There once was a girl named Sar-a!

She laughs and grabs her hand free, hits the keys that she's already hearing.

She comes from the present er-a!

She hums hard, whacking as many keys as she can reach.

The future had better beware-a!

Yes, she screeches: That's it. That's exactly what I'm saying.

He goes back into his bedroom, to his own keyboard, where he steals from her, those scattered fa-do-sol-la fragments of deep origin. She toddles in, tries to help, pushes keys for him. *No, darling,* he says. *This is daddy's piece.* But it isn't, really. Everything is hers.

By day's end, he has the start of a new berceuse, which he tests on her at bedtime. She's the only hearer the piece may ever have. Who else would listen to such a thing? It's too wild for the billion lovers of radio tunes, too blissful for the handful who need their music recherché.

But his daughter likes the song, and she's all the audience he needs. Sara is his experiment in what the ear might come to hear, when raised on sounds from a happy elsewhere. She giggles at his sudden melodic turns. Her face crinkles in puzzled glee. Her turn now to ask him: *What are you saying?* But it's only music on a summer's evening, even as a bouncy ballpark organ floats into the window, blown through the air from Fenway, the bat's crack, the distant whispered roar of a crowd, and a berceuse that leaves the saucer-eyed girl squealing in primal delight.

Outside the apartment, there are gas lines, wildfire inflation, the Middle East heading to Armageddon again. But inside, their days bring the real dramas. A cough. A fever. A fall against the coffee table that makes her bite through her lower lip. Two short years ago, he wanted to write music that changed what music was. Now he just wants to keep his daughter from changing too much, too fast.

Pushing Sara's stroller through the Victory Gardens, Els sees with terrible clarity the hubris of his twenties. He can't for his life imagine why he ever signed on for the full Faust ride. For years, he's struggled to write something thorny and formidable, as if difficulty alone ensured lasting admiration. Now he sees that what the world really needs is a lullaby simple enough to coax a two-year-old to lay down her frantic adventure each night for another eight hours.

On the playground near the art museum, Sara stands and chants to the sky: "This Old Man." The words are babble, the rhythm rough, and the melody little more than a crayon smear. But to Els, the old man is as recognizable as God. Rebelling is itself a passing fashion, as fragile as any. Hemlines rise and fall, but the present is forever convinced it has found the Tailor's pattern. The manifestos of Peter's twenties—the movements and lawless experiments, the crazy climbs up onto the barricades—feel like a tantrum now, like his daughter refusing to take her nap. Who can say what the academy champions these days? Els has been away too long to know. But he knows that cool will give way to warm, form to feeling, as surely as a leading tone tilts forever toward the tonic. Music cut from new whole cloth? No such material. The emperor will always be as naked as a jaybird, as nude as Sara slapping the waves of her bath, shrieking those patty-cake melodies she makes up on the spot.

The girl is in love with music. At four, she blossoms with solfeggio. By four and a half, she stumbles through the Mozart Sonatina in C with what strikes her besotted father as real feeling. She plays for him, improvised instruments: Horns made of rubber shower hose. Oatmeal boxes strung with rubber bands.

The game must always go a certain way, and she never gets tired of playing.

What am I saying, Daddy? she demands, and lays into the piano with every finger she has.

He listens. *You're saying, "Okay, Mom; I'll eat green food."*

Yes! Maddy calls from the kitchen.

No! Sara shouts, and tries more furious chords.

I know! You're saying, "I'm tired and I want to go to bed."

Wrong! she says. *Try again!* And her tune goes as frantically jagged as anything Els has written.

Wait, he says, tipping his head to hear. *Keep going. I almost have it. You're saying, "I'm loved, and life is good!"*

The music collapses, suddenly bashful. She turns her face away from him, her mouth crumpled in a shy maybe.

FIVE YEARS IN the Fens apartment pass like the *Minute Waltz*. His fellow Illinois grads have scattered into university music labs across the U.S. He listens to their gnomic tapes, studies their gnostic scores. Musical resistance still strikes him as worthy. Between Nixon, the endless war, and a radio spectrum filled with bland self-pity and sales jingles, there's more to resist than ever. But he listens, and can't get traction.

One night, bent over the low kitchen radio, nursing a bowl of butter pecan while the ladies sleep, he hears the spectral wails of Crumb's *Black Angels*, for electric string quartet. Thirteen images from the dark land, barbaric and glorious, a system of proportions in the service of a spiritual impulse. The sounds come from another galaxy. Infinite sonic possibility unfurls in front of Els, and he can't move. He can't even think which way he *would* move, if he could.

The very next night—heaven's DJ toying with him—it's

George Rochberg's third string quartet. Rochberg, rigid seri-
alist, now serves up a bouquet reeking of lyric consonance,
right down to bald-faced imitations of Beethoven, Mahler,
and Brahms. It's like a heretic giving the benediction: a serious
composer surrendering, turning his back on the last hundred
years, and sinking into prettiness.

And yet: what courage in this backsliding. Els shakes his head
at the loveliness of the florid finale. It makes him remember
old pleasures condemned for reasons he can't now retrieve.
The piece sounds naïve at best, at worst banal. But strangely
willing to sing.

Afterward, the announcer explains: Rochberg's young son,
dead of a brain tumor. Now the archaic tonality makes perfect
sense. The real mystery is how Rochberg could write anything
at all. If something happened to Els's daughter, fast asleep on the
other side of the bedroom wall, composing would be done forever.

MUSIC GETS AWAY from him. In this one town alone, fantastic new inventions premiere every week at dozens of venues
on both sides of the Charles. From a distance, it's hard to tell
the Brahmins from the bohemians. Els no longer needs to; he
and his daughter wander hand in hand through the rose bower
in the Fens, chattering to each other in a secret language, collaborators in a whole new genre of spontaneous invention.

Let's make something, he tells her.

Make what? she asks.

He picks a fallen flower out of the dirt. *Let's make a rose
nobody knows.*

She pouts, lip like a slug. *What do you mean?*

Something good.

Good how? she says, but her face has already begun to guess.

Good slow, he suggests.

No, she corrects. *Good fast.*

Okay. Good fast. Something that's never been. You start.

She sings a little. He adds some notes. They walk and invent, and the day is the song they're making. They finish the piece at the keyboard when they get home.

IT BECOMES THEIR rolling litany. Let's make something. Make what? Something good. Good how? Good and grumpy? No: Good and gentle. Good and treelike. Good like a bird.

Maddy catches them out one evening, giggling at some private nonsense over dinner.

What is it with you two? What's the big secret these days?

Secret what? Els says, words that send his daughter into hysterics.

Sara holds her finger up, japing. Tips her head. *Secret good!*

Maddy swats at them. *Fine! Be that way.*

Jealous? Els asks.

Maddy stands and clears the dishes. *Forget I asked.*

Sara, anxious: *No, Mom! You can know. We're making things.*

What kind of things?

Songs. Songs that nobody knows.

HE FINDS THE girl on the day after Christmas, under the small blue spruce filled with popcorn strings and paper ornaments, laying out her new alphabet blocks in patterns on the floor. She spaces them at varied distances, in gaps that she adjusts and readjusts until each one is perfect.

Els watches awhile, but can't break the code. *Bear? What are you making?*

They're our songs, she tells him. *Look.*

And she shows him how the system works. The distance between blocks, the height in the line, the colors like the keys of her xylophone: she's invented notation. Written down secrets for the distant future, for no one, or for anyone who wants to hear. Els can't stop looking—at the blocks, at the score, at the girl. It's music from out of something that, a few dozen months before, was nothing but the sequences hidden in a single cell.

I wanted music to be the antidote to the familiar. That's how I became a terrorist.

We need a bigger place, Maddy says. *She's six. She can't keep sleeping in a walk-in closet.*

Beyond arguing. Yet moving out of their apartment for a larger one, down the Green Line toward Coolidge Corner, feels to Peter like a perp walk out of Eden at angel's sword point.

Sara starts school at New Morning, where Maddy is now assistant director for the arts. Quilting has fallen by the wayside. Els returns to part-time at the museum. He picks up more copy jobs; he spends weeks at a time transcribing other people's notes and articulations, bar by bar, into clean, perfect systems of staves. He loves the work, a chameleon trying on alien colors.

But at night, in an office carved out of the Brookline apartment's guest bedroom, Els starts work on his first real piece in three years. He tinkers after midnight, teetering between splendor and defeat. Over several weeks, a new style takes shape, one he only slowly begins to hear. Except the style isn't new at all. He remembers describing it to Richard Bonner almost a decade ago, on a dark, frozen campus in the middle of the cornfields.

He talks Maddy through the sketch—a piece for piano, clarinet, theremin, and soprano, to words from Kafka's "The Great Wall of China." The piece consists of regions of mutating rhythmic fragments dominated by fixed intervals, constantly cycled and transposed. The intervals build to a peak of dissonance before relaxing into something like denouement. There's no fixed tonality, but the sequence still propels the listener's ear through a gauntlet of expectation and surprise. The method feels like a way forward, a middle path between romantic indulgence and sterile algorithms, between the grip of the past and the cult of progress.

"The Great Wall" fits together, stone by stone. He plays sections for Maddy on their little forty-four-key electric piano, trying to get her to sight-sing. It's not hard, even for a voice that hasn't sung much in recent years. And it's interesting enough to go over well at one of the contemporary music venues in Cambridge or Kenmore. They'd only need two other players; Peter could manage the clarinet part himself.

You do not need to leave your room.
Only sit at your table and listen.

Don't even listen;
simply wait, be quiet,
still and solitary.

The world will offer itself to be unmasked.
It has no choice; it will roll in ecstasy at your feet.

Maddy nods at the guided tour. She smiles at his crimes and clever reconciliations. Her eyes spark with the memory of old campaigns the two of them waged together, not all that long ago. For a moment, her face is that humming girl's, the pageboy who was game to run through anything. But when they reach the end of the read-through, she's the assistant director of New Morning School's arts program again.

It's very intense, Peter. I wish I had time to learn it.

He finds a group of whacked-out New England Conservatory classico-jazzers, who program the piece on an evening at Brown Hall. The audience is the usual hardy few who frequent such premieres, hungry for some transcendent thing that the human mind may never produce. On the night of the premiere, Maddy begs off. *We can't take a six-year-old to a two-hour avant-garde concert. She'll melt down.*

Why should she be any different than everyone else? Peter asks.

His wife wants to smile, but can't quite manage. *I'm sorry*, she says. *We'll listen to the tape? Later?*

Sure, he answers. *All the time in the world.*

Wish me luck, he tells his daughter, on the way out the door.

No! Sara says. *No luck without me!*

The piece goes over better than Peter hoped. In fact, seated in the audience, he hears the clarinet slip free for a moment of the churn in the theremin and set off on a line that surprises him with its grace. He can hear all the sparkling false relations, the spin of a piano sequence that wants to get out and see the world. Edgy yeses; chance deliverance. And then, that glorious downbeat when the soprano wades in to wash it all away. For a moment, something: Something good. Good free. Good growing. The world at his feet.

The serialists in the audience smirk. The aleatory people are nonplussed. But two or three of the nonaligned are . . . well: call it moved. A fierce, redheaded ectomorph wrapped in a black knit shawl corners him afterward, her eyes alight.

It's about isolation, isn't it? The power of indifference.

She's a luscious vampire, craving anything with warm blood. Els's brain issues emergency orders to all provinces: drool, gape, grovel. It boggles him that a woman like this could want anything from any composer, let alone him.

Music isn't about *things,* he says. *It is things.*

She scrunches her face, flinches, and before Els can clarify, she corners the theremin player and asks him for a demo.

Peter comes home with phone numbers and dates for future concerts and even a business card from a conservatory dean, with a dangled half promise of a commission. He shows Maddy. *Musicians with business cards. Like little kids with car keys.*

Sara jumps, grabbing for the paper trinket. *I need that for me!*

He toys with his little girl, spider-style, then gives her the card. He doesn't need it, anyway.

Maddy puts a palm on Peter's chest, to slow him. He's flying, it's true. But he has received more adult attention tonight than he's gotten since he left school. Shocking, to feel how much he's missed it. A germ motif blows through his cortex, an old prophecy that he somehow forgot.

Maddy takes the dean's business card back from her objecting daughter. She studies it, excited. But she doesn't hum.

You think they might have something for you?

Two beats, and he decodes her. She means: a real job. She makes no open charge. She doesn't have to. He hasn't pulled his weight in their little workers' cooperative since Sara started preschool. Not unless you counted the hours spent staring at the brutal blank page, pushing note heads around on five-lined paper, trying to recover a fugitive language that no one would understand, even if he did discover its grammar. Clear, now: his wife has no reason to count those hours as anything other than an expensive and self-indulgent glass bead game.

The key was futility. Music, pointless music for a while, will all your cares beguile.

Trees, rolling hills, hours of speckled light, and a cottage stocked with food all confused him into forgetting he was a criminal. On the second morning, he walked at random into the national forest and found himself on a trail along a swollen creek. The trees were still leafing, and the stream cut through sandy outcrops the color of indolence.

Three miles down the trail, the gravity of his situation hit home. He imagined the charges against him. Obstructing a federal investigation. Evading arrest. Cultivating a known pathogen. Indulging in patent insanity. Even as he hiked, investigators pored over their labeled biohazard bags, looking for links to the multiple hospital deaths. Farce, calamity, and government agencies: it would make a great sequel to his one foray into opera.

He sat down on a rotting log gilled with lichen and fungi. All around him, new hardwoods greened out from the carpet of last year's dun leaves. The creek scouring its rocky bed sounded like things Els once made with computer-doctored tape loops.

A young couple came down the trail, waving a furtive hello. They glanced away, caught in guilty pleasure on this stolen weekday. When their high-tech jackets disappeared into the undergrowth, a great emptiness took hold of Els. He felt as thin, flaked, and shiny as gold leaf on a reclining Buddha.

He stood and stumbled back the way he came. The woods
were far from wild. Where deep blends of hemlock, oak, beech,
and pine once ran all the way to the seaboard, only a few managed stands of black cherry and maple remained. The public
owned the thin layer of topsoil, but the subsurface mineral
rights were in private hands. Drilling had started up again—
fracking, shale extraction—more ingenious gleaning, for fuels
ever harder to reach.

Chopin's prelude greeted him as he came through the cottage
door. The device went mute by the time he found it. Its screen
showed three missed calls from Klaudia, no messages. His finger
hovered on the callback button. But he couldn't cope yet with
any new developments.

He punched in his daughter's number. The keys bleated—a
retro audio joke—with the old dual-frequency touch tones
that had once delighted little Sara. Often in Brookline he'd
played phone-pad tunes to make her laugh, until a comic jig
he invented rang through to Emergency Services. Perhaps that
false alarm, decades old, still sat in some ancient police database.
There were composers from as late as the eighteenth century
who left behind no record beyond a baptismal entry. Even Beethoven had no birth certificate. But Els's footprints were everywhere. People three hundred years from now could discover
which performance of *The Rake's Progress* he'd bought online.

He needed only to hear Sara's voice. When they'd last talked,
he still had his house, innocence, and anonymity. His life's biggest crisis was choosing music for his dog's funeral. Since then
his brain had become a sustained cluster chord. Two minutes
of his fiercely sensible daughter would clear his head.

His finger stopped on Sara's sixth digit. He killed the device
and set it down. From what little Els had read, Patriot legislation

had ended the restrictions on search and seizure. If Joint Security
Task Force was trawling for his chatter, they'd be listening to
his daughter.

Els launched the phone's browser and searched again. Hits
on his name were growing as fast as any virulent culture. The
president of Verrata College promised full support for the
investigation and called on Peter Els to surrender for questioning. The online site where Els bought his custom DNA
claimed he'd given them a college lab procurement number.
That was a lie; anyone with a Visa could have bought everything he did.

A pop culture blog linked to a list of books raided from
Peter Els's house. *Good Germs, Bad Germs. Plagues and Peoples.*
Someone had cherry-picked the titles, out of a thousand books
in his library, for maximum fear and thrill. Coldberg, Mendoza,
and friends were leaking him. The government wanted him
hung in public.

He pecked terms into Kohlmann's phone—Els, *Serratia*,
Naxkohoman—until it dawned on him, late again, that his
every keystroke was settling forever into multiple server logs
that the FBI would comb through on no more grounds than
they'd used to raid his house. Somewhere out East—Maryland
or Virginia—and elsewhere out West—in the Bay Area, near
Sara—there were buildings, white and boxy, multistory, concrete, and windowless, where people at workstations in fluorescent cubicles eavesdropped on all the world's suspicious searches,
watching for patterns in the flow of hot words, a list that now
included *Els, Serratia,* and *Naxkohoman.* The logs would record
the machine that sent the queries. And the querying machine
had GPS tracking. If Klaudia's device could lead Els to this
cabin, it could lead the FBI to her device.

Els powered down the smartphone and pushed it across the breakfast nook. When he shut his eyes, he could see a cadre of hazmat suits dismantling the Kohlmanns' little house in the woods.

Heard melodies are sweet, but those unheard are sweeter.

The books on Els's shelves did tell a secret history, but one beyond any government's ability to control. Once he discovered the suppressed evidence, all the standard accounts of human affairs turned comical and self-serving. Trade, technology, nations, migrations, industry: the whole drama was really being orchestrated by Earth's five nonillion mutating microbes.

A year of reading, and the scales fell from Els's eyes. Bacteria decided wars, spurred development, and killed off empires. They determined who ate and who starved, who got rich and who sank into disease-ridden squalor. The mouth of any ten-year-old child housed twice as many bugs as there were people on the planet. Every human body depended on ten times more bacterial cells than human cells, and one hundred times more bacterial genes than human ones. Microbes orchestrated the expression of human DNA and regulated human metabolism. They *were* the ecosystem that we just lived in. We might go dancing, but they called the tune.

A short course in life at its true scale, and Els saw: Humanity would lose its war of purity against infection. The race now bunkered down behind the barricades, surrounded by illegals and sleeper cells of every imaginable strain. For two centuries, humans had dreamed of a germ-free world, and for a few years, people even deluded themselves into thinking that science had beaten the invaders. Now contagion was at the gates, the return of the repressed. Multiple resistant toxic strains were rising up like angry colonial subjects to swamp the imperial outposts. And in a way that Els could not quite dope out, the two nightmares infecting the panicked present—germs and jihadists—had somehow found their overlap in him.

None of the sites reporting on Peter Els's raided library mentioned those other books in his possession—battle manuals that agitated for all-out assault on the general public over the last hundred years. Boulez's *Orientations*. Schoenberg's *Harmonielehre*. Messiaen's *Technique de mon langage musical*. That war had ended long ago, and its struggles were of no consequence to any but the dead. When the body was under attack by invisible agents from every direction, why worry about a thing as vaporous as the soul?

Does it hurt to know that any piece of music, however sublime, can be turned into a unique large number?

A knock on the door and there's Richard Bonner, on the threshold of the Brookline apartment, which all at once feels like a bourgeois doll's house.

What's for dinner?

Peter can only stand and gape. At last his arms grapple at the ghost. *Jesus God, Richard! What are you doing here?*

If you don't love me anymore, I can leave.

But faster than Els can stand aside, the choreographer breezes in. With the briefest upbeat, Bonner is seducing the wife, pulling the daughter's pigtails and getting her to bark like a seal, criticizing the art on the walls, and rearranging the secondhand furniture to better effect.

At the sight of his old friend, arcs of color and readiness well up in Els. Summer camp tumbles down from out of the sky, and a thousand urgent projects enlist him. Years too late, the new decade comes to town. Richard is here; and with Richard near, a man might make anything.

Maddy is cross, behind her woozy smiles. *You might have given us a little warning. I'd have cooked you a real meal.*

Bonner leans his forehead against hers. *Zig when they think you'll zag. Creation's Rule Number Two.*

What's Number One? Els asks, willing to be this bent soul's straight man.

Zag when they think you'll zig.

Soon enough, over impromptu gin fizzes, the impresario gets everybody dressed up—a hobo tux for Peter, a feather boa for Maddy, and a crocodile tutu for the girl. He makes Sara fetch her long-outgrown toy piano. *Ready? The Twinkle Variations. Like there's no tomorrow. I'll sing!* What the duet lacks in grace they make up for in decibels. Sara slaps the plastic ivories, laughing like a banshee.

They sit down to leftovers. Richard never stops chattering, even to breathe. He brings the New England hicks up to date on every fad that has fluttered through Manhattan in the last few years. Stunned Sara can't even eat. She sits with fork halfway to open mouth, gazing at this trumpet-lipped, tangled-hair messenger who fills their dowdy apartment with news of a world so much wilder than hers.

Maddy suggests an after-dinner walk, but Richard waves her off. He produces a backpack full of other seductions—reel tapes, half-finished scripts, sketches, notations like secret code.

He pulls Els to the corner desk and commences the composer's reeducation.

He plays the spawn of Terry Riley's bit of West Coast craziness, *In C*. Gibson, Glass, Reich, Young: a whole school has formed while Els wasn't looking. Sara spins around giggling with her eyes closed in the middle of the living room, trancing out to the trippy hypnosis. Maddy, cleaning the dishes, stops long enough to cock an eyebrow at the proceedings: Relentless, no? Her look is schoolmarmish. But schoolmarming is what she does for a living. The former soprano, once game for any tune, now grins and shakes her head.

Richard lies back on the sofa, shifting in ecstasies. *You hear what this is, don't you?*

Boring? Els ventures. Banal arpeggios of little harmonic interest, looping over and over. Czerny on acid.

The first real revolution in music for fifty years.

Els tips his head and shrugs. But he keeps listening. If something is boring after two minutes, try it for four. If four, try eight. Music was never what he thought it was. Why should it start behaving now?

They listen as if the world is lost. They're back in school again, with all life's root discoveries still before them. The music makes time wax and wane like a fickle moon.

Maddy sweeps through the room, scooping up her daughter from her listening post on the rug. *Sorry, gentlemen, we need to sleep.*

No, gentlemen, Sara shouts. *We need more!*

Go ahead, Richard tells the ladies. His hand traces obeisant rococo curls. *Sleep away! You won't bother us a bit.*

Maddy kicks his shins, and the men kill the music. Mother

whisks her daughter off to her bedroom and the night's last story. But the men don't budge from their improvised atelier. The scores come out, and the two old collaborators go on murmuring by lamplight, long after both girls are safely asleep.

Bonner says: There's something going on in New York. The city is headed to hell. Homeless everywhere. Basic social fabric, unraveling. But the downtown performance scene has never been stronger. It's sprouting like toadstools on a grave.

Richard's sales pitch unfolds like one of those minimalist glaciers. The director has found a fairy godmother, appearing from an aerie in the upper altitudes of Central Park West to throw him some cash. She was waylaid by a piece of Bonner street theater involving one hundred volunteer dancers dressed in ordinary work clothes, planted throughout a square-block area of Midtown, who, at synchronized intervals during rush hour, turned to stone, as in a child's game of statue maker. The guerrilla ballet played for three straight days and ended without explanations just as word of the performance began to spread around town.

From the tenth-story window of her foundation's office on West Fifty-seventh, the fairy godmother chanced to glance down on dozens of sudden fossils. They gave her that goose-flesh feel of shared doom she looked for in art. She was moved, not so much by the freeze-ups themselves, but by the logistics that had gone into assembling so anonymous, ephemeral, and near-invisible a work. It took her three dozen phone calls to trace the insurgent dance back to its demented maker.

Now she's throwing money at me to turn it into a film!

Els shakes his head. *A film? Doesn't that defeat the whole purpose?*

But Bonner has no purpose. Bonner is pure energy, a taste

for prankish novelty, and a sense of bottomless despair when he isn't, as he still insists on calling it, *working*.

The two men take the crackpot notion out onto Beacon Street. They walk inbound, back toward the Fens. Bonner maps out a plan involving video cameras with long-focus lenses dangled out of forty-story windows, zooming in and out on the street below. He needs a musical score that can also zoom in and out on demand. He wants cycles within cycles, intricate, interlocking instrumental figurations, each recorded on separate tracks so the whole piece can materialize and dematerialize at will, the parts fading and surging, splitting off, then swelling again into a churning whole.

Sounds brilliant, Els says. *But why not get one of those New York minimalist guys to write it for you?*

Bonner freezes on the bridge over the MassPike, a sudden statue.

Well, fuck you, too.

Els recoils, stunned. It has taken him years to grasp the obvious: Richard Bonner is as thin-skinned as a child. The critics are powerless to harm him; he thrives on their attacks—the more vicious, the better. But a friend might scar the man for life without even knowing he'd drawn blood.

I happen to have, Els says, improvising, *several beautiful ideas that might work.*

Bonner starts up the parade again. *We don't need beauty, Maestro. We need music.*

Package deal. Just to be safe.

Safety will kill you, you know.

I'm aware. Creation's Rule Number Three.

They make their way home an hour before dawn. Els fashions a little nest for Richard on the sofa. The impresario sleeps

through the family's morning rituals and the departure for
school. And he's gone, on a train back to the city, by the time
Maddy returns home.

Does it help to know that any large number, however random, hides a masterpiece? All you need is the right player.

What can Els remember about that night's duet?

It's a real commission, he tells his wife, over the remains of a
curt ratatouille. They sit at that rickety green-painted table with
the Dover Thrift Edition of Emerson's *Nature* shimming up the
short leg. *A thousand bucks. Can you believe it?*

She looks at him over her drained wine glass, a nick in its cheap
rim. The look says: Really? The look says: Don't bullshit me.

*Of course, I'll have to spend a little time down there. Rehearsing
and recording.*

Peter, she says. The word is ancient. Weary.

Peter turns to his daughter. *Hey, Bear? Want to play something?
Maybe your new* Mikrokosmos *piece?* Sara pokes off to the other
room and its little upright piano, in that slurry of bliss and
caginess, the prelude to youth.

Maddy holds his gaze. *We can't live like this. You need to find
a job.*

A job? I've had six jobs in four years. I've been earning . . .

Something full-time, Peter. A career.

He looks through the window on the twilight neighborhood,
as if the threat emanated from outside. *I have a career.*

Maddy inspects her hands. *You have a daughter.*

The words enrage him. *I am a good father.*

Her fingers go up into her hair, rooting. She doesn't want to do this, either. It strikes Els then, or somewhere near then, that he hasn't heard her hum for more than a year.

She goes to the sink and fills it with pots and pans scavenged from a trio of thrift shops.

Look, Els says. *It's real money. A high-profile project in New York.*

Maddy sighs in the rising steam. *You could make more per hour by tuning pianos.*

He tries to remember when he last saw her quilting. A Romanian folk tune, harmonized in modal contrary motion, issues from the other room. The tune sounds to Peter like the final word on longing. Maybe he *should* make a living tuning pianos.

It's a step, he tells his wife, more gentle than defensive. *If the film runs . . . it might lead to . . .*

Woman washing dishes. Not softly.

Maddy, he's paying me . . .

Really, Peter? She turns to face him. *A thousand dollars? Minus commutes to New York? Train tickets, restaurants, hotel rooms . . . ?*

WHAT'S THE TIMBRE of this piece? Two slight instruments, say oboe and horn, their intervals trickling out through the open window into the vacant autumn courtyard. Two parents, keeping their voices low to keep from disturbing the rustic song their little girl plinks out in the adjoining room.

Peter's words are flinty. He tastes them as they leave his mouth, the tang of things to come. *You never liked him, did you?*

He feels himself serpentine. Creation's Rule Number One: Zag when they think you'll zig. But Maddy's surprise is honest, flushed out in the open.

Who—Richard? Richard's a perfectly charming poseur. He'll have all the fame he wants, soon.

I can't believe I'm hearing this. The man's our closest friend.

This isn't about Richard. You've had . . . you've been at this how long? And you've written half a dozen short pieces that have been played a total of five times.

His hands marimba. He reaches across the table for hers, then stops. For two measures, nothing.

And now I have a commission for something substantial. This is what we've been sacrificing for. A chance to break out.

Break out? She laughs a single, sharp high A. *Peter: It's experimental music. The game's over. Nobody's listening. They never will.*

So what are you saying? You want me to pitch it all?

Her head takes two full swings before he sees she's shaking it. Her lips form a stillborn smile. *Adulthood, Peter.*

The provable world holds her hostage, and she can't cross back over to him. Raising a child has brought her to this brute pragmatism. Any one of her needs make his look like puerile fantasy.

The girl wanders in, her body hunched and furtive. She takes his hands. *Dad? Can we make something?*

Make what? he's supposed to say. Instead, he says, *Soon, sweetie.* She goes back to the living room and pounds on the keys.

From the sink, Maddy says, *You could do what every other living composer has to do. Get a university job. And on your summer breaks . . .* She turns and holds her hands up, dripping dishwater. *Write whatever music floats your boat.*

The folk song from the other room breaks off in midphrase. Els cups his ears, then his nose. He breathes into the mask he's made. Then his fingers push up and over his forehead.

I could, he concedes. *But I'd need more pieces on my résumé. More performances. This film score would make me more competitive.*

Competitive! You've never even tried. How many positions have you applied for, in the last six years?

He feels no need to answer. He has fallen into a place equal parts panic and peace. He searches for a line of Cage: "Our poetry now is the realization that we possess nothing. Anything therefore is a delight." But the line won't save him.

What are you afraid of, Peter?

Failure. Success. The wisdom of crowds. Knowledge of what his notes must sound like, to everyone who isn't him.

Calamity from the living room: Sara slamming her patty-cake mitts across four octaves. In one smooth ball-change, Maddy turns back into supermom, gliding into the living room. *Hey, hey, hey. What are you doing, lady?*

I'm playing something and nobody's even hearing it!

That's as good as it gets, Peter Els wants to tell his daughter. Creation's Rule Number Four. Little girl, anywhere, without an audience: so long as no one listens, you're better than safe. You're free.

There is another world, the world in full. But it's folded up inside this one.

He couldn't stay in the cottage. If the Joint Task Force tracked him here, they'd trash the place without hesitation. Kohlmann would be drawn into the middle of his nightmare. She, too, might be held until cleared—an accessory to terror, the hidden half of the Naxkohoman sleeper cell.

For one more night, Els slept in the bed of his unmet bene-factors. He kept off the Web and ducked all calls from Klaudia. No more data hostages. The next morning, he scavenged a last breakfast and took stock. He had half a tank of gas, the clothes on his back, and Klaudia's smartphone, which he was now afraid to touch. In his wallet was the two hundred dollars he'd taken from the cash machine the morning of the raid.

The moment he used his credit card or withdrew more cash from an ATM, they had his coordinates. His every transaction went straight to searchable media—part of an electronic com-position too sprawling for any audience to hear.

He got in the Fiat and took the interstate back toward Nax-kohoman. On the outskirts of town, he followed the familiar state highway spur until he was twenty miles northeast of his house. And there, at the drive-through of a bank branch he often used, he took out another five hundred dollars, the most the machine allowed. From behind a window of smoky glass, a video camera turned him into a short film with no soundtrack aside from the Fiat's furtive engine.

The thousands of moving parts of the digital passacaglia, the packets of proliferating information, circulated in a way that he couldn't hope to understand. His plan was crudeness itself: keep moving, and leave as few footprints as possible. He pocketed the ejected stack of cash, glanced sideways into the dark lens, and rolled the Fiat back onto the road.

Two blocks from the bank, he stopped and gassed. He paid with his card, since his bread-crumb trail already led to this block. Do you need a printed receipt? No, thank you. Then he got back on I-80 west. The shallow meanders of highway focused him. He drove for a long time, emptied of thought, as marked as an endangered creature wearing a tracking tag.

In the afternoon, almost back to his Allegheny hideout, he pulled into a convenience center off the interstate. He bought gas again, paying in cash this time. Security cameras seemed harder to search than credit card databases. The store's smells left him faint with hunger. Amid the aisles of saturated fats and corn syrup he found a shelf of omegas and antioxidants, stranded through some demographic miscalculation. He stocked up, feeling oddly excited, as if on a long-delayed holiday escape with his national parks passport waiting to be stamped. The meal went down in four minutes, in the corner of the truck stop parking lot.

At the intersection with I-79, in a Zen trance, Els turned south. He followed the signs to Pittsburgh, guided by shaped chance. A rush hour construction snarl slowed him to a crawl. At last he broke and resorted to the radio.

The dial swarmed with ecstasy, dance, and rage. Els shied away from music, keeping to the shallows of talk. But the talk washed over him, unintelligible. Two think-tank economists had written a book arguing for the abolishment of the Department of Education. A congresswoman likened the EPA to al-Qaeda. A spokesman for a citizens' action group called the New Minutemen threatened reprisals if the President's fascist health care bill wasn't trashed. The spliced-together monologues played in his ears like an experimental radio theater piece from 1975.

The shakes set in as he hit that narrow finger of West Virginia. The sun had fallen, and his body was succumbing again to the absurdity of hunger. Somewhere in the dusk of eastern Ohio he pulled off at a rest stop. He ate dinner out of vending machines and slept in the reclined driver's seat, using a rain poncho he found in the trunk for warmth. Sleep went no

deeper than a series of loosely affiliated stupors. The envelope
of noise in which he floated—the grind of eighteen-wheelers,
the vampire cleaning crew who readied the facility for the next
day's assaults—combined in a spectral chorus. He came awake a
little after four a.m. hearing Penderecki's Hiroshima threnody,
a piece he hadn't listened to for twenty years.

Morning was long, flat, and straight, with the sun at his back.
A double dose of coffee, donuts, and headline radio powered
him through Columbus. The fragile alliance between Cairo's
Copts and Muslims was falling apart, days after they'd protected
each other from the regime's police. A twenty-five-year-old
Korean beat his mother to death for nagging him about computer games, then played on for hours, charging the session to
the dead woman's card.

Toward noon, outside a town called Little Vienna, long after
the AM chatter plunged him into his own chronic focal difficulty, Els heard his name coming out of the radio. Fatigue and
malnourishment couldn't explain the hallucination. A Pennsylvania college professor was wanted for questioning regarding
the deaths of nine Americans by bacterial contagion. And as
exhibit one of evidence against him, music poured out of the
car's five speakers. Twelve measures of baritone aria:

Nothing is more beautiful than terror,
More terrible than His coming.
All that is high will be made low . . .

The second act of *The Fowler's Snare*: John of Leiden, King
of the New Jerusalem, reaching his crazed zenith. The sole
recording Els knew of had sat in the bottom of a cardboard
box in his various closets for eighteen years. Some enterprising

journalist had found another copy and discovered the incrim- inating passage. The music had long gone unheard by all but a few listeners. Now it made its belated radio debut, for a panicked audience of hundreds of thousands.

Eighteen years on, Richard's libretto—that pastiche of Rilke and Isaiah—made Els wince. But the singer's expansion of the germ motif sounded righteous, even brazen. A good melody was a miracle, with all the surprise inevitability of a living thing. A strange sensation warmed him, and it took Els a moment to name it: pride.

The orchestration cut through his interstate haze—eighty people blowing and sawing away, while a lunatic praised the beauty of terror. The tune was a clear incitement to violence, and Els felt himself being hung in the court of public opinion. Contemporary opera making it onto AM radio: such was the power of threat Level Orange.

After twelve seconds—a broadcast eternity—the aria faded out. The news went on to a story about the boom in black market Adderall sweeping America's high schools. Els killed the radio. His hands bounced on the wheel. All at once, seventy seemed perilous. He eased his foot off the accelerator. A lion- maned woman on a cell in a dinged-up Volvo pulled out to pass him. A bulging Ford Expedition shot through behind her; two towheaded boys in the backseat flicked obscene gestures as they passed. A caravan filed by, each occupant turning to gawk at the gray-haired moving violation. Els looked down at his speedometer: he'd slowed to forty-eight. A lone highway cop, running his plates for going too slow, would finish him. "Prophet of Beautiful Terror, Apprehended."

By pure will, he forced the car back up to sixty-two. He flipped the radio on again and fished for pop tunes. He didn't stop until the gas tank made him. At a truck stop, he stocked up on shrink-wrapped sandwiches. Then he pressed on through Indiana into eastern Illinois. He pulled off for the night at a roadside motel on the north edge of Champaign-Urbana, not ten miles from where he met his wife, conceived his daughter, and befriended the one man in all the world whose opinion still mattered to him.

It seemed as good a place as any to be caught and held forever.

Listen deep down: most life happens on scales a million times smaller than ours.

He spent his nights composing for Richard. First the film soundtrack, then a pitched percussion accompaniment for a brittle but thrilling piece of voice theater that never made it beyond a few Village apartments. By then Els was going down to New York every few weeks. Maddy never tried to stop him; she was just his wife, after all. But she refused to drive him to the bus station. *This is your baby, Peter. You do what you need.*

At home, he worked at the electric piano, under headphones, deaf and muted to the world. Sara stamped on the floor in the next room, jealous of this thing he was trying to raise from the dead. Once she came to him and demanded, *Let's make something.*

Daddy is, Daddy said.

No, she shouted. *Something good.*

Good how?

Good like a rose that nobody knows.

They tried, but the rose had plans of its own.

Then one night Maddy, too, stopped by with a commission.

She came into his study, so much more slender and circum-
spect than she'd been in her grad student days, and grazed her
fingernails across his back. She glanced at his score in progress
and smiled, all their proxy skirmishes of the last few months
forgiven. *Write me a song,* she said.

She meant: Something singable, not art. No occult noises
for gatherings of alienated prestige-mongers. A tune that could
play on the radio, steeped in desire and mystery. The kind that
most people need and love.

Come on, write me something, she said. Almost soubrette again.
Something simple. Her eyes said: One last romp. Her mouth said:
Bet you can't.

PETER TOOK THE dare and slept on it. The next morning,
while guarding Titian's *Rape of Europa* from vandals, he fash-
ioned a melody out of all the rules from Intermediate Theory
that he'd long ago discarded. He built his air on top of an
expansive descending bass. Anchored by a stirring pedal point,
it leapt free to a surprise stunning chord right before the half
cadence. The irresistible hook, like a bruised cloud blowing
off in a June breeze, left behind a blue swathe that caught the
heart and lifted it into a bird's-eye view of things to come.
Song, just song, the enigma of it, the warmth and longing.
The three-minute forever.

He took the melody home with him, planed and trued it,
fitted it up with irresistible harmonies, and played it for his
wife. He had no words: only scat, on a melody that sounded
more discovered than invented. By the end, he had his two girls
singing descant on the chorus and laughing out loud.

Sara couldn't get enough of the trivial tune. Even Maddy was
caught humming the hook around the apartment. The earworm

was as brutal as a bad case of flu. Maddy shook her head at the song's total delight. *Oh, you missed your calling!*

So he had. A dozen such tunes over the course of a career, and he might even have saved lives.

The realization softened and saddened them both. *It's good, Peter*, Maddy admitted. *It's really good.* And for the first time in months, so were they.

Two days later, Peter told his wife that he needed to head down to New York again for a few days, to talk with Richard about a new ambitious work. Maddy recoiled from the announcement. She looked like he'd French-kissed her, only to bite through her tongue. But she recovered quickly enough.

Do what you like, she told him. But be ready to like whatever you do for a very long time.

Richard had secured funds from his fairy godmother to put together a chamber ballet oratorio based on the transhumanist Fyodorov. The plan called for five veterans from the Judson Dance Theater, eight Tribeca new music militants, and four singers—SATB—performing in shifts over the course of twelve hours. Els would do the music, of course: he was now part of the Bonner package deal. They called the project *Immortality for Beginners*.

Some new, brutal urgency was taking shape in a Lower Manhattan slammed by an oil crisis, mugged by inflation, tattooed with Day-Glo tags, whacked out on blow, buried under uncollected trash, and sliding into bankruptcy. Punk had blown the top of pop's skull off, and downtown concert music was on high alert. The scene was stripping down—postminimal, pulsed, machinic. The music grew a skin of brushed steel and smoky glass. It sounded to Els almost nostalgic, like a holy cantillation for a city slipping down into the East River ooze.

Richard kept a bed for Els in a third-floor studio above a junk shop on the Lower East Side. So long as you came and went in sunlight and kept the lock bar wedged against the front door, the place was as safe as houses. Els squatted there when he came to town to hammer out his cosmic collages with his collaborators. He could have stayed anywhere; he lived, in those days, inside his swirling Fyodorovian choruses, with their vision of an evolved future that would come to know all things, control all atoms, perfect the body, stop death, and revive every person who ever lived. The mad Russian's Common Cause spelled out everything Els had once wanted from music: the restoration of everything lost and the final defeat of time.

But immortality proved lethal. Maddy met every new announcement of another New York trip with stoic and pleasant nods. He'd spend the train ride down in awe of her, of her growing, no-nonsense poise. Her self-possession seemed the equal to every upheaval. She'd given him years to make his mark—so many of them—and he hadn't delivered. And yet there was nothing, absolutely nothing at all he could gift her back, except this holdout search for what the world wouldn't give.

One evening back in Brookline, Peter looked up from his score-in-progress to see New Morning's new principal across the room in a baggy cardigan, at work at her own desk on urgencies he knew nothing about. Camped at his feet, which she clung to these days, his third-grader was busy drawing maps of Umber, an invented world that Sara spent all her free time populating. Umber had races and nationalities, politics and languages, catastrophic wars and great eras of peace. It survived contagious pandemics and man-made depressions. It had folk songs for every race and an anthem for every nation.

Maddy worried about the girl's obsession with the place. But Peter wanted to tell his daughter: Yes: make something good. Live *there*.

And sitting at his desk, scoring his systems for half a handful of listeners, Peter realized that he lived on the very best planet available. Music was pouring out of him, music that danced and throbbed and shouted down every objection. Composing was all he wanted to do, all he *could* do, and he would do it now with all he had.

Maddy? he said.

She looked up, alerted by his gentleness.

We could live there. Start new. Just like—

Where? Sara asked, excited. *New York?*

Maddy's mouth twitched, ready to smile at the punch line. She didn't say: Don't be ridiculous, Peter. She didn't say: You know I can't leave my job. She didn't ask what the hell he was thinking. She just stared at him, incredulous and very, very tired.

The way he'd remembered it, everything happened in that shared glance. On that downbeat, he left a wife who'd given him a decade of unearned patience, abandoned a daughter who wanted only to make things with him, and stepped out into free fall. For nothing, for music, for a chance to make a little noise in this world. A noise that no one needed to hear.

For years, he blamed Fyodorov, those choruses from the growing oratorio, with their slow, progressing ecstasies as inevitable as death. Whatever we love will live again. Every disastrous adventure in this life would be cloned and resurrected. Everyone who ever lived would get a better second act. All his vanished lake-splashing cousins, his loner father and lonely mother, the teachers he needed to impress, the friends he never dared open to, the endless parade of museum visitors, mute and motionless as the paintings he guarded: all would be brought back to life and made whole. Countless failed hopes, forever redeemed by the right sequence of notes.

The way he saw it, Els was leaving nothing; there was nothing in life he *could* leave. He and his daughter would walk once more through the Victory Gardens, giving all the rose varieties ridiculous theme songs. He and his wife would sing together again, old inventions from student days. *Sooner or later, all men will do and know all things.*

All dead wrong, of course. Life turned out to be one shot, stray and mistaken, a single burst scattered on the air.

He held his wife's eyes, waiting for her to see.

Yes! his daughter shouted, from her pads full of scribbles on the floor. *Let's go someplace. Someplace good.*

But Maddy heard another tune, nearer and louder. *No,* she said. *Not me. I live here.*

HE TOOK HIS girl to her favorite soda fountain to tell her. He ordered her a Black Cow: a work of art that demanded every atom of her eight-year-old attention. He told her, *Your mother and I still love each other. And we both love you more than ever. It's just. She has work she has to do. And so do I.*

Hold it, the girl said.

Nothing's going to change. We'll still make things together. Still be like we always were.

Wait, Sara shouted. Soon the shout was full-voice shrieking. He couldn't make her stop, and when she did, the silence was worse. It said, as clear as silence ever said anything: Never ask me to make things with you again.

A grammar but no dictionary, sense but no meaning, urgency without need: music and the chemisty of cells.

Richard consoled Els, when he got the news. *Sorry, Maestro. I truly am. We loved that woman. I thought the three of us would be together forever.*

Thought wrong, Els told him.

Lost the one with the vagina, Richard said.

Looks that way.

And the kid. Oh, geez.

Bonner palmed his face and pressed long and hard. At last he said, *Well, you have your work. Maybe she'll come around.*

Peter Els joined the community of souls in orbit around Richard Bonner. He surrendered to a collaborative excitement not altogether distinguishable from panic. Inspiration came at him from the strangest places, and there were days when he could pull marvelous sequences of notes out of a subway conversation. He had his work, and there was no end of work, work so good that it felt, sometimes, like death.

ELS STILL SAW them often, his wife and daughter. But Maddy was no longer his wife, and six months on, Sara had fled to some farther, imaginary planet. Maddy wouldn't take the girl to New York. Els had to come up to Boston, staying in rentals in Somerville and Jamaica Plain. On his third visit after the separation, he asked the sullen child for the latest news from Umber. He always did. It was like asking how things were with her friends.

The girl gave a pragmatic shrug. *Bingo and Felicita went to war.*
Yes? Els said. *That's happened before, right?*

She shook her head. *They didn't stop, this time.*

By autumn, Sara asked to quit piano. Maddy, enlightened
educator, didn't resist. She and Peter fought about the decision
over the phone.

What a waste, he said. *She's twice as musical as I was at her age.
And . . . ?*

And she'll kick herself later, when she grows up.

His ex-wife said, *You want to give her adulthood without regret?*

Soon other crises made the piano seem child's play. The
girl swallowed a fistful of aspirin—*to see how it would feel*—and
wound up in the ER. She poured fingernail polish on a friend's
new platform shoes and called another girl she knew a limp
dildo.

A what? Peter asked his ex-wife. *Does she even know—*

I asked, Maddy interrupted. *She was a little hazy on the details.*

Peter's suggestions for how to handle the girl no longer
counted. He'd thrown away his vote the day he packed up his
four crates of salvage from the Brookline apartment. He was
the cause, and never again a cure.

Maddy stayed perfectly pleasant over the phone, and, in person, the most cheerful of distant acquaintances. The posture,
impeccable: Here's your daughter; have her back by dinner.
Graceful, stately. Maddy, too, had missed her calling. She should
never have left the stage.

She broke the news to Els long-distance, with the studied
levelheadedness that was now her art. She'd married Charlie
Pennel, the longtime superintendent of New Morning. Peter
knew the man. His wife had worked for him for years.

The ink on their divorce papers was still wet. *You might have told me in advance.*

Really, Peter? Why is that?

How long has this been in the works?

He could hear Maddy's amusement in her mouth's small muscles. *Peter! What are you suggesting?*

Not suggesting anything. You do what you need to.

I thought I might.

Every playful thing in her now disgusted him. He hung up. Ten minutes later he called her back to wish her well. He got her machine, and left no message.

He spent a week humiliating himself, calling old friends and neighbors, pretending to be catching up after years of neglect. Then he'd ask, stony-casual: *Did you make it to the wedding?* When at last he found a guest, he insisted on being tortured with a full description. The music was straight-up Mendelssohn, played by a small ensemble of gifted students from New Morning.

IMMORTALITY FOR BEGINNERS came to life, a vigorous corpse flower. Twelve hours of music was an eternity. Els wrote long, slowly mutating, terraced fantasias that pulsed and sighed and exploded. He scattered the peaks and valleys. He borrowed from voices dead for centuries and made them chatter posthumously. And he repeated, recombined, and looped everything until the whole was wide enough to stretch from dawn to dusk.

Bonner loved the finished score. He pointed to a favorite extended passage. *It's hilarious, Peter. I didn't know you were so nasty.*

What are you talking about? Els asked.

The question surprised Richard. *I thought . . . you mean this part isn't a parody of reactionary crap?*

No, Els told him. *It is reactionary crap.*

But Richard adored the eclectic score. His choreography was in-your-face, rancid, and divine: slung hips and puzzled arms, heads twisting in synchrony, glances raised and lowered like divine lunatics reading a celestial tabloid. He had to cycle the performers, who spelled each other out, relay-style, over the course of the monster marathon.

The piece took most of a year to put together, and it was over in a day. From sunrise to sunset on a Saturday in July, bewildered listeners filtered through a renovated warehouse loft in the old butter and eggs district, watching crazies proclaim the coming reconstruction, from pure information, of everyone who ever lived. Most stayed for a while and left shrugging, but a few souls camped out, lost in the endless middle of things. The *Times* review ran five hundred words. It admired the choreography's giddy novelty and called the music of thirty-nine-year-old Peter Els evasive, anachronistic, and at times oddly bracing. But this reviewer admits to leaving after an hour and fifty-three minutes.

The party afterward, in the gutted loft, lasted almost as long as the performance. Everyone was spent. Els pushed his way into the drained celebration. The Velvet Underground growled out of someone's cheap boom box, homesick and way too loud. Richard started throwing stuffed grape leaves at the bottles of wine lined up on a long sideboard across the room. Each time he knocked one down, he'd do a little Martian hornpipe and spout obscene rhymed couplets. The cast stood by, watching the show. Two male dancers started a color commentary.

That's what happens when you stop sleeping for two weeks.

And add some creative pharmacology.

Bonner heard the pair and began pelting them with crudités. A young, splay-toothed oboist named Penny came up to Richard, touched his elbow, and asked if he was okay. Bonner flipped the back of his hand as if to return a Ping-Pong ball and slapped the girl across her face. The room went dead, and Els, who'd known the man longest of anyone, stepped up to Richard and took his arm. The choreographer reeled on him.

Oh, fuck me with a rubber mallet! Look who's here. If it isn't the morals police.

Come on, Richard, Els said, working an arm around Bonner's shoulder. *Closing time.*

Bonner shoved him. *Don't touch me! Get your little chickenshit hands off* . . .

Els recoiled.

Richard pointed at him, his thumb a gun site. *You, my friend, will never be more than a polite mediocrity.*

The whole ensemble froze in a ring around the two men. Stunned dancers with daubs of face paint still rimming their eyes looked on as Lou Reed purred, "Shiny, shiny, shiny," into the echoing air. It might have been a coda to the Bonner staging that had just played for the last twelve hours.

Have I done something to you? Els asked. *Hurt you in some way?*

Someone said, *Finally lost it.* Someone said, *Make him puke; he'll be fine.*

Bonner aimed at Els and clicked off a shot with his finger. Then another.

Els said, *You didn't like the score? You should have told me months ago, when I could have done something about it.*

Bonner reeled on him. *You, my friend, will never make anything but steamy, creamy, lovely shit. Know why? You need to be loved too much.* He turned on the tittering audience: *Who wants to give*

*Tune Boy here a little love? Somebody? Anybody? Come on! He'll
trade you pretty things for it.*

Els held up his palms, like some medieval Jesus stepping from
the tomb. He turned and threaded his way out of the room,
pulling free of the few pairs of hands that tried to stop him.
And so beginner's immortality came to an end.

A WEEK LATER, Bonner traced Els through mutual friends
to the tenth floor of a Brutalist apartment block in Long Island
City and sent him a singing telegram: four white suburban
kids in tuxes crooning "You Always Hurt the One You Love."
Els didn't bother to reply.

He got a job working nights as a cake decorator for a bakery
in Queens. By day, he apprenticed as an unlicensed plumber's assistant, knocking around in a blasted van through the
Upper East Side, repairing the fixtures of the rich and famous.
Once he helped rebuild a shower stall for James Levine, who
looked frailer in person. He fraternized with no one but his
two plumber bosses, his geriatric neighbors, and the Domini-
can grocery cashiers who rang up his cold cuts and cereal. On
bad nights, when his body demanded release, he used the past:
Maddy as she was the night she sang his Borges songs.

From time to time, melodies occurred to him, broad melancholy phrases from places he'd forgotten—listening with
Clara, lessons with Kopacz, those years of war with Mattison,
the songs he and Sara used to improvise. He never bothered to
write the phrases down.

He did write one piece in those months, an odd, glinting setting of Pound's "An Immortality." On the day they met, Maddy
had coached Els on what a soprano could and couldn't do. Now
he took everything she'd told him and threw it away. He wrote

for a voice that could reach any note, one that might levitate the Pentagon if it wanted. He added two parts for unspecified instruments, lines that billowed like ribbons on the page. The harmonic language was a wash of things old, new, borrowed, and blue. It sounded like a troubadour song come loose in time. It sang of love and idleness; nothing else was worth the having.

He copied the chanson on cream-colored parchment and mailed it to his ex-wife. He dedicated it "To Madolyn Corr, on the occasion of her marriage. May the future change the past for the better." She never acknowledged receipt. Not long after Els sent the gift, he learned that Maddy, Sara, and Charlie Pennel were moving to the western suburbs of St. Louis to start an alternative school.

OUT IN THE void of the Central Time Zone, Sara rediscovered music. At eleven, Andy Gibb. At twelve, Anne Murray. Then came thirteen's key change. When she next came to visit him in New York, she was a torn T-shirted fake anarchist with "London Calling" on her Walkman, and he, an old guy whose music was worse than a museum. They were supposed to spend ten days together. They ran out of things to talk about in ten minutes. He took her around town. The only place that interested her was CBGB.

The second night of her stay, he told her, *Let's make something.*

She looked at him puzzled. She doped out the question and shuddered. *I'll pass, thanks.* A long week later, she was gone, and he didn't see her again for another year.

HE WORKED ON the edge of the city, celibate, for almost four years. He saved money. He listened to everything he could put his hands on. He stopped anticipating, stopped making edicts, stopped planning. Mostly, he waited. For what, he wasn't sure.

One April Saturday night, he swallowed half a hit of acid that he'd gotten two years earlier from the percussionist for *Immortality for Beginners*. Peter had hidden the tab away in his sock drawer, for when he felt equal to extinction. At some point in that year-long night, he found himself on top of a high-rise near Gantry Plaza, looking out over a silk sheet of water on a shimmering green quilt of a city. While he watched, the great, urgent message of the future took shape and revealed itself to all who could peel free from themselves and hear. Life was infinitely clear, infinitely redeeming. He scribbled the message into his pocket notebook, where he kept all his musical ideas. The words were a perfect mnemonic, and just rereading them would forever rejoin him to the endlessly brocading transfiguration. He would need only look at the words again a year from now, or fifty, and they'd turn his every anxiety into a matter for laughter and embrace.

The next day, he lay still and did nothing as his cells knitted back together. Then work took him up again. A week went by before he glanced into his notebook. There he discovered the magic reminder: "Keep living."

He heard about a cabin up in New Hampshire in the foothills of the White Mountains that a friend of his boss was trying to rent. The place was tiny, and a year's rent was less than he now paid every three months. All he needed was a reference, and his boss supplied one without reservation.

No offense, Mozart, but you aren't cut out for plumbing. You always struck me as more of the mad backwoodsman type.

Els packed up his half a dozen boxes of salvage. Clothes that would serve him for a few more years, until they dissolved from washing. Polaroids of his father and mother, sister and brother. A picture of a woman who had been his wife, with a gecko skull on her chest and a cicada in her hair. A stack of printed parts and handwritten scores. A quilt: Night in the Forest. Reels and cassettes of music of his that he no longer recognized. A song his seven-year-old daughter had written for him called "Good Days Are Best." And a scrap of torn cardboard that had once been part of an improvised toboggan. And still something in him waited to scribble down the tune that would raise every-one he ever knew from the dead and make them laugh with remembering.

If a lion could sing, we'd know it right away as a song.

Els went to New Hampshire to escape New York for a sea-son. He stayed ten years. Later, he could recite everything he did in that decade in a little under five minutes, and leave out nothing crucial.

And yet those years in the woods were the most productive of his life. He got stronger. He believed, for a while, in his body. In spring, he'd walk up into the White Mountains, into the vistas of Cole and Kensett and Durand. Twelve-mile days were his specialty. He composed as he hiked, and he kept his ideas intact until he got back to the bungalow. In summers he biked; in the autumn, he chopped wood. In winters, he shoveled out by hand the two-hundred-foot gravel drive that connected him to civilization.

He ate well, by the standards of the day. He read every work of eccentric history that the North Conway Public Library owned. That's how he met the librarian, Trish Sather, who soon began to visit Els at his bungalow twice a week, on nights when her husband and son had hockey practice. Trish would park a quarter mile from the house, fooling no one. Peter cooked for her, they'd have gentle sex, and if time remained, from their hundred minutes, they wound up talking books or playing backgammon. It was a kind of love, although neither ever used the word. Afterward, Trish would shoot home, push her bookmark forward thirty-five pages in *War and Peace* or *Crime and Punishment*, and settle at the kitchen table, ready to cheer her returning boys' triumphs and nurse their tragedies. Like the making of strange musics—their affair was a victimless crime.

Trish liked cowboy songs, and she played Els no end of the old high lonesome. Three sad ballads and they were stupid with desire, taking no more than the rest of the album side to find what they each needed. This happy arrangement lasted until the night, some twenty months on, when Trish, under the flannel sheets and topped by Maddy's quilt, stroking her pill-swollen breasts, said, *You don't really trust me, do you?*

What do you mean? he asked, knowing already.

You write music all day long, every day. Even Sundays. And you've never played me a single song.

Els went limp and sighed. The sound angered her.

What? I embarrass you? You think I'm too big a dipshit to get what you do?

He sat up, suddenly middle-aged. *There's nothing to get.*

You won't even let me try.

He looked around the room, his cabin. His soul was a house on fire, and he had to get out.

I don't have a tape player, he said.

She squinted at him. *In my car.*

They sat in her Gremlin, windows up and engine idling, surrounded by autumn and listening to warped, years-old tapes on a cheap deck. He played her the work he'd saved from the last quarter century. Greatest hits—maybe an hour's worth in all. He knew it would make her late, that she'd have to lie her way back into her own home. The last piece was a clear, high-voiced girl he once knew, singing, *Time is a fire that consumes me. But I am that fire.*

Bright sparks going over a mountainside. *Whelp,* he said, when the concert ended. *That's my life.*

She sat behind the wheel in the dark cab, her teeth clamped to a fingernail. She seemed more stymied than chagrined.

Well, shucky darn, Peter. Sometimes it's fine. But other times? It just sounds . . .

Like noise? he suggested.

Outside, the geese were heading south.

Els ended things two weeks later. Thereafter, he bought his books in garage sales and dime-store bins. Only when he heard that the Sathers had moved up to Burlington did he return to the library reading room.

CABIN ECCENTRICS WERE common in those parts, and the villagers knew his species. Word got around that he'd been some New York bohemian who had some kind of breakdown. One night, half crazed with loneliness, he wandered into a bingo game at the American Legion. His ear had grown acute with so much silence, and he heard a vet at a nearby table tell his wife, *Look who's here! The burnout artist.*

He lived simply, earning a little money as a builder's assistant and handyman for the elderly. He spent almost nothing, except for food and his criminally low rent. For a while, he tried to send Maddy child support, but she never cashed his checks.

When Sara was a sophomore in high school, she sent him a letter accusing him of being the reason why people thought she was a freak. He flew her out for a visit. For three days she lay on the couch, fiddling with a Rubik's Cube, answering his every suggested activity with, *No thanks; I'm good.* She listened to jackhammer, monochordal drones that he could hear through her earbuds from the other room.

The day before she flew back to Missouri, she asked, *Could you buy me a personal computer? Mom doesn't think I need one.*

You're interested in computers?

Her eyes swept up behind her lids. *Why is that so hard for people to believe?*

It's not at all, he said. *You can do amazing things with them.*

She lifted her head from the armrest of the couch, trying to spot the trap.

I once wrote music algorithms on some of the earliest mainframes.

Huh, she said. *That might have been cool.* And the duet was over for another year.

In New Hampshire's lost notch, Els's music abandoned all pretense of system. He fell back on a diversity that bordered on plagiarism. He'd lived all his life under the tyranny of originality. Now he was free to be as derivative as he needed.

The sketches began to flow again: a double concerto for bass clarinet and sopranino sax. *World Band*—a juggernaut symphonic pastiche that ran a fourteen-note motif through a dozen ethnic styles. A setting of Rupert Brooke's "Safety," for tenor and brass quintet:

Safe though all safety's lost; safe where men fall;
And if these poor limbs die, safest of all.

Els sent the score of *World Band* to an acquaintance from grad school who ran a festival in the Low Countries. Something in the piece—perhaps the virtuoso kitsch—caught on with a European audience tired of having to work so hard for pleasure. The new music ensemble that premiered it in Utrecht took it on tour, playing it throughout the Île-de-France and Rhineland. One day he got a royalty check for a little over four hundred dollars—about a tenth what his boyhood paper route paid him for the same number of hours' work. He pranced around the cabin cackling and rubbing his hands. Then he remembered God taunting the rabbi after his Sabbath hole in one: *So? Who you gonna tell?*

HIS BROTHER CALLED, out of the blue. Els hadn't spoken with him in three years. Paul's voice still sounded like a punk of ten, but with a finger dragging on the record.

Paulie! Jesus, how are you? I can't believe you're calling. Who died?

After five fat seconds of nonplussed silence, Paul replied, *Mom.*

Carrie Els Halverson had been visiting London with a high school girlfriend she'd rediscovered after her second husband Ronnie came out and left her. The two were inseparable, traveling together twice around the world. But this was Carrie's first trip to a country where they drove on the left, and on a pretty June morning in 1986, she stepped off a curb in Westminster and was hit by a cab that didn't even have time to sound its quaint horn.

Peter flew to England. Paul met him at Heathrow. He'd

grown so large, slow, and sallow that Peter didn't recognize him. Between them, they managed to contact their sister, in an ashram in Maharashtra. Susan sent back a muddled telegram, the last Els would ever receive, about how their mother hadn't died but was simply becoming something else. The brothers had the body cremated, and they spread the ashes illegally in a corner of Chelsea Physic Garden. This was on the second day of summer. The sky was ridiculous with blue. Peter tried to say a few words and found he couldn't. His brother touched his shoulder.

That's okay. I knew her, too.

In the three days they spent handling death's logistics, Peter was surprised to discover how much he enjoyed his adult brother. Paul swam in a sea of theories. Everything from the morning's headlines to the license plates of buses had hidden significance. But Paul's torrent of interpretations had something joyous to it. Buried patterns everywhere. It sounded, sometimes, almost like musicology.

They sat in a pub in Holborn the night before Paul's return home, drinking viscid beer and eating gravy-doused pastries. Paul shared some insights into the *Challenger* explosion and its relation to the Soviet adventure in Afghanistan. Peter gazed upon his brother's still-woolly head, now flecked with gray, and he regretted all the years they'd been out of touch. Paul had met his niece only twice. It took death to bring the brothers together.

Why is this, Paul? Peter asked.

Why is what?

Loners should stick together, shouldn't they?

The idea baffled the giant man. *They wouldn't be loners then, would they?*

Across the oaky pub, people at pushed-together tables sang

club football songs, swaying to more communal pleasure in three minutes than Peter's music had created in thirty years. Another sing-along poured from a television above the bar. Paul examined the bottom of his dinner plate for any revealing fragments of text.

Peter said, *Remember how angry you got, that I didn't understand rock and roll?*

His brother stopped investigating and frowned. *What are you talking about?*

You tied me up and forced me to listen.

Did I? Sheesh.

You threatened to wash my ears out with soap.

No, no. That must have been your other brother.

You were right, Paulie. I was deaf.

Paul waved him off. *Just as well you never got into that stuff. A lot of those songs use subliminal persuasion techniques.*

Serious?

Paul nodded. *The whole industry employs a fair amount of thought control, these days.*

Paul had never heard a note of Peter's adult compositions. He put Peter's vocation on par with their sister Susan's esoteric vision quests. It would have been fun to sit with Paul and some Boulez or Berio, to learn whatever secret messages he might hear.

What do you listen to now? Peter asked.

Paul set down the dinner plate, shook his head, and shot his little brother a quizzical smile. *I'm an adult, Petey. I listen to talk radio.*

THAT NIGHT, AS they went to bed in their shared room in a Bloomsbury B and B, Paul asked, *So how have you been making ends meet?*

I'm not, really, Peter confessed.

Well, you're all set now.

Peter stretched out on his lumpy twin bed. *What do you mean?*

Mom was sitting on a lot. Ridiculously overinsured, too. Even split three ways, you've got enough to keep on writing any weirdness you want for a good long while.

Peter sat up against the headboard, his hands cupping his ears, listening to the music of chance. His actuary brother lay in a bed three feet away, annotating newsweeklies in tiny, all-caps letters. A tune materialized in Peter's head from across a great distance. Placing it wasn't a problem. He could name that tune in one note.

'Kay, Paul announced, when his scribbling hand got sore. *Lights out.*

Peter lay in the dark, listening to the sounds of a Hammond chord organ as his parents sang. *There's a bower of roses by Ben-demeer's Stream*. His voice shocked the muted room.

What was Mom listening to these days?

From Paul's bed there came a muzzy, puzzled grunt. *I don't have the foggiest*. A snort of embarrassment turned into the simplest sob. Then nothing. Then a steady, pitched snore that kept Peter company long into the night.

Insecurity will always be a growth industry. The economy now depends on fear.

The evening had turned icy when he entered Illinois. Now he sat in the motel parking lot with the engine off, sealed in a cocoon of fogged glass. Starving, woozy, and saddle sore, he wiped a portal in the windshield and looked outside. Six feet above the car, against the wall of the faux-folksy chain motel, was a thing that looked like something NASA might send to the outer planets. Security camera. In another life, Els had read that the average city resident appeared on video a few hundred times a day. The fact hadn't bothered him, then.

Els flipped his collar up around his face, calling even more attention to himself, and stepped into the cold. Cars thrummed from the interstate and frontage road to the south. To the north, towering halogen streetlights illuminated a fairyland of chain stores. Down a car-choked gauntlet of stoplights there spread a copy of the same preassembled strip that seeped northward from Naxkohoman, emblazoned with logos that every toddler in the country learned along with her ABC's.

A street sign shone in the distance: Town Center Boulevard. When Els lived in this town, there'd been nothing here but the richest topsoil in the world, all the way to the horizon.

The lobby of the motel was a cartoon Southwest: quarry tile, muted earth tones, and above the reception desk, pastel paintings of Pueblos. He'd somehow wormholed through into Arizona. A circus-colored popcorn machine stood between the reception desk and a small breakfast area. The room stank of synthetic butter. A bowl of apples so perfect they might have been props for a musical about Eden sat on the reception desk. On the wall above, a flat-screen newscast split into three simultaneous video feeds with two text crawls and a title box beneath.

A twenty-five-year-old in T-shirt and blue blazer looked up from his computer and smiled. Els braced, but the clerk kept grinning.

Hey, there! What can I do you for tonight?

Els glanced over his shoulder, gauging the distance to the lobby door. *Would you have a single free?*

You might be in luck, the clerk said. He punched some keys and bugled victory. *Smoking or non?*

The clerk produced a sheet for Els to fill out. Name, address, phone, contact info, driver's license, make and model of car, plate number . . .

Els took the form and held it in front of him. *I'm paying cash.*

No problem! the clerk assured him.

Els stood, pen in hand, regarding the form. The clerk looked up from the computer and swiped the air.

Not to worry. It's just for the files.

Els filled in the form, inventing freely.

You have a loyalty card? the clerk asked. *Triple-A? Anything?*

Els blinked.

AARP? Maybe you left your card at home? No problemo. Ten percent off, for the man with the honest face.

Els traded his money for a key card. On the molding behind the desk, another little webcam glared at him with a cyclops eye.

The room was like the afterlife in a French existentialist novel. Bed, chair, bedside table, clock-radio, wall-mount TV. You could sail to the next galaxy in it, or serve out a life sentence in its minimum-security oblivion. Els showered, almost scalding himself. He lay in a towel on the bed and flipped on the television. He found the news channel, cowering between fourth-generation reality shows. The day's events unfolded in twenty-second clips. The screen filled with shaky footage from Cairo. Tens of thousands of people fanned out across Liberation Square, clapping, chanting, and marching. As in every large production Els had ever worked on, chaos called the tune. The demonstrators, after dwindling to a trickle, were back in force, in numbers beyond anything the nascent Arab Spring had yet seen. The military were changing sides; the protesters sensed triumph, and all because of one infectious melody.

With a quick crosscut, the scene turned into a Bollywood musical. A singer drifted his way across the square, singing an upbeat tune that could have been the theme song to a sitcom about young cosmopolitans enjoying their star-crossed lives. People held up hand-lettered signs. Vendors proffered food while lip-synching along. Old men in knit caps and women in headscarves mouthed the hopeful, defiant words, which scrolled across the bottom of the screen. The anthem had gone viral over the weekend, saving the revolution.

One more government brought down by a catchy hook. Another crosscut, and the song morphed back to reality. The crowd of euphoric protesters probed each other for clues to what would happen next. Els saw why Socrates wanted to ban all those modes.

But for now, the Cairo correspondent said, *this revolution seems to have turned around . . . on a song.*

Els stood, shut off the television, and found Kohlmann's phone. Merely powering it up created more traceable data. He didn't care. The phone played a little tune and reported eight missed calls and a dozen texts. He dialed.

Where are you? Klaudia said, before he heard a ring. *Are you all right?*

That had all the earmarks of a trick question. *I'm fine. I'm alive.*

Have you heard the latest?

Probably not, Els said.

All the IV bags from the Alabama deaths came from the same pharmacy.

Of course, Els said. *But let me guess: somehow that story isn't getting as much coverage as the first.*

They still haven't ruled out malicious tampering at the pharmacy site itself.

Oh, for God's sake.

The authorities are advising increased vigilance at similar facilities.

Giving the all clear, while asking everyone to stay terrified.

Your man from the FBI dropped by to talk. Somebody here must have alerted them about the class.

Oh, Christ.

He asked if we knew your whereabouts. He wanted to know if you were preaching anything crazy.

What did you tell him?

We told him it doesn't get crazier than Messiaen. Lisa Keane had some pretty good notes, which she shared with the man. Turns out he had someplace he needed to get to. You'd think we Q-tips terrified young people.

Did they ask about your phone?

Don't worry. If they do, I'll tell them you stole it.

I, too, had nothing to say, and I tried to say it as well as I could. What harm could so small a thing as saying nothing do to anyone?

Els stayed on in England after Paul flew home. Expense no longer mattered. He could stay for years now, without any sacrifice.

He saw the poster on a notice board in the back of St. Paul's. He might have created it by imagining. A concert: prestigious Baroque chamber ensemble playing works by unknown composers at St. Martin-in-the-Fields that Saturday. The music had no interest whatsoever for Els. But in the middle of the photo—a dozen musicians in concert dress—holding a cello, was the mother of Clara Reston.

Then the mother turned into the child. The girl had cut her four-foot fall of hair. She wore a tight perm now, silver-blond. Els rejected the evidence, until the evidence rejected every explanation except Clara.

He went to the concert. The two hours of formulaic music were shot through with fleeting, wild phrases and startling harmonies that wouldn't occur again until the twentieth century. Els couldn't decide what was clumsiness and what was neglected genius. It didn't matter: the night held out a string of misshapen pearls that might have gone forgotten forever.

All he could hear was the *Firebird*. Els couldn't take his eyes off the cellist. She stroked her instrument as she had at twenty, her graceful neck nuzzling the fingerboard. Something was different about her, aside from the hair and weight and middle age. It took Els many measures of Sweelinck to name it: she had turned mortal.

She was bolting from the church with her packed instrument when he found her. He stepped in front of her. She stopped, annoyed, and then, with a cry, she wrapped him in a bear hug without letting go of her cello. She stepped back, girlish, flushed, palm to her forehead, taking her own temperature. *I can't believe it. It's you!* Her accent had drifted British. Els wondered if she'd forgotten his name.

She pulled him down into a pew. *What are you doing in England?* The timbre of her voice said: You found me.

Els felt the strangest impulse to lie. To say he'd sought her out, that she was the reason for this, his first ever trip abroad.

But he told her of his mother. She cupped her mouth in pain, although Clara and Carrie Els had never been more than wary rivals.

But how did you know about the concert? she asked, when Els was done.

Pure chance.

Her eyes went wide, as if adulthood had taught her, too, that chance was an order no one could yet see.

They sat in the pew, racing through the last quarter century. Clara had lived three years for each of Els's one. She'd taken a First at Oxford. A year after their final disastrous phone call, she married a Rhodes Scholar, whom she divorced soon after, when he returned to the States to enter politics. Two years of graduate research at Cambridge; then something happened that she couldn't talk about, and she took off for the Continent. After a stint in the pit of the Zurich Opera, she bounced around Germany for a decade, playing with various broadcast orchestras. She auditioned for the Baroque ensemble, which had been her family for the last four years. She remarried, a British conductor six years younger than she was, with a growing reputation.

We're more good friends than . . . man and wife, anymore.

Els thrust his juddering hands into his pockets. *No children?*

She smiled. *When was that going to happen? You?*

A daughter, he told her. *Very bright. Angry at me. Studying computer science at Stanford.*

Not chemistry? Clara fixed her eyes on Els's shoulders.

No. It's machines, for her. At least they're predictable.

He looked away, into the cavernous space emptying of people. Up in the galleries and behind the choir, the wide window lancets were sheets of black. Buzz from the departing audience floated up into the flattened barrel vault and echoed off the clouds, shells, and cupids. Els gazed around the frowsty barn—half meeting house, half wedding cake. And he told her of his life.

Twenty-four years, and almost nothing to say. He'd studied composition, taken on the fierce cravings of the avant-garde. He'd worked a dozen jobs of no significance. He'd married, had a family, and abandoned it for a pile of mostly unplayed creations now almost four feet high.

All your fault, he said, warmed by a strange joy. *I would have been so much better off playing chamber music with my chemist colleagues on Saturday nights.*

Her bow hand found her neck. *I shipwrecked you!*

For years, all I wanted was to write music that would twist your gut.

You're doing pretty good now, she said.

But then . . . I got caught. You know: a certain rhythm, a sequence of intervals. And something would spring open, like the tumblers of a lock . . .

It was, he suddenly felt, as good a life as any. Spin the wheel, roll the twelve-sided dice, push them around, hoping to find the future. Even a three-minute piece could run to more permutations than there were atoms in the universe. And you got three-score years and ten, to find one that was sublime.

He heard himself bungling this, the explanation he thought he'd never get a chance to give. But Clara nodded; she'd always had a good ear. She stared off into the bare, paneled aisles. A laugh tore out of her, and she stood. She took him in one arm and her cello in the other, and hustled them from the church through the admiring thank-yous of the thinning crowd.

They wound up in a subterranean restaurant in St. Martin's Lane. It was dark, noisy, and indifferent, with candles and a tiny

Persian carpet on the table. Clara managed to be both measured and giddy. She ordered an expensive Bordeaux and offered a toast: *To unearned forgiveness. I was a monster, Peter. One confused little shit of a girl. Forgive me?*

Nothing to forgive, he said, but clinked her glass anyway.

They tried to talk music, but their worlds were separated by three centuries. They had no more common cause now than cannibals and missionaries. It stunned him; he'd misread her love of music from the start. Not revolutionary: recuperative. He'd gotten the whole game wrong. Still, her eyes were soft over the rim of her glass as he spoke of their old discoveries. Her mouth curled up with happy embarrassment.

What are you thinking? he demanded. *Where are you?*

At my house. Summer before college. Two babies! Listening to those Strauss songs.

He cringed in the dark, but corrected nothing. *I remember.*

Tell me about your music. I want to hear everything.

There wasn't a single score or recording on this island he could show her. At best, he could whistle her bits of tune—like selling your car by scratching off a few flecks of paint to show prospective buyers.

Funny, he said. *Right before I made this trip? I was just beginning to learn how music really worked.*

Clara's eyes widened. She pressed two fingers against her lips. *You have to come home with me! Oh, not . . . There's something I need to show you.*

She wouldn't tell him. They settled up and left the restaurant like runaways. Els sat on the wrong side of her Ford, driving with no steering wheel. He leaned back in the tunnel of London lights. Soon enough, she pulled up in front of a row of Georgian terraced houses. The inside felt like one of those London pocket museums. Old engravings covered the walls and the heavy furniture sprouted festoons. Even the foyer was a wonder cabinet. She'd stepped from their shared Levittown childhood into the highborn eighteenth century.

She nudged him into the sitting room and sat him in stuffed leather. Then she addressed a wall of floor-to-ceiling bookshelves. The thing she sought lay on an upper ledge, in a system of labeled cardboard coffers. She had to climb up a trolley ladder to reach it. The sight of her legs from under her concert black, ascending the rungs, threatened to kill him.

At last she waved something aloft, singing the first few notes of Bach's *Et Resurrexit*. She descended triumphant, crossed the room, and put the prize in his hands.

The sheets were a letter he'd posted to himself, into a distant future. His adolescent musical penmanship ambushed him. What do you think has become of the young and old men? And what do you think has become of the women and children? They are alive and well somewhere. But *somewhere* was an awfully big place.

He followed the staves of his first apprentice piece, laughing at all the car wrecks and crazy inspirations. Every choice seemed tender green and bumbling. But how much life the music had! How much hunger to give and excite. All his adult sophistication would never get it back.

All he could do was stare and grin. Young Turk, full of groundless optimism. Every single element of his style had changed. Music had been ground up in the mangle of years. And still he studied the notes, and learned.

He looked up, incredulous. *You kept this?*

Her head bobbed like a teenage girl's. Behind her, her shelves sagged under the legacies of a life richer than he could grasp. And yet, she'd saved this student sketch.

Why?

She took the score back and tugged him to the baby grand that dominated the adjacent room. She slipped off her concert heels and sat him on the piano bench.

Come on. Let's try it.

Clara laughed her way through the upper lines, leaning into the turns with gusto. Their hands collided as they staked out the keys, struggling to catch the boy's buckshot notes. Their shoulders pressed together, as if this four-hands act were their standard Saturday night ritual. They resumed the little phrase that they'd had to set aside for a moment, a quarter century before. All went onward and outward; nothing at all important had collapsed.

They crossed the finish line together in a rough approximation of what the boy might once have had in mind. Clara, gleeful, shook her head and patted the pages. *Great, isn't it? For a first go?*

Els shrugged. He needed to show her a quarter century of work that could vindicate this first attempt. She had shipwrecked him. But he wanted to prove that shipwreck might still be luckier than anyone could suppose.

Again! Clara insisted. And the second time through, the thing breathed.

She grabbed his wrist when they finished. *Peter! I'm so happy. I feel . . . retrieved.* She fell into a cloudy silence, head bowed, stroking the keys. *I'm surprised you'd even say boo to me.*

She took him into her tiny galley kitchen and opened a Château Margaux. Wine in hand, they toured her collection. Her walls were crowded with Renaissance woodcut processions and copperplate Baroque fêtes. Four small oils depicted saints in a rainbow of surprise. But the photos were what grabbed Els. He couldn't stop looking: Clara from every missing year. At twenty-five, in a sleeveless black dress, ridiculously confident and free. At thirty-two, in front of the castle in Prague, gemütlich but wary. A woman of thirty-nine, kissing the hand of Arvo Pärt, before anyone knew the man's name.

She returned to the kitchen and retrieved the bottle. *Come on,* she said, taking him by two fingers. *Something else to show you.* And she led him up the half-width staircase toward another forgotten thing, put on pause awhile, a lifetime back.

She sat him on her four-poster. They lay back, on top of the nineteenth century eiderdown. She kept his fingers. Els felt the wine, the distance of the past, this woman as familiar as breathing. He bought time, entertaining her with accounts of SoHo spectacles, Richard Bonner's paranoid flamboyance, the Brooke sonnet to safety that would never be heard. When he ran out of material he made things up, almost like a real composer. She laughed and drew his hand up underneath her concert shirtwaist.

They fell silent in the woozy warmth. Sobered, she took his hand away and studied it. *You could stay a bit,* she said. She flinched as she spoke, waiting to be berated.

Els steadied his glass and leaned against her. Alertness coursed through him. She was right: He could. There was nowhere in the world he had to get to. His passport was in his inside jacket pocket. No one waited for him anywhere. Home was a technicality, and the future held no real obligations aside from filing taxes and dying. The one inexplicable wound of his past had spontaneously healed. Nothing left to prove, and no one to impress or punish.

He felt impossibly cold. He heard her say, *You're shaking.*

Yes, he said. His arms and legs convulsed and wouldn't stop. Clara bent forward, then lowered herself to him. They clung without thought. She shifted to fit, and he matched her—a minimalist ballet. Both were where they had to get, and they stayed in that place, free from time, until the doorbell rang.

Clara leapt up and smoothed down her silk wrinkles to no effect. It was well after midnight. Her face flushed with apology. She pulled back her hair, pleaded with her eyes, and padded down the narrow stairwell in her stockings.

Els lay alone in the bedroom of a woman he didn't know from Eve. He looked up: triglyphs and metopes ringed the room, and below them, a light floral frieze. The cultivated serenity resembled something he might have guarded once, in his museum days. This was the room of the fearless girl of sixteen who'd taught him how to prize the new above all things. He rose from the bed and straightened the eiderdown. On the Belle Époque nightstand next to her pillow was a set of silver hairbrushes and an old edition of Jowett's Plato. Something clicked, and Els saw what he hadn't, all those years ago. Even as a girl, Clara Reston had hated the real world.

Voices issued from downstairs: two people, speaking low. Els heard only the cadence, but that was enough: a short comic opera of chirrups and murmurs. Warmth turned to confusion, then furtive explanation, then annoyance, wheedling standoff, and a tense good night. The door shut. Feet padded up the stairs, and Clara eased back into the room.

Her eyebrows rose as she crossed to him. *Sorry about that. Where were we?*

She took his fingers, the same fingers that had once frozen to the faceplate of a public phone, feeding it quarters on an arctic night weeks after the Cuban Missile Crisis. Now, through the walls of her Georgian terrace house, came elevated doses of radiation from Chernobyl, thirteen hundred miles away.

That was nothing, she told his hands.

He held still and supposed she was right.

This matters more.

For years, he'd tried to write music that would make this woman say those words. Now he didn't believe them. They were no better than that boy's apprentice piece—passionate but clumsy. The Clara he'd imagined for decades would have laughed at them.

Peter. You looked me up. Despite everything. It's astonishing.

He freed his hands. Hers patted the air between them.

I want you to know that nothing is off the table. Nothing is impossible.

I should go, he said.

Later, he couldn't remember getting downstairs. He did retain an image of her standing in the foyer saying, *Peter. This is wrong. Something brought you here. Don't throw this away.*

But he'd thrown away much worse already in his life, and the real cleaning hadn't even started. He scribbled his New Hampshire address on the back of his ticket stub. She didn't want to take it. He left it on the Empire guéridon at the foot of the stairs.

Thank you, he said. *For everything.*

He had a thought bordering on elation: even death was lucky, and no real loss. But nothing short of music could explain that thought to her. She was still shaking her head, unbelieving, when he pulled the door shut behind him.

·   ·   ·

HE NEVER SAW her again—not in this life, nor in any other, except on those nights when he lay awake sensing the piece he was supposed to write but had so far failed to find. But he did hear from her one more time. A package reached him in New Hampshire two years later, covered in Her Majesty's pastel silhouettes. In it was his apprentice piece, the song from "Song of Myself," the dare he'd taken from her once, at twenty-one. With it came a card, a picture of Mahler's composing hut at Maiernigg. Inside the card was a signed blank check drawn on an English bank. The note read, "This is a formal commission. I want you to set the next stanza. For clarinet, cello, voice, and whatever else you need. Three minutes minimum, please."

He'd known the poem by heart once but now had to look it up. The lines jumped off the page, setting themselves to a preexisting music. I depart as air. I bequeath myself to the dirt. If you want me again, look for me under your boot-soles.

He filled in the check for forty pounds, which he figured would cover the frozen phone call, twenty-five years of compounding interest, and international transfer fees. But he didn't cash it. He put it in a manila envelope along with his apprentice piece, Clara's card, her letter of commission, the Whitman lines, and a few quick sketches. He carried the packet around with him over the next twenty-five years, and it was sitting at peace in a four-drawer steel filing cabinet in Naxkohoman when the FBI raided his house in search of dangerous materials.

I hoped my nonsense pattern would have no effect at all.

It wasn't possible—getting lost in a simple grid where he'd lived for almost a decade. Like fumbling the notes to "Happy Birthday."

But the place had changed much more in forty-two years than Els had. New buildings everywhere, the visionary projects of discredited decades. The whole arts ghetto of shabby bungalows had been wiped out. Els searched for the house where he and Maddy first slept together. He couldn't even find the block it had stood on. The blocks themselves had been rearranged, taken over by behemoth enterprises of steel, stone, and bulletproof glass.

He stood on a small plaza in front of what claimed to be the Music Building. It looked like the love child of a logic problem and a crossword puzzle. Across the street, the fly towers of a massive performing arts complex stood against the night sky like three container ships on a collision course.

A string quartet carrying their instruments picked their way around him where he lingered on the sidewalk. They were all Asian and impossibly young. Two of them massaged four-inch touch screens with their thumbs. The violist slowed as she passed. *May I help?*

Els shook his head and tried to grin. He wanted to ask what they were rehearsing. Nothing from his era—of that he was sure. Those old manifestos would sound to these children like the crude stabs of a dulled cutting edge.

He ducked into the corner coffee shop—a watering hole for bohemians since long before Els arrived in town. He'd sat inside it a thousand and one times, hammering out the future of American music with those who were going to shape it with him. Everything about the place had changed, starting with the name. But it was still filled with twenty-year-old makers, plotting the revolution.

Els stood at the counter, staring up at a menu of hot beverages that took up the whole wall. Nine-tenths of the offerings hadn't existed the last time he stood in that spot and ordered. The current barista sported a spectacular geometric tat that ran like the Andes from the nape of her neck down into her chartreuse tank top and reappeared in the naked small of her back, above the drawstring of her pajama bottoms. Earth had nothing like her, in his youth. To go through life as a living work of art: it seemed to Els a splendid thing. He asked for a recommendation and she made him an echinacea.

Four dozen people spread through the dim rooms. No one so much as glanced in his direction, let alone pegged him as the deranged Pennsylvania bioterrorist. Bystander effect, Genovese syndrome. He was safest now in crowds. And crowds of the young, who tended to look away, embarrassed, from anyone careless enough to have let himself get old.

He found a corner and nursed his concoction, listening to ambient dub coming over the speakers. The tables were painted with wispy enamel scenes that spoke of psychosis or hallucinogens. Els's depicted a girl turning into a tree. At the next table—a pulsing bull's-eye—two earnest young Apollonians, one of each sex, pored over a score. Els eavesdropped and spied on the pages. The score—like every score these days—looked like a published work of art. Such typesetting would have cost him four months' rent, when he was the age of these children. The work was for chamber orchestra, lush with melodies that everyone in the audience would leave the hall humming. It contained just enough passing dissonance to reassure listeners that it had heard the rumors about the previous century.

Even little Darmstadt in the prairies: colonized by the same neoromantic loveliness that the whole world now embraced. Who gave those signals? *Everybody to the other side of the boat.* The boy pointed out ingenious features of the work while the woman studied and nodded. The piece's comeliness sounded in Els's ear, even over the café noise and the looping ambient dub. At twenty-five, Els would have found the thing insipid and reactionary. At seventy, he wished he'd written it at twenty-five.

Then, as if from embryo in Els's own fugitive mind, a solo soprano launched an open vowel on the air. *How . . .* The voice, like a sterilized needle. *Small.* The melody wove through the contours of a harmonic B minor scale, one word per note:

How small a thought it takes to fill a whole life.
How small a thought.

The boy at the next table stopped, ruffled by the sound. Then he returned to the systems under his hands. But the woman who'd no doubt share his bed tonight shushed him and pointed skyward. *What* is *this?*

Her lover glared and shook his head. After two more beats, Els said, *Reich. Wittgenstein. Proverb.*

The boy swung toward Els's table, glowering at a noise from the fourth dimension. The woman turned to Els and murmured, *Thank you.* She caught his eye a moment, confused about why she should recognize this total stranger.

The odds against my sequence doing anything biological were almost infinite. But *almost* doesn't count.

The soprano starts up again, repeating the same falling line. But now a second voice echoes her, a beat and a half behind. The two lines clasp and catch, throwing off sparks of consonance and dissonance, shocks made by a melody out of phase with itself. They cadence on a perfect fourth, joined by a ghostly double.

In the night café, students flirt and study and browse. They sit on barstools at a counter along the plate-glass window, each with a private clamshell, checking on the ten million Facebook frenemies they will meet in heaven. In a cushioned pit behind them, an apprentice engineer in down vest and cargo pants holds his head in his hands as equations proliferate on canary legal sheets all around him. A couple in the far corner are in tears. On an overstuffed sofa ten feet from Els, a woman presses her face into an old baize-bound book. The barista pins her tumbling hair back up with a chopstick. The music might be cha-cha, for all anyone hears. But it's a proverb from the year 1995: Dayton Accords. Oklahoma City. Nerve gas on the Tokyo subway. The first planet discovered outside the solar system. It's all, to Els, just yesterday, but to these café denizens, as quaint and sepia as any *March of Time* newsreel.

The echoing lines slow to half speed, reprising the song's first measures. Augmentation, it was called once, worlds ago, before MIDI. The two-part canon turns into a trio. Choirboy clarity thickens, then smears out as thin as gold leaf. The posters on the walls, the painted tables, the bodies huddled in booths and stretched out on sofas—everything around Els dissolves into wet crepe. The couple at the next table freeze, alerted. The woman's soul is all up in her ears. The boy leans forward in a frightened crouch; someone is doing a thing better than he ever will.

Voices align and interfere. Bliss starts to jar. The lines weave a standing wave, a sonic moiré. Then those pulsing chords cadence again at another perfect fourth.

An organ emerges from nowhere. It blends into the held pedal point while two tenors bob in parallel above. Els's lips twist in unwilling joy. The ancient harmonies spread through his bloodstream like an opiate. He grows light-headed on the parody, the imitation Pérotin, these sounds from the Notre Dame School, from the dawn of harmony. The bar lengths keep altering; Els can't hear how to count them. Soon counting doesn't matter. Time is nothing; only these changeless changes are real. The soprano lines echo and multiply:

How small a thought
It takes to fill
a whole life.

The twin tenors lift free above the organ's drone. There was a time—as recent as the year this music was written—when such an exercise in smoky nostalgia would have appalled Els. For years these canons would have sounded like pure kitsch, needing only a drum machine, a scratch track, and a little over-dubbed rap to become the latest caustic mashup.

Tonight, he finds it rebellious, even radical. Sopranos again, in unison: tandem seraphim floating through each other's lines, even slower now, at wider intervals, without a single breath. They sail up and above a vibraphone whose dotted rhythms turn the long sustains into a pocket infinity.

The raucous café—industrial frother jet on the espresso machine, clink of mugs and cups from the kitchen, laughter and shouted politics from the back room's upper loft—has no need of forever. Half the clientele have their own earbuds, the other half use this music, if at all, only as protection from the terrors of silence.

But these canons at unison glide on. Voices unfold above the driving vibes. Their intervals cycle through clashing dissonance. The collisions start to sound like a requiem for the millennium-long search for novel harmonies, a search now done. The sounds could be an elegy for those scant ten centuries when chant became melody, melody blossomed into harmony, and harmony pushed outward in ever more daring border raids on the forbidden. This innovative phasing piece, collapsing back into ars antiqua. Organum again: the sound of possibility, after the map of the possible is all filled in.

A girl at a nearby table bows over a textbook filled with symbols. She curls her hands around her mug campfire-style, warming them in the steam. She frees one hand to drag a highlighter over a crucial formula. She grabs the mug and sips, deaf to the record of that reckless rush of Western music that ran too fast from Dorian mode to Danger Mouse. But her head nods to the changing bar lines, under the spell of something she doesn't even know she hears.

Above the room's two dozen contrapuntal conversations, over the relentless vibraphones, the singers harp over and over on their lone idea:

How small
a thought
it takes
to fill
a whole
life.

The words rock and breathe. Els has seen the idea leaping through texts across two and a half millennia, from Antiphon and the Dhammapadas on through Maddy's beloved Merton. He himself has set those texts to music, banged on the doors of that smallest thought for his whole life without ever getting in. He'd wanted to be a chemist, to add to the world's useful knowledge. He'd wanted to repay his first love, the one who taught him how to listen. He'd wanted to see the world with his wife, to grow old with her; but he'd abandoned her after a dozen years. He'd never dared to want a daughter; then he had one, and afterward, he lived solely to make things with her. She'd grown up a thousand miles away, a holiday visitor, shoulders hunched and eyes wary, her hair hacked into different geometrical shapes each time he saw her, forever resenting that small thought that had taken over his life.

Pitches cluster above the throbbing vibes. The piece has lasted twice as long as any self-respecting song and shows no sign of stopping. A voice at the next table says, *Let's get out of here.* The boy points his rolled-up score at the ceiling. *Can't hear myself think!* The woman he'll lose but never quite forget smiles back, demurring. The boy stands and slips on his coat, halfway gone already. His friend takes longer to saddle up her backpack. Els watches, caught in the snare of these tangling lines. It's clear in the way she follows her love to the café's side door. She's reluctant to leave with the thousand-year secret about to be revealed.

She turns at the door, surprised by the song's sudden brightening. She catches Els's eye and frowns. He holds up two fingers in a covert wave. She waves back, baffled, and disappears into the night. She, too, will die wanting things she won't even be able to name. Her shed boyfriend will look forever for a music that will revive this night. A few steps into the embracing air outside this café and they'll both be bewildered, old.

Outside the picture window, a copper moonrise. It hangs above the horizon, four times bigger than it should be. A fist wheels and flickers in front of the reddish disc: a bat, hunting by echo-map, flying in paths so skittish they seem random.

A change of color pulls him back into the music. After so much phasing, circling around the same unchanging key, the switch to E flat minor comes like a thunderclap from a cartoon sky. Wittgenstein's proverb—that one small thought—darts off into unprepared regions. The effect electrifies Els: one simple veer that changes everything. Where the replicating voices once chased one another down broad meanders, now they turn and flow back upstream.

Melodic inversion: the oldest trick going. But it hits Els like naked truth. The sopranos chase each other up a cosmic staircase, driven higher by the lurching vibraphones. The phrases shorten and slow, like one of those boggling Einstein thought experiments with trains and clocks Els could never wrap his head around. Leading tones clash, hinged on the half step between natural and harmonic minors. How can simple, pulsing lines build to such tension, when they run nowhere at all?

Voices leapfrog into chords that alternate between hopeful and unbearable. He glances up again, but the music has made no more imprint on these rooms than would a stranger's death on the other side of the globe. The girl with the baize book searches the bottom of her mug for evidence into the theft of her cappuccino. The students with clamshells lined up in front of the plate-glass window haven't budged. The barista flirts

with the dishwasher, a Latino with a ponytail down to the tip
of his scapula. The engineer in cargo pants sleeps like a baby,
face pressed against his canary-yellow pad.

A stutter in the vibraphones propagates itself. And now the
meter, too, starts to evade Els. This phasing motor pattern
mutates, a slow metamorphosis, slipping from one crystal lat-
tice to another and another, turning into diamond under the
constant pressing. The three high voices braid upward, stepwise
by minor thirds, in a triple canon:

How
Small
A
Thought
It
Takes

Then the parallel tenors rush back in. Twelfth and twenty-
first centuries alternate, competing with each other. Those two
broad streams flow together into a further sea.

That glimpse of open ocean, at six minutes, lasts no more than
a few sustained measures. When the splendor passes, it beaches
Els again in this place, a visitor from the future come back to
intercept his own past. He sits here, years too late, knowing
everything. Music has turned out to be the very thing he was
taught to scorn. All his fellow composers have scattered on the
winds of changing taste. But the young are still here, still in a
hurry for transcendence, still ready to trade Now for something
a little more durable . . .

Through the picture window, the bat hangs motionless in

front of a frozen moon. Before Els can decide that he can't be
seeing right, the bat is gone. The sopranos start to swell again,

To
Fill
A
Whole
Life . . .

The words turn into open syllables. A moment of uncer-
tainty, a wavering between keys: Does that D want to return
to B minor, as in the beginning? Will the road lead back to
E-flat minor, or leap free into a wilder place? The path bends
again; E-flat in the soprano, followed immediately by a half
step lower, and he's flooded with loss, the sound of something
said that can never be taken back.

The dim rooms—these painted tables and ratty sofas, the
window-long counter, the sunken mosh pit, the booths with
their tawny lamps—fill up with generations, sitting beside Els.
He feels the hundreds of years of café debate, the thousands of
lives spent arguing over perfection. He hears the musical turf
wars that will rage on long after all the debaters are gone . . .
Those countless twenty-year-old songwriters, dead before he
came here, and those eager heirs who won't arrive for centuries
yet: they're all chattering on to each other, in the trance of these
phasing canons, the slowly changing chords of all the adamant,
brute-beautiful songs of the young still to come.

Another modulation, and the ghosts disperse. He wants the
piece to be over. Not because of the thrilling sameness: monotony could almost save him now. Because of the waves of connection lighting up long-dark regions in his head. He knows

better, but can't help it: these spinning, condensed ecstasies, this cascade of echoes, these abstract patterns without significance, this seamless breathing leaves him sure, one more time, of some lush design waiting for him.

Eleven minutes in—the endless dominant pedal point in the organ, the scraping seconds in the tenors—and the piece breaks through into a clearing. The three sopranos slow so much that their message stretches out almost past hearing:

H

o

w

s

m

a

l

l

a

t

h

o

u

Each change in the phased melody, now falling again, as it did in the beginning, flows through the bobbing tenor line. Figure swaps with ground, and back again. Tenors and sopranos envelop one another. Canon and organum at last merge. The two halves of this braid, across their eight-century gap, weave together so seamlessly it's clear now how they were shaped from the start solely for this reunion.

The piece spreads outward, its pitches like recombinant germs. The notes condense, incandescent. Shifting harmonies blaze into an old man's head. Layered parts swell and fall, split and multiply, collide and detonate, filling a life too small to hold them.

At a booth six feet away, a balding student of thirty sits in front of a brushed silver laptop, staring at Els. He's one of those brilliant Asperger cases who come to town to study political economy and stay forever, working for the rest of their lives as bag boys at the Co-op. He squints through his Lennon glasses, taking Els's measure. Then he bows his head and taps his keys.

A moment later, he peeks again. A glance at Els, a glance at his browser. Maybe it's nothing; Els has lost the ability to figure. He rises and drifts across the room, a diagonal feint toward the orders counter. There he comes about, back to his surveillant, and heads for the door. As he reaches it, the interminable quarter hour of proverb ends. Voices that poured in waves out of the café's speakers fall silent. Els keeps walking, past the creamery station, along the orders counter, through the packed and noisy tables, out into the bracing air.

He trots to the car, head down, feeling eyes on him. He reaches the Fiat and realizes where he is. Two hundred yards to the south is the Old Music Building, where he once lived. In a minute, he's standing in front of the Beaux Arts temple with Bach, Beethoven, Haydn, and Palestrina carved in the pediment. Palestrina no longer seems so laughable. Haydn now seems the odd man out. Another hundred years, and who knows? The group mind may scoff at that interloper, Bach.

He drifts behind the building to the Quad, that spot where the two long southern diagonals cross. The place where, once, in another life, on an ice-bound January night at the beginning of creation, a young man told him, *Half of life's problems would be solved if only one of us had a vagina.*

They form in front of him: his friend, his wife, his daughter. People who loved him, who believed he'd do good things. In the mild April mist, he thinks: All I ever wanted was to make one slight noise that might delight you all. How small a thought it took. How small a thought.

He stands on the X and stares down the long diagonals at the prospect of a life sentence. He can die in prison a public enemy, a musical Unabomber, reviled and ridiculed for a simple act of curiosity. Or he could try again.

Stray undergrads, their smartphones glowing, drift through the dark. The Asperger political economist in the Lennon glasses has already called in his coordinates. Someone has tracked the Pennsylvania plates and staked out his car. But for a moment, nothing can touch him. He was made for this fugitive life, destined for it four decades ago. Made to return here, da capo, after so long a time away. Made for art, made for memory, made for poetry, made for oblivion.

THE RECEPTION DESK is empty and breakfast not yet out when he comes down before dawn the next morning. He leaves his key card on the empty counter. And he's fifty miles west on I-72 before he admits to where he's going.

The only harmless works are sterilized, and the only safe listeners are dead.

His music changed during those years in the woods. He embraced those gestures that had threatened him only a few years before. Minimalist, with maximal yearnings. He layered ecstatic melodies over driving syncopations, as if something unparalleled were coming, right around the corner. Now and then, a piece got heard in New York or abroad. By the end of the globalizing eighties, Els had developed what, in the dim light of a few cryptlike new music venues, looked almost like a reputation.

Stretched out in a rocking chair one evening in the North Conway Public Library, taking a break from reading about medieval heretics, he spotted a baby-fat face sprouting out of the collar of a batik shirt on the cover of an arts magazine on the wall-length rack. The hairline had eroded and a pair of ridiculous blue goggles gave him the look of a cartoon professor. But the face japing at Els from across the room was as familiar as shame.

He crossed the room like a dancer in a trance and opened to the cover article. His eyes skipped across the page.

> Bonner's violent elation is among the few games in town grandiose and surreal enough to compete with this year's headlines . . . His limb-jutting, head-swiveling choruses dance through Tiananmen, chain across the Baltic states, and climb on the sledgehammered Berlin Wall, before most of us have even registered the events.

The list of the man's achievements read to Els like parody: a revival of Gershwin's *Oh, Kay!,* with the Prohibition bootleggers changed to South Bronx crack dealers. A Handel *Xerxes* that came straight from Idi Amin's Uganda. A Glimmerglass *succès de scandale* casting Nancy and Ron Reagan in a phantasmagoric

Verdi *Macbeth*. Bedlam-filled ballets featuring Iranian revolution-aries, prancing running backs, and camouflaged Sandinistas—spastic kaleidoscopes of rapture and cataclysm. A sidebar in large type quoted Bonner: "The best art always feeds gossip." The idea seemed to have earned him an international reputation.

In disbelief, Els tracked down every magazine mention of Richard Bonner that the library owned. So when, a couple of months later, early in the new year, Bonner came stumbling up Els's gravel drive near dusk, it seemed like just another *coup de théatre*. The diatribe started from twenty yards away.

How the fuck is anyone supposed to find this place? There aren't any house numbers. No damn street names. And you're living in some kind of reconditioned chicken coop.

Els stood in the door of his besieged home. Bonner jogged up and bear-mauled him. He kissed Els Russian-style. Then he shoved him back into the cabin.

Look at this: The works! Electricity. Furniture. Running water. I'm crushed, Maestro. I thought this was supposed to be the woods.

What are you doing here? Els asked. *How did you get my address?*

Bonner twisted Els's head one way then the other. *Hmm. This whole nature fad agrees with you.*

Els tore free. *Thought you'd just pop in, after six years? Seven?*

Bonner pouted and dropped his hand. *Could be.*

You remember the last thing you said to me?

Hey! Statute of limitations.

My music was shit and always would be.

I know. I'm a pig, aren't I?

Bonner broke away and toured the room. He picked up and sniffed a fireplace log. He ran his fingers down the spines of Els's books. He glanced out the window at some invisible assailant. The man had put on maybe thirty pounds.

Amazing trip up here, he said. *Got me a five-hour education in West Coast hip-hop.*

Bonner stopped fiddling, crossed to Els, and rested an elbow on each of his shoulders. *How would you like to help ruin my career?*

I take it you're staying for dinner, Els answered.

ELS POACHED A WHITEFISH. Richard contributed a bottle of Malbec out of the trunk of his car, two fistsfuls of dietary supplements, and an account of his latest coup. Els listened in monosyllables.

It seems, Richard said, *that City Opera wants a work for their 1993 season.*

Els had to laugh, and did.

I know, Bonner said. *Not possible, right? The kind of thing they offer to real artists. Not punk boho kids.*

Bravo, Richard. You've arrived. What's the piece?

You're not listening, dickhead.

And then Els was. The opera board had decided that a bankable iconoclast of Bonner's rep might revive a dying house on controversy alone. They'd given him carte blanche to settle on a libretto and choose a composer.

I told them I want you. They think I'm nuts.

Only when his chunk of fish went down did Els bother to say, *They're right.*

But they hired me to be nuts. You see the beauty here?

Night had fallen. Outside, above the town's holdout lights, the mountains darkened. A raiding raccoon clicked across the roof shingles. An owl sang half a mile away.

Don't make me beg, Bonner said.

When could I ever make you do anything?

Richard slumped back in the Shaker chair, his neck against

the top slat. *Something's happened, Peter. The game's gone flat. I'm playing myself. Formula transgression. Turn the crank, and out come the little predictable spurts of stylized outrage.*

Els stacked the dirty dinnerware, studying the problem as if it were the Sunday crossword.

Doesn't sound like anything I can help you with.

Richard manacled Els's wrist. *Don't game me, asshole. You want me to tell you I need you?*

Els withdrew his trapped wrist, sat, and steepled his fingers to his lips.

Don't give me that Buddha shit either, Bonner said. *You remember everything. We used to discover things. Laws of science. We worked for God, once, you and me. And anyone who didn't like it could go save themselves.*

As Els remembered it, God's preferences had been largely unknown to them. Yet he held still and listened.

Bonner slipped into a fantasia for the audience of one. *The whole globe's convulsing. But this country is walking around in a gauzy, super-sized, antidepressant-laced, MTV-fueled cocoon. Game Boys and Party Girls. Fuck: I'm not making art. I'm just the next consumer-friendly dose of distraction for people who're bored by halftime spectacles.*

You want something, Els said.

Bonner looked at him, startled by the insight. *Dying for it.*

And you don't know what.

Oh, but I do. I want to wake people from their dream of safety.

And you think I can help you do that.

You're the only person I've ever met who wants more than I do. Look at you! Not afraid to torch your entire life. Writing for no one.

Els didn't bother to correct either lie. He stood and took the dirty dishes into the kitchen. He returned with two cartons of ice cream and two spoons. Bonner grabbed a spoon and set to work on both cartons at once. Els just watched, thinking the man might be abusing some prescription drug.

He said, *You are a miserable human being. Why should I put myself through that again?*

Bonner nodded mid-scoop, agreeing with everything. *Because your stuff with me is the best work you've ever done.*

You've got a problem, Richard.

You don't say. Bonner raised his spoon in the air and sang, *News, news, news, news, news, news, news has a . . . has a . . . has a kind of mystery . . . !*

So what is it? You're a repressed queer? Is that your great secret?

Bonner swung the spoon like fencing foil. *Oh, fuck off. Queer, straight: Who makes these things up? Is anybody anything?*

You're manic?

Bonner dove back into the box. *What does that even mean?* He fished for bits of nut in the melting mass of cream. *We're either hungry or dead. Don't talk to me about finer distinctions.*

Els went back into the kitchen to put the kettle on and fill the sink with hot suds. A large mammal was foraging around the trash on the back porch. He didn't bother to scare it away. When he returned to the dining room with tea, Bonner was still launching his frontal assault on the melting cartons. Els picked up the other spoon and started in. He leaned on his elbows and poked at the butter pecan, as if conducting a flea orchestra.

Every time we've worked together, you've ended up insulting me.

Every time? Oh, come on. That's bullshit.

Els flipped the spoon across the room and stood. Bonner grabbed his hand.

Peter. I have to. Everything satisfying disgusts me. I have to keep . . .

Els sat and rested his hands in his lap. He stared at his small white draftsman's table in the next room. Bonner followed his gaze. A thought drifted through Els like a crane across a Chinese landscape painting. He held up a finger, and vanished. After some minutes, he returned with a square of torn cardboard.

Bonner took it. *What the hell's this? Some kind of concept piece?*

Els waited. Recognition was slow in coming.

Oh, Jesus. You're kidding me. You saved . . . ? Bonner started to laugh—stress hysterics. *Didn't I say you were the one person crazier than me?* He sobered, looked up at Els, and squinted.

Els squinted back. *How do you plan to sell City Opera on an unknown composer?*

I told them you were the only person I'd work with. Now shut the fuck up and let's make something.

Bonner tugged Els down the dark road where he'd left the rental. Then the two of them drove the quarter mile back up the hill into Els's driveway. Richard got out and took two hulking green duffel bags from the trunk. He offered one to Els. Peter looked at the vintage military issue stenciled with a long Polish name.

Are you moving in?

What's it to you, Maestro? Come on. Could you give me a hand, here?

Yes: I'm guilty of playing God. But thousands of such creatures have already been composed, and millions more are coming.

In the morning, when Els came out to the kitchen, Bonner was in the front room jabbing and thrusting. Els thought

another squirrel had come down the chimney at night and
Richard was chasing it. Richard loped around in a vulpine circle, then made several klutzy lunges. He looked like a teenage
boy writhing in a private sports fantasy. Els fought back a horrified laugh. The man was inventing. Coping. Call it dance.

That morning, they packed a lunch and walked through snow
calf-deep up into the mountains. Els figured Bonner would be
gasping for air after twenty minutes, but Richard held tough.
He talked straight through the two-hour climb, his words
steaming in the January air. He laid out what he wanted for
the opera. He'd spent his entire life fleeing from narrative, and
now he discovered, to his surprise, that it might not be too
late to embrace the kind of storytelling that the world craved.

Els proposed biography. The life of Thomas Merton—the
contemplative mystic who inspired millions with his thoughts
on inner divinity but who never contacted his own illegitimate
child. Bonner shot down the idea without explanation. Els then
suggested the chemist Gerhard Domagk, who tested his newly
discovered sulfa drug on his dying daughter, was arrested by
the Gestapo for winning a Nobel, and ended up aiding the
Nazi cause.

Where do you come up with these things? Bonner asked.

A guy can read a lot when he lives alone.

Bonner plowed through the drifts, considering. At last he
said, *No touching human intimacy. Let's face it, Maestro. Neither one
of us knows shit about being a human. Not our thing.*

Richard knew only that he wanted something epic—a story
that swept the cast up into a collective fate. Something that
would shatter the audience. Something with sweep.

Historical drama, Els said. *People at war with things as they are.*

That's it, Richard declared. *I knew you were my monkey.*

In the snow, dotted by long stretches of silence, Bonner's vague fancies solidified. Els listened, now and then interrogating. He led them up to a ledge overlooking Crawford Notch. They stopped to share hot noodle soup right out of the thermos. The gorge was luminous, blanketed with snow. Els kept telling Bonner to look, but Richard was busy.

Maybe the Challenger *explosion,* he said. *No, okay, you're right. How about the fall of one of these Eastern strongmen? Ceauşescu. Honecker.*

After half a dozen slugs of soup and several more proposals—Jonestown, the Red Brigade—Bonner grew fidgety. *I'm dying here, man. And you aren't helping.*

You want ecstasy, Els said. *Transcendence.*

Is that asking too much?

You want real opera.

Bonner nodded.

Real, all-out, outrageous opera, a hundred years out of date. But you're trapped in current events.

The words struck Bonner like a revelation. *Jesus, you're right. I'm stuck in the damn headlines.*

In the death grip of the present. When what you really want is Forever.

Maestro. Bonner put down the thermos. *I'm listening.*

Els gazed out on the pristine vista. *No contemporary politics. Something old. Alien. Uncanny.*

Go on, Bonner commanded. And Els did.

Siege of Münster, 1534.

Bonner held his frozen hands in the soup's steam and grinned. *Let's hear.*

They broke camp and headed back. The snow started up again, and darkness fell well before they reached the car. But by then both men were deep in details, lost to the clock. When they got back to the house, Bonner was faint with hunger. But he refused to break for dinner until Els finished the story.

Els sent him to bed with books. Richard read all night and didn't wake until noon the next day. Despite the hour, he insisted on his loping workout before the day could begin. Afterward, the two men began to outline a three-act libretto.

When they finished the outline two days later, red-eyed and covered in salt-and-pepper stubble, they looked like twin prophets of their own deranged sect.

I knew this already, Bonner said, tapping the sheaf of paper and shaking his head. *I was looking for this, before I even knew I was looking.*

He was still mystified as they packed the car. *This is it, Peter. Euphoria versus the State. Like the damn thing was waiting for us. How the hell did you ever come across it?*

I told you. Live alone, and you come across a lot.

The two men stood by the rental in puffy down coats, planning to meet again in another month, after Bonner had briefed the City Opera brass. Bonner wanted to draft the libretto himself. Using primary sources, he could have a first draft in three months. Els assured him that there was plenty of music to write, even in advance of the first words.

Richard got in the car and started it. The rental's tailpipe spit a plume into the clear air. Then the director got back out and grabbed the composer, as if they were still young.

Peter? Thank you.

Els waved him away. He stood until the car disappeared down the tree-lined road. Then he went back inside the cabin to the piece he'd been working on for months—the stacks of staff paper on his drawing table with their hundreds of sketches for the first act of that same opera the two men had just mapped out together.

Life fills the world with copies of itself. Music and viruses both trick their hosts into copying them.

The radio names him twice in the first two hours out of Champaign. A government spokesperson says that scientists are trying to determine if the bacteria taken from the home of Peter Els, the so-called Biohacker Bach, have in fact been genetically altered. Els waits for the speaker to admit that the strain that killed the patients in Alabama wasn't his. Instead, the announcer returns to say that, in yet more bacterial news, the deadly outbreak of *E. coli* in Germany may have come from tainted Spanish vegetables.

Through the Fiat's windows, miles of stark black tillage begin to green. Nothing about the spare beauty looks like a country under any kind of threat. But at ten a.m., on a syndicated public radio interview program, Els learns just what he has unleashed.

The show is on the dangers of garage biology. *A rash of hospital deaths*, the host begins. *Supermarket contaminations in several countries. A do-it-yourself genetic engineer working with toxic microbes, now on the run from the authorities.* The sounds reach Els from a great distance, as if the whole segment is one of those sampled, chopped-up, looped, and reassembled song quilts that are again all the rage, half a century after their invention. *How scared by all of these stories should you be?*

For insight, the host welcomes a Bay Area writer whose book on the growing amateur microbiology movement Els has read. The man talks of garage scientists numbering in the thousands.

Who are these people? the host asks.

The writer gives a frustrated chuckle. *Lots of folks. Libertarians, hobbyists, students, entrepreneurs, activists. They're old-style citizen scientists in the spirit of Jenner and Mendel. This is cheap, democratic, participatory biotech. Closing it down would be a mistake.*

The show turns to the director of a safety watchdog group, who maps out the worst-case scenario. *The problem is,* she says, *between mail-order synthetic DNA and a kitchen stocked with a thousand dollars of gear, an amateur could create a new lethal pathogen. Given how many people want to harm this country, biopunk is one of the greatest threats facing us.*

The writer laughs her off. *Skiing is hundreds of times more dangerous.*

A bipartisan Washington commission on WMDs and terrorism predicts a major bioterror attack in the next couple of years, the watchdog says.

The host asks, *What can we do to prevent that?*

We need to build on the success of the TSA, the watchdog answers.

The writer howls. *The TSA hasn't detected a single terrorist action since its inception!*

That proves their effectiveness.

The host throws open the call-in lines. The first caller asks if this killer *E. coli* in Europe is a terrorist act. Both experts say no. The caller hangs up unconvinced.

Els hears the next caller's fury before she speaks three words. *This man,* she says, *creating germs in his own laboratory—people have died, and this man needs to be found and stopped before he harms anyone else.*

The host asks his guests to comment. The watchdog says, *At very best, this is a case of an amateur modifying a toxic microorganism without really knowing—*

The writer cuts in: *Amgen does that all the time. Monsanto. Half our corn and ninety percent of our soybeans are biohacked, and we put them in our mouths on blind faith.*

Amgen is run by trained scientists, not a retired musician working at the kitchen sink with no idea what he's doing.

Trained scientists have produced more disasters than all the amateurs combined.

The blast of an air horn like something out of *Götterdäm-merung* drives Els across the lane. In his rearview mirror, an eighteen-wheeler rides up his tailpipe. He jerks right. The semi blasts past him, wailing. When the truck pulls back in front of Els, the driver hits the brakes. The front of the Fiat kisses the truck's bumper.

The watchdog is talking. *He has panicked the whole nation.*

The nation has been panicked for ten years. And if spreading panic is the measure, every news anchor is a terrorist.

The host patches in another caller. A trembling woman says that scientists were behind the earthquake and tsunami in Japan.

Els pulls one stuck hand off the wheel and kills the radio. An exit floats into view, and he takes it. He hits the rumble strip twice on his way up the ramp. He follows a local road for a long time, trying to regain control of his body. He pulls into a gas station in Vandalia that clings to the intersection of two empty state highways. He fills the tank and hands the cash to a bearded anarchist who looks like he wouldn't turn in Hitler.

Els sits at a picnic table behind the station, under a blue spruce, nursing a turkey wrap and flipping through a copy of the *Times* that the convenience center stocked by accident. He finds himself on page A10: "Homebrew Genetic Modifier Heard

Beat of Different Drummer." The article psychoanalyzes Peter
Els's biohacking by considering his decades of audience-hostile
avant-garde creations. A little vomit spasms into Els's mouth. He
folds up the paper and leaves it on the picnic table, under a stone.

He opens the door to the Fiat, and a voice shouts, *Hey!* Els
turns, hands rising. The wild-bearded anarchist stands in the
doorway of the gas station, rigid. It's a relief, almost, caught at
last. The fugitive motif has gone on too long. He's tired. He
smiles at his accoster, surrendering.

I forgot, the man says. *You get a free drink with that turkey thingie.*

Els sits in the parked car, his hands revolting. The free drink,
his alibi, splatters when he brings it to his lips. Through the
windshield, he watches a family of four parade into the convenience mart. The little girl, her sweatshirt advertising a mega-
church, fixes him in a telephoto gaze. Arrest is just a matter
of time. What he has done and what he has failed to do must
both be paid for. The good of the many demands it.

Kohlmann's phone has ridden beside him on the death seat
since Champaign. He takes it and turns it on. Too late for the
traceable device to hurt him. He has only eighty miles to St.
Louis, and his destination. The Joint Task Force can have him,
once he finishes there.

His fingers flail at the on-screen keys. He punches in an
address memorized years ago. It has always been a little fictional,
no place he would live to see. But the Voice figures out the
route in seconds, door to door. All he needs to do is accept the
GPS's higher power.

The route unfolds in front of him—an hour and a half. His
limbs are clammy and his skin metallic. He pries open the glove
compartment. A stack of loose CDs spill out onto the passenger
side floor, none of them what he needs. He leans over into the

chaos-strewn backseat and rakes through dozens more cracked and unhinging jewel boxes, finding nothing that can help him.

Then he remembers: all the tunes in the world are his. He plugs the smartphone into the car stereo and pecks in his search. The piece bubbles up with a few pokes of his index finger. It's music that will get him as far as he needs to go. Shostakovich's Fifth—a condemned man writing the accompaniment to his own execution.

Serratia can split several times an hour, when conditions are right. Double a few times, and soon you're talking real numbers.

The overture begins with almost nothing: one oboe, one English horn, and one bassoon. They play in unison at first, a theme filled with anticipation borrowed from a mass by Ockeghem. The unison divides; one melody becomes two, then two become four, rising and stretching. Dawn in the free city of Münster, Northern Rhineland, January 1534.

The first tradesmen trickle through the Prinzipalmarkt. Vendors set up their stalls, and customers congregate. Two violas join the reed trio. An ermine-trimmed noble draws a retinue across the market square to a swell in the trombones and cellos. Over the course of several dozen patient measures, dawn turns into full-on morning.

Streets radiate from the prosperous plaza, lined by step-gabled houses and pinnacled façades. To the east, the commanding Gothic Rathaus. To the north, the cathedral spire. Brisk commerce fills the marketplace. The orchestra begins a vast prolation canon—copies of a single germ, sped up or slowed down, pitched at various intervals. The tangle of lines gives way to pulsing chords. Then the shock of a baritone cuts through the sound:

Fire, air, the rain, the sun—the Lord made all things common,
    for our shared joy.

The fireplug preacher Rothmann, in his dark robes, mounts the stone bank rimming the plaza's fountain.

Whoever says "This is mine, that is yours"—that man steals
    from you!

Some of the chorus stop their buying and selling long enough to shush him. They sing of recent calamities throughout the empire that must not reawaken. Rothmann's baritone shines out above them.

God gave us the world, whole. We've wrecked it, and fight over
    the crumbs. No wonder you're miserable—all of you!

A trio of merchants caution the preacher, above the massed strings. They say the years of chaos must stop. The city needs peace and prosperity; all else is rabble-rousing noise. The words form islands of triadic consonance in the orchestra's atonal surge.

Others come to Rothmann's defense. *The man hurts no one. Let him preach what heaven tells him.* The merchant trio become a sextet, a plea for harmony, productivity, wealth. But the preacher laughs them off in a swelling solo:

Peaceful? Productive? The Prince-Bishop wants you productive!
    Producing for the Prince. Fools! For peace, you've traded
    away your souls.

The ill, the oppressed, the unemployed, and the merely spiritual begin to flock to Rothmann's side. Old clashes break out across the stage. The cast splits into a freewheeling double chorus, its two factions feeding the rising excitement. Chords stack up and melodies clash above a turning ground bass. Each time the cycling figure returns, its texture thickens. Rothmann shouts above the fray—curt and thrilling melodic anagrams of the original, aching theme.

> *God put joy into your body—real joy! Live in the light. Live*
> *in full beauty. Live in the common air.*

A sudden modulation into a remote harmonic region, and four men on horseback appear from the wings. At their head is the tailor's apprentice, John of Leiden, a charismatic man with a flowing beard. To a brass fanfare, in a heroic tenor, he leads his posse in a motet. They come from the Netherlands at the bidding of Jan Matthias, the baker turned prophet, who has identified Münster as the place where God will begin the world's end. Rothmann, they sing, is clearing the way for the long-delayed heavenly kingdom.

Rothmann embraces them, and together, in long, brazen lines of modal melody, they sing in ecstatic counterpoint:

> *Mine and Thine, Thine and*
>   *Mine?*
> *Live in light! Live in beauty!*
> *There is no life without dying*
>   *into the One.*
> *Where else to place your hope,*
>   *your joy, your love?*

> *One false world is ending,*
> *The true one will soon arrive.*
> *No fulfillment but in hunger.*
> *No safety but through danger.*
> *Ready yourself: the day is*
>   *here.*

In the building passacaglia, Rothmann works his way downstage to join John of Leiden. He asks the prophet to baptize
him again, to give him the danger of rebirth. He and John
sing a buoyant duet, each line based on a different tetrachord.
John leads Rothmann to center stage and into the marketplace
fountain. The singing stops and the orchestra falls silent.

A solo cello starts up Luther's baptismal chorale, *Christ unser
Herr zum Jordan kam*. The two men enter the fountain up to
their waists. A second cello harmonizes the first in simple fifths
and thirds. The Dutchman lowers Rothmann until the preacher
goes under. Strings now play all four lines of the chorale, its
harmonies nudged by accidentals into a mad experiment. Rothmann stays underwater way too long. He lunges back up, gasping and dripping. The orchestra launches a triumphant treatment
of the chorale in the driving harmonies from the early 1990s,
the sounds of the falling Wall.

The spectacle awes the market crowd. An old woman asks
for her own full immersion. She sings the most haunting aria
of the first act: *So near the grave, I find this birth*. Together, John
of Leiden and Rothmann baptize her. Two weeping girls in
their teens demand to be next, while tradesmen stop to witness.

A trill in the flutes alerts the stage. The woodwinds rush
forward through a flurry in the horns. A march unfolds, so
forceful that even the skeptics are caught up in it. More bodies
plunge into the fountain. The reborn emerge from the water
and wander offstage in a state of grace. Once in the wings, they
run back behind the flats, slip into dry clothes, and reenter stage
right, as newcomers to the commotion. So the chorus multiplies
until belief is everywhere.

The march carries the crowd along on a public flood. A clear
key—E major—emerges, rich with the vengeance of shared

faith. Believers and unbelievers, foreigners and natives, prophets and merchants, the elect and the damned, swirl together in a frenzied tutti.

By now even the untrained ear can hear how all the scene's material—the opening theme, Rothmann's aria, John of Leiden's motif, and Luther's chorale—fit together into this gathering chorus. As the ever-renewing crowd plunges into the pool, Rothmann and the Dutch messengers, lifted up by the circling strings, sing a simple, unison, Gothic lullaby drawn from the words of Saint Paul:

Darkness is passing,
The night is over,
A new dawn makes its way.

My piece might be all around you, and you'll never know. Cellular songs everywhere, by the hundreds of millions.

The terror of an empty auditorium, two weeks before opening. Two thousand five hundred empty seats. Four and a half rings of balcony, stacked up like a beehive. Scattered bodies dot the sea of red. Els cowers near the front of the house while, onstage, dozens of builders put the last touches on the City of God.

He has needed forty months to deliver 170 minutes of music. During those years, the war that has lasted since his childhood comes to an end. The evil empire crumbles into a dozen-plus countries. All the world's data weaves together into a web. In the desert on the far side of the planet, Els's country goes to war, made godlike by technology. The apocalypse of smart bombs and computer screens would all have made for dazzling opera if Els hadn't already been busy with one—an opera as strange to the present as the present has become to him.

His work is over now. The brainstorming, the interminable phone conferences, the fights over cuts and simplifications. The score has been frozen for weeks, past fixing. Still, he hangs around in the cavernous hall, sitting twenty rows back from the orchestra pit, keeping the final stages of production together on the sheer force of his teeth-gritting will.

Behind the singers, in the recesses of the great stage, carpenters complete the cathedral's west portal. Siege engines slide by on dollies. Artisans in overalls snap a pair of volutes into place on a towering flat that hangs from a batten. It panics Els, still, to count the people employed to bring to life something that began on his cabin's drawing table. He still can't quash the urge to jump up and shout, Oh, no, thank you! Please don't bother.

The goal seemed simple enough: raise the dead and make them sing. And Els has done that, these last three years. His ghost dictation filled hundreds of pages. For forty months, he has hoarded the pile of manuscript, showing it to his collaborators only under threats of violence. Every few months, he glimpsed something worthwhile in the growing score. Once, near the finish, he caught his breath at the sounds of real inspiration.

Bonner and his thugs came and took the pages away from him by force. And somehow in the course of a few more months, the team of craftsmen have turned his obscure secret formulae into theater. He's stunned, sitting in the crepuscular hall, to discover how good the first act sounds—how often it captures the bright, poisonous, ample world he lived in during his thousand-day trance.

The pit orchestra is a special forces team. Four decades ago, Els's tricky polyrhythms and kaleidoscope of keys would have been unplayable. But these seventy crack musicians, raised from infancy on perfect recordings, tear through his score as through a show-tune medley. The leads, too, are superb. The self-styled prophet and his sexy consort, the ousted bishop returning at the head of a powerful army, the demented tailor-king: all sung by shining young singers.

Bonner is everywhere at once—upstage, downstage, offstage in the wings, charming, berating, flattering, cajoling. He seduces the singers of both sexes, reblocks their entrances and exits. He sinks into dark reveries or belts out their arias the way he hears the phrases in his mind's ear. The man strides through the theater the way the bedecked prophets parade through rebel Münster, and the awed cast regards him with that same wavering reverence that Münster gives the rogue Anabaptists.

He confesses to Els, far out of earshot of the cast, *Every show I've done in the last two decades has been warm-up for this. You've served me up the perfect pitch, and I intend to hit it out of the park.*

And a city rises up at his bidding: walls and towers, council chamber, the nave of a great cathedral. The set has all Bonner's favorite mechanical gimmicks. It rotates and reassembles itself. There's scrim projection, of course, with thousands of now digitally driven images. The costumes are way over budget. The production adds several hundred thousand dollars of debt to the company's already shaky ledger. The businessmen try to rein in the uprising, but Bonner tells them what any good rebel prophet knows: every rich donor on earth will follow you to the stars, if they think you can reach God on His unlisted number.

Three months into composing, Els discovered that the opera

had already been written: Meyerbeer's *Le prophète*. Any real composer would have learned the mid–nineteenth century drama in school; but Els's education was hijacked by the avant-garde. He called Bonner in a panic.

Richard, I've sunk you. We're finished.

When Els calmed down enough to give the details, Bonner just laughed.

Peter, are you shitting me? Meyerbeer? That piece of fluff? It's a damn love story.

It's John of Leiden, Matthias, the siege. Everyone's going to think we ripped it off.

Your point? Bonner asked. *Of course it's a rip-off! The cave paintings of Lascaux were a rip-off. Everyone who's ever made anything is ripping off somebody, living or dead.*

More fires followed, which Bonner had the time of his life running around putting out. He turned an angry cast uprising into a cathartic breakthrough. In three days of shuttle diplomacy, he resolved an ego war between the conductor and the choral director. He threw the crew's continuous litany of insults and injuries into Münster's cauldron and let the flavors simmer.

Now Els settles in to watch the master work an eleventh-hour miracle on the second act. Bonner channels the scene as if he'd been there when it first unfolded, four and a half centuries ago. The prophet Matthias and his raven-haired wife Divara stand in a plaza blue with night. The music is an ethereal vesper. They and their disciple, John of Leiden, strike a pact with Knip-perdollinck, the leader of the guilds. Together, the men dash through the streets, urging the populace to repent. And in one quick fantasia, the Anabaptists occupy Town Hall.

The council takes no arms against the uprising. They mean to exploit the chaos for their own ends. They pass a law protecting liberty of conscience. The rebels rise up ascendant, and sanity is finished.

A brass fanfare launches the crowd into a midnight saturnalia. They tear through the cathedral smashing paintings and sculptures. To a deep, carnal surge in the strings, they set the city library ablaze. Matthias sings his scourging aria, *Get out, you godless ones, and never come back!* In the dark auditorium, the tune again sounds to Els like a gift from nowhere, a thing he wrote from dictation.

The chorus picks up where the aria leaves off. By scene's end no one is left in the city but the Children of God. They make the rounds, pilgrims of the future, greeting each other as *Brother* and *Sister*. They sing, a community forging itself anew on pure love. Els springs from his seat and staggers up the aisle to hear how the madness sounds at the back of the house. It sounds good. Scary good. Even inspired.

Knipperdollink, Matthias, and John celebrate inside the seized palace. In a noble trio, they praise the divine plan that has handed them an entire city. From a balcony above a crowded square, Knipperdollink decrees that all property will be held in common, in warehouses, to be given to the poor. The crowd takes up the decree in a gathering fugue. Those who object are seized by soldiers and led away.

On the thrust stage, a solo messenger sings of the spread of the millennial dream across the north. *Scarcely a village or town where the torch is not glowing in secret* . . . But in fact, Münster is surrounded. A coalition of neighboring states sends armies and digs earthworks. Els paces in the aisle, watching the noose close around his breakaway city. The siege music needs more horns—he can hear that now—more glee for the Prince's armies, closing in on the believers. But the measures are set, and they seem to be flying.

On the city ramparts, Matthias receives an Easter order from God. The world's end is under way. He leads a handful of men on a sortie against the entrenched invaders. They're cut into bloody chunks and scattered for vultures. Poetry, prophecy, and slaughter run together in an interlude so beautiful Els can't believe he wrote it.

The city devolves to John, the bastard, failed tailor. When the man sings, his words almost don't matter. From childhood, he has loved only theater. He has wasted years writing, producing, and performing plays, acting the hero in his innermost fantasies. And now fate gives him an entire city as a stage on which to turn that fantasy real.

From the back of the cavernous auditorium, Els flinches from the coming attack. One swift downbeat releases a percussive hailstorm that sends the playwright prophet screaming naked through the streets. The eerie lighting, Bonner's projections, and Els's manic music leave the man flat on his back, staring up at heaven, mute with ecstasy. When he comes to, Act Three has begun, and with it, the end.

The failed tailor proclaims himself King. He sings, *All the works of men give way now to the work of God*. He establishes polygamy and takes Divara, Matthias's stunning widow, as the first of his fifteen new wives. One quick change of tempo, and the communal kingdom of God on Earth embraces free love.

Prepared by a life of amateur theatricals, John assumes military command. He beats back an assault by the Prince Bishop's forces in a scene that leaves even the stagehands holding their breath. His followers pour into the Town Hall square to sing one more broad chorus of belief: *The Word has become Flesh and dwells in us. One King over All . . .*

A dim thought forms at the base of Els's brain. He has been

here before. He himself has taken part in this ecstatic uprising gone wrong.

The breaking wave of this music pulls him back down the aisle. He lowers himself into another seat, mid-house, testing the scene from yet another vantage. It's still good. It dizzies him to think: This time, the revolution might just work. Two hundred people have combined to revive a story half a millennium old, and tonight, in this late dress rehearsal, the tale feels ready, at last, to open.

Then Bonner slides into the seat next to his. Three beats ago, the director was deep in the wings, climbing the scenery and herding the cast with a list of rehearsal notes longer than God's grievances against humanity. Now he holds a folded-over newspaper in one hand and smacks it with his other. There's glee in Richard's eyes. Vindication. Fear, maybe, and a little true madness. *Maestro. You're not going to believe this. You're a damn prophet. Art predicting life, with two weeks to showtime!*

You'll walk by as if there's nothing there: In the grout of your bathroom tiles. In the air you breathe.

Moderato, to begin with. The opening measures of a condemned man's testimony played across a landscape of black earth and brown stubble. Relentless midwestern farmland and Shostakovich's Fifth: both spread in front of Els, pliant, empty, and terrifying, made for each other.

The jagged theme and its canonic echo tore out of the Fiat's speakers. He'd heard the movement too many times in this life to count. He knew how the thing was built; he'd long ago analyzed every phrase to death. He'd memorized the spare counterpoint, the canonic echoes, the chromatic ambiguity, the concision, the relentless reworking of that blunt first theme. But the piece that played across three Illinois counties was altogether new to him.

Once, when he was young, Els had believed that music could save a person's life. He could think of nothing now but all the ways it might get a person killed.

From the first leaping figure in the strings, Els heard again the problem with music. Even the slightest tune sounded like a story. Melody played on the brain like a weather report, an avowal of faith, gossip, a manifesto. The tale came across, clearer than words. But there was no tale.

Despite himself, in that first bleak figure in the strings, the one that would reappear in so many guises before the end, Els made out the maker's miserable life: driven into the public arena, forced to choose between penance and revolt, heresy and faith, while his life hung on whatever story the state imagined that it heard.

Els piloted the car toward the setting sun, back into the firestorm of 1936. An adventurous composer, at the top of his Orphic game, brilliant, unpredictable, admired by everyone. For two years, *Lady Macbeth of the Mtsensk District* played to near-total acclaim. Then the *Pravda* article—"Muddle Instead of Music"—a rabid, all-out attack on Shostakovich and everything his music stood for. Problem was, the anonymous author turned out to be that culture fan and amateur music critic, Stalin.

From the first minute, the listener is shocked by deliberate dissonance, by a confused stream of sound. Snatches of melody, embryos of musical phrases drown, escape, and once again vanish in rumbling, creaking, and squealing . . . The music grunts, moans, pants, and gasps . . . leftist muddle instead of natural, human music . . .

In one clean sweep, the killer of millions names the twenty-nine-year-old composer an enemy of the people.

The people expect good songs . . . Here is music turned deliberately inside out in order that nothing will be reminiscent of classical opera, or have anything in common with symphonic music or with simple and popular musical language accessible to all . . .

Stalin saves a final flourish for the end. *This is playing at things beyond reason that can end very badly.*

Overnight, the official press is thick with condemnations. It calls for an end to formalist cleverness. It commands Shostakovich to reform and embrace a simple, affecting realism. The opera—*a farrago of chaotic, nonsensical sounds*—drops from sight, worse than dead.

Nothing for the man to do but pack his bag and wait for the two a.m. knock on the door.

Disappearance is epidemic that year. Mass arrests and exiles—the Kirov flow. Tens of thousands are plucked from their apartments every month. Artists, writers, directors—Erbshtein and Gershov, Terentyev, Vvedensky and Kharms. The poet Mandelstam, jailed for terrorist acts. Shostakovich's own mother- and brother-in-law, arrested for sedition. *The NKVD does not make mistakes.* And all of society, guilty of complicit silence.

Then the shadow falls on Shostakovich. The composer asks his powerful admirer Marshal Tukhachevsky for help.

Tukhachevsky appeals to Stalin to spare Shostakovich. Soon the marshal himself is arrested and executed.

Brittle, tense, and close to suicide, Shostakovich works on. But the piece that comes out of him is worse than the first offense. The Fourth Symphony: filled with audible treason. Days before the premiere, Shostakovich suppresses the piece and chooses to go on living.

To call any music subversive, to say that a set of pitches and rhythms could pose a threat to real power . . . ludicrous. And yet, from Plato to Pyongyang, that endless need to legislate sounds. To police the harmonic possibilities as if there were no limits to music's threat.

Through the windshield to the west, Els looked out on a featureless gulag only waiting for him, the latest public enemy.

Shostakovich: *Cut off my hands, and I will still write music holding the pen in my teeth.* But kill him, and the only tunes left would be the ones the state picked out for his funeral. Forced, then, to surrender or die. And so, the Fifth: *A Soviet artist's creative response to justified criticism.*

For a few dozen miles, Els followed that response into its final, surprise freedom. He kept to the speed limit; every car on the road blew past him with scorn. Light traffic headed back East, from where he came. The futility of the interstate came over Els: you all stay there, and we'll stay here, and let's call an end to it.

The ominous tune and empty miles concentrated him. Deep inside a traumatized country still dreaming of security, he listened. The sounds would soon be like those stone-carved glyphs so eroded no one could read them anymore. But over the Fiat's worrisome new rattle, for one last time Els heard the Fifth choose between truth and survival.

The tune wandered as if in shock: strident minor sixths and thirds, then murmuring fourths. Fragments flared up, alternating between fight and surrender. At last there arose something like a pulse, a timid motor rhythm driving toward a goal as amorphous as the one Els now chased. There came a lassitude, a yielding to chance. The music pressed on toward some still-deniable *cri de coeur*. It barreled forward, now a march, or perhaps a parody of one, lumbering on like a huge, blind beast.

The movement offered up anything Els might want to find in it—hope, despair, stoic surrender. A reprobate crawling back into the fold. A flaming blow for conscience. The towns clicked past: Stubblefield, Pocahontas. But the music was all Leningrad, the night of the premiere—the whole city listening through Stalin's ears, waiting for judgment. Waiting to hear whether the rogue composer would stay true to his art or beg for mercy, be spared or disappear.

The sun slipped below the line of the windshield, and Els flipped down his visor. In the field to his right, a hulking green machine bigger than a summer dacha dragged itself down the black grooves of earth, over a slight hummock, all the way out to the horizon. The deranged Allegretto started up. The desolate theme from the first movement turned into a lurching waltz, a deep-woods Russian folk tune, a triumphal horn call, a halfhearted military band. Vintage Shostakovich: a cavalcade of perky, grim, mocking, and sardonic snips, reaching for the one freedom that would always be available, however complete the disaster: the condemned man's dance.

Then the Largo. Strings and light winds, harp and celesta, spun a long, eerie elegy, pushing the first movement's theme into a place beyond further harm. Tremolo played against a figure of rapped-out alarm. Els had heard the movement too many times to make out anything new. But for a quarter hour, the naked pain stretched out in front of him, a virgin outing. It spoke of whatever was left, after the worst that humans did to each other.

At the premiere, they cried openly, not caring that they wept. The whole audience—victims of the present's catastrophe—knew what the Largo said. Millions dead, tens of millions sent to the gulag. And no one had dared speak the fact in public, until this music.

Those who showed up that night to hear the accused man grovel heard, instead, this. Here was music simple and populist, just as Stalin commanded, and in a language whose anguish everyone recognized. Naming the crime so bluntly should have been suicide. But to convict Shostakovich for speaking out, the state would have to admit to crimes worthy of this Largo.

The hard midday light began to soften. Stubbly farmland gave way to the edges of urban sprawl. Traffic thickened. He passed a semi stopped on the shoulder. The Fiat shuddered from the shock wave. A laugh tore out of Els at the huge downbeat of the final movement. He caught his own glance in the rearview mirror, and beyond that, toward the vanishing point, flashing red lights.

For one last time, the pound of tympani launched Els into that demonic march: driving brass punctuated by skittering winds. Crescendo, accelerando, then the flood of strings falling into formation. The car crept up above seventy, ready to break for it. Els scouted the gathering traffic. What was this hell-for-leather madness? This shrill joy, never so crazed, so inevitable.

The march: Russian to the bone. Easy enough to hear triumph—hip-booted regiments of Cossacks, heads sideways, goose-stepping past Lenin's mausoleum. That's how Els's teachers had taught him to hear it. Kopacz, Mattison . . . That's how

Western listeners had heard the march, as late as the nineties: Shostakovich throwing together a blast of Soviet Realist bombast, a sellout finale to save his neck.

The lights in the Fiat's rearview swelled and gained, even as the strings released a torrent of screeching bats into the air. Clear now: a squad car, pursuing its prey. Els's foot pumped on the accelerator. The bats gave way to demented jubilation, and the ancient car shuddered. He was going well over eighty when, all around him in the sealed compartment, martial grandiosity exploded into forced festivity.

He eased off the pedal. The flashing lights closed the distance in a couple of measures. From the moment he'd fled his cordoned house, Els knew he'd be caught. But he never imagined he'd be plucked off the highway outside of Marine, Illinois. Satellites could read license plates from geosynchronous orbit. Any vehicle on the road ended up on spy cam several times an hour. Kohlmann's phone was as good as a tracking anklet. Someone in a windowless cubicle in Langley had tipped off an Illinois state trooper in real time.

The lights swam up in his rearview mirror. Els signaled and slowed. As he pulled over onto the shoulder, the cop blasted past in the left lane. The lights vanished in a pretty twinkle half a mile away before Els stopped his brittle giggling.

He pulled onto the shoulder, quaking. The music turned into scattered night whispers, rumors in a dark minor. Through banks of doubt, a grim snare drum. Then something burst through the miasma and galloped to a sudden finish. Triumph, or its bitter parody. The People, perhaps: their directed, collective will. Or perhaps the outlaw artist, exit laughing.

Els pulled back out onto the interstate. In the sealed car, aftershock hung in the air as it must have done in Leningrad on the night of the public trial. The audience on its feet for thirty minutes, the conductor holding the score above his head . . . And long before Czar Joseph and his Central Committee even have a chance to reach a verdict, the sentence is passed: set free—free to write again, free to be muddled, formalist, esoteric, and unclear, free to satirize, to disgust, to offend, free to pursue whatever shape the notes might take.

    • Yet the secret police are never wrong, and the work of security is never done. It will all happen again, the ambush from above, the public attack by the engineer of human taste. Shostakovich, sentenced to a lifelong cat-and-mouse game, perpetual target in the war against dissonance, dissidents, and discontent. His music, always variations on the dead man's jig. Decades later, long after Stalin's death, the composer will still wear a packet around his neck containing the full text of the article "Muddle Instead of Music." The words will give him the freedom that only an enemy of the people can feel.

Els merged left, into the lanes feeding toward the Mississippi. The shakes dampened and disappeared, replaced by a great lightness. The siren of the squad car, the germ of a musical idea. The last echo of the Allegro died away, plunging him into the hum of engine and wheels. Once it might have sounded like silence; now the road noise was symphonic.

The smartphone chimed and a window popped up on the screen. He swerved onto the rumble strip, trying to read the message there. The music player was asking him to vote. Two bright icons presented themselves: thumbs up or thumbs down. He had only to click—a swift judgment from his box seat—to decide the fate of the piece again.

He made it to the gathering outskirts of St. Louis. A strip

mall, a housing division. Before long Saarinen's great arch soared up from the horizon, the gateway to the West.

The trained ear can hold up an empty shell and make out the sea it came from.

He reads through the newspaper article that Bonner thrusts at him. A sect of property-sharing polygamists has proclaimed an autonomous city of God somewhere in central Texas. At first he thinks it's a demented marketing campaign that Bonner has dreamed up for *Fowler's* opening: the ecstatic believers, camped out in the desert, singing, praying, and waiting for time to end. The bungled raid by the ATF. The FBI laying siege to the believers' compound in a cordon as tight as the Prince Bishop's earthworks around Münster.

Too familiar to take in. *What is all this?*

Bonner's doing something with his mouth: call it smiling. He glances at the stage, where John of Leiden, sword in hand, heads into Act Two's closing barnburner aria, *The glory of all the Saints is to wreak vengeance . . .*

Yeah—how about that? Been going on for weeks. Who knew? Shit happens while you're busy.

Els scrambles out of his seat and turns up the aisle. Bonner grabs his wrist.

Where you going?

Els doesn't know. To the nearest television set. To the library. To the office of the artistic director of City Opera to plead innocence.

He lowers himself back into the chair. *What do you know about this?* He sounds absurd, accusatory.

Only what I read in the papers.

Els stares again at the fulfilled prediction. *This can't be happening.*

Bonner's face lights up. *I know, huh? Total gold mine. Somebody's watching over us.*

Els wants to punch the man. Instead, he scrambles back to his feet. Richard doesn't bother grabbing him again. Els jogs up the aisle and out of the hall, just as the run-through of Act Three begins.

In hours, he knows as much about Waco as anyone. He holes up in his room in Richard's apartment, camped in front of the TV, surrounded by newspapers. He watches the standoff escalate its nightmare logic: The empire's war machines. The siege works, cutting off the rebels from the outside. The core of believers huddled around their messiah, living on rainwater and stockpiled rations. He hardly needs to watch; he's spent three years composing it.

Richard finds him that night watching videotape of the compound taken from an Army helicopter: a few dozen religious zealots bunkered down against the most powerful government on Earth. A voice-over says that the siege is costing the taxpayers a million dollars a week. The camera pans across a nearby caravan of RV vehicles—campers who show up to see how the standoff will play out. They sit along the road in folding chairs, playing cards and barbequing, waiting for the climax of this live theater.

Els speaks in a spectral treble, without turning to look. *This isn't coincidence.*

Bonner's arms are full with pad thai and the day's rehearsal notes. *Peter. Turn it off. Let's eat.*

What does this mean? It has to mean something.

It means we're a genius, you and me. Absolute psychics.

People will think we . . .

There's no end to what people might accuse them of. Unearned luck. Very bad taste. Opportunism. Some Faustian bargain.

Richard, Els says. *We have to stop this.*

Right. I'll get right on the horn to Janet Reno.

Els doesn't hear. He's staring at his fisted knuckles. The news segues to a story about the World Health Organization declaring TB a global emergency. Bonner eats; Els watches him. It's not the siege of Waco Els needs to stop. It's the siege of Münster.

Two days later, ATF forces overrun the compound. Armored assault vehicles, engineering tanks, tear gas, grenade launchers. Then fire. Els might have told them: everything will burn. Scores of adults and two dozen children, shot, exploded, and immolated, and every detail of the finale beamed around the world on live television.

No need to watch through to the end. Els knows the end; he's already written it. He stands in Bonner's apartment in fetid clothes, fingers pressed to his head, waiting to be told what to do. Receiving no commands, he heads out into the blazing day and hops a cab uptown to Lincoln Center.

Richard is in row three, laying into the starving throngs of Münster. *I want to hear hope!* he shouts. *You still believe that God is going to come down and fuck the Prince Bishop and his entire paid mob up the ass!*

Els drops into the chair across the aisle. When Bonner sets

the onstage planet revolving on its own again, Els tells him the news. The director stares as if Els were a college intern on the lighting crew who has started to give him blocking advice.

Peter, I'm kind of busy. We have previews in six days. Is there something you need?

We can't do this, Els says.

Bonner blows a raspberry and twists his palms toward heaven. He hoots. His smile is brighter than it has been since Knipperdollinck's understudy went over the edge of the orchestra pit and smashed his coccyx.

You're out of your damn mind.

Okay, Els says. *We just have to postpone . . .*

Bonner snickers. There's no other reasonable response.

We can go next season, Els says. *Or later this—*

Peter. Get real. We've put these people three-quarters of a million dollars in debt. Even a two-night delay would kill them.

Truth is, since the standoff in Texas became a headline, sales for the show have gone from poky to brisk, and opening night now has a reasonable chance of selling out. Marketing has gotten behind the opera with renewed vigor; they've started plastering stickers across the existing posters and flyers: *Come See the News That the Past Already Knew.*

Innocent children, Els says. *Burnt to death by American law enforcement agents.*

There's confusion onstage, an altercation over the scene's blocking. Bonner trots toward the crisis. Els dogs him.

Not our fault, Bonner tells him, without turning.

Els grabs him by the elbow. *Listen to me. The minute people see . . . We can't capitalize on this. It's obscene.*

True bafflement crosses the director's face. The accusation is so bizarre it interests him. *This is your story, Maestro. You want to quit, now that it's real?*

THERE'S SOMETHING TO say for a short third act: rapid rising action and a race to the finish. It takes only a recitative and two arias for the Prince Bishop to rally support in the north and tighten the snare of death around the crazed kingdom. The City of God can do nothing but play out its fate in a succession of otherworldly choruses. The siege seals up; food vanishes. A gentle siciliana in the harps and flutes predicts starvation. The believers hold out by eating every dog, cat, and rat within the walls. Then grass, dirt, and moss, shoe leather and old clothes, and finally the flesh of the dead, all to a lilting 12/8 dance.

John, the Messiah, the World's King, retreats into his beloved amateur theatricals. He turns the final days into a great masque. Revels fill the town square, and the cathedral hosts an obscene Mass. Raunchy figures in the high winds grope and snipe at each other. Chopped-up snatches of sacred chant circle and rise until the entire orchestra turns into a spinning bacchanal.

In a flurry of brass, a group of the tailor King's starving subjects flee the city. But the Prince's armies pin them in the shallow meadows between the siege works and city walls. The refugees drag about, foraging the grass like desperate animals until they coat the ground with corpses. The music goes mad; sul ponticello harmonics slither through the strings.

Every player in the orchestra plunges into the surging tutti. The attackers enter a city turned to walking dead. They offer the citizens safe passage for surrender, then slaughter them the moment they lay down their arms.

Knipperdollinck and John, the amateur thespian, are tortured with red-hot irons and hung in cages from the tower of Saint Lamberti. But throughout his ordeal, the fallen savior makes no sound. His final aria—his last public performance—is total silence accompanied by a halo of strings.

The music falls away to a pianissimo mime. Then, from nowhere, it comes back glorious. The anticipation theme from the opening bars of the opera returns, anchored by the cellos and trombones. Augmented now, it unfolds in growing astonishment. A chorus of dead souls fans across the stage singing the *De Profundis*. The tune bends ten centuries of musical idiom into stunned wonder. Few in the first-night audience can follow the harmonic vocabulary. But the house breaks into applause as soon as the conductor drops his arms.

His colleagues force Els up onstage. He stumbles up in his white tie, blinded by the shining blackness. There's sound everywhere, like the hiss of his father's records that he woke to, as a child, on those nights when he'd fall asleep listening. He can't make out what the static is saying or what this audience has heard. He hears only the cries of burning children, the snickering of fate, the great sucking sound of his endless vanity.

He looks out over the audience, sick. This is what he has wanted his whole life—a roomful of grateful listeners. And now the room wants something from him. An explanation. An apology. An encore.

Someone to Els's right—a crazy man, an old friend—takes Els's fist and lifts it into the air. To his left, a resurrected John of Leiden beams. The conductor, the choral director, the choreographer, all the assembled leads and chorus flank him. Massacred believers and besieging mercenaries hold hands and bow, smiling at each other and at Els, the maker, celebrated at last, vindicated after all his long years *outside*. Els turns and plows through the happy cast, trying to escape into the gap in the velvet curtains before the contents of his gut come up into his mouth. In this, too, he fails.

How small a thought it takes to fill a whole life.

The man-made peak of Monks Mound loomed up from along the interstate. Once it had been the center of a city larger than London or Paris, a site for communal and dangerous art. Now it was part of a museum visited only by schoolchildren under duress. Its massive cone made Els want to turn off the highway, get out of the car, and climb. Cahokia seemed as good a place as any to be captured. But he was too close to his goal to be taken now.

The road bore hard to the right, and the Mississippi, without warning or comparison, spread in front of him. Water filled the landscape in both directions, and he saw that flowing lake as if he were the first fugitive ever to stumble across it.

The Voice took him by divine convolution deep into St. Louis's southwestern suburbs. All Els had to do was stay on the road and obey. The neighborhood, when he reached it, surprised him: so different from what he'd pictured for thirty years. Stately homes sat back from the street behind moats of lawn. Brick and dressed stone, half-timbering, Federal, Tudor, Greek Revival, Queen Anne—houses as adept at faking styles as Stravinsky.

A weekday afternoon, and the streets betrayed no habitation. Even the corner park was empty. Everything human had taken itself indoors. The capering gray squirrels might as well have inherited the Earth.

The Fiat nosed up to the empty curb. Els had seen pictures over the years—his daughter and her parade of misfit friends, standing in front of the house in all seasons. Soft yellow lights shone out from the discreet façade. He sat in the car, thinking how this ambush might be the worst idea he'd had since setting up his home microbiology lab. He dialed the long-memorized number.

The phone rang, but the lights and shadows in the house didn't change. At last, a deep, professional, and suspicious voice demanded, *Hello?*

The once-soubrette had turned contralto. *Who's calling?* Two accented eighth notes and a quarter: a descending fifth followed by a rising sixth. The soothing three-note tune turned exquisite, and Els took two beats too long to answer, *Maddy.*

The rise and fall of her breath reverberated in the air of her cavernous house. Far away, Els heard what sounded like an exercise tape, the spritely orders of health fascism.

I'm sorry, she said, unapologetic. *Who is this?*

It's Peter, he said, not recognizing his own voice.

Silence came from the other end, in timbres beyond Els's powers to orchestrate. That was the thing about sounds. Even their absence had more shades than any ear could hear.

Peter, she said.

He wanted to tell her: It's all right; life happens.

But the ID says Kohlmann.

Yes, he said, in a way that suggested how many parties might be listening in. She'd always had a good ear.

Where are you? Maddy asked, her voice thick.

Half a laugh came out of Els. *Funny you should ask.*

For some seconds, she said nothing. Then the teal drapes in the front bay window pulled back, and there stood the partner of his youth, the one who'd believed in the mind's ability to levitate the Pentagon. She put her hand to the glass. He did the same, from the driver's side of the Fiat. She hung up.

All life long, he'd had that composer's gift of being able to tell exactly how long a minute lasted. He counted four of them. At last he shut down the phone and started up the car again. There was no more plan. He'd drive until caught, in a motel somewhere in the Dakotas.

The car nosed from the curb. Then the house door opened. She had on a long olive shirtdress and gray tailored vest. She was thicker and shorter than he remembered. Her feet edged down the front flagstone path like the taps of a blind person's cane.

She let herself into the Fiat, slid down into the passenger seat, and swung to him. She looked at his ragged face and shook her head.

Rule Number One, he said. *Zag when they think you'll zig?*

The corner of her lip twisted. Neither leaned in, in the slightest.

What are you doing here, Peter?

He stared at her, flooded with the past. She flicked the back of her hand toward the windshield and said, *Drive.*

He drove, to her direction. They followed a suite of quiet residential streets, emerging onto a commercial boulevard. They said nothing, as if they were a sunset couple taking their ten thousandth car ride together in this life. He wanted to give her the wheel, to see if she still drove like she was sailing an ice boat across a windy northern lake.

I've missed you, Maddy.

She sniffed and scratched her nose. *Please. No nostalgia. It's unbecoming in a bioterrorist.*

She guided him into the parking lot of a mall the size of a breakaway Balkan state. Els panicked.

I can't.

You'll be fine, she said. *No one's looking for a couple.*

He angled the Fiat into a slot and killed the engine. He turned to look at her.

You're beautiful, he told her. *Perfectly unchanged.*

Oh, Christ! You never could see, could you? She held her sagging arms out and tipped her head forward, revealing her roots. The lines around her lips and eyes were cuneiform cuts in baked clay. Els shrugged.

Seeing is overrated.

They sat in the parked car, hands in laps. Down the lane in front of them, a woman pushed a cart loaded with a cardboard box big enough to live in. Maddy peered forward, intent on something Els couldn't see.

Well, she said. *You can't have done what they're saying you did.*

I think I must have, Els said.

You've just turned some stupid misunderstanding into a federal offense by acting like a criminal.

A foolish hope welled up in Els. She was always so wise. The windows were fogging up. Maddy painted idle petroglyphs on the passenger-side glass.

Modified bacteria? Phht. You can't even microwave a bowl of tomato soup.

No, Els said. *I did that.*

She shook her head. *Impossible.*

Any intelligent college kid—

Oh, Peter. I don't believe this. Her hand snaked out, fending off the fact. They were seventy years old. They'd been divorced for a third of a century. But here they were, fighting on their first date.

Have they charged me with anything specific?

The hand came back down over her eyes and massaged her forehead. *Lordy. And I thought you were naïve at twenty-five.*

You thought I . . . ? You were the wild idealist.

She looked out the window, at a different past. On the sidewalk in front of the burnished brass and black granite entrance, three women riding Segways handed out red, white, and blue tote bags. Half a dozen children dressed as boarding school wizards trotted into the mall, late for some arcane experiment. Maddy shook her head.

And you're the biggest threat to national security since that propane-filled Pathfinder in Times Square.

He started to cackle. Maddy turned to him, and the fear in her face fed his laughter. His eyes watered at his absurdity, and he couldn't stop. She put a hand on his knee. The shock of her touch sobered him. He raised his arm and caught his breath.

Sorry. It's the stress. Losing it.

She tugged on his trouser crease. *Come on. Let's get some food into you.*

A carousel spun in the center of the food court, a swirl of colored lights, mirrors, and a calliope. At one end of a large ellipse of food stalls, four bulky men clad in denim and sweatshirts played guitars and sang into mics, songs to listen to while driving across desiccated places in trucks very high off the ground. At the other end, a chorus line of child wizards were getting gunned down one by one by the voice vote of a merciless crowd.

With awful ease, Maddy secured two slices of pizza and a

pair of fizzy drinks. They sat across from each other at a red molded table that would still be around long after the race had cooked itself to death. Four dozen people ate at nearby tables. A few hundred drifted around the ring of franchises. Most of them had seen his picture all week long. But none noticed him.

From across the table, he looked at the woman who had driven to Boston with him in a seventeen-foot rental truck, while carrying his child. A minute of gazing, and it seemed she'd had crow's-feet and paper skin and liver spots for as long as he'd known her.

So how much trouble would you say I'm in?

Maddy considered the question from a vantage far away. *Oh, they want to put you in jail for a very long time. You're the perfect bogeyman.*

Graves, her placid features seemed to say, were just the thing for dancing on.

People are buying gas masks. Purification pills. You're the toast of the Internet.

Yes, he said. *Finally famous.*

She flipped a piece of melted cheese back onto her slice and squinted at it, a horoscope. *So you really did this thing.*

What thing?

Genetic whatever.

Yes.

You modified the DNA of a living thing?

He shrugged. *Hundreds of companies do that every day.*

Why, Peter? What ever possessed you?

A tune he couldn't name issued from the twanging guitars of the old men in denim on the soundstage.

It's astonishing, he said.

What is?

The things that happen down there.

I have no idea what you're talking about.

He couldn't begin to tell her. Life. Four billion years of chance had written a score of inconceivable intricacy into every living cell. And every cell was a variation on that same first theme, splitting and copying itself without end through the world. All those sequences, gigabits long, were just waiting to be auditioned, transcribed, arranged, tinkered with, added to by the same brains that those scores assembled. A person could work in such a medium—wild forms and fresh sonorities. Tunes for forever, for no one.

He pleaded with her, palms bared.

Not you, Peter. You're doctoring toxic organisms?

More throbbing counterpoint poured out of the PA system from down the concourse in the heart of the mall. It collided with the power rock from the stage, the calliope, and the chorus of beeps and chimes from a hundred smart and mobile devices. He could no more hear his thoughts than he could see the constellations at noon.

A middle-aged couple sat down at the next table, sharing a soft-serve cone and holding hands like teenagers. But Maddy didn't lower her voice.

Was this some performance piece? Some kind of avant-garde stunt? Getting your revenge on the thankless public by scaring them shitless?

He barked a single-syllable laugh. *That would be an idea.*

Then what? Have you broken any laws?

None. There aren't many to break.

Hope flashed across Maddy's face. *Then turn yourself in.*

The answer: so simple, so obvious. For a moment, he was ready. Then he remembered.

I believe I've burnt that bridge.

Why, Peter? I don't understand.

She looked up across the ellipse of eateries and pointed. There, near the food court entrance, two men in uniforms, a slant rhyme for *police,* nosed through the unnoticing crowd. Mall security. Panic filled Els. But he needed only fifteen seconds to do what he'd come here to do. He leaned forward, but didn't touch her.

Mad? Before I met you, I thought I was going to be a chemist. That's what I studied in college.

I know this, Peter. I was your wife, you know.

I'm sorry. I'm rambling.

So, what are you saying? That this was all some kind of vicarious fantasy? The road not taken?

In a way. I was . . . I was trying . . .

Oh, shit. Her hand rose and her eyes widened. *You were composing. In DNA?*

It did sound ludicrous. But what was music, ever, except pure play?

She stared at him as she'd done once, the night they broke. The night she'd said, *The game is over. Nobody's listening. They're never coming back.*

What is *it you want?* she hissed.

Her anger surprised him. The stored years. He'd never wanted anything but to give back something as fine as he'd been given. To make something worth hearing, and to send it out into the world.

Listen, he told her. *I made a mistake.*

She smoothed back her thinned hair. *Apparently.*

No, he said. *Not the genetics. I'd do that all again.*

The mall security officers looped up the concourse. They stopped to flirt with the Latina fast-food counter help. In another moment, they came abreast of the seating area, scouting

the crowd. Els braced and hid his face. Maddy smiled at the
heavyset officer as they passed the table. The man saluted her
with one finger to the brow. The two guards ambled on, toward
the wizard talent show. Maddy blew out her cheeks and exhaled.
She would have made the greatest accomplice that any musical
terrorist could have wanted.

When he could talk again, Els said, *I think I must have been
mentally ill.*

Maddy swung to face him, twisted her head. *This is what
I'm wondering.*

*No. Back then. I never should have left you and Sara for music.
Even to change the world.*

He'd said the last thing he needed to say in this life. Peace
came over him, one he hadn't felt since Fidelio died. She looked
away, her gaze now as blank as the past. The middle-aged lovers at the next table—married, but so obviously not to each
other—stood and walked away, giggling and licking ice cream
off each other's fingers.

We already had music, Els said. *All the music anybody might want.*

The high lonesome denim band went into some kind of
finale. The child wizard contest was coming down to the final
four. Maddy inspected the food court—the sounds they had—
then turned back to the sounds he still wanted.

This cell thing. You were trying to live forever?

Could be, Els admitted.

Her chest rose and fell. *That was always your problem.* She
looked for something in the bottom of her cup. *I only ever
wanted now.*

They sat in the cauldron of sound and light, as they once had
in Cage's *Musicircus.* He held his pepperoni crust aloft. *This was
our first meal.*

Was it? She asked.

You'd just read through my Borges songs. I'd posted an ad at the Music Building, promising pizza for an hour of woodshedding. You answered.

Did I? I was always hungry back then.

I was mad at you for not loving them at first listen.

Oh! She looked up, surprised. *But I did!*

He fell back, puzzled. He'd driven here to admit to this woman the central mistake of his life. But more mistakes than he could number filled the air around him. Something loosened in him, a landslide of dread. *Your quilt,* he said. *I buried it with the dog.*

She shook her head, not getting him.

I was in bad shape. I didn't know what I was doing.

Oh, for God's sake. She pawed the air. *I'll make you another while you're in prison.*

Really? You're quilting again?

Retirement. Something to do.

Careful, he said. *That's how it starts.*

She reached across the red plastic table and covered his fist in her palm. Her hand was cold. Her shot skin no longer held in heat. *Peter. They're going to use you. Make a lesson out of you.*

He opened his hand and took her finger. His life had been full of fearless music. The trick was remembering the sound of it, now that it was no longer playing.

She squeezed his hand hard, then flicked it away. *Speaking of which. Your daughter is beside herself. She's tried every possible way of reaching you for the last three days. She told me last night she was afraid you might kill yourself.*

Tell her I'm good. Tell her I'll be all right.

You want me to lie to her?

His eye fell on a kiosk near the center of the court. Its

banner read Because there is no such thing as natural beauty . . .

Tell her what I told you.

All right, she said. *I can do that. But you should tell her yourself.*

Maddy stood and stacked the trash, the plastic plates and disposable silverware.

It was all fear, she said. *Fear got us. By the way: Who's Kohlmann?*

The name came from another planet. So did the note of jealousy. Els glanced at Maddy, but his ex-wife was taking a last, too-large mouthful of now-congealed cheese and trying to hide her pleasure.

Friend. With a phone.

She led Els to the garbage station, where they jettisoned their final meal. Then they ran the gauntlet of shops back toward the entrance, Maddy leading, Els stumbling two steps behind her, through the world's endless profusion.

Outside, it had begun to drizzle. At the car, Maddy said, *Let's blame Richard.*

Els snapped a finger. *Perfect! Why didn't I think of that?*

They slipped into the Fiat as if they'd just made a pit stop and it was now back to the highway, license plate bingo, and the annual trip to Yosemite. She fiddled with his shoulder, absently, as he cranked the engine.

How does he seem to you these days?

He goosed the pedal. *You hear from him?*

Wait. You don't?

He backed out of the parking slot right in front of an SUV, whose driver laid into his horn for a full ten seconds. The Fiat lurched forward. The lot was a maze of perverse and pointless turns, leading nowhere but toward more shops.

He said, *I haven't spoken to the man for seventeen years.*

She took her hand back into her lap. *He called me a few months back. He's in a clinical field trial out in Phoenix. New Alzheimer's-arresting drug.*

Phoenix? Els asked. His head was wrong. He was driving at random. *Why Phoenix?*

Because that's where the old people are.

He turned toward her, but she looked away. He looked back to the parking lot, crisscrossed with hazards.

She said, *He calls sometimes.*

He's calling *you?*

Only at night. When he's terrified. Mostly around two a.m. Charlie wants to kill him.

Does he . . . is he . . . ?

Much the same, Maddy said. *For now. A little flakier. Early-stage. That's why he's in the trial. He's pinning everything on this drug. He calls me up to prove that it's working. He talks like the two of you are as thick as ever.*

Els didn't even see the stop sign until he was through it. He pressed on, his field of vision narrowing to a brown tube.

You're in touch. I thought you hated him.

Richard? I loved Richard. And I loved you. I just hated the two of you together.

After two more capricious right turns, he asked, *Where exactly am I going?*

I was just going to ask. Peter? Her chin rose and fell; her eyes shot down the road. *What are you going to do? You don't think I can shelter you, do you?*

Of course not, he said.

I can help you, she told the glove compartment. *Get you a lawyer. Run interference. Character witness. Whatever you need. There's still the law, isn't there? You are innocent, right?*

He caught her eye. Too late for foolish optimism. She closed her eyes and held up one hand.

Let's not go there yet.

He'd gotten them onto a quiet residential street full of modest ranch houses. He nosed the car to the curb along a maple-lined parkway. The rain had turned real and the sky was indigo.

I . . . he began. *I don't need anything. Just your forgiveness.*

Maddy grinned, a grim Minnesota girl's grin. *You're an idiot. How am I supposed to forgive that?*

He couldn't hold her look. He said, *Mad. Meeting you like this . . . ? Ten minutes ago, I was ready to surrender.*

Yes, she said. She placed a palm on his shoulder and turned away. *But now you need to get to Arizona.*

SHE GUIDED HIM to another chain motel, not far from westbound 44. This one looked like a Swiss chalet. An early start the next day, and he'd be in Amarillo by nightfall. She went in to rent the room. He waited in the parking lot, underneath a streetlamp that buzzed like something Ming the Merciless might use to torture freedom fighters on Mongo.

She came back to the car with the room key, laughing. *Why do I feel like I'm cheating on my second husband with my first?*

She gave him Richard's address. Then she guided him to her bank. She made him park on the street while she walked up to the machine and drew out enough money to get him to Arizona.

Thank you, he said. *I'll pay you back as soon as I can.*

If you don't, I'll get the law on you.

You know . . . they might pay you a visit.

You think?

Fearless, she was now. Or very tired of fear. Tired of giving it everything she was afraid it might take.

He, too, was exhausted. *You need to get back home. Charlie must be starting to worry.*

Peter! Are you trying to save my marriage?

Small twists in her pitch and rhythm told him: she was autonomous. And she had been for a long time. Her melody insisted that everyone ended up autonomous in the end. Had they known as much when they were young, they might have grown apart together.

On the way back to her house, he remembered he had something urgent to ask her, but couldn't remember what. Instead, he said, *When was the last time you sang?*

Three hours ago. While showering. You?

He pulled up to the curb where he'd phoned her a lifetime before. Night had fallen. The past that he needed to atone for had vanished. He killed the engine and they sat a moment in the dark. Maddy patted the dashboard of the Fiat.

Can I go with you tomorrow?

She grinned at his confusion, until he found her.

You always do, he said.

She undid her seat belt and shook her head. *It was a good piece, Peter. The two of us. I'd sing it again.*

She leaned over and kissed him. *We're good,* she said. *Really.* Then she opened the passenger door and flooded the little remade past with light.

I depart as air.

He wanted to destroy the opera and start again, now that he knew what it meant to be burnt alive.

He couldn't stop a single performance. The three-hour exercise in transcendence got dragged into the shit-storm of human events. He fled back to New Hampshire, but the noise about *The Fowler's Snare* followed him. Bonner gave interviews on his behalf. Art, Richard proclaimed, didn't take moral stands. All opera did was sing.

The production made the cover of *Opera News*. The *Times* reviewer called *Fowler* "visionary" and labeled Els "the mad Prophet's prophet." An article in *New Music Review* by one Matthew Mattison concluded, "One stroke of luck has turned a nostalgic exercise into something electric."

Reporters couldn't get enough of the eerie coincidence. They praised Els for an artistic bravery he never possessed. They faulted him for failing to exploit the full political significance of an event he couldn't have predicted.

City Opera extended the run. Dallas and San Francisco wanted to mount productions while the freakish story was still hot. Els refused all requests, and for a few weeks his refusal itself became industry news.

Bonner drove up in mid-June, to bully Els into compliance. Even the next day, Els couldn't remember the details. Richard got no farther than the driveway. The altercation happened there, on the obliging gravel. The talk started out civil enough. Richard spoke of creative duty, of all the people Els owed, of the moral cowardice of abandoning one's work.

There were words, rich, inventive, and pitched. Someone shoved the other, and shoving became punches. All Els could remember in any detail was Bonner dusting himself off and getting back in his car. He promised to sue Els for everything he was worth. Worth nothing, Els only laughed.

All further contact between them went through a lawyer.

Els stood his ground. He made sure *The Fowler's Snare* would never be performed again. The fight merited a moment of gossip in musical circles. Then those circles moved on to morbid Eurotrash productions of Mozart with underwater nudity and thrilling new hybrids of rock and rave, Broadway and Bayreuth.

Els didn't follow those developments. He was done with musical progress. He was done with Richard Bonner. This time the break was permanent. That much was obvious, the minute the dancer stood up bloodied from the gravel drive.

Two years after *The Fowler's Snare* closed forever, the Murrah Federal Building in Oklahoma City went down. Els heard the news on public radio while making dinner. There was talk of Arabs and hidden terror cells. But anniversaries are no accident, and Els knew at once just what slow war this attack continued. For the first time in two years, snatches of robust music formed in his mind. Lush instrumental passages, pushing outward in a mad rush: Act Four, he guessed, or Act One of an unwelcome sequel. The story was dark and resonant—worth splendid music. But by then Els believed that music's job was to cure listeners of drama forever.

A letter arrived one day, forwarded from City Opera. It was from the pianist who'd premiered Els's *Borges Songs* in graduate school. Once a weed-loving closet jazzer, the man now signed himself the dean of fine arts of Verrata College, a small liberal arts school in eastern Pennsylvania. *Fowler* had blown him away. "If you're ever looking for a way to make ends meet," the dean said, "you can always do some teaching for us."

He didn't need cash so much as he needed protection from the psych ward. Structured activity might keep at bay all the thoughts brought on by extended silence.

Verrata saved him and gave him the sustainable oblivion he

needed. He moved back down to the Mid-Atlantics and took up the gristmill work of an adjunct professor. He taught five courses a semester: a mix of ear training, sight singing, and basic theory and harmony. His days were a gauntlet of Fixed-Do slogs, with him as tonality's drill sergeant. Like every adjunct, he was a stone-dragging serf helping to build a very wide pyramid. But exploitation suited his need for penitence.

He threw himself into the crushing routine. A few semesters of teaching the rudiments of music made him realize how little of the mystery of organized vibrations he'd ever understood. The whole enigma unfolded in front of him, and he stood back from it as baffled as a beginner. He tried to tell his freshmen the simplest things—why a deceptive cadence makes a listener ache or how a triplet rhythm creates suspense or what makes a modulation to a relative minor broaden the world—and found he didn't know.

Not knowing felt good. Good for his car.

He still composed sometimes, at his desk between student conferences, or sitting in the thick of the college commons, although he never bothered to put any notes to paper. Tiny haiku microcosms spilled out of him, five-finger exercises in peace that fragmented into lots of beautiful, fermata-held rests.

Students came, learned, and left. Some suffered through their solfeggio exercises, masters of the taciturn eye-roll. But others he changed forever. To the best of his student composers, Els said, *Do not invent anything; simply discover it.* One or two of them understood him.

The years went by, and he worked as hard and well as he could. He gardened. He learned how to cook. He took up long morning walks. One day, his daughter called him out of the blue. She was passing through Philadelphia for a conference her

start-up was attending. Els met her at a noisy chowder house.
The diffident girl of twenty who'd spent long, secluded hours
on dial-up bulletin boards in multi-user dimensions was having
a ball inventing whole new imaginary worlds again. Only this
time it was called entrepreneurship.

Five minutes of conversation with this short-haired, soft-
suited, velvet-shirted stranger, and he was in love all over again.
And weirdly comfortable, as if they'd gone on chatting away
in their own language for all those missing years.

So what exactly is data mining? he asked.

Okay, Sara said, wiping the white linen napkin across her
twisting lips. *Say you wanted to know how many hours a week midwestern urban professionals between the ages of twenty-five and thirty
spend listening to crunk.*

Wait, her father said. *Start from the beginning.*

A very good place to start.

She'd ended up much like her mother: solid, flourishing, in
love with work. She came back out East four months later, and
they went to New York to look at paintings together. Then
the calls started. First every Sunday evening, then expanding to
two or three times a week. She did enjoy him. But he was her
project, really. She seemed to feel some need to look after him,
a fix for all those years when he failed to look after her. She sent
him a dog for his birthday. She bought him books and sent him
discs and concert tickets. She vetted his television viewing and
took him with her once to Hamburg. She did everything but
say: Let's make something, Daddy. Something good.

All the while, he worked. He had the esteem of his colleagues,
the respect of his neighbors, and the occasional affection of his
better students. After some years, it shocked Els to discover that,
for the first time in his life, he was almost happy.

I bequeath myself to the dirt.

Near Amarillo, the sun dropped huge and bronze below the
horizon. Els kept to the radio. One hundred outbreaks of avian
flu throughout Bangladesh and Southeast Asia. Fatal cases
in Egypt and Indonesia and Cambodia and Bangladesh and
Dakahlia. Infected wild birds were showing up in the abandoned radioactive wasteland zones around Fukoshima. The
newsreader couldn't suppress the thrill in his voice. Something
was happening, at last. If not this flu season, then the next.

Els pressed on past the city. The plan was to make it to
Phoenix in one more push the next day. Anxiety stained his
clothes, and he would have no fresh ones anytime soon. Home
and comfort were no more than nostalgic folk songs. He'd badly
misjudged the vast, callous vacancy of the West. The featureless
Panhandle stretched out in front of him, da capo ad nauseum.

A flyspeck town near the New Mexico border beckoned,
and he pulled off. A mile and a half up a dark road he found
a mom-and-pop place with a sign whose half-darkened neon
letters read like Martian script. A Holiday Inn Express beckoned
from across the way, but Els chose the churlish motel without
a second thought. Fifteen hours of solo driving: the sensation
was not unlike sitting through a fifty-year-old experimental
art film five times in a row. His vision swirled, and the asphalt
of the parking lot as he baby-stepped across it bobbed like the
sea. Only the thought of lying down forever kept him moving.

A single-story elbow of rooms bent around the weed-shot
parking lot. The building had seen better times, but the times
could never have been too good. A line of windows hid behind

heavy curtains, and the roar of retrofitted air conditioners kept up a steady drone. The insects in the air, the plane overhead, and the blood coursing in his ears combined into a spectral masterpiece.

A bouquet of Pine-Sol filled the tiny lobby, with its walls of stucco and knotty pine. Behind the ironing board of a front desk, a sun-beaten old man in chinos and a tee reading Outta My Face preempted the guest before he could say hello.

Cash only, tonight.

The man's voice was a wondrous, geared machine. Els said, *Deal.*

The proprietor didn't even pretend to paperwork. The eleven most hated words in the English language: I'm from the government, and I'm here to collect your receipts. But politics and art made strange bedfellows, and Els was fine with allies wherever he found them.

The room smelled of tobacco and microwave popcorn, but the bed was soft, and Els felt lucky beyond saying. He opened the particleboard closet and stood in front of it, feeling the urge to unpack. The absence of a bag made that difficult. His head buzzed and in his ears, the slap of tires against the seams in the highway continued to beat out a steady andante.

A TV tilted from the wall like an altarpiece. He flipped it on, for tranquilizing. The headline news channel featured a pet care business that was booming in the advent of the Rapture, only weeks away. He turned on the smartphone. The FBI could zero in on the device and raid the room, so long as they let him take a hot shower first. Searching on his name produced too many citations even to skim. It left him vaporous, diffused, and a little exhilarated. He chucked the phone on the bed, stripped, went into the funky, pine-paneled bathroom, and got under the spray.

The pelt of hot water against his skin sizzled like cymbals. The ringing in his ear changed pitch as he clenched his jaw. Toweling dry, he heard the great night music from Bartók's *Concerto for Orchestra* so clearly that he was sure it came through the motel walls. He stood and listened. The piece, its thick brocade of brass, seemed to him uniquely worth saving from the last century's runaway bonfire. Making such a thing could justify a life. But the piece was a charity commission, and the maker died a miserable pauper's death a year and a half later, mourned at his funeral by eight people including his wife and son.

Fatigue pulled Els down to the bed. With what strength remained, he set the clock radio for five a.m. The minute he slipped under the coarse, pilled sheets, he heard Chopin's *Vision*. Groping on the bedstand to shut it off, he saw his own name on the glowing screen: Els, S.

He fumbled the phone on and mumbled, *Sara*. Something like his daughter's voice came back at him.

Daddy. Oh, God, what are you doing?

He thought he might still be sleeping, his head on the pillow. Maddy must have given her the number from off of the caller ID. Technology, family, love: prisoner of them all.

He said, *Hey, Bear. You okay?*

Daddy, what's wrong with you? Her voice was strange and hoarse.

Don't worry. I'm fine.

Where are you? Wait. Don't say anything.

Your mother told you that I—

Shut up, she said. *Don't, don't, don't.*

He held the phone in a stunned silence. Data everywhere.

What the hell did you think you were doing? she said. Then: *Don't answer that.*

She said nothing more for a very long time. At last she bleated, *You haven't done anything. You're innocent.*

He sat up and flicked on a light, as if there were a reason.

I don't think so, he said. *Not anymore.*

They have nothing on you. Nothing that would stand up.

Google me, he said.

God! I'm Googling you ten times an hour.

His daughter, his ducats.

It's all garbage, she said, desperate. *Scared people spouting shit.*

That's just it. I've panicked millions. I'm going to release a new killer strain.

Dad. Shut up and listen. Just tell them the facts.

If he'd ever possessed something so quaint, he'd long ago mislaid it.

You have support. Powerful people. They're saying you're the victim of a paranoid culture.

Serious?

Plead ignorance. You got sucked up into a stupid hobby. Naïve and misguided. It's obvious. Your whole . . .

She didn't need to complete the thought. His whole life—naïve and misguided. A long apprenticeship for this final act of bad judgment.

I've found you representation, she said. *The best. The firm that defended that microbiologist performance artist in Buffalo. They'll work pro bono, for a cut of any damages. Hold on. I need my notes.*

Something rose in him through his fatigue: the spiraling perpetual motion of the Bartók finale. He filled with pride for this remarkable woman, his one perfect composition, however little credit he could take for the finished work.

Her phone clunked as she picked it up again.

The sooner you do this, the easier it'll be to clear things up. You were frightened and ran. They'll understand that.

Yes, he thought. If they understood anything, it was fear. Lightness came over him and he said, *You used to write music, remember? You invented a whole system of notation using your colored blocks. You were amazing.*

Please, she said.

I just saw your mother.

She mentioned.

I told her I made a mistake.

You did, Sara said, the words skidding in pitch. *Stop making more, and we'll forgive you.*

Okay. I can do that. I can surrender.

Don't call it that.

What should I call it?

Fixing things, she said.

He must have started to doze already, even before goodbyes, because the next thing he knew, it was five a.m. and the clock radio was playing "Smells Like Teen Spirit," so soft and sad and slow and minor and faraway that the haunting tune might have been Fauré's *Elegy*.

If you want me again, look for me under your boot soles.

Her face is a Renaissance profile against the October sky blazing through his office window. She waves two fingers at the score on the screen in front of her, and a sinuous duet pours out of the speakers, sung by a MIDI patch of sampled human voices standing in for virtuoso singers who don't yet exist.

Jen, this one: not the first Jen he has worked with in this sunny room, and she won't be the last. But by every useful metric, surely the most magnificent. Tall, clunky, voluble, half goof, half gazelle, and her dyed-fuchsia curls fly everywhere, however often her fingers rake the mane. Her laughs are per-cussive, her questions mellifluous. She breathes in instruction and breathes out ingenious freedom. And for one hour every week, he gets to watch her breathe.

He's written no real music in the eight years since *Fowler*. And yet, she's here to study composition with him. He's sixty. She's twenty-four, eight years younger than his daughter, and starved for anything he can tell her about sound. She wants to squeeze out of him the last thousand years of harmonic discoveries. But he has little to teach that isn't already within her hungry reach.

Jen's duet swings upward into a sequence of stunning chords before settling into a cantabile. Then the cantabile broadens. He once put something similar into an ancient octet—the appren-tice piece that won him the chance to work with Matthew Mattison. Back then, he still clung to the vestiges of Neo-Romanticism. Now Neo-Romanticism, unkillable vampire, is back with a vengeance. His student outpouring was reactionary, anachronistic; Jen's is hip and current. Other than that, the gestures are much the same.

He listens to her irrepressible waltz, as familiar as yearning. Then, just when Els has it pegged, the tune explodes into a wild fugato, leaving young Peter's precious student tinkerings in the dust. He turns toward the girl, amazed. She sneaks a glance his way, mugging a little, impish, a conspirator's grin. She's pleased, not with herself but with this marvelous mechanical bird she has stumbled across while out wandering.

They sit shoulder to shoulder, facing the music, nodding to the beat. Now and then he jots something into a pocket notebook. When his pleasure in her devices overflows, he'll flick her elbow or kneecap with his fingernail.

Four weeks earlier, a quartet of passenger planes turned the dream of the present into a greasy plume. The whole world watched the cycling images in narcotic dread and could not look away. Days passed when even buying a dozen eggs felt like hubris. People kept saying that life had changed forever, but Els couldn't see how. He'd lived too long for the fallen towers to seem like anything more than history's next nightmare installment. Terrors as large had struck every decade he'd lived through. Only they'd always happened somewhere else.

On day five, Stockhausen called it the biggest work of art there ever was, compared to which every other composer's work was nothing.

On day six, Jen came to her tutorial. She sat in her usual chair, her face bloated and red. *Oh, man!* she told him. *Every note I put down seems grotesque. Self-indulgent, after this.*

It took all the self-control of a swami at sixty to keep from holding the girl's jittery hand. Simply wait, he wanted to tell her. Be quiet, still, and solitary. Music will offer itself to you, to be unmasked. It has no choice.

Now, a month on, she's in full sail again, and the world lies in ecstasy at her feet. She hasn't forgotten anything; she's *remembered*. Who will tilt this footrace from Death to Love, if not her? And these full-out, cascading kaleidoscopes, their interlocking syncopations, are her weapons of mass enchantment. Her duet darts like swallows; soon, the voices are joined by ondes Martenot, contrabassoon, and bass clarinet in manic motor rhythms. Then a battalion of spiccato cellos and double basses. Tubular bells, of course. How not? And fanfares served up by a double helping of trombones.

The music works its way to a whirling waterspout, then explodes into strobing suspensions. Jen leans forward into the breakers of her own ocean, grinning like a demon. She's managed to delight herself again with her God-given right to strike a pose, to play on the fantasies of any willing listener.

The piece plunges off a cliff into blissful silence. In the aftermath, the maker can't suppress a satisfied giggle. *Huh?* she teases him. Where does such confidence come from? *Whadya think?*

I have two words for you, he intones. *And one of them is* Holy . . .

The praise makes her levitate. He stands and crosses to the piano, where he demonstrates for her a better way to handle a clumsy moment near the piece's climax. She has reinvented a kind of quasi-fauxbourdon, lush and archaic, like the kind Brahms might have used. But her voice leading is all wrong. She doesn't know the models, the ones that have solved all her problems already. There's too much more to hear than the mere past. She listens to music all day long; her tastes are catholic and indiscriminate. She has shown him the tunes on her player, scrolled through the titles in her promiscuous trove. Now and then she leaves gifts in his in-box, music for the end of time: Radiohead, Björk, the Dillinger Escape Plan. The songs startle Els. They're jewels, rich with dissonance and unstable rhythms. They sound like the experiments of half a century ago—Messiaen or Berio—reborn for a wider public. Maybe that's how long it takes to go from germ to general acceptance in this world. Maybe the key to acclaim is simply to live long enough.

But then, maybe acclaim is just the foyer to death.

For every solo discovery Jen makes, Els must point her toward dozens more. The world's bounty has overflowed, and the young are washed away in it. Human ingenuity was doomed from the first, to do itself in with abundance. Of the making of many musics, there is no end.

His fingers step through the keys, spelling out his proposed alternative. He glances up as he plays. His gaze locks onto her chestnut eyes as he talks her through the solution. The girl shakes her head.

God, I wish I could do that.

Do what? He's done nothing but trace out a well-mapped progression, one known for centuries.

Stand at the keyboard and knock those things out. While talking!

Oh, stop. You just played me a fifteen-minute piece with a billion notes in it.

That's not me, she says. *That's Sibelius!*

Confusion lasts only an instant. Not the Finn: the composition software. The program that turns an average tunesmith into Orpheus. And if a student were to ask Els where to put her energies—into mastering the past or mastering that interface . . .

He recrosses the room and sits next to her again. He waves his finger at her screen. *Time for surgery.* For him, Jen is always ready to repair. She goes to work on her own keyboard, like a kid releasing global thermonuclear war. He marvels again at the sheer power of the tools: cut-and-paste harmonies, point-and-click tone painting, one-button transposition. With a few deft flicks, a handful of raw building blocks becomes a new two-minute stunning tutti. Els wags his head in sad astonishment: five weeks of work for him, back in the day.

Oh, you children are like gods.

Children? she asks, her eyebrows aerobic. *Is that how you see me?*

It's the most coquettish thing she has ever said. She's still high on the power of her piece, the sheer trip of playing it for her mentor. Yes, he thinks. A child with breasts. With brains. With the most delicious insouciance he has come across in decades.

When I was your age, he tells her, *we used to have to find a nice flat stone, polish it up, get a chisel . . .*

She listens, brows furled. Then she tsks and shoves his shoulder. *Sure, Gramps.*

Again, he says, pointing at her machine. He feels himself enjoying her, enjoying this, enjoying even music again. *From the top. Once more with feeling.*

She does as commanded, and though the reprise of the revised piece sends their lesson into overtime, neither of them gives the minute hand a second thought. Sounds fill their ears and the notes scroll past. The music is everywhere again, lush and naïve and searching out the best in both Apollo and Dionysus.

For a few short measures, the layers turn strange and cold as moonlight. *Oh!* Els says, clapping. *I like that bit!*

You should, she says. *I ripped you off!*

He thinks she's joking. She's not. The pulse drives on ahead, but his ears turn wary. He waits for the piece to end before confronting her.

You did what?

Her face is shaped for grinning. *I found it in a piece you wrote . . . Your Borges songs?*

We are made for art, we are made for memory, we are made for poetry, or perhaps we are made for oblivion. He's forgotten the work was ever published, and if she's gone and ordered a copy of the score, it will be the first dollar of royalties Els has made in years.

I owe you an ice-cream cone.

What's that supposed to mean?

Means she has done something good with his old obscure formulas. Putty, sanding, and a paint job, and the thing is all shiny again, better than new.

What were you doing, hunting down my old stuff?

The words scare her, a key he's never seen. *Gramps?* she asks. She looks at the offending passage. *It's pretty beautiful.*

Oh? So beauty's back, is it?

How much must have changed in the world of musical taste, since he last took its temperature, for those old provocations to be accused of such a crime. He smiles at sounds from very far away—the antics at the piece's premiere, Maddy and the players dancing around the little auditorium to Richard's imperial bidding.

What? Jen says. She's ready to laugh along, if she should. *What'd I say?*

He shakes his head. *Old friends,* he says. *Crazy people.*

She frowns, wondering if she's supposed to understand. But perplexity rolls off her as easily as recent history. She belongs to the first generation to use the mantra *whatever* without exasperation. It doesn't matter to her what he's babbling about. His words are nothing; she wants his tunes.

It's Monday, 6:20. She's late for something—dinner at the dorm, a lover's tryst, a week-starting pub crawl with friends. But her eyes search upward in the air, as if the score of his old songs were printed there. *I learn so much from what you write.*

Wrote, he wants to say. Her zeal seems genuine enough. But then, she's capable of extracting instruction and delight from a ten-second ad jingle.

He wants to tell her: Hold on to what you know right now.

Let no one persuade you of a single thing. Study your hunger and how to feed it. Trust in whatever sounds twist your viscera. Write in the cadences of first love, of second chances, of air raids, of outrage, of the hideous and the hilarious, of headlong acceptance or curt refusal. Make the bitter music of bumdom, the sad shanties of landlessness, cool at the equator and fluid at the pole. Set the sounds that angels make after an all-night orgy. Whatever lengthens the day, whatever gets you through the night. Make the music that you need, for need will be over, soon enough. Let your progressions predict time's end and recollect the dead as if they're all still here. Because they are.

He folds his hands behind his neck. *We had some strange notions back then.*

I know. The sixties! Even the name excites her. A daughter of a revolution that did not happen as she imagined.

We did some silly things. We thought people could learn to love anything.

She braces. *They can't?*

They can't, Els says. *God. We had energy. We had ideas. We had daring. We had invention for every need. The dreamers outnumbered the charlatans. Then we woke up.*

His words slap her, and her face falls. He can't imagine why his apostasy should bother her. Her music is so lavish and satisfying it's closer to the 1860s than to the sixties in question. Still she hangs her head, mourning iconoclasm. She'll never have the pleasure of creative destruction. Nothing to break anymore. Everything already broken and glued back together in a mosaic of pretty bits, too many times to count.

Nobody wanted that stuff. Very little of it will ever be played again.

Through the window, October stretches out, cloudless and amnesic. According to this blue, nothing significant happened last month, with more lovely nothing in the extended forecast. Els stretches. There's a tune in his ear like the fifties rock and roll his brother force-fed him after tying him to a chair in the family basement.

Turns out that people want a very few things.

He's a boy again, listening to his father's hi-fi. *Young Person's Guide. The Orchestra Song.* The tympani's two tones are always the same tones: Do Sol, Sol Do. Do Sol Sol Sol Do. And now the long, strange trip of his sixty years, all that wandering through distant keys, doubles back to tonic, that exploded home.

He can't for the life of him figure out how, but he's upset her.

Gramps? Jen's voice wavers. *It sounds so generous. Fresh.* She pouts with the same force that drives her music on into badass brilliance. *Like you don't give a shit who comes with. I love that!*

He can't even pat her on the head. There are laws against that, and laws beyond those laws. He waits too long to say anything, and his silence humiliates her.

You tried so many things, she blurts. *Why'd you stop?*

He says, *Not your business.* And at once regrets the words as much as any music he has ever written.

Her eyes blink and her head snaps back. She closes the clamshell of her computer and shoves it in her pack.

Jen, he says, helpless to say what he should. She stops, waits, vacant, her hand fighting her Amazon hair.

Go to the piano, he commands. She sneers, but does.

Hit a key.

She shrugs—whatev. She, at least, doesn't bother to ask which one. She chooses G-sharp. Lovely, intense, *and* perverse. This one will have a future.

Tell me what you hear.

She shrugs again, stone-faced. *G-sharp below middle C.*

Again. What else?

Nothing at first. But awareness spreads through her, ten times faster than it dawned on him, back in the day. She hits the key, snorts, pounds the thing again, three times in a row. Then she starts the long arpeggio, plunking her way up the overtone series.

So what? she says, trying to scowl and failing miserably.

She knows. It's all over her face, a message already charging into her future. For every pitch that ever reaches your ear, countless more hide out inside it. The things he can never tell her, the music he never wrote: it's all rolled up, high up there, in the unhearable frequencies.

You will hardly know who I am or what I mean.

They slaughter infected poultry all across Asia. A holocaust of birds. Birds die by the millions, infected or not. Safety is a concept piece, at best.

Human cases break out by the hundreds: Egypt, Indonesia, China. The numbers are small, still, but the real outbreak will start just like this.

Meanwhile, in Rotterdam, researchers breed variant strains of H_5N_1 in generations of ferrets. Three months and five small mutations later, they'll succeed in turning the virus airborne. It's a simple enough experiment, one that tens of thousands of DIYers could re-create at home. A disease that kills half of those it infects, grown as contagious as the common cold. Governments and agencies will try to suppress the data. But soon enough, the recipe will spread around on the Internet at the speed of thought.

This happens in the Age of Bacteria, which began about 3.5 billion years ago.

Out East, in Cambridge, Massachusetts, a molecular geneticist makes a novel organism from scratch, one with its own genetic code. It won't be dangerous, a panel of scientists says, unless it escapes the lab. Everything gets loose, a panel of historians says. Life is an escaped experiment, say the artists, and the only real safety is death.

The guardians carry on flying their nightly sorties. Drones gather data from all the planet's hotbeds. Recon units comb those last few holdout places that elude the grid. Virtuoso interpreters of chatter listen in on all frequencies. Everywhere, agents break up attacks before they're even planned.

In another few weeks, an airborne squad will drop into the compound of the supreme artist of panic—fugitive these last ten years—and slaughter him. That death will change nothing. Panic, like any art, can never be unmade.

But I shall be good health to you nevertheless.

Sixty-one came, and sixty-two subito, a few days later. For two years, Els worked at Verrata and listened to nothing but Bach. He taught ear training and sight singing, then came home and listened each night to everything the old contrapuntist ever wrote. Nothing else. It was a discipline, like jogging or doing crosswords. An escape from the night sweats of his own century. *The Well-Tempered Clavier* became his daily bread. He

went through the suites, concertos, and trio sonatas. He pored
over the two-hundred-plus cantatas three times through. The
study focused him. He felt like a student again, a beginner in
his own life.

After two years of listening, Els woke one morning and
realized that he was done, even with Bach's bottomless buffet.
The surprises were over. The brilliance had gone routine. He
could anticipate every outlandish dissonance hidden in those
independent lines. And where do you go, once you've memorized the sublime?

He went to Mozart. He pored over the *Jupiter,* as a scholar
might. But even the cosmic finale was lost in familiarity, or
something worse. The notes were all still there, audible enough.
But they'd flattened out, somehow, lost their vigor. And the
phrases they formed sounded metallic and dun. It took him
some weeks to realize: His hearing had changed. He was just
sixty-five, but something had broken in the way he heard.

Els made an appointment with a specialist. His symptoms
puzzled Dr. L'Heureux. The doctor asked if Els experienced
any changes in coordination. Any confusion or disorientation.

Oh, probably, Els told him. But only the musical confusion
worried him.

Are you having any trouble finding the right words?

Els had never in his whole life been able to find the right
words.

Dr. L'Heureux made Peter walk a straight line, count backward by sevens, arm-wrestle, and stand still with his eyes closed.
He didn't ask his patient to sing or name a tune.

Dr. L'Heureux ordered a scan. The scanner was a large tube
much like one of those Tokyo businessmen's hotels. It hummed

to itself as it probed, a microtonal drone that sounded like La
Monte Young or the cyclical chanting of Tibetan monks.

Doctor and patient sat in a consulting room examining slices
of Els's cortex. The scallops and swirls looked like so much cau-
liflower. Dr. L'Heureux pointed at bits of Els's spirit and heart
and soul, naming regions that sounded like vacation spots in
the eastern Mediterranean. Peter followed the magic lantern
show. He nodded at the doctor's explanations, hearing another
libretto altogether. What was it about music's obsession with
Faust? Spohr, Berlioz, Schumann, Gounod, Boito, Liszt, Busoni,
and Mahler, down through Prokofiev, Schnittke, Adams, and
Radiohead. Centuries of bad conscience, long before the Nazis
burnt the temple of High Music to the ground.

It seemed to Els, as another slice of his brain filled the screen,
that classical music's real crime was not its cozy relations with
fascism but its ancient dream of control, of hot-wiring the soul.
He pictured Faust looking at his own neurons on a monitor—
his bottomless hunger laid bare, his desire for mastery swirling
through his brain like cigarette smoke curling in the air. As
full knowledge filled the seeker at last, Mephistopheles, at his
elbow, would sing, *Now we're both paid in full.*

Once such an infant opera would have flooded the folds of
Els's brain in spikes of color. Now he looked at a stilled sea.

Els pointed to a speck of gray-black Sargasso. *What's that?*

Dr. L'Heureux nodded, confirming a diagnosis Els didn't
even know he'd made. *That's a lesion. A small dead spot.*

Dead?

A small transient ischemic attack.

The doctor pointed out another.

The scans of many people your age show the same thing.

Ah, Els said. *So there's nothing to worry about.*

Dr. L'Heureux nodded. *Perfectly normal.* Perhaps a lesion had taken out his sarcasm detector.

Els asked how much of a person's brain could be dead and still qualify as normal. The question confused Dr. L'Heureux. He seemed not to make a strong distinction between normal and dead. And all the medical evidence was on his side.

Yet the tiny gray islands in his silver brain reassured Peter. Whatever musical facility he'd lost was not his fault. He wasn't being punished. The scattered dead spots on the screen joined together into a pattern. The islands of silence shaped the still-surging ocean of noise around them. He'd always told his students that rests were the most expressive paints in a composer's palette. The silences were there to make the notes more urgent.

Dr. L'Heureux described the virtues of exercise. He mentioned possible medications and dietary changes. But Els had stopped listening. He asked, *What about my musical facility?*

Dr. L'Heureux's shoulders made a helpless appeal. He mentioned a name: acquired amusia. It had a variety of possible causes. There was no treatment.

Something in his words tipped Peter off. A tone he could still hear.

This is going to get worse?

Dr. L'Heureux's silence suggested that it would not get better.

Els went home, into a world of changed sound. Listening to music felt like looking at a flower show through sunglasses. He knew when the intervals shocked or surprised, soothed or blossomed. He just couldn't feel them.

Rain and thunder, the sides of mountains bathed in flowing orange, frantic delight, the sizzle of cities at night, feasts of

self-renewing tenderness, the heaven of animals: the most rav-
ishing harmonies turned into secondhand, summarized report-
age. Music, the first language, direct transcription of inner
states, the thing words used to be before they bogged down
with meaning, now read like a curt telegram.

For a few days, he could still tell what sounded different.
Then, little by little, he couldn't. The brain got used to anything, and soon Els's new ears were all he'd ever had. He listened less for subtle rhythms and harmonic contour, more for
melody and timbre. Everything he heard was new and strange.
Two-tone, four-by-four garage, rare groove, riot grrrl, red dirt,
country rap, cybergrind, cowpunk, neo-prog, neo-soul, new
jack swing . . . He'd never dreamed that people could need so
many kinds of music.

A year of listening to the new world confirmed him. He'd
waited his whole life for a revolution that he'd already lived
through and missed. The airwaves were full of astounding
sound—a spectrum of grief, craziness, and joy so wide he
couldn't step far enough back to make sense of it all. As more
and more people made more and more songs, almost every
piece would go unheard. But that, too, was beautiful. For then,
almost every piece could be someone's buried treasure.

His students grew younger and the music wilder, but Els went
on teaching the same basic rules. While he trained students
how to hear seventh chords in the third inversion, the globe
went over the financial brink. The entire web of interlocking
con jobs came unraveled. Trillions of dollars disappeared back
into fiction. The college lost half its endowment. They asked
Els to retire. He volunteered to keep teaching for free, but the
law forbade it.

He returned to the life of a sole proprietorship, but now

without a way to pass the days. Still, the days passed, many in a major key. He had his phone calls with his daughter, whose every word delighted him. He had her gift, Fidelio, his elated companion on long walks nowhere. There was nothing more pressing to do all day, every day, except think about the question that his whole life had failed to answer: How did music trick the body into thinking it had a soul?

At sixty-eight, Els could think about the question only a little at a time. He read what he could find—the distilled knowledge of hundreds of experts. He couldn't follow all the physiology. The body had evolved to feel fear, hope, thrill, and peace in the presence of certain semi-ordered vibrations; no one knew why. It made no sense that a few staggered chords could make the brain love an unmet stranger or grieve for friends who hadn't died. Nobody could say why Barber moved listeners and Babbitt didn't, or whether an infant might be raised to weep at Carter. But all the experts agreed that waves of compressed air falling on the eardrum touched off chain reactions that flooded the body in signals and even changed the expression of genes.

Deep in his stuffed armchair, Els read about the chemical cascades that music set off inside the body of a listener. Sometimes, he felt as if that night with Clara by the banks of the Jordan River back in Bloomington had never happened, and he'd stayed a chemist instead of heading down music's mirror fork.

People now made music from everything. Fugues from fractals. A prelude extracted from the digits of pi. Sonatas written by the solar wind, by voting records, by the life and death of ice shelves as seen from space. So it made perfect sense that an entire school, with its own society, journal, and annual conferences, had sprung up around biocomposing. Brain waves, skin conductivity, and heartbeats: anything could generate surprise melodies. String quartets were performing the sequences of amino acids in horse hemoglobin. No listener would ever need more than a fraction of the music that had already been made, but something inside the cells needed to make a million times more.

In the fall of 2009, while fast-walking Fidelio around the long loop of the arboretum, Els watched a wet oak leaf fly through the air and stick to his windbreaker. He peeled it free, studied its surface, and saw rhythms inscribed in the branching veins. He sat down, a little dazed, on a boulder at the side of the path. His hand grazed the rock's surface, and the pits played pitches like a piano roll on his skin. He looked up: music floated across the sky in cloud banks, and songs skittered in twigs down the staggered shingles of a nearby roof. All around him, a massive, secret chorus written in extended alternate notation lay ripe for transcribing. His own music had no corner on obscurity. Almost every tune that the world had to offer would forever be heard by almost no one. And that fact gladdened him more than anything he'd ever written.

Fidelio strained at the leash. The tug pulled Els to his feet and dragged him toward the duck pond. The dog splashed into the water, her paws churning up a pattern of dotted rhythms and accented attacks. Duets, trios, even a brash sextet spread outward across the pond's surface. The tiny maelstrom of intersecting ripples contained enough data to encode an entire opera. Find the right converting key and the score might tell any musical story there was: Man uses tunes to bargain with Hell. Man trades self for a shot at the lost chord. Man hears his fate in the music of chance.

His whole history, recorded in a few haphazard splashes of water: the idea was mad. But music itself—the pointless power of it—was mad, too. A six-chord sequence could chill a soul or make it see God. A few notes on a shakuhachi unlocked the afterlife. A simple tavern sing-along left millions longing for their nonexistent homes on the range. A hundred thousand years of theme and variations, every composer stealing from every other, and none of it had any survival value whatsoever.

Grace was pouring out everywhere, from hidden sounds, into Els's damaged auditory cortex. And all that secret, worldwide composition said the same thing: listen closer, listen smaller, listen lighter, to any noise at all, and hear what the world will still sound like, long after your concert ends.

Fidelio pulled at the leash, a more present need. The banks of the pond were damp, and Els's shoes sank into the muck. He took a stick and scraped the mud from his soles. Each scrape flung away millions of species of bacteria, fungi, protozoa, micro-algae, actinomycetes, nematodes, and microscopic arthropods—billions of single-cell organisms, each pumping out tens of thousands of different kinds of proteins. This torrent, too: chemical signaling, mind-shattering tone clusters, deafening festivals of invention for anyone who cared to attend.

Somewhere in the billions of base pairs in those millions of species there must be encoded songs, sequences that spoke to everything that had ever happened to him. Music to abandon a wife and child by. The lifelong rondo of a friendship gone wrong. Hermit songs. Songs of love and ambition and betrayal and failure and repentance. Even the evening hymn of a retired industrial chemist whose one regret was living so far from his grandchildren.

Els turned from the pond and tugged the dog back onto the macadam loop. Cars shot up and down the nearby street. A low-slung Mustang slunk by, spilling over with a cranked-up anthem of pounding love. Fidelio dashed about in ecstasies, chasing butterflies, barking at phantoms that operated on frequencies Els couldn't hear. Panting to keep up, with only half the animal's legs, Els slipped the leash off the retriever's neck—a little violation of the law that hurt no one and carried at most a nuisance fine. The dog shot toward a sycamore a hundred yards away and stood at the base, barking, as if her happy, pitched howls might induce her prey to hurl itself out of the branches and sacrifice itself to the circle of life.

And in that moment, the idea came to him. It assembled itself in Els's head as he stood and watched Fidelio baying: music for an autumn evening, a ring of thanksgiving, with no beginning or end. He'd signed on for the full ride long ago, and all that remained was to be true to the dreams of his youth and take them to their logical extreme. He could make his great song of the Earth at last—music for forever and for no one . . .

A few days earlier, on the radio, lying in bed before falling asleep, he'd heard soundtracks extracted from DNA—strange murmurings transposed from the notorious four-letter alphabet of nucleotides into the twelve pitches of the chromatic scale. But the real art would be to reverse the process, to inscribe a piece for safekeeping into the genetic material of a bacterium. The precise sounds that he inscribed into the living cell were almost immaterial: birdsong, a threnody, the raw noise of this arboretum, music spun from the brain that those self-replicating patterns had led to, four billion years on. Here was the one durable medium, one that might give any piece a shot at surviving until alien archaeologists came by to determine what had happened to the wasted Earth.

Digitize a composition into a base-four strand, then put the tape inside the player. You'd have to allow for the slow drift of mutation that reworked every genome. But that endless change in the musical message would be more like a feature than a bug. As far as Els knew, the medium was virgin territory. Soon it, too, would be covered with graffiti. But he could get there early and play for one last moment in a newfound land. No storage medium longer-lasting than life.

He would spend his remaining days seeing what might be done in the form, and learning to hear a little of life's great ground bass along the way. With a little time, patience, a web connection, the ability to follow instructions, and a credit card, he might send a tune abroad again, into the very distant future, unheard, unknown, everywhere: music for the end of time.

Els dropped to his knees, patted the ground, and whistled. Fidelio came bounding back, delirious with frantic and unqualified love. Els leashed the dog, bundled her back into the car, and drove home with an urge to work that he hadn't felt since his opera had fallen into earthly politics years ago. He'd heard a way that he might redeem, if not the past, then at least his youthful sense of the future. Making things felt strange again, and dangerous. Patterns might yet set him free.

That evening, he set to work ordering parts for a home laboratory.

And filter and fibre your blood.

He's sure the game is over the minute he walks into the clinic. The night clerk looks up from the reception desk, alert. Els gazes back, with the courage of one already lost.

I'm here to see Richard Bonner.

The clerk keeps eying him. *I'm sorry. We're closed for visits.*

I'm his brother. It's a family emergency. I've driven all the way from Texas.

The clerk gets on the phone. In a moment, he says, *Mr. Bonner? Chuck here. Sorry to call so late. Your brother is here? To see you? From Texas?*

In the endless pause, Els edges back toward the foyer. The clerk cradles the phone to his face and examines Els. *Which brother?*

Els rolls his eyes. Pure Verdi. *Peter,* he says. *How many does he think he has?*

The clerk repeats the name into the phone. He waves his hand while talking, for no one who can see. Invisible gestures—like music for the deaf. The wait stretches out. The clerk shakes his head and listens. Els gauges the distance to the front door.

The clerk hangs up and smiles. *I'm supposed to send the bastard through.*

The facility is opulent. A central lounge with leather couches and a beaded cathedral ceiling opens up onto a cactus garden. There's a tiny library with magazines and paperbacks. The women's wing leads down a pale raspberry hallway; the men's is hunter-green. Dozens of ink and watercolor washes of animals in a peaceable kingdom line the hall. Past the nurses' station, through a half-open door, is a small lab, its shelves full of glassware and boxes of medication.

Els passes a room with a movie screen, then a small gym where a handful of ancient women grind away on treadmills while youthful aides take their vitals. In a sunny atrium, four gray-haired men in golf shirts and khaki slacks hunch over a table playing an elaborate board game involving thousands of colored cubes. Two younger men with stopwatches and clipboards observe.

Richard stands in a doorway at the end of the long hall. He looks like he's wearing stage makeup, the greasepaint formula for old age. He grabs Els by the shoulders, scrutinizing the effects of seventeen years. He wags his head, refuting the evidence.

You're supposed to be in hiding. Did I get that wrong?

It's Bonner, but it isn't. He's inches shorter. Something around the eyes has been ravaged. Els looks down and sees the interstate still sliding by beneath him. He's too blasted to form words. Bonner pulls him to his chest in an awkward clutch. The release is abrupt and a little confused.

Richard's mouth comes open, laughter without sound. He studies Els, puzzled. *Look at you. Quite a pickle you've gotten yourself into, Maestro. Come on. I've got stuff to show you.*

He pulls Els into the room. Number 18 is a narrow country. There's a twin bed, a desk and chair, a tiny dresser, a wall-mount TV, and a wheelchair-accessible bathroom. Richard crosses through the deluxe dorm room to a stack of papers. He picks through the teetering tower. Nothing is what he's looking for. Els sits, unbidden. An intentional tremor takes Richard's hands—a vibrato so wide it can only be a side effect of the experimental drug. He's beyond frail, hulled out, fighting for that lone resource of any consequence, focus.

A shout of triumph—*Ha!*—and he waves the prize aloft. *Here we go.* He crosses to where Els sits and hands him the article. It's about a squad of CIA analysts—self-styled "vengeful librarians"—who spend their lives combing through several million Web posts a day.

What do you think? Richard says. *Our next . . . our next thing. Show.*

Before Els can even stammer, Richard shoves more recent clippings into his hands. There's an article about the installation artist Ai Weiwei, now languishing somewhere in a Chinese prison for tweeting a post that played on the word *jasmine*. There's an article on a blockbuster film about a runaway pandemic, set to be released on September 11. There's an article about a man arrested for building a nuclear reactor in his kitchen. And, of course, several articles about the Biohacker Bach.

They all fit together, Richard says. *We just have to find out how.*

His words are rushed, shorthand. There's not much time, and the task keeps getting bigger, the longer they put it off. He implores Els, ambitious, impatient to knuckle down and concentrate, while concentration is still possible.

Els's tinnitus starts to blare. Yellow highway lines pulse in his eyes. He can hear Bonner's words, but he can't understand them. He looks back down at the articles in his hand: Someone's trying to send him a message, but in a language of weird blips and bleeps. Some unreadable, avant-garde thing.

Wait, he says. *You knew I was coming?*

Richard blinks. *No. Did someone say I did?*

They look at each other, an arms race of bewilderment.

Richard breaks first. *Oh. You mean . . . come here, eventually? Oh, eventually, sure. I knew.*

He pats the provinces of his body, looking for a hidden cookie to pop in his mouth. He's the kid from the stands of the University of Illinois Stock Pavilion on a cold night in 1967, shouting lunatic manifestos into the maelstrom. Under the paving stones, the beach.

Richard grins, reading his collaborator's mind one last time. *Forgiven? Again?*

Nothing to forgive.

I'm sure there is, Richard corrects. *I just can't . . .*

No. You were only . . .

Els doesn't know how to say what his friend was. What this one aggravating, insufferable man managed to bring into his life.

You were an asshole, is all. Always.

Richard shrugs. *How was I to the music?*

I think you might have loved it, Els says.

Bonner walks to the window and peeks out through the blinds. *What was the big one called? The opera?*

Early Alzheimer's looks, to Els, much like his old friend. *The Fowler's Snare.*

That's it, Richard says. *That's from the Bible or something? And there was one, lasted for hours, in New York? Something about bringing dead people to life?*

Els himself needs half a minute to remember. Bonner turns back into the room, searching again. *Why did you want to quit all that?*

He stops to stare at his hands, and the search ends. *You know what our problem was? When you want Perfect, even Magnificent seems shabby.*

This is the case, Els says.

The old dancer swats the air. *Never mind. New project. You've gotten us off to a fantastic start. Killer Theater. I've been dreaming about somebody doing this for a long time.*

Els hides his bafflement in a coughing jag. It's the Phase One wildcard drug babbling. Or maybe it's the last thrashing of a mind that never committed to anything so trivial as sense. Els

lays the clippings down on the student desk and studies this
alien man, his one friend.

Richard, I don't know what you're talking about.

Come on, Bonner shouts. *Who gets this kind of audience? Millions
of people are following your act. You can't afford to refund that many
tickets, Maestro.*

He puts his arm around Els's shoulders and leads him out
into the hall. The pair of them wander back down the corridor
toward civilization, leaving the door to Number 18 hanging
open. There's nothing in the room to steal except a stack of
project ideas, and nobody to steal them except for three dozen
human guinea pigs.

You may find this worth . . . worth seeing, Richard says. *The
drug is called Consolidol. The disease is called shit. God knows what
anybody else is called. They all have interchangeable little names, the
fuckers. Lots of women named Leslie.*

From down the hall comes a man as large as both of them,
with a Marine buzz cut and a goiter like a grapefruit. He waves
from a distance. Drawing near, he shouts, *You can never bring in
a wall. What say you, Bottom?*

Els is lost. Richard answers, *Some man or other must present
Wall: and let him have some . . .*

The giant draws close enough to muss Richard's hair. Richard, incredibly, abides the attack. The giant waves at Els and
mouths, *Hi, hi!*

Richard starts again: *and let him have some plaster . . . some . . .*

Or some loam, the giant supplies, his goiter shaking with
pleasure.

. . . or some loam, or some rough-cast about him, to signify wall . . .

Bruno, the giant says, sticking out his hand.

Els takes it and suffers the massive crushing. *Paul,* he says. *You visiting?*

. . . or some loam, or some rough-cast about him, to signify wall . . .

Yes, Peter says. *Just leaving, in fact.*

And let him hold his fingers thus. The giant holds up his fingers in a sideways chink of V in front of his shining eye.

Shut the fuck up, Richard barks. *Right. And let him hold his fingers thus, and through that cranny shall Pyramus and Thisby whisper.*

If that may be, the giant says, *then all is well. Come, sit down, every mother's son, and rehearse your parts.*

He waves, and ambles on past, down the hall.

Richard turns to Els and asks, *So what dose do you think he's getting? Twenty thingies? Five? Or salt water? Those are your three choices.*

Els shrugs. *If we're betting, I'd say twenty.*

Oh, we're betting, all right. Hundreds of millions of dollars. And I'd bet the same as you. So tell me. What dose you think I'm getting?

I don't know, Els says.

The fuck you don't. I've spent forty years reading that damn play. Four hours a day, this last month. More hours than all these other jokers combined. It's about fairies, you know.

He stops to turn his pockets inside out. He births up a handful of forest-green jelly beans and studies them like they're pebbles from the moon. He pops a few and staggers down the hall again.

The worst of it? Memorizing Dream *was my idea.*

You . . . Els stops, thinking better. Then plunges in anyway. *You directed it, in graduate school. Set in an old folks' home.*

I didn't! Richard exclaims. *Did I?*

He walks oddly, listing toward port. They pass the small weight room, and a trio of old, broad women call to him. In a moment, they're out in the hall, headbands and jerseys soaking,

taking turns pressing their sweat to Bonner's body. The shortest
of them purrs and says, *What angel wakes me from my flowery bed?*

The fuck is this? Bonner snarls. *Summer of Love? What are you
supposed to be—the three whosits?*

Isn't he adorable? the short one asks Peter.

The oldest of the Graces frowns at Els and taps her temple.
I know you from somewhere.

The middle one takes her wrist. *No, you don't, Jean.*

*Did you grow up in Glencoe? Did you go to New Trier? You look
so familiar.*

Els grins and shakes his head.

Let's go, Jean, the middle one says. *Come on, babe.*

Were you in the Peace Corps, by any chance?

Richard ambles away, singing, *Good night, ladies.* Els tags
along in his wake.

O, how I love thee! the short Grace calls after them from down
the hall. *How I dote on thee!*

Richard waves without turning, over his shoulder.

Jean shouts at Els from down the hall, *Are you a musician or
something?*

They meet more subjects in the central lounge. The talk is
all variations on their one shared theme: Is the stuff working?
They're bound together in a fierce pharmaceutical camaraderie.
The whole facility feels like one of those sci-fi stories set on an
interstellar craft, with generations of travelers who are born,
live, and die in transit, creeping across the galaxy in search of a
new star system. Everyone greets Richard like a long-lost friend,
and Richard greets them all in return as if he's just discovered,
too late in life, that friendship may be a comfort to a man. The
disease has gentled him.

They duck out together on the back deck. Richard paces.

You see how it goes here. We work out. Take tests. Play games. Every twitch monitored. Memorize whatchama . . . Shakespeare. We're doing a little run-through next week.

He shakes his head, dismisses his bottomless despair with a flick of his fingers.

And we wander around trying to guess who's getting what dose. Watching for a sign that we're not hosed for eternity. The damned and the saved. Every day it gets a little more obvious. I know what they're giving me, anyway. And there's no placido effect, I can tell you.

Placebo, Els says.

Placebo, Richard drawls. The natural Texas accent he spent a lifetime suppressing. *My father wanted me to lead a normal life. He just couldn't pronounce the word* normal. He thrusts his hands into the pockets of his sagging jeans and nods, nods again—*Placebo, placebo*—turning in tight circles on the redwood deck, a philosopher at last, a Peripatetic, spiraling into enduring dusk.

Give it time, Els says.

Got no time.

But if the drug is working for these other . . . if nobody's getting sick . . .

On my bad days? I hope someone strokes out, so no one gets what I can't have.

But once the test is over . . .

Phase Two, Richard says. *Then Phase Three, and Phase Four. Final approval by the FBI—the whatnot.*

Els can't think of the agency's name, either.

Then they have to set up factories for making the stuff, big time. I'll be drooling on myself years before it comes to market.

He grabs Els by the wrist, pulls him under the halogen deck light. *Hell of a finale, isn't it? Yours is better. We need to work on yours.*

He drops Els's hand and signals him to wait. He ducks back inside the facility and is gone for a long time. Els can't say how long. His metronome is shot by stress and three days of driving. At last Richard comes back, carrying a telescope as if it were a large Torah. He pats the instrument. *My alibi.*

A tripod dangles under his arm; Els grabs it as it slips.

They hate when we leave without signing out, Bonner says. *They think we're going to wander off and forget where we live. Can you imagine?*

He stumbles down the deck stairs, arms full of optics, gleeful again, getting away with something. Call it art.

Come on. Star party. Once you hear the music of the spheres, the stuff you earthlings make is a bore.

Bonner leads the expedition across the back parking lot, down half a block, into a parkway a tiny bit darker than the surroundings. There's a ring around the moon tonight—cold and huge and blue, a halo against the gauzy black. Els can't stop staring at it, monstrous and beautiful. Richard wrestles the telescope up onto the spread tripod, to a running commentary.

I'm going fast, Peter. Like a sugar cube in water. I write myself notes in a little notebook. To remind me of things. Then I can't figure out the note.

Els stands by helpless, understanding the man at last.

That's why you had to come now, Bonner says. *While there's still time to do this.*

Els asks, *Do what?*

Richard hoists the scope and secures the mount clamps. He swings the sighting scope into place, inspects the objective, and bends down to peer into the eyepiece. *The long day wanes*, he recites, singsong. *The slow moon climbs.* He hunches next to the tube, his eye to the cosmic keyhole, and peers into the universe. He might be waiting for a bus that comes around to this part of the galaxy once every epoch. *Come, my friend, it's not too late to seek a newer world.*

Now and then, Richard tweaks the right ascension control knob. He almost looks like he knows what he's doing. A massive sigh escapes him, as wide and filmy as the night sky. He straightens and steps back. *Have a look.*

Els does. The field of view is black.

Once you hear the music of the spheres, Bonner says, as if the idea has just occurred to him, *the stuff you earthlings make is a bore.*

What am I looking at? There's nothing there.

Look harder.

Els does. There's still nothing there. There's nothing there for a long time. Then there is.

From behind him, in the dark parkway, Richard says, *So tell me what you have.*

Els pulls his face from the eyepiece. Seconds pass. *What do you mean?*

What's the piece?

What piece? Els says.

Richard smirks at the evasion and won't be taken in. *You're saying you were doing real genetic engineering? Trying to create a new form of life?*

No, Els says.

So out with it. What do you have for me?

Too many miles have passed since home for Els to be sure. *I didn't get very far.*

That's where your collaborator comes in.

I was trying to put music files into living cells.

A pause, a last flare-up of telepathy, and Richard laughs like a hyena.

What's wrong with eight-tracks? So what does it sound like?

Richard. There is no piece. This was all proof of concept. They raided me before I could learn how.

Bonner scowls, puzzled by how a smart man can have such trouble with the obvious. *There is. There is a piece.*

No.

You're not listening.

Bonner gazes through the scope again. Els stands nearby. He tunes in to the night, the cars and air conditioners. He listens, a little quieter, a little harder. Sounds everywhere, but still no piece. There'll be no piece forever.

Then there is.

Oh, he says. *Oh. You're saying . . . You mean . . .*

But Bonner, like music, doesn't mean things. He *is* things. Things that can never be unmade.

The two of them start in again, like they'd only paused the old project for a moment, long enough for it to ripen. Bonner has been tinkering with an idea since first hearing of Els's flight. Els has been working on the thing since childhood, his chance encounter with *Jupiter.* They talk, Els to Bonner, Bonner to the stars, through his lensed tube. They hum to each other, and the piece takes shape. Richard dials the pitch and yaw and roll of the scope in tiny increments, checking the eyepiece after each minor adjustment.

This is your baby, he tells his friend. *Make it live.*

The piece turns lethal. Music to panic a whole country. A thing of silence and nothingness. Required listening. Els feels the madness of it, and the brisk Phoenix night, the lights from the clinic, the traffic whipping back and forth on the nearby boulevard all say: Hear, and be afraid forever.

Use that Web thing—Tweety Bird. Tell the whole world, in short little bursts.

Bonner points across the way, to the glow of the clinic. *We can use the machines in the lobby. Say that it's all out there, spreading. Everywhere. Released into the wild. An epidemic of invisible music.*

Els laughs, but it's not a laugh. *They'll kill me, you know. The minute I . . .* The idea rushes away from him, like the five recombining lines of the *Jupiter.*

You got a problem with that? You weren't doing anything else, were you?

Els presses his skull with both hands. Fatigue and the fugitive life catch up with him, because this all suddenly sounds suicidal and very, very doable.

Tell me, Bonner says. *What was it that you wanted from, from . . .* He cranks his right hand, spooling up all the music Els ever tried to write.

There's a place Els has been to, a few times in this life. A place free from the dream of security, where the soul beats to everything with a rhythm. And every one of his few visits there has reminded him: We're entitled to nothing, and soon to inherit. We're free to be lost, free to shine, free to cut loose, free to drown. But part of a harmony beyond the ear, and able, for a moment, to move.

I wanted awe.

Richard claps his hands. *Done. Living music, swimming around in the water supply.*

Surprise, Els says. *Suspense.*

Oh, they'll be hanging on every measure.

Refreshment. A sense of the infinite.

Fear, you mean.

And change, Els thinks. Eternal mutation. For a beat, he forgets the piece isn't real.

He comes clean. *Beauty.*

Richard's eyes crinkle at the mention of the guilty secret. His lips twist up. *Fine. What's more beautiful than music you can't hear?*

Els looks up at the clear desert sky, speckled with light, even above this suburban sprawl. *They'll crush me like a bug.*

Richard steps toward his friend and lays one hand on his shoulder. His eyes soften into something like sympathy. The words he wants evade him. But the look says: They'll crush you anyway, even if you never make a peep.

He waves back toward the scope. *Have a look.*

Els puts his eye to a burst of stars. They cluster, a blue star nursery, spraying out new worlds. He feels like he did two years ago, when he first looked at a glowing stain of cells under the 1,000x objective and realized that life happens elsewhere, on scales that have nothing to do with him.

He calls out. Behind him, Richard chuckles. *Once you hear the music of the spheres, the stuff you earthlings make is a bore.*

The stars come toward him in a stippled rush. He pulls his head away. Richard is staring at the clinic half a block off—at the experiment that offered him hope and served up saline. He says, *How much can they hurt you, anyway?*

Els doesn't answer. Words are for people who know things.

Richard squints into the distance. *You have to do this. The largest audience for an experimental piece in history.*

You always wanted me dead, Els says. *Didn't you?*

Bonner is elsewhere. *Eye of man hath not seen,* he says. He stops, muddled. *The eye of man hath not heard, the ear of man hath not seen . . .*

The words dissolve. There's an agonizing gap, which Els is powerless to fill. It strikes him, the one small compensation to where Bonner is going. Every look, every listen, will be like the first.

Something, something, nor his heart to report, what my dream was.

Richard points: Flashing lights. A van and three cars, one of them unmarked, slink into the circular front drive of the clinic. Men in riot gear issue from the vehicles and fan out. A dozen of them rush the main entrance. Challenges ring out in English and Spanish. The clerk at the reception desk has at last remembered the face on last night's news.

Bonner surveys the piece of theater as if it's something he once choreographed. By the look on his face, the blocking is all wrong.

He turns to Els. *You ready for this?*

Whatever *this* is, the answer is no. Richard beckons and Els follows. They head around to the far side of the clinic buildings, to the long-term parking lot, leaving the telescope and mount in the middle of the empty field.

The building screens them from the officers a few dozen yards away. Shadows of shock troops dart down the windows of the men's wing while two old men stumble toward a rented Accord. Bonner bends down near the right rear tire, like he's hiding behind the vehicle or praying. He reaches up inside the wheel and withdraws a key.

This way, I can always find it. If I can find the car.

He hands the key to Els. Els can't take it. His arms are numb. Freedom has come for him, impossible, huge, cold, blue, and he'll drown, way out in the middle of it, out of sight of all land.

Take it, man. It's just a rental. What's a little grand theft auto, once they have you for terrorism? You're doing the world a favor. They should have taken my license away four months ago.

Richard closes Els's fist around the key. One last recital, his eyes say. You can do this. Make it something even this distracted world will hear. It will only hurt for a moment.

Els presses the fob and slips into the driver's-side door. Panic slams him, but he surfs through it. He pats his pocket; the smartphone is still there. Giddy with fear, he starts to laugh. He rolls down the window. Bonner looms above the door.

If only one of us had a vagina, Els says, *half of life's problems would be solved.*

Richard recoils. *What a very curious thing to say.*

Els backs the Accord out of its slot, points it toward the curving parkway, a stone's throw behind the assembled police cars. He turns to wave to Richard. But Bonner is already walking, back turned, hunched, hands in pockets, headlong into the drama, ready to direct it, if they'll let him. Creation's Rule Number One. Zag when they think you'll zig.

Failing to fetch me at first, keep encouraged.

On the shoulder of an old state highway in Barstow, California, Peter Els, terrorist, stops to examine the railing. Looking is pointless. The scribbles on the guardrail that he's looking for are long gone. Even the railing itself must have been replaced, maybe more than once. God knows how many hundreds of miles of highway rails must run through Greater Barstow. The scribbles exist nowhere except in the music that remembers them. Still, he stops to look. He has never stopped to read a guardrail before.

The Mojave sky is as lustrous as a painted backdrop. Heat ripples off the scrubland that runs in every direction around the crater of the city. A few hours earlier, over lunch—a sack of steaming ground meat picked up at a drive-through off the interstate—he began to tweet. Figuring out the system gave him childish pleasure. He created an account and chose a user-name—@Terrorchord. He spent a few tweets proving that he was this year's fugitive. Then he moved from exposition into the development section.

I did what they say I tried to do. Guilty as charged.

I was sure that no one would ever hear a note. This was my piece for an empty hall.

What was I thinking? I wasn't, really. I've always been guilty of thinking too much . . .

The year has had no real spring. Much of the country jumps straight from December to June. In Barstow, it's August already. The freak weather may be nothing to worry about. Not for extremophiles, anyway. Bacteria need worry about almost nothing.

After the burger joint, Els pulled into a gas station run by the company that recently put five million barrels of oil into the Gulf. For the last several miles, Richard's car had been running on fumes. Els stuck his credit card into the pump and surrendered his location. No alarms sounded. As the gas flowed into the tank, Els imagined that he might be charmed, that he might, in fact, get the four more hours he needed to redeem his whole life.

In a corner of the station's lot, near the air pump, he sat in the driver's seat of the Accord and tweeted some more. The phrases rolled out of him, dozens at a pop, no more than 140 characters each.

I was after the kind of music that reminds the brain what it felt like, back when we lived forever.

I wanted a piece that would say what this place would sound like long after we're gone.

He tweeted like that white-throated sparrow in the arboretum just days ago, reinventing tonality a triad at a time. By midafternoon when he pulled into Barstow and tweeted again, he had almost eighty followers. The messages were spreading by themselves.

Coming to this place would feel like design, if he were a better designer. The Voice brought him here. The name popped out from the smartphone map: Barstow. He'd always wanted to make the pilgrimage. Stumbling on this town was like those few times—the frantic dance in the middle of the *Borges Songs*, the awful dead-drop in the middle of Brooke's sonnet, the slow build through the last twenty minutes of *The Fowler's Snare*—when the music wrote itself and all Els had to do was take dictation.

The highway is narrow, and the backdrafts of passing cars rock him. Els edges along the shoulder, probing another stretch of rail. On such a spot, eight forsaken Depression hitchhikers scribbled bottle-messages to no one. Eight anonymous pleas, turned into an ethereal, banal, subversive, conservative set of microtonal mini–folk songs, Harry Partch's signature piece: *Barstow*. Easy place to land in, hard place to get out of.

> *It's January twenty-six. I'm freezing. Ed Fitzgerald, Age 19. 5 feet 10 inches, black hair, brown eyes. Going home to Boston Massachusetts, It's 4 p.m., and I'm hungry and broke. I wish I was dead. But today I am a man.*

His scour of a hundred yards of rail turns up a wasp's nest, a bumper sticker for a towing service, an obscene rhymed couplet, several pairs of initials, a chiseled tumorous phallus, and a broken heart. Also, many sphinxlike scratchings that might as well have come from another planet. Els climbs back into the Accord. Before turning Richard's key in the ignition, he sends off another tweet, by the hobo Partch, now an accessory before the fact:

American music has one of its greatest bulwarks in bumdom.

He'd read the words in graduate school, half a century ago, in another backwater town, one where Partch lived and left right before Els arrived on the scene. The words have stayed with him, through everything. Maybe he botches the exact phrase. Mutation happens.

Partch, if anyone, knew that. Burned the first fourteen years of his music in a potbellied stove in New Orleans and started over at twenty-nine, cutting himself off from the mainland forever. A Carnegie grant to visit Yeats in Dublin, where he sold the old poet on a revolutionary setting of *Oedipus*. A few months later: homeless and broke, thumbing for rides and begging meals across the length of 1930s California—"California! Land of oncoming Los-es and Las-es, Sans and Santas, Virgins, Conceptions, and Angels!" Eight years adrift, sleeping wild or camping in hobo shanties, jumping freights, catching diseases, going hungry, and reinventing music.

Gentlemen: Go to five-thirty East Lemon Avenue, Monrovia, California, for an easy handout.

Tramp Quixote, visionary bum, indigent in a collapsing country. Prophet in the wilderness, sure that only an outsider could find the way *through*. A man of no compromises. A mean drunk. Gay, for what that was worth, like so many of the century's best composers. In any case: Did not work and play well with others. And convinced that the salvation of music required cutting an octave into forty-three pitches.

Marie Blackwell. Age nineteen. Brown eyes, brown hair, considered pretty. One-eighteen East Ventura Street, Las Vegas, Nevada. Object: matrimony.

Even to hear his spectral music, Partch had to invent a whole orchestra of outré instruments. Forced by visions into carpentry. Hence the Zymo-Xyl, built of hubcaps and liquor bottles. The diamond marimba, bass marimba, bamboo marimba, mazda marimba, and quadrangularis reversum. Adapted violas and guitars. The harmonic canons, with their sliding bridges, tuned anew for every new piece. The kithara, the gourd tree, the cone gongs, the spoils of war. A whole series of chromelodcons, organs whose keys sliced half-steps into slivers. And of course the cloud chamber bowls, a copy of which sat in Els's living room and helped alert the federal government to the fact that here was a house worth raiding.

Dear Marie, a very good idea you have there . . .

A new railing swings into view, and Els hits the brakes. Behind him, a Ford Expedition honks and veers out to avoid slamming him. The vehicle screams past. Els pulls up onto the shoulder and stares at the stretch of pavement across which, in another world, he's lying smeared.

Then he rises from the dead, pulls out the smartphone, and tweets again. He tweets the formula for his homebrew. He tweets program notes about how the piece was made. One flick, and a new wave of messages heads out into the world's largest auditorium.

Possible rides: January sixteenth, fifty-eight. January seventeenth, seventy-six. January eighteenth, nineteen. January nineteenth, six. January twentieth, eleven. To hell with it—I'm going to walk!

Els steps from the car and inspects every inch of the guardrail as if it's the score of the *Jupiter*. And it almost is, so full of scratches is it, both random and deliberate. He can't stop looking. People, nature, and chance have scrawled all over the metal bumper. Sleeper cells, covert messages everywhere. Who knew how much is going on, written down into these invisible inches?

Pencil on paint, from 1940: of course his hitchhikers are long gone. Every railing in Barstow postdates them. But every railing is full of their offspring, millions of scribbles from descendant generations. With the sun starting to drop and the traffic picking up, the search feels senseless and urgent, and everything it turns up seethes with life.

Jesus was God in the flesh.

Partch was right about so much. Twelve chromatic pitches are nowhere near enough. They doom a composer to a series of already explored phrases, progressions, and cadences. They slip a straitjacket over the continuous richness of speech. "The composer yearns for the streaking shades of sunset. He gets red. He longs for geranium, and gets red. He dreams of tomato, but he gets red. He doesn't want red at all, but he gets red, and is presumed to like it."

But the man was wrong, Els decides, in thinking that forty-three pitches put you any closer to infinity than twelve.

Els leans back against the dusty hood of Richard's leased car and pulls out Klaudia Kohlmann's smartphone. He tweets:

Partch on the piano: "Twelve black and white bars in front of musical freedom." I found an instrument free of all such bars.

Partch again: "I heard music in the voices all about me, and tried to notate it . . ." That's all that I tried to do, as well.

All my life I thought I knew what music was. But I was like a kid who confuses his grandfather with God.

As he types, somewhere under a viaduct, in the hard rain of memory, other travelers wait for a ride.

Looking for millionaire wife. Good looking, Very handsome, Intelligent, Good bull thrower, Etcetera. You lucky women! All you have to do is find me, you lucky women. Name's George.

Els tweets:

The key was futility. Music, pointless music for a while, will all your cares beguile.

He remains like this, leaning on the hood, tweeting, almost comfortable, almost at peace. Every minute he stays out here raises the risk of a state cruiser stopping and picking him up for vagrancy. But he's charmed now, protected by the god of harebrained schemes.

A text arrives and fills his screen: *The class wants to know if all this will be on the final exam. KK.*

He smiles and sends off a reply: *Believe it.* Then another chorus of tweets, and he gets back in the car.

From Barstow he turns north into the Central Valley, up the length of the state where Partch once bummed rides and transcribed the speech of strangers into notebooks filled with hand-drawn staves. He heads north, toward the spot that once made Partch scribble down in ecstasy: *In the willowed sands of the American River, within the city, I gaze up at the enthillion stars and bless the giver. And she shall be multiply blessed, for at every approaching dusk I shall thumb my nose at tomorrow . . .*

At nightfall, he orders huevos rancheros at a diner in a truck stop near Buttonwillow off of I-5. Word of mouth has pushed him over the thousand-follower mark. Readers retweet his messages. A comment posted under a feature on bioterrorism at a prominent news site is the first to announce the fact to a wider public: The biohacker Bach is improvising in public. Confessing to his crime.

All night long, discovery lights up in scattered nodes across the Net. A sound engineer calculates how many DNA base pairs it would take to encode five minutes of symphonic music. Someone uploads five minutes of old VHS footage from a performance of *The Fowler's Snare.* A couple who live a mile from Peter Els's house in Naxkohoman fall violently ill, and detail their symptoms in their blog. A mass email starts to circulate,

with links to information on what to do if you suspect you've
been exposed to *Serratia marcescens*. "Please send this information
to anyone you think might need it."

A journalist wonders out loud on his Facebook page whether
@Terrorchord is in fact Peter Els or just another anonymous fear-artist aiming for a couple of minutes of power. A
semi-prominent morals policeman posts an eloquent rant on
how music has been taken over by frauds: "Music that can't be
read, played, or listened to: now I've heard everything." The
post starts sprouting contrarian comments within ten minutes.
Two mathematicians debate how hard it would be to decode the
base-four music and play it back. Someone reports that government scientists have already isolated and sequenced the variant
strain, which contains a gene for multiple antibiotic resistance.
A young woman composer describes having heard the file that
Peter Els spliced into the genome—a piece for small ensemble
that's breakneck and free.

By morning in California, the lines are humming. An activist
from Maine argues that anyone who has altered a living germ
line so recklessly should be put to death. A law student argues that
the tweets themselves are a form of terrorism, and that by current practice, the perpetrator can be held in indefinite detention
without trial. Writers on an obscure new music zine decide that
for the first time in years, someone is singing a whole new song.

*Here's wishing all who read this, if they can get a lift, and the
best of luck to you. Why in hell did you come, anyway?*

Els sleeps in the Accord, in a slot behind the rest stop north
of Lost Hills. He dreams of bumdom, that bulwark of American art. In his dream, ordinary people chatter to each other,

millions of massed solos, in pitches and rhythms so rich that no scale or notation can capture them. All night long, the orchestra of long-haul freight whipping up and down the interstate accompanies him.

He wakes and heads north. He can reach his daughter's place by evening. There is no plan. There's only that old hobo tune: Make me down a pallet on your floor. When I'm broken and I got nowhere to go.

Missing me one place, search another.

A man sits in his car in a roadside rest area and types into a phone. He writes: *I started with a rhythm that said: "Move now. You'll be holding still for a very long time."* Then he presses post.

He tells about a piece that he wrote, a melody from a time that speech can no longer reach. He types of harmonies spreading through the piece in long, self-replicating chains. The messages go out to satellites and back down to servers that send them all across the face of the planet.

He says what the piece sounds like: Like the porous edge between hope and fear. *I tried to make my germ sound like the music I loved at sixteen, discovering a new monument every few hours. I tried to make it sound like a tune my five-year-old daughter once spelled out in colored blocks across the living room floor.*

Every message, a melody. He tweets how he hired musicians, rehearsed and recorded the song for no one. Cars pull up next to his. People amble past his hood, suspecting nothing. They use the facilities. They buy lunch out of vending machines. They get back into their machines and drive away.

He goes on writing, of music converted into a string of zeros and ones, then converted again into base four. He writes of *Serratia's* chromosome ring, five million base pairs long. He tweets how he divided those two numbers to produce a short key. Of how he had that key custom-made for him. Nothing you can't order online these days.

The account grows happy, almost prolific. All in short, joyous bursts about how he turned a living thing into a jukebox—a sequence of meaningful patterns to add to the ones scored by billions of years of chance. He presses a button and the message sets out into the biosphere, where it will live and copy itself for a while. He tweets of how he let his music go. Of how it's spreading in the air all around, in the grout of your bathroom tiles. A tune you might be breathing in right now, one you'll never be able to hear.

The tweets condemn him.

I left the piece for dead, like the rest of us. Or for an alien race to find, a billion years after we go extinct.

I haven't a clue what the piece will do. Nothing, probably. Maybe you'll forget the thing is even there. After all, it's only a song.

I stop somewhere waiting for you.

The listener gets red and feels the beating sun. The listener gets blue and sees the sky. The listener gets green and sets out to sea.

Colors pour into the mobile concert hall. They come from the radio at first: Strings in a rocking sigh. A long sustain, the sound of the day ending. Nothing left to be frightened of; nothing left to discover. But seven chords in, a shimmer of horn, and on the next measure's pickup, a soprano sings:

Amor mío, si muero y tú no mueres,
Amor mío, si mueres y no muero,
no demos al dolor más territorio . . .

Love, if I die and you don't,
Love, if you die and I don't,
let's not give sadness any more ground . . .

The words meander like a languid river. But soon enough a swirl of unstable harmonies pushes the sound into a wider place. This music, half a dozen years old, could be a hundred. It's shot through with Mahler at his most serene. The few dissonances it admits to are dappled and transient, as if the perfected terrors of the last century changed nothing, and even now, even in this year, home might still be intact, and nearer than you think.

The rocking figure returns, doubled now by horn. In that pulse, the soprano finds her way back to the wide first theme: *no hay extensión como la que vivimos.* No place is greater than where we live. And for a few measures, down this stretch of generic interstate, it's as good as true.

You've heard the piece before, three years ago, and on first listen, it sounded like mere sentiment. Movie music. Sprinkles of South American hue and charm, Villa-Lobos via Ravel. A place we couldn't get back to anymore, even if it still existed. Now comes this radio reprise, served you by a programmer who likes to insist that first hearings are always wrong.

The culprits are known to you: Peter Lieberson, Pablo Neruda. But such names are at best composite pseudonyms. These phrases assembled over centuries, the work of more anonymous day laborers than history will ever credit. You're in there yourself, down a branch of the self-spreading Net, stepfather of a fleeting mood or modulation, vector for new infections.

What might a listener never know about this song? How it was composed for the woman who sings it now. How she led the composer to this love, this poem. *Love, if you die* . . . How the singer died just months after this premiere.

And does it change anything in these phrases, so shameless and lavish, to know that the composer is next? He'll be dead in a few days. That's why the radio plays these songs: a eulogy in advance. But listen, and the music forecasts another passing, one even older than the harmonies it uses.

Decades ago, this man, too, wrote like a believer in the infinite future. He studied at the feet of fearsomely progressive masters. Music poured out of him, splendid with math and rigor, music like a formal proof, heady stuff admired by dozens, perhaps even hundreds of discerning connoisseurs. He reveled in all those once-required shibboleths, now given up as so much discredited zeal. But *this* song—ah, this one will travel, go everywhere, get out and see the world, and even the tone-deaf will hear something forgotten in it.

So what to do with that failed revolution, the hundred years of uncompromising experiment? The need for something beyond the ordinary ear: Disown it? Discipline and punish? Shake your head and smile at the airs of youth? No: Strangeness was your voluntary and your ardent art. You fought alongside the outsiders for something huge, and knew the odds against you. No take-backs now. No selective memory; no excuses. There's only owning up to everything you ever tried for, here at the end of the very long day.

But what to do with *this*—these love songs, the autumnal harmonies hurting your chest? What to call it? A repudiation. A return. A hedge. A sellout. A deathbed conversion. A broadening. A diminishment. Music to kill the last fifty miles of a cross-country drive.

Call it nothing, then, or call it music, for there are no movements or styles or even names for the sounds that wait for you, where you're headed. Listen, and decide nothing. Listen for now, for soon enough there'll be listening no longer.

The music tenses. A quick raising of stakes, a nervous drawing in: a gesture stolen from somewhere, sure, but where? From no one in a position to sue. The touch of conventional suspense breaks the spell; you would have built a different contrast. And that's the curse of a life spent looking for transcendence: nothing real will ever suffice, nothing that you won't want to tweak. And yet, and still—another swell, a rhythmic fault line, a change of instrumental color, and you think: Why not? Then even approval gives way to simple hearing.

El tiempo, el agua errante, el viento vago . . .

Time, flowing water, shifting winds. The dying composer has gone on record: he wants to apologize to generations of his students for leading them down a mistaken path. Wrong back then, the music says, but righted at last, here at the finish line. It's a happy enough story, and one that should hold until the flock wheels next and the changing winds of fashion declare again who's in, who's out, who loses, and who wins. There will be reverses still; that's how music works. Listen, only listen, and do not worry too much about keeping score. Reunion has you now, for a while, and a while is all you get. The grip of this enchantment lasts no more than a moment. *Pudimos no encontrarnos en el tiempo.* Love, we might never have found each other in time.

They thaw you, the rays of this late sun. But soon enough these harmonies, too, will set and cool. Even beauty exhausts itself and leaves the ear wanting other sounds. Need will turn to something harder, some training ground for the difficulty to come. But for a while, this song, *this* one.

The first, expanding figure returns one more time. All the notes align, and it's like you've written them yourself. Not here, not in this life, not in the world where you worked and lived. But maybe in the one you might have reached, in time. *Esta pradera en que nos encontramos.* In this meadow where we meet. The long, luxurious lines forecast your past and remember your future in detail. You can't imagine how you missed the fact, for all those years. It might have been okay, even fine, to have written something so simple and pacific. To have made a listener want to be more than she is.

And yet: You did what you did and made what you made. Here you are. And to tell the truth, this meadow had its moments. *Oh pequeño infinito!* O little infinity! We give it back. We give it back.

YOU STAND IN the evening rain, on the steps of her trim gingerbread. The Voice got you here, a last, best act of navigation. She opens, a woman in the foyer of middle age. Her face freezes in the happy irritation she's prepared for someone else. She, your cells' lone heir and executor, is busy with joys and fears you don't even have the right to ask about. But now her whole task is you. She swallows her half scream back down her throat and pulls you inside.

There's anger and there's excitement. Hurried questions, distress and fuss thrust at you, along with a serving of noodles left over from a dinner for one. She towels dry your hair. The words pour out of her, unbearable. But they won't need bearing for long. *Are you feverish? What happened to your lip? What's wrong with you? Jesus, Daddy, try to eat something.*

She's living in a two-page spread from a furniture catalog. The townhouse is as clean as a C major scale. The curtains have just been ironed. The throw pillows pile up on the sectional in chilling symmetry. Photos of her crossing finish lines in tech clothing and various stages of pain grace the walls. Four posture-correcting ladder-back chairs surround the dining room table as if they've been lined up with a ruler. An umbrella stand flanks the front door and, next to it, a shoe rack with several identical coral-colored running shoes. All a gift from you, this rage for rational management. It's what happens when you teach an eight-year-old that nothing—nothing at all—is secure.

But there's a piano, too. A six-foot baby grand, its keyboard open, Schumann's *Scenes from Childhood* on the music rack, and the lid open on the short stick. It doesn't seem possible.

You're playing again? Why didn't you say anything?

She doesn't answer. She's at the window, glancing up and down the street, then pulling shut the curtains.

On the near side of the music rack is a photo: A young man and woman amusing themselves together. The man crouches over a toy piano, arms above his head, fingers poised to pounce on the tiny keys. The woman holds up one hammy palm, eyes closed, her mouth a ringing *O!* You knew those kids, knew the photographer. How long did it last, that amateur duet? Not even ten years, from start to finish. *Pero este amor, amor, no ha terminado.* But this love, Love, has no finish line.

In the background of the photo grins a fearless girl. She's in the kitchen now, making tea with an electric kettle and tea bags taken from an elegant roundel. Two vanilla wafers for each of you. She comes back into the dining room where you sit, her brows a single mound of worry in the middle of her forehead.

You think: My only decent composition.

Other photos on the sideboard tell the truer story: preteen and her fledgling half-sister, at the foot of a bumper Christmas tree. Mother, stepfather, and happy grad, her mortarboard caught in midair. Young woman and her feckless man in front of Half Dome, their walking sticks raised in a mock-joust. All the dense, long years of daily being, the real heft of it, not the mere soundtrack you imagine. You know nothing of her causes, the pulls on her compass, what she does all day to pay the mortgage on this trim place. In her life, you were mostly an itinerant sower of pain. And still she came and found you out in your self-made wilderness, kept you phone company every week when you had none, bought you a dog.

She sits and pours. First the tea, then a cookie go into her mouth like she's blowing on a pitch pipe.

Please tell me you didn't write those things.

The ones that proliferate like living things, all over the Net. You'd like to tell her that. You almost could. It's almost true.

You shrug, and the shrug makes her curse you. The pent-up stress of forty years. More profanity, and she starts to cry. You take her hands, but she flicks yours away and pulls hers to her neck. She closes her eyes, bows her head, pinches the bridge of her nose. You see wild gray strands in her hair. You, who never see anything.

Her voice wavers like a student violin. *I don't* get *you. What are you trying to do?*

But music doesn't do. It is. Dust in the wheat, sand among the sands.

So many noises abroad tonight, it's hard to add a thing. The air fills with trivial ecstasies. And here, at last, it's enough to attend, to keep still and add nothing to the mix. The spring wind takes the metal blinds and scrapes them against the window casement. There are sirens, miles away. Fire or violence, someone's life ending. A trickle of radio from a passing car. The chirping of gadgets. The chime of a glockenspiel broadcast from an ice-cream truck three blocks and sixty-six years away. The television of neighbors through the townhouse walls, tuned to the eternal national talent show. The hum of air conditioners, like frogs in the trees. A cheering crowd, an echoing PA. A cloud of buzzing insects and the silent pings of bats that hunt them in crazy knots across the sky. The coursing of blood in the capillaries of your ears. No place is greater than where you lived.

I wanted to make you proud.

She shakes her head, incredulous. Proud? *I thought you were God.*

Until I left.

She shakes her head, denying the denial.

The phone rings. She finds the offending device and kills it. But not before you hear the ringtone three times. It's as familiar as breathing, but you can't place it. Then you can.

What is that? Where did you . . . ?

She doesn't answer you—you, the one person on Earth who doesn't need that ringtone identified. Instead, she rises and whisks the tea service away before you can finish. No lingering, this one. There are problems to solve, systems to work, old nightmares to keep from reprising.

You can stay here. I'll hide you. We'll call that lawyer tomorrow, the one I told you about. He'll figure out something.

You hear the first van pull up and a door open. She looks at you, thick with hope, ready to believe that even now, every misguided public confession might still be called back. Then her face clouds over again with pain. *You really did that?*

You squint: Did what? There's much to plead guilty to. But you want to be sure.

She can't stop looking, scrutinizing you for evidence. Her eyes say: You turned a living cell into a music box? A CD? Something in the look could almost pass for excitement.

Somebody says they've isolated it already. Somebody uploaded . . .

No, you say. *Not possible.*

The rattle and thump of another van, on the other side of the house. Boots hitting pavement. You can't make out how many. Then your daughter asks what she hasn't asked since childhood.

What does it sound like?

Her eyes shoot toward the piano. A shy request: Play it for me, this thing that the world will only ever be able to guess at. Once, on another coast, you told a terrified eight-year-old, *Nothing is going to change. We'll still be like we always were.* Now your frightened forty-two-year-old triathlete data miner needs another lie.

A cordon assembles around the house. The pound of boots, the sawtooth whine of something electronic.

It's a fine piano, better than any you've ever owned. You try out a few chords. They ring like the brightest future. Your fingers say: Love, let's not give sadness any more ground. They remember something, your digits, a song you wrote for her mother, way back when, on a dare. After a few stumbles, it comes back. Resurrected.

She laughs in surprise. *Oh, no! You didn't. You didn't use that.*

No; you smile, a little puckish. No, you're right. It seems important to be as far out of the house as possible when they reach you, as free and clear as you can get. You say, *I can't believe you remember that one.*

On the far side of the music rack is a bud vase filled with fresh-cut lily of the valley. It's ready-made, if a little theatrical. Useful to have something in your hand, and the bud vase will look much like lab glassware in the dark. You pick it up and hold it to you.

You'd be surprised, she says.

You look down at the keys, those twelve repeating black and white prison bars. There's something in there that you'd still love to jailbreak, even here, even this late, tonight. You will not find the key in this life. But the still-unfolding sounds, the music you felt and lost, the combinations you just missed finding, the dangerous songs still waiting to be made: *y así como no tuvo nacimiento no tiene muerte.* No birth, and so no death. That river of remembered futures will go on without you, changing nothing but its course, its lips. This love, Love: this love has no end.

Listen, you say. *Hear that?*

She goes to the window and lifts the curtain. A cry tears out of her. *Oh, shit.* Her body retreats from the glass and her arms fend off the fact. *Shit!* Her eyes dull and dilate. Her face goes gray. *Daddy,* she pleads. *No. Oh, please, no.*

Sara, you say. Safe though all safety's lost. *Sar? Let's make something.*

She shakes her head, sick with terror. Her eyes search yours:
Make what?

Something good. Good loud. Good lively. A rose no one
knows.

When she nods, even a little, you'll head to the door and
through it. Run out into a place fresh and green and alert again
to whole new dangers. You'll keep moving, vivace, as far as you
can get, your bud vial high, like a conductor readying his baton
to cue something luckier than anyone supposes. Downbeat of
a little infinity. And at last you will hear how this piece goes.